FLY LIKE A BIRD

A Novel

JANA ZINSER

Virginia

Published in the United States by BQB Publishing
(an Imprint of Boutique of Quality Books Publishing Company)
www.bqbpublishing.com

Printed in the United States of America

978-1-945448-24-9 (p)
978-1-945448-25-6 (e)

Library of Congress Control Number: 2019940447

Book design by Robin Krauss, www.bookformatters.com
Cover design by Rebecca Lown, www.rebeccalowndesign.com
Author photo by Amy Stephens Photography in Castle Rock, Colorado.

First editor: Caleb Guard
Second editor: Pearlie Tan

DEDICATION

My love for Iowa knows no bounds.

As a child, my small Iowa town offered me the freedom and safety of riding my bike all over town, the joy of the gently rolling hills, and the music of the colorful birds. It provided the comfort of a community that knew my name, the thrill and competition of sports, and the close-knit bond of friends and family who knew what I was up to at all times. Iowa gave me a great education and an expectation to succeed, access to the arena of state and national politics, and the ability to accept and appreciate the uniqueness in all of us.

We all see the world from our own limited perspective, but I remember as a child trying to understand racism and beyond that, the inequities of the world, sometimes right in front of me. I'm not sure I understand it any better today.

In *Fly Like A Bird*, I wanted to explore the awakenings of a young girl and her struggles to make sense of the artificial unfairness placed upon many of us with the invisible bars of race, sex, poverty, and family circumstances that frequently restrict our choices and our successes.

In this story, as in real life, it is often the cruelty of just a few that stops the freedom of many. We all shelter self-doubt and insecurity within our hearts, but if we could stand up for each other when we see injustices, we might find we end up accepting ourselves as well. We should not shy away from differences, we should embrace them.

In Iowa, if you listen, you will hear the melodious songs of so many different birds and they all belong in that glorious state that I love. *FLY LIKE A BIRD* means finding your freedom to be who you are, to stand up for yourself and others, and to soar to great heights on the winds of the Iowa prairie.

AUTHOR'S NOTES

Although *Fly Like A Bird* is inspired by musings told to the author, this is a work of fiction. Names, characters, businesses, places, events, and incidents are either the products of the author's imagination or used in a fictitious manner. Any resemblance to actual persons, living or dead, or actual events is purely coincidental or incorporated in a fictitious way.

CONTENTS

Prologue (1959)   ix

Part I: A Family of Sorts (1966)   1

    Chapter 1: Best Left Unsaid   3
    Chapter 2: The Sandwich War   9
    Chapter 3: The Cookie Jar Violation   19
    Chapter 4: Spooks   23
    Chapter 5: Eavesdropping Isn't Polite   29
    Chapter 6: Thrasher's Pond   39
    Chapter 7: The Dump   53
    Chapter 8: The Devil's Pictures   65

Part II: Finding Her Way Home (1970–1971)   73

    Chapter 9: The Garden Hoe   75
    Chapter 10: The Doll Baby on Mulberry Street   85
    Chapter 11: Another Holiday Tainted by Discord   95
    Chapter 12: The Barbershop   111
    Chapter 13: The Rosie Project   119
    Chapter 14: Mushroom Hunting   125
    Chapter 15: The Supreme Court Said You Could   131

**PART III: Mischief, Trickery, and
Disappointment (1975–1976)**   141

    Chapter 16: The Coffey Shop   143
    Chapter 17: The Dusty Library   151
    Chapter 18: The Corn Quicksand   159

Chapter 19: Where the Buffalo Roam   171
Chapter 20: Deadman's Woods   183
Chapter 21: The Lawn Creatures   197
Chapter 22: The Great Purple Dog   207
Chapter 23: The Rain Stopped   215
Chapter 24: Leaving Coffey   225

Part IV: Hearts Have No Skin Color (1979–1980)   237

Chapter 25: Losing Touch   239
Chapter 26: The Woman at the Window   249
Chapter 27: The Betrayal   257
Chapter 28: The Death Grip of Love   261
Chapter 29: Every Ending Creates a Beginning   271
Chapter 30: Patty's Day Out   281

Part V: The Great Hereafter (1984–1985)   291

Chapter 31: Preparing for Death   293
Chapter 32: Ivy Visits Her Past   305
Chapter 33: A Child is Worth Some Trouble   315
Chapter 34: The Rescue   327
Chapter 35: Play the Hand That's Dealt   345
Chapter 36: Rose Hill   351
Chapter 37: Sentimental Journey Home   359
Chapter 38: Will the Night Ever End?   371

Part VI: The Return of the Birds (1985–1986)   375

Chapter 39: The Geriatric Scuffle   377
Chapter 40: The Benches   389
Chapter 41: The Vanishing of the Ghosts   397
Chapter 42: The Halloween Heist   401
Chapter 43: Finding Your Spirit   407

Chapter 44: Nothing Worse Than Being Caucasian   413
Chapter 45: The Pies   417
Chapter 46: The Wings of Hope   423

Recipe for Angel Pie   **425**
About the Author   **427**

PROLOGUE (1959)

The violent December wind whipped the pelting rain and turned it to ice on the roads of southern Iowa as Robert Taylor pulled into the driveway of his mother's white Victorian house. He stepped out of the blood red Pontiac and into the storm, shielding his shivering baby in his arms. The moon lay buried deep behind the storm clouds and lightning flashed in the dark Midwestern sky, startling the baby. The crashing thunder and howling wind drowned out the little girl's cries. Robert was twenty-six and overcome with fear and panic.

Robert's tears mixed with the pouring rain as he kissed his daughter's cheek and handed Ivy into his mother Violet's waiting arms. Violet grabbed his arm as he turned back into the storm, but Robert pulled away. Her frantic warning evaporated into the thunderous night.

Violet Taylor tucked Ivy against her body inside the front of her big coat. The baby calmed and peered out from her Grandma's lapel. They huddled together on the front porch and watched Robert's car back down the driveway past the big maple tree that swayed and groaned in the storm. The old tree had survived many decades of Iowa storms by holding fast to the earth with its deep roots and bending with the power of the wind.

Cold rain poured from the porch eaves as Robert drove off. Fifty-four-year-old Violet pushed her short, wet hair out of her face and kissed the top of Ivy's little head. She stared into the darkness for a while as if she thought her son might reappear, but he didn't. Ever.

Later that night, someone reported that Robert's car briefly stopped outside the Coffey Shop then hurriedly drove back into the freezing rain that coated the roads with an invisible sheet of black ice.

The new Deputy Sheriff, Charlie Carter, said the car carrying Robert and his wife, Barbara, skidded and swerved as it approached the two-lane Highway 69. He reported their new 1959 Pontiac Bonneville did not stop in time to avoid the oncoming tractor-trailer. The truck's giant headlights must have appeared in the blackness of the storm-ravaged night, hazy through the cascade of freezing rain on their windshield. Bright-colored sparks exploded on the highway as the big truck dragged the mangled car beneath its belly.

And Ivy was left an orphan.

PART I

A FAMILY OF SORTS

(1966)

Chapter 1

BEST LEFT UNSAID

Iowa's late sunset showered bright colors of red, gold, and orange across the broad horizon like an explosion of fire in the summer evening sky, and the Iowa sun bowed behind the prairie skyline.

The hot summer night in 1966 produced only a slight breeze as eight-year-old Ivy put on a thin summer nightgown and pushed her sweaty strawberry blond hair off her neck. Grandmother Violet pulled back the yellow daisy-printed quilt and Ivy jumped into her antique sleigh bed.

"A little bird told me that you rode your bike out past the Thrasher place today," said Grandma. "I've told you not to go out there. If you do it again, you will be in deep, dark trouble with me. Do you hear me, little missy?"

"Why?"

"Never you mind. You need to do what I say because my job is to protect you."

"Okay, Grandma, but I don't—"

Grandma shook her head. "Uh. Uh."

The crickets serenaded outside Ivy's bedroom window and the glowing fireflies danced. Ivy kissed the black-and-white picture on her bedside table and snuggled into her bed. The old photo showed her father with curly hair and dark eyes. Beside him stood her mother, wearing a silver heart necklace engraved with a rose, the only possession of her mother's that Ivy owned. She never took it off.

In many ways, Ivy's parents only existed through Grandma's stories and a few photos. Most of Ivy's newly created images of her parents drifted thin and fuzzy, like half-remembered dreams, and the hazy thoughts of their tragedy haunted her.

Ivy held her Grandmother's hand and floated away on her dreams.

A few hours later, a nightmare of exploding colors, crashing metal and terrifying screams jolted Ivy straight up in bed. She felt the cold wetness of the sheets and her urine-soaked nightgown clung to her skin. She crawled out of bed and crept down the dark stairs to find Grandma.

She padded lightly down the expansive stairway of the old Victorian. When she reached the bottom of the wide stairs, Uncle Walter's voice boomed from the kitchen where he and Grandma played cards.

"She's just a little girl, but don't you think she has a right to know what happened? There's a few in town that have their suspicions. Someone might tell her."

Grandma muffled a growl in her throat. "Now, Walter, you know some things are best left unsaid. Even if anyone suspects anything, they'll stay quiet because I know too much about them. Everyone's got family secrets. Now that's the last I want to hear of it."

Uncle Walter mumbled something Ivy couldn't hear. She turned and tiptoed back up the stairs, and crawled into her wet bed. The pungent smell of urine pierced the humid air as she huddled in a dry corner of her bed. Her wet nightgown stuck to her skin. Grandma's words inflamed Ivy's worst fears. Were they hiding something horrible about her parents' accident?

The headlights of passing cars moved around the walls of her room as she picked up the picture beside her bed. Having no parents made her feel empty. She needed to find out what Grandma and Uncle Walter were talking about.

Ivy could hear Grandma's heavy steps climbing the stairs. She hurriedly set the picture down on the table just as Grandma peered in.

Ivy sat up. "I wet the bed again."

"Why don't I change your bed while you get on a new nightgown?"

Ivy pulled a clean nightgown from her drawer. "How come nobody ever talks about my parents' accident?" she asked as she changed her clothes.

Grandma finished tucking the clean sheets under the mattress and Ivy climbed back into bed. Grandma patted Ivy's cheek and sat down beside her, her weight making a deep dent in the mattress. "Too painful, I suppose. Time often stands still in families."

Ivy fingered the silver chain around her neck and Grandma shifted on the bed, making the old bed springs creak. Ivy tucked her hair behind her ears. "Tell me about my mom."

"Well, she grew up in Stilton and she was beautiful. You look a lot like her, you know." She patted Ivy's freckled cheek. "She liked to have her own way. Your father loved your mother more than life itself. Your mother had that effect."

Ivy fiddled with the ring on Grandma's finger. "How come my mother isn't buried in the cemetery with my dad?"

"Guess it just wasn't meant to be. You've always liked this ring, haven't you?"

Ivy nodded. She picked up the framed photo of her parents and lay it on the daisy-printed pillow next to her. Grandma pulled her soft housecoat around her ample lap and stared into the distance as if looking into the past.

"On my wedding day Sam Taylor gave me his ring and a bottle of lilac perfume. I've worn that fragrance ever since, and I've never taken this ring off." She sighed. "Sam Taylor and I thought we would always be together. But life changes your plans. When he died, he left me three grown sons and 4120." That was the nickname she gave to her big Victorian house on 4120 Meadowlark Lane. "But families survive tragedies. You have to go on."

Grandma touched the tip of Ivy's freckled nose. "Your Grandpa would have adored you. Now go to sleep. You promised Uncle Tommy you'd take the birdseed over to his place early tomorrow."

With no brothers or sisters, Ivy spent a lot of time with her two uncles who lived in Coffey, a small farming community in southern Iowa. She loved being with her Uncle Walter. And, at Grandma's insistence, she reluctantly spent time with Uncle Tommy.

Ivy's uncles hadn't spoken to each other since 1959. No one quite remembered the incident that started the silent treatment, except that a pastrami sandwich at her father's funeral was to blame. Ivy felt drawn to her uncles' feud, and she was driven to find out what had started the long-standing sandwich war.

Ivy nodded, clutching Grandma's hand. "You're not going to die tonight, are you, Grandma?"

Violet Taylor, who was sixty-one, gave the same response she had given every night since she had a breast removed because of a cancerous lump. "No, I'm not prepared for death. I'm only prepared for life. Death can't touch me. I have you to raise. God won't take me until you're ready." Grandma covered Ivy with the sheet and kissed her forehead. "I love you more than the great blue sky."

During the previous winter of 1965, Grandma had discovered a lump in one of her breasts. Two weeks later, the cancer specialist in Des Moines removed one of Grandma's breasts without much contemplation or concern. "As if it was just a moldy piece of bread," Grandma said. "Maybe he thought a fat old woman wouldn't miss her sagging breast. Fool. But life can't wait for breasts. My brassiere will never know the difference." She shook her head and rearranged the miscellaneous stuffing in her bra.

Grandma soon adjusted to the change. Loss was nothing new to Violet Taylor. She stuffed her large, vacant bra with socks, kitchen tea towels, or anything she could find, and went about her business.

That night, Grandma sat on the bed and sang the old Western cowboy song, "Red River Valley" like she did every night. The crickets outside chirped along in chorus. Ivy's sun-streaked hair spread tangled on the pillow. Her eyelids closed.

"Goodnight, Grandma. I love you, too."

Pushing the floor with her feet, Grandma bounced the bed until Ivy's breathing slowed and she floated on the edge of sleep. "I pray I'm doing the right thing and that you will have a forgiving heart, for all of us," Ivy heard Grandma say as if from a million miles away.

Grandma brushed the stray hair off Ivy's face, so much like her mother's, and put the photo back on the bedside table. The crickets' rhythm thumped like the heartbeat of the night. The fireflies played hide-and-seek, flashing in the darkness of the woods. The wild birds settled in the trees. But the squirrels never slept. Neither did Grandma. She cooked, cleaned, or watched TV at all hours. Ivy worried about Grandma dying, but hearing Grandma's constant sounds in the night, gave her the comfort to finally drift away into that deep sleep.

Chapter 2

THE SANDWICH WAR

The air hung thick and heavy a few hours after the sun rose. Ivy, dressed in a yellow sleeveless shirt and peddle-pusher shorts, came downstairs ready to ride her bike to Uncle Tommy's house to deliver the bag of birdseed.

She found Grandma in the kitchen. "Can I go over to Uncle Walter's after I drop off Uncle Tommy's birdseed?" she asked Grandma. "Luther Matthews is building him a cookie jar shelf today."

Grandma stirred a huge pot of red raspberry jam, cooling on the stove. A row of Mason jars stood ready to be filled. "Okay, but stay out of Luther's way, you hear? He's got enough on his mind, poor man."

Grandma scooped red raspberry jam into the first jar. She tilted her head and wiped the sweat off her forehead with a tea towel. "Best not to tell Uncle Tommy about Uncle Walter's shelf." She raised her eyebrows. "You know how he can be."

Ivy dipped her finger in the jar of jam and licked it. "Why do they hate each other?"

Grandma bent down and rummaged for the jar lids in the bottom cabinet. She set them beside the jars on the counter. When the jars were filled, she would take them to the canning room in the darkest corner of the cold basement where they also kept the pop for game nights. She placed her hand on her thick waist and slowly straightened. "They don't hate each other. They just tend to hold a grudge."

"You always say that, but why don't they talk to each other?" Ivy dipped her finger into the raspberry jam again and licked it, then pointed to the backyard. "I bet your bird friends would tell you if you asked."

The woods surrounding Coffey were full of hawks, eagles, owls, goldfinches, and other wild birds and Violet Taylor knew them all. She believed that if a person loved birds, he couldn't be all bad. Ivy was always on the lookout for the glimmer of a goldfinch, the Iowa state bird, because according to Grandma, it brought good luck.

"Well, the birds talk a lot, but they don't tell me everything." Grandma smiled and absentmindedly arranged the stuffing in her bra. "Something changed between the boys when your father died, but sometimes, we're best off not knowing. You see, some secrets are safe in the telling, and some secrets are safe in the keeping."

Goosebumps tingled on Ivy's arms. Her throat felt dry. Grandma guarded the secrets of her family very well.

"Now, go on," Violet smiled. "You better skedaddle. You're going to eat all my jam before I get it put away. Uncle Tommy's expecting you."

Ivy stole one more lick of jam before she rushed outside, hoisted the bag of birdseed into her bike basket, and pedaled the few blocks to Uncle Tommy's house.

Uncle Tommy, a big gruff man, worked at the Coffey Sewage Treatment Plant. He lived with his wife Hattie and their two children, Angela who was fourteen and Russell who was thirteen. Ivy tried to fit in, but she shared little in common with her older cousins.

That morning, Ivy greeted Uncle Tommy and Aunt Hattie on the back porch as they ate breakfast by themselves. Her cousins weren't there, probably still asleep. She sighed with relief as she dropped the birdseed on the porch by the door, biding her time before she could go to Uncle Walter's trailer.

Ivy pointed at Uncle Tommy's breakfast. "Why do you eat the same thing every day?"

Uncle Tommy slumped in his chair. He wore a sleeveless white undershirt, jeans, and black cowboy boots. He set his coffee cup on the metal TV tray next to him on the porch and clicking his tongue against his teeth, he sucked out bits of food. He pushed up his black-rimmed glasses. "I guess I'm just a man who knows what he likes."

"But don't you get sick of having an egg sandwich and black coffee every morning?"

Uncle Tommy tapped the pointed tips of his black cowboy boots on the worn porch floor. He scratched his chest. "Heck, no. I like my coffee naked." He grabbed the crotch of his jeans. "And my eggs covered."

Ivy grimaced and looked away.

Aunt Hattie slapped the arm of her chair. "Tommy, for the love of Pete."

Laughing, Uncle Tommy pulled a bag of salted sunflower seeds still in their shells from his pocket and popped a few in his mouth. He shucked them with his tongue and spit out the soggy, empty shells.

Aunt Hattie was a short, intense woman, with reddish-brown, frizzy hair that framed her round face. The buttons on her ragged housecoat stretched across her soft middle and she nodded her round chin. "Your uncle is a man of ungodly habits." She tipped her face heavenward. "Lord, have mercy on his dark soul."

Uncle Tommy turned to Aunt Hattie and stopped tapping his boot. Sunflower seed shells catapulted out of his mouth. He stuck two fingers in his mouth and whistled loudly like a bird, trilling low and high. Aunt Hattie put her hands over her ears, pressing her curls to her head as she gritted her teeth until he stopped his shrill whistling.

Uncle Tommy pointed to his disapproving wife. "That's bird-talk for 'Shut up, holy lady.'"

"You're as useless as those stupid birds you feed," Aunt Hattie said as she crossed her arms. "And now you're talking to the birds like your mother and you're almost as goofy as your brother."

Uncle Tommy snorted. "Nothing wrong with birds." He started tapping his cowboy boot again. "And no one's as goofy as Walter."

Ivy sat down in the chair next to Uncle Tommy. "Do you hate Uncle Walter because my dad died?"

Uncle Tommy's head jerked toward Ivy. A sunflower shell shot out of his mouth, just missing her. "Why'd you say that?"

"Because Grandma said that's when you stopped talking to each other."

Uncle Tommy sighed and settled back in his chair.

Aunt Hattie sniffed and twitched her little ski-jump nose. "Why don't you ask your . . ."

Uncle Tommy sat up and whistled his shrill bird call again, drowning out Aunt Hattie's words. Aunt Hattie's eyes narrowed to two angry slits.

Uncle Tommy leaned back and shook his head. "I just got dadburn tired of Walter's view of life, that's all. It was the last straw when he stole my pastrami sandwich at Robert's funeral potluck. Haven't missed the conversation none neither."

A slight breeze blew the sickly scent of Uncle Tommy's after-shave across the porch. Ivy sniffed and turned away, breathing in fresh air.

A black cat, trying to sneak across Uncle Tommy's backyard, drew their attention as it danced on its paws hurrying across the yard. Uncle Tommy grabbed the gun leaning against the porch wall. "Dadgum cats scare the birds."

He raised his gun and shot. Ivy cringed and looked away. She hated when he did that. Uncle Tommy reached into his jeans and got out his pocketknife. "The best way to stop a varmint is to shoot him in the head before he knows what hit him. Got ten points for that one because it was big and black, like Miss Shirley."

He laughed and cut a mark on the peeling back porch post. The pockmarked post proved Uncle Tommy's shooting accuracy.

Ivy fumed. She liked Shirley Roberts, the flamboyant black woman who cleaned houses for many of the wealthier families in town and lived next door to her friend Maggie. "Why don't you like black people?"

"Because they're black." Uncle Tommy scratched his head. His hairline showed signs of a surrendering retreat.

"The Bible says their skin was turned black to punish them," Aunt Hattie said. "The word of God brings me great comfort."

Uncle Tommy rolled his blue eyes. "Jack Daniels brings me great comfort."

Aunt Hattie made the sign of the cross with her stubby fingers and held it out at her husband. "I'm tired of trying to live a holy life with God, while you live an ungodly life with your friends. Mark my words, your day of reckoning is near,

Thomas Taylor. Jack Daniels won't save you from the end of the world."

Uncle Tommy tipped his head back and pretended to guzzle out of a bottle. "No, but I'll have a heck of a going-away party." He mimed, wiping his mouth.

"This November when the Holy Rapture comes and me and all the other truly righteous souls ascend to heaven, I'm leaving you with nothing." Aunt Hattie snatched up the empty breakfast dishes and marched inside the house.

"What? You plan on taking all this with you?" Uncle Tommy gestured around the porch.

Aunt Hattie slammed the door behind her.

"That ought to wake up the kids and ruin my peace and quiet this morning." He spat a shell into the backyard, then looked up at Ivy and made a clicking sound with his tongue. "Hasn't been all that quiet anyways, I reckon."

"But what's wrong with being black?" Ivy asked again.

"Oh, for crying out loud. Not again. Why you asking me? I don't know. They're just black, that's all. Okay?" Uncle Tommy peered down at Ivy over the top of his glasses. "Why don't you go bother somebody else? Go have your little touchy-feely talks with your Uncle Walter. I don't have time for your silly questions."

Ivy stood up. She'd rather be at Uncle Walter's anyway. "Okay." She jumped down off the porch, forgetting Grandma's earlier warning. "I got to go anyway. Luther's building Uncle Walter a shelf for all his cookie jars today."

"Crazy Luther's building Walter a shelf for his cookie jars? Now, that's a good one." Uncle Tommy leaned back and laughed.

Ivy hopped on her bike and started pedaling, relieved to get away from Uncle Tommy and Aunt Hattie. She couldn't wait to get to Uncle Walter's place.

Uncle Walter was two years younger than Uncle Tommy. He lived in the Prairie Hills Trailer Park. A collection of cookie jars in the shapes of vegetables filled his trailer and an odd assortment of lawn ornaments, including a deer, a turtle, a chipmunk, and an ugly gnome sitting on a mushroom, guarded the narrow strip of lawn between his and Bertha Tuttle's trailer.

Uncle Walter loved the tidiness of having everything he needed within the confines of his small trailer, and since he lived alone, nothing was ever out of place. Uncle Walter's need for precision and order gave him satisfaction and pride in sorting the mail which made him good at his job as a letter carrier at the Coffey Post Office. He delivered his route on foot because he liked to walk—in fact, he didn't own a car—but his knees often ached by the time he got home.

Uncle Walter worked every weekday and every other Saturday. On that particular Saturday, he had hired the local handyman, Luther Matthews, who had been in the same class at school as him, to build a shelf around the top of his trailer's living room and kitchen to display his favorite vegetable-shaped cookie jars and relieve the clutter on his counter.

Ivy rode the few blocks over to Uncle Walter's trailer. She knocked, and she could hear Uncle Walter unlocking the many locks on his door. She hurried inside and followed her uncle to the kitchen counter where the cookie jars sat side by side next to a neat line of Dr. Pepper bottles. Uncle Walter was much smaller than his big brother, Tommy. He hummed "Sentimental Journey" as he lined up his cookie jars on the counter.

Ivy handed him the carrot cookie jar. "When's Luther coming?"

"Hard to tell. He sort of works on Luther-time."

"I don't think Uncle Tommy likes Luther very much."

"Well, your Uncle Tommy's not much of a judge of character. Luther's suffered some hard knocks. His father was a mean drunk. He basically raised himself after his father was poisoned by mushrooms. You know they can be dangerous if you don't know what you're doing. After that, Conrad Thrasher tried to get the county to take Luther away and put him in the county home for boys. If you ask me, Conrad just wanted to get his hands on Luther's land. It was your grandmother who promised to look in on him. She talked the county folks into letting Luther live by himself and finish high school. Eventually, Luther found a way to get by. He learned to fix things."

A short knock announced Luther's arrival. He entered the trailer wearing an old sweat-stained handkerchief on his head like a cap, tied in knots at the four corners. His long, uneven hair jutted out like stubby cornstalks beneath his homemade hat.

He got to work quickly and began cutting the boards. His worn-out Levi's jeans fell below his waist as he sawed a board on Uncle Walter's patch of lawn. The sawdust flew as Luther talked to his saw. "Okay, Old Toothless Joe, do your stuff."

Ivy pointed in front of Luther. "Hey, look out for the gnome."

Luther jerked and looked up. Uncle Walter's decorative garden gnome rode motionless on top of a brown mushroom. "That's not a gnome. That's an evil pixie."

Ivy nodded. The gnome's tiny painted, disapproving face looked as if it accused the mushroom of unknown atrocities.

"You know, I've never liked mushrooms much," Luther said.

A thud sounded. Ivy looked up at the trailer next door. Bertha Tuttle, a secretary at a law office and the town snoop, watched them from her window. Bertha lived alone in the doublewide trailer next to Uncle Walter ever since her husband ran off with the dime store clerk.

Luther followed Ivy's gaze and pointed with his chin toward Bertha, who was an old classmate of Uncle Tommy's. "Looks like Bertha's nose is stuck to the window again." Luther turned his head and winked at Ivy. "That'd hurt, don't you think?"

Ivy covered her mouth and giggled. She kicked the sawdust on the ground. "Hey, Luther. Did you know my mother?"

"Not much. She moved here after high school to work in the office out at the packing plant, I think."

"You mean where they kill the cows?"

"Yeah, you know down by the sewage plant where your Uncle Tommy works." He scratched his neck. "Yeah, she sure was pretty though. You look a lot like her."

Ivy blushed. She lifted her sweaty hair off her neck for a second. "I wouldn't like a job at the packing plant."

Luther rested his hands on his tool belt which held a hammer, screwdriver, nails, knife, and a tape measure. "Knew your father though. Nice guy. Real nice guy. Too bad what happened. Tommy used to be pretty decent himself in the old days. I remember one day, your mom's dad, that'd be your grandad I guess, came to the plant and dragged her out of there. Wanted to take her back home. But she didn't want to go. Put up quite a fuss, they say."

"What happened?"

"Well, I heard Tommy came out of the sewage plant and told him to leave. There might have been a skirmish, but whatever happened, the guy left, and your mom went back to work."

Ivy bit her lip.

Luther nodded. "Your Grandma, she's good people. Don't come much better. I'd do anything for her. She saved my life when Thrasher tried to have the county take me away. Now, Thrasher, there's a bad guy."

"But he's the mayor and he goes to church all the time."

"The Good Lord ain't fooled. You know, I think your mother used to be friends with Mildred, his wife. Would see her going over to the Thrasher place from time to time."

Ivy kicked at the grass. "You know his son, Weston? He's mean, too."

Luther blew sawdust from the board. "Mean dads are kind of hard to live with. Might make you do mean things."

When Luther finished the job late that afternoon, Uncle Walter examined the completed shelf. "It looks great, Luther."

"I'm here to help. But you better thank Old Dan Tucker here." Luther tapped his hammer in the palm of his hand and slid it back into his tool belt. Then he pointed at the new lock he had just installed on Uncle Walter's front door. "Hopefully that'll keep your brother out."

As Luther gathered his tools, Uncle Walter and Ivy placed his cookie jars in alphabetical order on the new shelf. "Wait. My eggplant's gone. Why is Tommy always messing with my cookie jars? He knows how hard it is to find a purple vegetable and that one already had a broken lid."

Ivy looked at Uncle Walter. "Is he still mad about the sandwich?"

Uncle Walter stared at Ivy. "It wasn't his sandwich." He turned away and began straightening the cookie jars on his new shelf.

"That must have been a really good sandwich."

Uncle Walter didn't answer.

Chapter 3

THE COOKIE JAR VIOLATION

That night, Uncle Tommy and Reuben Smith, a local farmer, bowled and drank rounds of beer at the Blue Moon Bowling Alley and Bar. The corrugated tin structure with a flickering blue neon crescent moon included a bar, ten bowling lanes, and three pool tables against the wood-paneled wall by the snack bar. Charlie Carter, the deputy sheriff, joined them. There wasn't much of a need for police in such a small town as Coffey and since Charlie lived there, he became the only law enforcement in town. At Conrad's insistence, the town gave Charlie an office in the bottom of the courthouse with a couple of cells.

Uncle Tommy put down his beer mug and rubbed his balding head. "I heard Walter had Luther build him a new shelf for his dang cookie jars today. He's over at my mother's playing cards tonight." He stood up and slapped his hands. "Let's go mess up his veg-ta-bles."

Reuben Smith drank the rest of his beer and wiped his foamy mouth on the short sleeve of his green and yellow bowling shirt. He wound up, hiking his leg up like a pitcher on a baseball mound, and threw his bowling ball down the lane. It hit the center pin.

"STEE-RIKE!" he shouted. His sunburned ears stuck out beneath Reuben's John Deere cap. "I'm right behind you."

Charlie Carter, who was an old high school buddy of Reuben and Uncle Tommy waved them off. "You go on. I think I'll stay put and keep your seats warm for you at the bar." He sniffed. "Can't be involved in such mischief, considering I am the deputy sheriff and all."

"You never cared about the law when you were a kid," Tommy said.

Charlie's jowls lifted in a smirk. His bristly dark hair showed an unusual solitary patch of white hair starting at his forehead like a thin streak of lightning through the middle of his head. Aunt Hattie called Charlie's patch of white hair "the mark of the devil." The sheriff scratched the snowy patch of his crewcut. "Well, come back and let me know how it all comes out."

When they got to the trailer Reuben took out his pocketknife and picked the lock that Luther had installed on Uncle Walter's door that very morning. The drunken intruders staggered into the tidy trailer. As Reuben stumbled toward the shelf of cookie jars, he tripped on a mousetrap concealed under the skirt of the avocado-green recliner.

He hopped around the trailer trying to shake off the mousetrap snagged on his boot. His wild jumping made him dizzy. The mousetrap flew off and he fell into Uncle Tommy, who fell into the flimsy paneled wall. The bump shook the small trailer. The zucchini cookie jar tumbled from the newly built shelf and shattered into tiny shards of green vegetable ceramic.

He shook his head and pushed his glasses back up his nose. "Walter's got so many dadburn vegetables, he won't notice if one's missing." Uncle Tommy flipped his finger at the broken cookie jar and wrinkled his nose. "What was that green thing supposed to be anyway?"

Reuben hooked his thumbs around his overall straps and kicked at the broken pieces with his big farmer's boot. "Zucchini. My zucchinis won first prize over at the county fair two summers ago."

Reuben liked to tell Ivy how he'd been a farmer all his life. He grew abundant crops of corn and soybeans and had a big garden with all kinds of exceptionally large vegetables which won blue ribbons every year at the McKinley County Fair. The extraordinarily large crops grew in the fertile fields directly behind his house. He swore his high-yield crops resulted from his expert farming methods, but many local people believed that his crops grew so large because dead bodies lay buried beneath his fields. The fact that the Weeping Willow Cemetery at Deadman's Woods was a short distance away only added to the spooky rumors.

For decades, he had farmed the acreage that belonged to his family. But the family line stopped with Reuben. As much as he wanted them, he and his wife had no children.

The two tipsy friends swept up the remains of the ceramic zucchini and buried the evidence of their crime in the trailer park dumpster so Walter wouldn't be tipped off to the zucchini murder. Then they headed back to the Blue Moon to tell the sheriff and their drinking buddies about their latest hilarious prank.

As they snuck past the window of Bertha Tuttle's double-wide trailer next door, the red gingham curtains moved a little.

Later that night, Uncle Walter and Ivy came back to his trailer to get more bottles of Dr. Pepper for their weekly Saturday game night at Grandma Violet's house. As soon as they walked in the door, Uncle Walter stopped.

"Ivy, my trailer's been violated again." He pointed to his green recliner, which was never out of place. "Somebody moved my chair."

Ivy grabbed Uncle Walter's arm and looked up at him with her blue eyes. Her nose twitched. "It smells like Uncle Tommy in here. It was him and Reuben again, wasn't it?"

Uncle Walter pursed his lips. He sniffed the air. "Yep, that's the stink of Old Sage."

After a quick roll call of Uncle Walter's cookie jars, they discovered the zucchini, the last vegetable in the alphabet, was missing.

"First my eggplant and now my zucchini. Cookie jars aren't safe in this world anymore and no number of locks can keep Tommy from his mischief."

Uncle Walter picked up a small ceramic fragment off the floor. He showed Ivy the broken bit of zucchini, resting it in the palm of his well-manicured hand. "Evidence of foul play."

Ivy hugged him. "I'm sorry, Uncle Walter. Why can't Uncle Tommy and Reuben just leave you alone?"

Uncle Walter ran his hand through his thick black hair. "It's hard for Tommy to let a good rivalry die." He shrugged with a heavy, exasperated sigh. "And Reuben, well, he's just Reuben."

Chapter 4

SPOOKS

The next weekend, Grandma asked Uncle Tommy to take Ivy over to Reuben Smith's place to deliver one of Grandma's burnt-sugar cakes.

Reuben and his wife, Patty, lived in an old white weathered farmhouse on the way to Hawks Bluff. Conrad Thrasher's farm was a mile down the road and the house after that belonged to Luther Matthews.

Ivy followed Uncle Tommy to the paint-peeling front porch. He opened the rusty-hinged screen door without knocking. No one locked their doors in Coffey except Uncle Walter, but he was justified because of Uncle Tommy's constant troublemaking and thievery.

Buckshot, Reuben's high-spirited golden retriever, came bounding toward Ivy, wagging his tail. When Buckshot howled, it sounded like he was wailing the words, "oh, no." Ivy laughed and stroked him as they entered the living room.

A clothesline strung down the middle of the living room displayed a load of drying laundry. Reuben's wife, Patty, didn't like to leave the house unless absolutely necessary. Uncle Tommy ducked under Patty's huge underwear and extra-large pink nightgowns dangling on the line. He picked up an open bag of Doritos on the couch and stuffed a handful in his mouth, pointing his Dorito-dusted fingers at Patty's drying underwear.

"You know, that reminds me. Ivy, did I ever tell you about the time Reuben and I got suspended from high school for stealing Edna Jean Whittaker's underwear from the girl's locker room and hoisting it up the library flagpole on Halloween?"

Ivy nodded. "Yeah, you've told me that like a hundred times."

Reuben came in from the kitchen as Uncle Tommy scratched his armpit. "Well, Edna Jean's eyesight was so bad she couldn't even tell the underwear-flag was hers. It wasn't hardly worth the dang trouble."

Reuben smiled, took his John Deere cap off and scratched his short hair. "The week off from school sure was nice though."

"Only Coffey would have a librarian that's blind as a bat and looks like one, too," said Uncle Tommy.

"But don't forget," Reuben imitated Edna Jean's high-pitched voice, "she's got a developed sense of smell." He tapped his ear. "And exceptionally keen hearing."

Edna Jean Whittaker, almost forty, had become the persnickety town librarian. She cleaned the books and furniture until the drab library smelled of lemon furniture polish and the books slid off the waxy tables and shelves. She kept cleaning because she couldn't see that it was already spotless. The lemon scent of the polish covered up the dusty smell of the old books which was important because Edna Jean had a sensitive nose.

Miss Whittaker did kind of look like a bat. Her dark wig looked like unkempt fur, and her thick glasses enlarged her tiny bat eyes. Edna Jean lived in a small house with a big front lawn only a few blocks from the library. She walked to and from work, opening the library before the sun rose and closing it after the sunset. During the day she lurked among the shadowy stacks of books. The darkness of the library made reading difficult for the town's patrons, but Edna Jean worked best in the dark. The light hurt her eyes.

Ivy stood up and peered around one of Patty's pink nightgowns. "What's wrong with Miss Whittaker?"

Uncle Tommy shoved more Doritos into his mouth and wiped his dusty fingers, making Doritos tracks across his white undershirt.

Reuben looked at Ivy. "Well, nothing really, I guess. She's just mad at life. Her high school boyfriend married her best friend and they moved away. Edna Jean stayed in Coffey."

Uncle Tommy reached into his mouth to dig out the Doritos stuck to his teeth. "I need a beer," he said, going into the kitchen.

Ivy dodged the hanging laundry and walked across the room to where Buckshot stretched out in front of the couch. The dog nudged her and she scratched his ears. She looked up at Reuben. "Why do you help Uncle Tommy play tricks on people like Edna Jean and Uncle Walter?"

Reuben rubbed his sunburned neck. Sprigs of hair grew out of his large ears. "I guess it's just something to do."

"Cause you're mad at life?"

Uncle Tommy came back into the living room with the bag of Doritos and a beer. "Walter deserves it. He's always looking down his nose at me."

Heavy thuds coming down the stairs announced Patty's arrival. Although it was late in the summer afternoon, Patty Smith still wore a pink flannel nightgown, identical to the ones drying in the living room. Ivy remembered a time when Patty didn't wear her nightgown during the day. But Grandma had told Ivy that as Patty grew larger and sank deeper into her sadness, she stopped dressing. Since she rarely left the house, changing out of her nightgown didn't seem necessary.

Grandma often urged Uncle Tommy to take Ivy to visit Patty and Reuben. She explained to Ivy that Patty hadn't always been so withdrawn. Barely eighteen years old when she married Reuben, Patty used to love running in the fields behind their farmhouse. She had helped Reuben wrestle the calves to the ground for ear tagging. She desired nothing more than to raise a family with Reuben on their small farm. Patty planned on six children, just for starters. But each year she didn't get pregnant, she sank deeper into a depression. All Patty wanted was a baby, and when no baby came, Grandma explained, all she wanted was food. Patty couldn't get filled up.

Reuben tried to soothe his sad wife the only way he knew how. He filled the shelves with groceries from the Hy-Vee store. He brought home pizzas from the Pizza Shed and fried tenderloin sandwiches and French fries from the Coffey Shop.

Ivy understood Patty's emptiness. She wanted parents.

Patty snatched the bag of Doritos away from Uncle Tommy. Reuben helped her over to the couch where she slumped into her well-worn seat and stuffed Doritos into her mouth. "I agree with Ivy. You shouldn't make fun of people. Nobody should have to endure torment."

Reuben waved his hand high in the air. "Tell that to the spooks."

While forty-year-old Patty was heartbroken over not having any children, Reuben understood why they remained childless. It was the ghosts.

Reuben held the spooks responsible for every power outage, roof leak, door slam, missing sock, cold draft, creaky floorboard, and broken furnace in the house, and when Patty didn't get pregnant, he blamed them for that, too. The spooks became a daily part of Reuben's life. He spoke about them as if they were a commonplace occurrence. Reuben constantly talked about the spirits to his friends as they drank coffee or ate lunch at the Coffey Shop. His friends enjoyed hearing Reuben's ghost stories as much as he enjoyed telling them. The only difference was that Reuben believed them.

Patty licked Dorito dust from her chubby fingers. Reuben patted his wife's shoulder and sat down beside her on the couch. "It wasn't your fault. Those ghosts made my seed unfruitful."

Ivy shivered every time Reuben talked about the spirits roaming the hallways and filling up the empty spaces of his small farmhouse. It didn't help that the tombstones of Weeping Willow Cemetery loomed eerily in the distance across Reuben's fields.

Ivy held onto Buckshot for comfort, but he stretched his legs, gripping the carpet with his paws and howled his signature "oh, no" dog-sound before sauntering upstairs.

"Why are the ghosts here?" Ivy asked.

Reuben tucked his hands in the pockets of his overalls. "I don't know. I remember the ghosts came right after my little brother died. I was just a kid. Can't remember the funeral or where he was buried, only the cold spell that winter and not having my brother. I reckon the ghosts came to get my brother's soul and take him to the world beyond. But the spirits never left. Must've gotten stuck here among the living. Anyhow, something got real messed up, and no new souls can come to our house."

A loud thump sounded upstairs, and Ivy jumped. She looked up at the ceiling and then back at Reuben.

Reuben raised his eyebrows. "See?"

"Probably just Buckshot's tail banging against something," Uncle Tommy said.

"Why didn't you move?" Ivy asked Reuben.

Reuben stood up and walked to the back door. "Come here."

Ivy followed Reuben onto the small back porch with Uncle Tommy trailing behind them. Patty stayed on the couch eating Doritos. She'd heard him talk about this many times.

Reuben swept his arm across his acreage. "This place is my home. Lived here all my life. I know it. It knows me. I reckon, sometimes, your home is worth the sacrifice." He cleared his throat and spat over the side of the porch, barely missing a chicken pecking in the dirt yard.

Ivy looked at Reuben's fields and the weathered red barn that had stood there since Reuben was a little boy. The Weeping Willow Cemetery appeared on the horizon as if waiting for something. The cemetery was in no hurry. Everyone came to it eventually.

"You know my dad's buried over there," Ivy said, pointing to the cemetery.

Reuben nodded. Uncle Tommy stared at the cemetery in the distance.

"But my mother isn't. Do you know where she is, Uncle Tommy?"

Uncle Tommy shook his head. "Nope." Then he hurried into the house.

Reuben patted Ivy's shoulder. "Anyway, sometimes you got to stay to keep your home. The ghosts be danged."

And although Ivy saw Patty's empty spirit, she hadn't seen any ghosts—yet.

Chapter 5

EAVESDROPPING ISN'T POLITE

In Iowa, the seasons are distinct and certain. Summer brings a humid, sweet-smelling heat. Fall carries a cool misty breath of frost. Winter blows cold and blustery. Spring grows a windy fresh rebirth. Each season creates its own beauty in its own time. But as soon as one season arrives, the earth yearns for change and a new season emerges.

Ivy grew up with that same intense yearning for change.

The air hung heavy on that hot summer day in 1966. Rivers of sweat left eight-year-old Ivy's sleeveless white shirt and blue shorts damp and sticky. She couldn't wait for fall. She parked her bike in the metal rack outside the library. She'd come to see if her best friend, Nick Jerome, was hanging out at his father's law office on Main Street.

Nick's mother, Ellen, who was thirty-three years old but looked much older, had suffered from what Grandma told Ivy was a nervous breakdown. She kept mainly to herself while her husband Peter and son Nick took care of her. She refused to talk to anyone else. But she was often seen out walking the streets of Coffey alone, sometimes at night. Ivy and everyone else in town got used to her adventures on foot and began calling them "Ellen's walkabouts."

Ivy would often see her walking by 4120 in her layered, mismatched clothes and unkempt hair. She looked extremely lonely sometimes, yet other times she seemed determined and bold like a lone explorer on an important mission. Nick seldom mentioned her except to say he needed to go home to check on her.

She had spoken to Ellen late one summer night when Ivy was in her front yard, catching fireflies in a mason jar. The fogger, a tractor that sprayed huge billows of bug spray throughout the town to get rid of mosquitoes and other insects, headed down Meadowlark Lane.

Ivy watched Ellen stride onto Meadowlark Lane in the path of the oncoming fogger, but what Ellen didn't see was a huge poisonous timber rattlesnake, coiled up and enjoying the warmth of the road.

To avoid breathing the toxic fumes, Grandma always made Ivy run into the house and shut the windows and doors when the fogger came. But that night, frightened for Ellen, Ivy ignored the fogger and ran toward Nick's mother, pointing and yelling, "Snake!" The loud fogger was nearly upon them and Ellen didn't hear.

Ivy grabbed a stick. "Snake!" she yelled again. She hit the snake until it slithered away just as the fogger arrived and Ellen looked up. When the smoke cleared, Nick's mother was gone but saved from the snake. Ivy could see her continuing her walkabout down the road. Ellen turned and waved her thank you. Ivy waved back. Then Ellen had continued her solitary exploration into the night like a ghostly apparition.

On that hot summer's day, on her way to find Nick Jerome, Ivy saw the usually homebound Patty Smith shuffle down the sidewalk toward the Hy-Vee grocery store. She stared at her friend, who was wearing a pink nightgown beneath a long stretched-out sweater in the thick summer heat. What was Patty doing out of her house?

Before Ivy could call to her, she heard someone yell. Weston Thrasher, the mayor's son, was leaning against the dime store wall. "Fatty Patty, her big butt's sore, 'cause she can't get through the bathroom door."

Ivy flushed with embarrassment for her. The heartbroken Patty turned and glanced at the young taunter for a moment before lumbering on alone. Ivy dashed after her and threw her arms around the women's soft, sweaty middle. She buried her face in Patty's old sweater, which smelled faintly of Doritos and her dog Buckshot.

"Weston's mean and hateful to everyone," Ivy said.

Patty bent down and cupped Ivy's freckled face in her hands. "Don't worry about Weston Thrasher. I don't care if his father is the mayor. That boy is nothing but a backwoods hooligan."

Ivy glanced over at the thirteen-year-old boy across the street. "My grandma says Weston's soul left with his mother when she died."

"Well, in that case, I'm sure we've got an extra soul floating around our place he could use."

Ivy giggled. "What are you doing in town?"

"Reuben's in the fields and I was out of Doritos." She breathed heavily. "Oh my, I'm not used to walking. I need to keep going. Goodbye, dear. Stay away from those Thrashers, if you can."

Patty tottered on toward the store to buy more chips to fill her cupboards and her empty heart. Alone on the street, Ivy spied on Weston out of the corner of her eye. Patty Smith wasn't the only person Weston tormented but most people in

Coffey overlooked the boy's cruelty because his father was the mayor and the banker, and because of the tragic circumstances surrounding his mother's death.

Ivy had overheard the story from Edna Jean the librarian when she was talking to Bertha at the library. One chilly winter day about a week after Ivy's parents' car accident, Conrad had reported that his much younger wife, Mildred, was missing after unexplainably being gone for several days. Sheriff Carter and his two deputies formed search parties and volunteers from town combed the woods at Conrad's farm and nearby Hawks Bluff as well as Reuben and Luther's fields. But they found no trace of Mildred.

A week later, a few days before Christmas, Conrad found something floating under the old swimmer's dock in the middle of the placid lake behind his house. It was his beloved wife, drowned but well preserved by the frigid water.

George Kelsey, the county coroner and town doctor, examined the body. He found that Mildred Thrasher had drowned in the lake. Locals speculated that the slight rocking motion of the floating dock kept the ice from forming in that part of the pond, leading to the discovery of her body. Otherwise, they might not have found her until spring. But how exactly she came to be floating in the peaceful lake remained a mystery that was often whispered about out of earshot of the Thrashers.

The Baker Funeral Home held Mildred's service and when the casket closed, so did Sheriff Carter's investigation. After asking only a few questions, he left his friend Conrad alone with his grief. Without any witnesses, nothing more could be done.

Conrad raised his son, Weston, without much guidance in the big farmhouse by the lake that took his wife, and Weston soon ran wild.

Today, Ivy wanted to avoid Weston, so, she took the long way. She crossed the street and headed down the alley between the dime store and the bank to see if Nick was at his father's law office.

Weston followed her, chanting in a sing-song voice. "Here comes Poison Ivy. Don't let her touch you. She poisoned her parents, and they died."

Weston scratched imaginary itches all over himself and fell over, clutching his throat. He lay on his back in the alley, writhing desperately as his hands pawed the air.

Ivy kept walking. "Weston, you're weird. You know that?"

"That's better than being poison." He ran ahead of her and blocked her way down the gravel alley. "Poison Ivy."

Ivy narrowed her dark blue eyes and tried to push past him. "Get out of my way. You're nothing but a backwoods hooligan."

Weston grabbed Ivy and pinned her arms behind her back. He kicked her leg and she fell to the ground, scraping her knee on the gravel. "My dad says you're just like your mother. Worthless."

Weston triumphantly spat on the ground next to where Ivy was sprawled. Then he darted across Main Street and disappeared around the corner of the Farmer's Co-op. Ivy got up and tucked her tangled hair behind her ears. She knew where he was going. Behind the Farmer's Co-op towered the huge grain silos where the corn was stored after it was weighed. Ivy and her friends often played "king of the mountain" in the massive piles of corn, despite the danger of sinking deep in the avalanche of dusty grain. Ivy had learned to climb the shifting hill of corn by stretching her limbs out wide like a spider. This way, she could safely maneuver her way up the golden corn mound.

She knew Weston would hide in the silos, sneaking in

through the grain bin door because it wasn't full of corn since the harvest hadn't started. She clenched her fists and chased him across the street. When she reached the library, she stopped. Weston disappeared around the corner of the Farmer's Co-op office. He wasn't worth the trouble. Besides, her scraped knee hurt.

Ivy brushed away the gravel stuck to her elbow. Her leg hurt where Weston kicked her. She sat down on the bench outside the Coffey Shop and looked at her scraped knee. When she glanced up, she noticed Conrad Thrasher, Weston's father, standing under the big bank clock on the corner, watching her. He threw down his cigarette and ground it out with his boot. Conrad was the banker in town that approved loans for cars and houses. Without much oversight, he never approved loans for the black people on Mulberry Street to purchase a home beyond the railroad tracks.

Weston had called her mother worthless. How dare he? Luther said she was friends with Weston's mother.

The door to the Coffey Shop opened, and Nick and his father, Peter Jerome, came out. She limped over to them.

"Hi Ivy. You okay?" Peter asked.

"Just scraped my knee but it's okay."

Peter had become a good friend to Ivy's grandma after he settled some legal matters when Ivy's Grandpa Sam died. Since then, Peter's investment advice had allowed Grandma to live in relative comfort.

"Well, you kids have fun," Peter said as he hurried across the town square and up the steps of his law office.

The county courthouse, the centerpiece of Coffey, was located in the town square. It held the sheriff's office, the jail, and the county offices. Many of Coffey's businesses were also

located in the square around the courthouse, including the
dime store, a vacant beauty shop, the bank, the post office, the
library, the Hy-Vee grocery store, the Coffey Shop, and Peter
Jerome's law office.

Ivy and Nick followed Nick's father to his building.

"What do you want to do today?" Ivy asked.

They leaned against the two-story brick building and threw
pebbles onto the Main Street. "Let's ride out to Hawks Bluff,"
Ivy suggested.

The two eight-year-olds climbed up the steep flight of
wooden stairs to the law office. The door was open. Before they
reached the top of the stairs, they could hear Peter's secretary,
Uncle Walter's nosey neighbor, Bertha Tuttle, talking on the
phone at her desk.

"I wouldn't tell him to his face, but I hate those ugly things,
whatever they are, on his lawn. They bring down the value of
the mobile home park—too tacky." Her tongue clicked the roof
of her mouth. "But he's just as proud as punch of them." She
paused. "I know. Walter lets Tommy and his friends go in and
out of that trailer at all hours of the night. I tell you, it just isn't
proper."

Ivy stopped on the stairs unseen and held up her arm to stop
Nick from going any further. She put her finger to her mouth
and they backed up against the stairwell. They quickly peered
around the corner and watched Bertha through the open door.
Her makeup made her look a little like a jack-in-the-box clown.
Her bright red lipstick was smeared a little at the corners, her
powder ended abruptly at her fleshy chin, and her cheekbones
were highlighted with two round, red circles.

Ivy swept her bangs off her sweaty forehead. "Is she talking
about Uncle Walter?"

Nick nodded and put his fingers to his lips.

Bertha's voice boomed down the stairwell. "It's not gossip, mind you, Edna Jean. I saw it with my own eyes."

Ivy and Nick sat down on the wooden stairs as Bertha droned on about other offending Coffey social crimes as Ivy wiped the sweat off her neck.

"Why would she want to spy on Uncle Walter?"

"My dad says she's lonely. She goes to all the funerals in town whether she was friends with the dead people or not."

Nick ran his hand across his bristly butch haircut. Porcupine hair. The only barber in town had moved away years ago. So, Nick's father used his clippers to cut Nick's hair, which left only a little stubble of light brown hair on the top of Nick's head.

Ivy tenderly touched her scraped knee and then looked at her finger to see if there was any blood. "How does she know who's dead?"

"I don't know. Maybe she reads the stories in the paper."

"I wonder if she went to my mom's and dad's funerals?"

"Probably."

Ivy and Nick stood up and watched Bertha from the top step. Bertha finger-fluffed her hair, which was piled high on top of her head like a beehive. The brassy red color was the result of a bad do-it-yourself dye job. The barber, Edna Jean's boyfriend, had left town with the local beautician to find a town that would appreciate their skills. Bertha had to make do. So did Edna.

The two kids slipped past Bertha's desk. She was too busy talking to pay any attention to them. "Tommy's never been the same since his brother's crash. No-account woman." Bertha clicked her tongue and tapped her bright red fingernails on her desk.

Ivy froze and grabbed Nick's arm. "What did she say? She's talking about Aunt Hattie."

Bertha heard her and turned, finally noticing Ivy over the top of her cat-eye glasses. "Eavesdropping isn't polite." She shook her finger. "No one likes a snoop."

Ivy walked over to Bertha's desk. "Mrs. Tuttle, did you go to my parents' funerals?"

Bertha cupped her hand on the phone's mouthpiece. "Edna Jean, I'll have to get back to you." She hung up the phone and sniffed. "Well, yes, I did go to your father's funeral. Lovely spread of food. But as I remember it, your uncles got into a ridiculous squabble over some silly turkey sandwich."

"It was pastrami."

Peter appeared at the door of his office, just past Bertha's desk. He tugged at his white starched cuffs, fiddled with his red bow tie, and cleared his throat.

"So, who was the no-account woman?" asked Ivy curiously.

Bertha adjusted her glasses before leaning forward. Nick's father took a few steps toward them and tapped Bertha's desk, interrupting her.

"Bertha, shouldn't you be getting back to work?"

Bertha, her nose high in the air, clicked her tongue and turned back to the typewriter.

Peter rubbed Nick's bristly head. "What are you guys going to do today?"

"Can we ride our bikes out to Hawks Bluff Park?" Nick asked.

"Sure. Just be careful."

They headed out of the office, passing Bertha's desk again. At the top of the stairs, Ivy turned back. "How's your nose, Mrs. Tuttle?"

"My nose?" Bertha pushed up her blue cat-eye glasses and rubbed her large round nose. "There's nothing wrong with my nose."

"I heard it was stuck to your trailer window."

"Well, I never!" Bertha blushed the color of the ruby rouge circles on her cheeks. She tapped her brown chunky sensible shoes beneath her desk. Peter quickly stepped back into his office, hiding his smile.

Ivy and Nick scampered down the steps to the street. Ivy's pink rubber flip flops slapped the heels of her bare feet, making a loud clicking sound. When the heavy door shut behind them, Ivy and Nick burst into uncontrollable laughter.

The robin sitting on the library flagpole watched them, cocking his head back and forth. Nick leaned against the old brick building, his brown eyes sparkling.

"Ivy Taylor, you've got spunk."

Ivy held her stomach and giggled. "I know. I got it from my grandma. She says us Taylor women are known to be a little surly."

Ivy knew when the robin told Grandma that one, she would throw back her head and laugh for a long time.

Ivy and Nick got on their bikes. Ivy's knee still hurt a little, but she soon forgot about it as they raced through town toward Hawks Bluff Park. As they rode, Ivy kept an eye out for the yellow glimmer of the goldfinch. Grandma always said that the goldfinch, the Iowa state bird, brought good luck.

Chapter 6

THRASHER'S POND

A mile outside of town, a steep grassy cliff rose a hundred feet, blunt and rough but not unkind. The hawks flew magically in the sky above it, soaring, it seemed, to the clouds and gliding back to the earth. A big lake with a muddy bottom and a short expanse of beach spread out at Hawk's Bluff's base—the only place Coffey kids could cool off in the summer. They rode past the lake filled with swimmers enjoying the water as they headed to the ball fields.

Their friend, Raven Montgomery, waved to them from the gray metal bleachers of the baseball park. Nick and Ivy dropped their bikes and hiked up to meet her. Her magenta nails flashed as she waved again. Grandma never let Ivy paint her nails.

Ivy and Nick sat down next to Raven on the old metal seats, hot from the summer sun. Raven got up and wedged her way between them. Ivy leaned across Raven to talk to Nick.

"That was weird at your dad's office, wasn't it? Did you hear what Bertha said? Do you think she knows something about my parents' accident?"

"No. If she knew anything, she'd tell. She can't keep a secret," Nick said.

"I wish I knew what really happened that night."

Raven flipped back her long straight black hair. "You're

a kid. Nobody's going to tell you anything. Anyway, there's nothing you can do about it."

"Be quiet, Raven," said Nick.

Raven, wearing a sleeveless top, shrugged her tan shoulders. "I'm just saying she's stuck here with her grandma."

Ivy put her hand up to block the bright sun. She looked at Raven. "No, I'm not. I'm going to travel around the world after I get out of high school. Then I'm going to college far away—maybe even New York City or London."

"Doubt it. You'll probably end up at Warner College." Raven picked up a rock and threw it at a bird eating a piece of popcorn on the ground. The rock hit the bird's wing, causing it to stumble before flying away.

"What'd you do that for?" said Ivy.

Raven tipped her head to the side and flipped her long black hair over her shoulder. "I just wanted to see if I could get it."

Coffey's five o'clock whistle sounded, part of its intricate communication system of blaring loud sounds across the town. The constant screeching, high-pitched five o'clock whistle announced the day's passing and marked the end of the workday for many locals. A wailing siren, starting low and going high, meant a tornado had been sighted in the area, while a lower pitched horn called the town's volunteer fireman to a local fire.

"There's the five o'clock whistle. I got to go. Grandma doesn't like me to be late."

Nick jumped up. "I'll ride with you part of the way."

Raven brushed the dirt from her magenta-painted toenails sticking out of her new leather sandals. "I can stay as late as I want. Stay here with me, Nick. We can have fun."

He shook his head. "Nah, I got to go check on my mom."

Ivy and Nick climbed down the bleachers and got on their

bikes while Raven stayed at the park. Ivy envied Raven's carefree life. Why did Grandma always tell her what to do? Grandma didn't want her to have any fun.

Ivy and Nick rode home on the back roads because a sign said the road to town was being tarred and graveled. Ivy tucked her sweaty hair behind her ears. They pedaled past the turnoff to old Highway 69, close to where her parents had died. Ivy stared back at the road that changed her life. Her wheel hit a rock and the bike wobbled. She gripped the handlebars to keep it steady. Nick squeezed his bike horn to warn the sparrows gathering in the gravel road. The birds exploded in a burst of flapping wings as they rose into the air.

"I don't think it's fair that your parents are dead," said Nick.

"I know. My mom and dad would have let me do anything I wanted; but they're not here and Grandma's got too many rules."

The birds circled in the air.

Ivy and Nick reached the turn-off for Deadman's Woods which surrounded the Weeping Willow Cemetery. Nick waved goodbye and headed through the shortcut to town to meet his dad before heading home. Although Ivy knew Grandma would be expecting her, she took the long way home in delighted defiance.

She waved as she passed Reuben, driving his tractor in his soybean fields that bordered the road. In the distance, the Thrasher farmhouse sat near the pond. Grandma did not allow Ivy to go near the Thrasher farm, but Raven went wherever she wanted, and her mother didn't care. Ivy pedaled faster. Raven was the youngest child and the only girl in a family of seven boys. Grandma said Raven's parents were simply exhausted and slightly uninterested, so Raven was left to roam.

Ivy rode past Conrad Thrasher's fields on the way home. Wild roses grew across the side of the ditch like a soft blanket of pink and green. Summer's hot breath gently waved their petals. Iowa stretched into many acres of flat fertile land, aching to be farmed. With smooth contours and gradual contrasts, Iowa's peaceful beauty soothed the soul and emboldened the spirit.

Ivy put her head down and pedaled faster. She turned off at Conrad Thrasher's pond near his farmhouse and hopped off her bike. Staring at the dark water where Conrad's wife was found dead, she walked her bike toward the forbidden pond. Grasshoppers popped up and down like popcorn in the tall summer grass.

Near the shore, cattails and lily pads grew from the dark water's muddy bottom. The deep steady croaking of a frog echoed across the water. Dragonflies hummed through the air, skimming across the still surface of the pond like tiny water-skiers.

Birds seldom visited the lake. Grandma said birds could smell the death still floating under the dock. Ivy laid her bike in the tall grass. A bumblebee buzzed in a white fluffy ball of clover nearby. Ivy kicked off her flip flops and walked through weeds and cattails before reaching the pond.

She stared at the deadly dock floating at the center of the pond. It remained in place by ropes attached underneath by hooks on the corners and tied to concrete blocks on the bottom of the lake.

She waded into the shallow water. With each step, the thick mud oozed between her toes. When she almost reached the dock, the bottom of the pond dropped off, and she slipped. Ivy sank, disappearing under the muddy water. The lake contained a power all its own. Immersed in the muddy pond, she was afraid she was going to drown and end up floating in the water like Mildred.

Kicking her legs, she swam toward the surface. She didn't have much air left. She popped above the water, gasping, and found herself underneath the old swimmer's dock.

Thin streaks of sunlight found their way through the old wooden slats. Ivy bobbed there, her head almost touching the dock as she treaded water. Although she had plenty of air to breathe, she panicked as she imagined Mildred's dead body caught under the dock in the cold for a whole week and Ivy breathed heavily as if all the air had escaped.

A flutter of wings and several chirps from above drew her attention. What were birds doing on the dock? Ivy took a deep breath and dove under again. She swam out from under the dock and climbed up on the floating platform with the bright sunlight hitting her face. The birds on the dock took flight and scattered across the darkening sky. She watched the birds fly away, scattering across the darkening sky. She stared down at the water's glassy surface. A frog jumped off a lily pad, sending circles rippling from its impact.

How could Mildred Thrasher drown in such a quiet pond? But Ivy still felt a hidden terror in that water. Goosebumps spread across her arms.

A car approached the farmhouse, leaving a smoky trail of dust behind it. Conrad Thrasher's big white Ford Lincoln Town car careened down the road toward her, like a giant whale breaking the surface of the ocean. She didn't want to be at the pond anymore and she didn't want Conrad to catch her there.

Ivy jumped off the old wooden dock and swam to shore. When she got to her bike, she picked up her flip flops and grabbed the bike's handlebars. She jogged beside the bike up to the gravel road just as Conrad drove by.

He slowed down and pulled the car up beside Ivy, rolling down the passenger window and leaning out. Sweat soaked his shirt.

"Well, well, if it isn't little Miss Ivy Taylor. All wet. Did you go for a swim in my pond?"

Ivy jumped on her bike, with her flip flops in hand. She didn't have time to put them on. "I just stopped for a second." She pumped the pedals, wobbling to get the bike straight. Why hadn't she listened to Grandma? She shouldn't have gone to the Thrashers' pond.

Conrad gestured to the back of his car. "Put your bike in the trunk and get in. You're soaking wet."

Despite the intense heat, a shiver ran through her body like an ice cube down her back. She suddenly knew that Conrad had killed his wife. She could feel it. "No thanks."

Her heart pounded, and the sound of gravel crunched under the car's tires. The big white car drove beside Ivy as she pedaled her bike down the side of the road.

Conrad pounded the roof of the car. "Hey, you think you're better than the rest of us, don't you? Just like your mother. Miss La-De-Dah couldn't get out of Coffey fast enough. She couldn't wait for nothing."

His face contorted, and spit flew out of his mouth. "I said get in." He swerved the big white Lincoln in front of her and stopped.

But Ivy didn't stop. She dodged his car by riding along the edge of the ditch on the side of the road and pedaled as fast as she could.

Conrad's car could not follow so he got out and ran after her. "You're not who you think you are, Miss Uppity." Conrad lunged and grabbed her.

Ivy screamed. Her bike wobbled on the loose gravel. She pulled away from him and stood up, pumping the pedals. She saw Ellen, Nick's mother, the perpetual hiker, emerge out of the ditch ahead of her and onto the road, carrying a walking stick. Ivy rode as fast as she could. She could hear Conrad's heavy breathing right behind her. She could smell his sweat and his cigarette breath.

Ellen stepped into the path and Conrad stopped his chase. Ellen waved her stick and yelled, "Snake!"

Ivy looked back and waved to Ellen as her knees quivered and her foot slipped off the pedal. For a moment the bike lurched out of control on the loose gravel.

Conrad flailed his arms at Ellen. "Have you lost what little of your mind you have left?" He moved around her.

Suddenly a flock of sparrows fluttered out of the cornfield near the road and flew low over them in unison, a brown cloud of birds. This distracted Conrad long enough for Ivy to make her move. She swerved off the path and rode into the middle of a cornfield. As Ivy disappeared among the stalks, Ellen turned and continued her walkabout as if nothing had happened.

The rows of corn swallowed Ivy and she merged into the rippling field. She barely noticed the pedals digging into her bare feet as the corn stalks whipped by. She breathed heavily and gripped the handlebars. Sweat dripped down her face. She didn't stop pedaling until she came out of the cornfield near the old hermit lady's house.

Rosie Buckley, seventy-one, a solitary woman of meager means, took care of numerous dogs and cats. She kept to herself and seldom came to town, but when she did, she went after dark, so she wouldn't have to run into anyone. She sequestered herself with her ill-mannered animals in a run-down shack with no running water or electricity. Her cracked and sooty fireplace heated the tiny house that looked as if it were built by disgruntled and unskilled gnomes.

Every fall around the end of October, Luther Matthews, Rosie's neighbor, brought enough wood for Rosie and her animals to keep warm through the winter. Luther neatly stacked the wood against the side of Rosie's little house. He brought it after dark, to spare her the embarrassment of having to say thank you. Rosie didn't believe in accepting charity.

Ivy rode out of the tall cornfield and into Rosie's yard. She didn't notice that the sparrows had followed her out of the cornfield, an umbrella of brown high in the air. She avoided the unruly weeds and took a shortcut to the road across Rosie's bare front yard.

The door to Rosie's shack opened and there she stood, looking like the witch from "Hansel and Gretel." A pack of barking wild dogs tumbled out her door and gave chase, nipping at Ivy's ankles as she rode past.

Rosie's wrinkled face was like an old dried-apple doll. "Get off my property," she scolded in a raspy voice.

Ivy gripped the bike's handlebars and turned to Rosie. "I'm trying."

The relentless dogs ran down the path and onto the road after her, barking and biting at her legs as she pedaled away. One enthusiastically vicious dog lunged at her bare foot, but his teeth clamped down on the bike pedal instead. Ivy screamed and held her leg out as the pedal whipped around. The dog tumbled into a ditch.

As she rounded the corner near Luther's house, she saw him walking out of the woods onto the road. He looked like a disheveled woodsman escaped from a nut house, his clothes drooping, his hair sticking up at all angles, and an ax in his hand.

He set the ax against a tree. As Ivy approached, he clapped and raised his hands toward the dogs.

"Wild dogs, cease."

The frantic dogs stopped their ferocious pursuit and trotted over to Luther, sniffing his feet. Ivy looked back gratefully at Luther and gave a quick wave. Her hair whipped across her sunburned face, but she pedaled on. The sparrows trailed above her, making circles in the air.

Ivy rode through town without stopping, going as fast as she could to 4120. Eventually her bike wobbled past the big maple tree in her front yard. The sparrows landed in an unorganized flutter in its big, comforting branches.

Grandma was waiting for her on the front porch with her hands on her wide hips. The birds must have already told her. "Little Missy, I hear you've been down at Conrad Thrasher's pond again and by the looks of it, probably in it. What's my rule about the Thrasher place?"

Ivy set the bike down on the ground, panting from the fright and her wild ride. Muddy pond water dripped from her clothes and down her legs and arms. "Not to go there. But I'm fine."

Grandma shook her head. "That's not the point. You disobeyed me. Go to your room for a while." Grandma tapped her tennis shoe on the porch.

Ivy narrowed her eyes. She threw down her pink flip flops and balled up her fists in frustration. "Those birds talk too much," she huffed. "They're like spies in the sky. You never let me do anything fun."

Her bare feet hurt as she stomped across the wooden porch. She slammed the screen door but Grandma marched in after her.

"You certainly can't do things that are dangerous, even if they are fun."

"I don't care what you say." As she walked away, Ivy flipped her hair like Raven did, but her hair fell tangled and wet against her sunburned neck.

Grandma grabbed Ivy's arm and turned her around. "Well, you should care. I'm your grandmother."

Ivy threw her shoulders back. "I don't want you. I want my mother. I need my mother."

Grandma's angry face flushed red and she let go of Ivy's arm. She pointed up the grand staircase, her flabby arm swinging. "Go to your room now, little missy."

Ivy pulled her mouth into a tight little circle. "You're not my mother. My mother would never be mean to me like you. She would've never gotten mad at me for having fun. Besides, grandmas are supposed to let you do whatever you want. You're not a good grandma."

Ivy dashed up the stairs to her room and slammed the door. She collapsed on the bed, crying and shaking.

A few minutes later, the polished wooden stairs creaked with Grandma's heavy bulk as she climbed the steps to Ivy's room. She knocked on the bedroom door before opening it and sitting down next to Ivy on the bed. Ivy turned away from her to face the wall. Grandma patted Ivy's back. Her wet shirt stuck to her skin.

"Ivy, sit up. I need to tell you something important."

The tears had left trails in the dust and sweat of Ivy's freckled, sunburned cheeks. She sat up.

"Ivy, you and I are taking this journey of life together. We're traveling side by side, sure enough. But you're at the beginning of your journey and I'm nearing the end of mine. Since I know the road, I'm your guide, your protector."

Grandma wiped Ivy's tears away with her thumb. "I wish I was the kind of grandma who could give you everything you want. But I don't have that freedom. There are some things in life we can change and some things we just have to accept. Having me in charge of you is just one of the things you have to accept. Please don't ever say those things to me again. I may be old, but my feelings still get hurt."

"I know. I shouldn't have gone to Thrasher's pond," Ivy said in a quiet voice.

Grandma stroked Ivy's wet, stringy hair. "Don't do it again. It's too dangerous. I don't want anything bad to happen to you."

"Like what happened to Mildred Thrasher?"

"Well . . ." Grandma shifted on the bed. "That man's soul is poison."

"Grandma, did Mildred Thrasher know my mother?"

"Mildred?" Grandma said, but the familiar warmth returned to her eyes. "Honey, in a town this size, everybody knows everybody. Why don't you come on down and get your supper? Warm up the television and set up the TV trays while I dish up the food. We'll eat in front of the TV tonight. Don't grandmas always let their grandkids do that?"

When they finished eating their dinner of meatloaf, mashed potatoes, corn on the cob, and green beans, they watched the night settle in from the covered back porch. Ivy ran around the yard catching fireflies in an old Mason jam jar with holes punched in the lid for air. When she was tired, she sat down next to Grandma on the porch swing to watch the moon rise high in the sky. The bright orb of light glowed through the gathering dark clouds of an approaching storm blowing in from the south—the direction of the worst storms and the strongest winds.

When Ivy got in bed that night, Grandma sat down beside

her. "Tommy's going to empty the trash barrels tomorrow. You can go to the dump with him, but only if you don't hang around that mangled car. It's a death trap. I wish Walter had never told you about it."

The twisted remains of her parents' Pontiac still sat at the town dump, a cold reminder of their last minutes. A tow truck had dumped it there after the accident.

"Okay." She picked up the photo of her parents and placed it on the pillow beside her. The Mason jar of fireflies was the only thing left on her nightstand. "Can Nick go with me?"

"I don't see why not. Nick's a sweet boy. Tommy shouldn't mind one more."

Ivy glanced out the open window. Rain bounced off the roof of the house, announcing the beginning of a summer storm. She pulled at the edge of the daisy quilt. "Grandma, why is Uncle Tommy always mad at me?"

"Oh, dear child, he's not mad at you."

Ivy inhaled the faint fragrance of lilacs from Grandma's skin. "Then why doesn't he like me?"

"He does like you. But not everyone you love will love you back the way you want. Some people hide their fears behind their meanness."

Ivy yawned. "What do you think Conrad Thrasher is afraid of?"

"Hush now. It's time to sleep." Grandma sang "Red River Valley," her voice competing with the sound of the summer rain, sprinkling the earth and soaking into the rich, black Iowa soil. A loud clap of thunder boomed in the distance.

Ivy gripped Grandma's hand. "It's not supposed to rain all night, is it, Grandma?"

"Don't worry, sweetheart, it's just a little rain. I know sometimes storms can sound scary, but they're really one of God's greatest gifts to the earth. Rain helps the farmers' crops grow and makes everything clean and fresh. The earth needs a good scrubbing every now and then. Believe you me."

Grandma patted Ivy's face and then stood up. "I love you more than the great blue sky."

"I love you, too."

The floorboards creaked as she left the room.

Ivy reached over to the Mason jar sitting on her bedside table. She opened the lid and released the fireflies. They flickered in her dark room—nature's own night-lights. The fireflies searched for their freedom until they found their way to the open window. She watched as they flickered, lining up on the windowsill, waiting for the rain to stop to clear their takeoff. She fitfully drifted away to sleep.

The storm picked up, the howling wind and pounding rain providing the backdrop to Ivy's nightmare of fear and fire and her parents' deaths. This time she dreamed that her mother, dressed like in the picture beside her bed, beckoned to her from a distance. Ivy tried to ride her bike to her mother, but Conrad Thrasher grabbed Ivy and wouldn't let go. Then her mother melted away into screams and exploding sparks until only darkness and silence remained.

Ivy woke up screaming. Her urine-soaked nightgown and sheets twisted around her. At the next booming crack of thunder she jumped up, pushed her daisy quilt to the floor, and cowered underneath her bed.

The heavy footsteps of her grandmother echoed down the

long hall. Ivy's bedroom door opened and Grandma padded over, slowly bending to look under the bed. "What are you doing down there?"

"I had a nightmare. It seems like morning will never come."

Grandma held out her hand. "Come on. We'll ride this night out together. I'll stay with you until the morning comes. That's what grandmas are for."

Ivy crawled out from under the bed. "I'm sorry I wet the bed."

Grandma waved her hand and pulled a clean nightgown from the dresser drawer. "*Pshaw*. It's only a little wetness. No need to worry. It's easily fixed, my dear."

After Grandma made the bed and sat down beside her, Ivy thought about her terrifying dream. It all seemed so real and left her with a sense of deep, terrifying foreboding. She reached out for Grandma's hand and played with her wedding ring.

Chapter 7

THE DUMP

The next day Uncle Tommy and his ghost-seeing buddy, Reuben, took Ivy and Nick to the town dump to get rid of the ashes, tin cans, and remnants of unburned trash in the rusty metal barrels from their backyards. The kids bumped along in the back of Uncle Tommy's pickup with Reuben's dog, Buckshot. The sun burned down on Ivy's freckled face as her hair flapped behind her in the humid, dusty air.

The dog howled his "oh, no" sound at the trail of gravel dust from the truck's wheels. Buckshot circled the trash barrels strapped to the bed of the truck with a Frisbee in his mouth as they drove past the rolling hills and woods interspersed with stretches of golden rows of corn. The tall stalks waved in the wind, like an accordion playing lively music.

About two miles east of Reuben's farm, they turned off on a gravel road that led to the town dump. The dump was home to discarded appliances and worn-out furniture, charred garbage, other people's junk, boards, broken glass, and old newspapers. Although it smelled of rotting and burned debris, the dump offered all sorts of treasures. It was also the place where Ivy felt closest to her parents.

The twisted heap of the red Bonneville remained half-buried among the other broken memories of bygone things that came to rest at the town dump. Uncle Tommy avoided his brother's mangled car, driving around to the farthest end of the dumping area. The pickup's wheels kicked up dust and ash as it eased down the slope to a spot where he could dump the burned contents of his trash barrels.

They got out of the pickup and Reuben and Uncle Tommy unloaded the barrels. Buckshot dropped the Frisbee and bounded over the piles of garbage into the trees to chase squirrels. Nick followed Ivy as she headed for the wreckage of her parents' red 1959 Pontiac Bonneville, out of sight of Reuben and Uncle Tommy.

Ivy leaned inside the car through the smashed window. The seats were burned and the steering wheel was strangely melted and twisted. She ran her fingers across the warped dash above the outline of the glove box. The brittle hinges of the handle snapped in her hand when she tried to open it.

Nick pointed. "Let's just pry it open."

She glanced behind her, but Uncle Tommy wasn't looking. Nick dug through the trash heaps until he found a metal rod from a broken baby buggy. He wedged it in the crack at the top of the glove box and pulled down as hard as he could. It didn't budge. He moved it more toward the center. He put all of his weight on it and yanked down. The misshapen glove box cracked open.

Ivy pulled out the contents—an old flashlight, a twisted and singed glove, and half of a charred envelope. As she picked it up, a flash of gold in the air distracted her. She tucked the burned envelope in the front pocket of her shorts and pulled her head out from the car. A goldfinch fluttered down from an old evergreen, like a shiny bit of tinsel shaken loose from the top of a Christmas tree. It perched on an old washing machine that peeked out from the mounds of rubbish. The flight of gold contrasted a mark of stunning beauty among the chaos of litter.

As Ivy and Nick watched the bird, a tall black man and an eight-year-old girl with braids appeared over the piles of debris. The goldfinch circled them before settling on the man's shoulder.

Ivy stared at the untamed bird. She knew of only one other person that the wild birds trusted—Grandma Violet. She elbowed Nick and then called out to her uncle. "Look, Uncle Tommy, can you believe that?"

Uncle Tommy finished dumping the trash barrel and turned around. He squinted at the black man and girl. "No, I can't. Trash going through trash. The dump is like their shopping center."

Uncle Tommy spat out the sunflower seed shells that he'd been chewing since he left home.

Ivy shook her head. "No, I meant the goldfinch on Maggie's father's shoulder."

Uncle Tommy squinted into the summer sun as he gazed around the trash heap. "What goldfinch? I don't see any goldfinch. And who the heck is Maggie?"

Ivy pointed to the little girl. "Right there. That girl is Maggie Norton. She's a friend of ours from school."

The black girl's braids almost touched her shoulders. A few shorter curls escaped by her forehead. Ivy knew Uncle Tommy didn't like black people, but Grandma forbid his use of derogatory racial language around her. Like everyone else, Uncle Tommy obeyed Grandma. But he felt unrestrained in showing his contempt when Grandma couldn't hear.

The pointed tip of his black cowboy boot sent a tin can flying over the trash pile toward the man. Tommy nodded his chin at him. "Oh, you mean Otis. He's as worthless as all those other losers on Mulberry Street."

Ivy ignored Uncle Tommy's tirades against the small

community of black people who lived in Coffey. She turned and grabbed Nick's hand and they scampered up the piles of trash to their friend.

"Hi, Maggie," Ivy said.

"What're you doing?" Nick asked.

Maggie smiled and flipped her braids back. "My dad's looking for some wood to repair our back porch. Miss Shirley fell through our floor." She covered her mouth with her hand and giggled.

Ivy and Nick looked at each other and smiled. They liked Miss Shirley. She was funny.

Maggie's father, Otis, a dashing forty-five-year-old black man with a pencil-thin mustache, tipped his brown plaid cap. "Hello, youngins."

Ivy waved at the tall man the wild birds trusted. "Hi, Mr. Norton." She looked at Maggie. "So, how'd Miss Shirley fall through the floor?"

Maggie swayed her skinny hips and waved her hands in the air. "Dancing to Leon Wilson."

Ivy's eyes widened. "Did he fall in, too?"

Otis chuckled.

"No, he's a famous singer," Maggie said, laughing.

"Oh," Ivy said as Nick danced around the trash heap and exaggeratedly fell down. Ivy and Maggie laughed even harder.

The pickup started behind them. Uncle Tommy called, "Ivy, get down here. Don't touch anything. It's time to go. That means you too, Nick."

"Okay!" Ivy yelled over her shoulder.

Reuben threw the Frisbee in the air and Buckshot chased after it at full speed. The dog knocked over a broken chair as he jumped for the flying disk and caught it in his teeth. Nothing stood in Buckshot's way when he was after a Frisbee.

Reuben walked backward with his hands in the air, gesturing. "Did you see that, Ivy? I got perfect aim or what?"

Ivy gave Reuben a thumbs-up and turned back to Maggie and Otis. "I guess we'd better go. I'll see you later."

Otis took off his cap and ran his hand along the top of his hair, patting his tight waves into place before putting his cap back on. "Nice to see you kids."

Ivy maneuvered down the trash heap. Then she remembered the bird and turned back. "Mr. Norton, that goldfinch landed on your shoulder for a little while, didn't it?"

"Yes, child."

Ivy clapped her hands. "I knew it. That means good luck, you know."

"Good. I need it." He put his arm around his daughter. Ivy looked longingly at his fatherly gesture before she and Nick hurried back towards the truck and the empty trash barrels. It was a goldfinch. She knew it.

As they ran past her parents' wreck, Ivy kissed her fingers and touched the crumpled car that had made her an orphan. She patted her shorts pocket, remembering the piece of burned envelope she had taken from the glove box. She would look at it as soon as she was alone.

On the way back, Uncle Tommy parked in front of the Coffey Shop for his usual mid-morning coffee with his buddies. Ivy and Nick jumped out of the truck and followed Uncle Tommy and Reuben into The Coffey Shop which sat across from the county courthouse in the town square. The restaurant had a Formica counter which accommodated eight red vinyl swivel stools by the grill. Booths lined the walls and a few tables filled the rest of the small restaurant. The warped wooden floor stuck to their shoes as if they walked on sticky flypaper. Charlie Carter, the deputy sheriff, was waiting for them at Uncle Tommy's regular corner booth.

Kitty Decker, a waitress who looked like Olive Oil, brought over carbonated lime drinks called Green Rivers for Ivy and Nick, and a pot of coffee for the men. Her light-blue waitress uniform hung slack on her thin body. The wooden ceiling fans hummed as they pushed around the hot summer air. After a minute, the screen door to the restaurant opened and Conrad Thrasher strutted in.

Charlie waved to him. "Well, if it isn't the dadburn dishonorable mayor. Hey, come on over here. You're just in time for some coffee."

Reuben slid over in the booth and Conrad joined them. Ivy shrunk down in the corner next to Nick, staring at the man the town respected. Conrad's piercing blue eyes stared at Ivy until she looked down at her drink. She stirred her Green River with a straw and pretended she didn't notice him glaring at the silver heart necklace hanging on her neck.

Uncle Tommy sipped his black coffee and turned to the waitress. "Hey, Kitty, what's Howard making in his workshop these days?"

The men bellowed with laughter.

The previous year, Kitty's husband, Howard, a short man with a huge beer gut, had lost his job at the meat packing plant after coming to work drunk and peeing in the meat rinsing trough, contaminating several hundred pounds of beef. The incident was the last in a series of fiascoes brought on by Howard's heavy drinking. He was fired and barred from being within a hundred feet of the plant.

Since then, the whole town talked about how Howard started drinking after breakfast. He chugged beer in a sleeveless white

T-shirt and boxer shorts and hid from his hardworking wife in his garage-turned-workshop.

He spent most of his days building a strange camper for the back of his pickup truck, using boards salvaged from the dump and discarded nails scrounged from construction sites. Crooked nails stuck out of the sides, but it somehow held together. Uncle Tommy and his friends often laughed about how Howard envisioned the camper's potential after finishing off a six pack of beer. The hodgepodge camper made sense when he was drunk.

Inside the camper he built sturdy benches along both sides and below the cab window and bolted them to the truck bed. The rest of the rattletrap camper could blow off with just a whisper of a wind, but the benches weren't going anywhere. He somehow attached the huge ugly camper top to the old truck, leaving the cab window open into the camper.

Every night, Kitty came home from her ten-hour shift at the Coffey Shop and checked on her husband to make sure he hadn't passed out on the cold concrete floor of the workshop while working on, as she called it, "The Monstrosity." The truck-camper's name stuck.

At the Coffey Shop, Kitty set the coffeepot on the empty table next to Uncle Tommy. "He's still working on the Monstrosity. But he's slowed down some since he got a job."

Kitty adjusted the bobby pins in her straight brown hair.

Conrad smiled. "I hired him to drive the fogger."

Uncle Tommy tapped his black cowboy boots on the floor. "Better stay off the roads then."

Charlie Carter scratched the silver streak in his dark hair. "You're letting Howard operate the fogger?"

They all looked at the mayor, who had hired a drunk to drive the fogger tractor. Conrad shrugged.

"What can I say? The stuff stinks. Nobody else would do it and Howard needed beer money." He laughed. "Everybody needs a job. I got you the deputy sheriff's job, didn't I?"

The swoosh of air brakes and the screech of a big engine outside interrupted their conversation.

The Greyhound bus came through town six times a day on its way to Des Moines and Kansas City. Three northbound buses and three southbound buses all stopped outside the Coffey Shop, one of many Iowa small-town stops.

Ivy slurped the last of her Green River. Then she and Nick followed the men out the door to watch the bus unload. Kitty Decker put her hands in her apron pockets as she watched them leave. "That bus has seen some folks come and go."

Ivy dashed out the door behind Nick just in time to see a pretty young woman step off the bus wearing tight black stirrup pants and a white sleeveless blouse knotted at the waist. Judy Marshal, twenty-seven, swept aside a loose curl and tucked it back into her short, teased hairdo. Bracelets tumbled down her arm to her elbow, tinkling like a back-porch wind chime on a whispery summer night's breeze.

Black diesel exhaust filled the air as the bus driver pulled four suitcases and several huge taped-up boxes from the luggage compartment in the belly of the Greyhound bus.

Reuben tugged at the straps of his overalls. "Must be that new beautician everyone's been talking about."

"Looks like she's not alone," Uncle Tommy said.

Sheriff Carter's eyes squinted as if examining the details of a crime scene. He raised his chin. "She's got a little crumb-snatcher."

Ivy stared up at the huge bus parked on the brick-tiled Main Street. She shaded her eyes with her hand, squinting into the bright sun. Jesse Marshal, a boy about Ivy's age, paused at the top of the bus steps. He stretched his arms and looked around.

"I'm here. But I won't be here long. I'm out of this place the first chance I get."

Nick frowned. "What's his problem? He doesn't even know Coffey. Hey, Ivy, let's get our bikes and ride out to the park."

But Ivy could no longer hear Nick. She was mesmerized by the arrival of the confident boy who would not be staying long and his beautiful mother with the musical bracelets.

Ivy soon found out that Judy Marshal had moved to Coffey to open Judy's Beauty Shop in the empty spot on the town square. She had escaped to Coffey for a fresh start after her husband disappeared in the middle of the night to get a pack of cigarettes and never returned.

On the day of the beauty shop's grand opening, Grandma Violet took Ivy with her to get their hair done. When they walked into the salon on Main Street, Conrad Thrasher was in the chair getting his hair cut. They sat down to wait in the chairs off to the side, out of Conrad's view, as Judy finished up.

Conrad grinned his fake, flirty smile. "So, I'm the banker in town. It's always good to know a banker. Let me take you to the Coffey Shop after you close tonight. Got the best tenderloin sandwiches around here. I promise."

Grandma caught Judy's eye and gently shook her head.

"Well, that sounds like a kind offer, but I've already got plans," Judy replied as she glanced Grandma's way.

Conrad turned and glared when he saw Judy looking at Violet.

"Best not to listen to old gossip in town."

"Not to worry. I only listen to myself." Judy swept the hairs off his neck, and took the cape off his shoulders. "There you go."

Conrad put some money on the counter of her station, glared at Violet again, and sulked out of the salon.

After Judy had finished trimming Ivy's hair, Grandma sat in the chair. "Ivy, help Miss Judy and sweep up the hair on the floor."

As Ivy swept, she could hear Grandma whispering to Judy about Conrad and the tragedy that had befallen his devoted, young wife in the pond behind his house.

From then on, Ivy often stopped by Judy's salon on weekends or after school to sweep up the hair clippings and fold towels. She liked spending a few hours with the glamorous and unconventional hairdresser, who was so unlike Coffey and so different from Grandma. She also liked to spend time with Jesse, Judy's son, who was often at the shop. Jesse said Ivy looked like a fairytale princess, the kind the woodland animals would help. From the first moment she saw him at the top of the bus steps, Ivy knew she would follow him out of Coffey.

When Judy hugged her, Ivy smelled her perfume and wondered what her own mother had smelled like. Judy put her to work and soon the new shop was buzzing.

Sometimes between clients, Judy grabbed Ivy's hands and they danced around the beauty shop. The light clacking of Judy's high heels on the black-and-white checkerboard tile floor and the tinkle of her wrist bangles and dangling earrings echoed across the salon. The pocket of Judy's pale pink smock held a pack of Wrigley's Doublemint gum, and her mouth snapped as she chewed.

Ivy loved to watch Judy apply a fresh coat of lipstick, toss her head back and laugh, or touch Ivy's cheek. This was what it must be like to have a mother. A great lonesome wind blew through her. She longed for her own mother, the beautiful woman who liked to have her own way, who she only knew from Grandma's sketchy descriptions and the wrinkled photo beside her bed. But Ivy felt connected to her mother from her own inner knowledge like a path long overgrown with weeds, yet its direction still unmistakable. She knew her life would have been so different if her mother had lived.

Chapter 8

THE DEVIL'S PICTURES

The August heat grew more intense. Dusk arrived muggy and stale. The birds splashed in Grandma's backyard birdbath, trying to stay cool. Inside Grandma's house, electric fans blew the hot air around. Uncle Walter avoided the trapped humid air in the house by sitting on Grandma's back porch where there was a slight breeze. "Let's set up the card table out here tonight. It'll give us more room since Tommy's family is coming over."

Ivy helped him prop up the old folding table and even-up the wobbly leg with a squashed Dixie cup. The last time the entire family played cards together, just a few weeks ago, it had ended in angry accusations and huffy exits. Every gathering of the Taylors threatened to start another intense family quarrel.

Uncle Tommy and his family lived a few blocks away from 4120, so they bustled down the path through the yard to the back porch as twilight's curtain closed.

"Okay, everybody, prepare to lose." Uncle Tommy pulled up a folding chair and set it at the head of the table.

Uncle Tommy's fourteen-year-old daughter, Angela, plopped down on a folding chair and crossed her tan legs. She adjusted the wide headband holding back her long brown hair. "How long is this going to take?"

"Won't take long for me to beat you all. Russell, are you

playing tonight?" Uncle Walter addressed Uncle Tommy's thirteen-year-old son, a gangly, inwardly driven, tormented boy.

"No, it makes my brain all squiggly to see the cards out of order," Russell said. He stood next to the game table, unable to be too far away from the disorderly cards. He vigorously patted his curly hair. The freckles sprinkled across his nose gave the impression that he was an All-American boy, but inside him, commanding compulsions controlled his young life.

Russell's fixations intrigued Ivy, but Uncle Tommy despised Russell's ritual checking habits. Uncle Tommy said Russell's lack of control was a sign of weakness and disrespect. Aunt Hattie found Russell's fussing irritating and bad mannered. Grandma never seemed to notice Russell's fidgeting.

Ivy handed Uncle Walter the deck of cards. "What are we playing tonight?"

"Let's play 'Oh, Hell,'" Uncle Tommy suggested.

"That's where you'll all end up," said Aunt Hattie.

"Oh, hell, let's just get this family fun over with," Uncle Tommy said.

"You go on and play this one without me. I'm going to get some drinks. It's not right to sweat without Dr. Peppers," Grandma said. She went back inside to get the pop from the cool basement canning room.

The rest of the Taylors crowded around the card table on the back porch. A lawn mower droned down the block. Aunt Hattie plopped herself in a folding chair on the edge of the porch as far away from the card game as she could get. "Well, I'm not playing. It's sinful." She crossed her arms. "Cards are just fifty-two invitations for the devil to visit."

Uncle Walter nudged Ivy with his elbow. "I told you, she's a fruitcake."

"I heard that, Walter." Aunt Hattie tried to stand up. "You're not getting anything of mine when the Rapture comes. God will not forgive your part in this family's treachery."

As she struggled to stand up, her foot slipped and her chair folded. She lost her balance and toppled off the back porch. Uncle Tommy laughed at his wife, overturned like a turtle with her chubby legs wiggling in the air. He folded his hands in prayer. "Oh, holy cow."

Grandma came out on the porch with bottles of Dr. Pepper and stared at Aunt Hattie upside down in the bushes. "What in tarnation? Somebody help her."

Nobody moved.

"Ivy, go," Grandma said.

Ivy ran over and held out her hand. Aunt Hattie narrowed her eyes and slapped away Ivy's outstretched hand. Her pursed lips barely moved as she whispered. "I don't need your help. I curse the day your mother stepped foot in this town."

"You hush up, Hattie," said Grandma. "Ivy's just trying to help you."

Ivy cocked her head to the side. She looked at her aunt, still tangled in the bushes. "What'd my mother do?"

Spit glommed in the corners of Aunt Hattie's mouth. "She brought evil into Coffey, and it's never been the same."

"That's enough," Grandma said to Hattie as she gestured for Ivy to sit down.

Ivy felt a chill roll down her back. She walked back across the porch and sat down at the card table. What was taking the Holy Rapture so long?

"Don't listen to her," Uncle Walter muttered. He made a circling motion with his finger at the side of his head. "She's the Mad Hattie. Loop-dee-loo."

Ivy tried to hide her smile. Uncle Walter shuffled the cards and dealt seven to each person. Grandma passed out the drinks before sitting down in her rocker to watch the card game.

Uncle Tommy looked at his cards. "Ivy, tell Walter that collecting cookie jars in the shape of vegetables won't get him a pass out of the Clarinda nut house."

Ivy lifted her hair from the back of her sweaty neck and tucked it behind her ears. She turned to Uncle Walter to relay the message. "He thinks you're crazy, and he doesn't like your cookie jars."

Uncle Walter wiggled his finger up and down his lips. "So, what? That doesn't hurt my feelings. Anyway, I'm not speaking to him. It wasn't his pastrami sandwich."

He flipped over the top card of the deck. Spades were trump. He checked his cards.

Ivy looked at Uncle Tommy. "It wasn't your sandwich." She picked up her cards. "And he's not speaking to you anyway."

Uncle Tommy's blue eyes flashed and he covered his ears with both hands. "Tell the mailman I haven't heard anything he's said since 1959."

The silence of the great sandwich war had grown louder over the years.

"Tell him I'm a letter carrier. He may not know that, working in the sewer and all," Uncle Walter said, referring to Uncle Tommy's job at the town sewage plant. "Can you smell the stink, Ivy?"

Aunt Hattie struggled back onto the porch and righted her chair. She sneered at the two men, her stubby nose high in the air. "And Cain smote his brother Abel down and was cast out of Eden."

"Oh, go pray in the bushes or something, Hattie, but leave us alone. I'm about to blow the stamps off of Letter Boy here," Uncle Tommy said, putting down the king of spades.

Aunt Hattie yelled from her corner protest. "Cards are just the devil's pictures."

"This is boring," Angela said.

Russell reached over and straightened the deck.

Uncle Walter glanced at his cards and winked at Ivy. "Looks like Hattie's right. The Devil got him." He laid down the ace of spades and took the trick. "I guess Tommy's going to miss the Rapture this time."

Uncle Tommy's face turned red. He stood up, scraping the chair's legs against the floorboards. He pointed at Uncle Walter. "He always cheats. He's just a big turd."

Uncle Walter raised his eyebrows but didn't look up. "If any man should know a turd, he should." Uncle Walter looked at Ivy out of the corner of his eyes and smiled. "He's so full of— "

Grandma hit her fist on the table. "Enough."

Uncle Tommy stomped his black cowboy boots across the porch. "As far as I'm concerned, I'm through with 'Oh Hell.'"

"Blasphemy," said Aunt Hattie.

"Oh, hell," said Uncle Tommy.

"That's exactly where you're headed," said Aunt Hattie.

"Forget this. I'm going down to the Blue Moon." Uncle Tommy stormed down the porch steps and around the house, leaving a trail of Old Sage aftershave behind him.

"The Lord hates a sore loser, right, Hattie?" Uncle Walter stretched his arms over the back of his head. "Now the rest of us can enjoy the game."

Grandma sighed and bit her bottom lip. "I wish you boys would get along."

Russell gathered up the loose cards on the table.

Aunt Hattie shook her finger at Russell. "Leave those cards alone. They're sinful."

"I can't stand the clutter." He realigned the cards into perfect order, counting them as he stacked them. When he finished counting, he sighed. "Fifty-two. They're all there."

Ivy took the cards. She shuffled and dealt the next hand.

Angela glanced up from her cards. Her light blue eyes, almost gray-blue like Grandma's, glared at Ivy. "These are terrible cards. You just want me to lose."

"No, I don't."

"Yes, you do." Angela shook her head. "Nobody is as perfect as you. I just hate it."

"Angela, that's enough," Grandma said sternly. "It's just the luck of the draw."

Angela threw her cards on the table. "If Daddy gets to leave, I'm going home. Are you coming, Mother?"

Ivy wondered why Angela always seemed so angry. Uncle Tommy gave her everything she wanted.

"Can we go?" repeated Angela.

Aunt Hattie stood up, slapping Russell's hand as he reached over to straighten Angela's messy cards. "Don't touch the evil. It's time for us to leave this den of iniquity."

Russell patted his hair. "I should've stayed swimming at the lake."

Ivy knew Russell felt most comfortable swimming at Hawks Bluff Lake. He didn't even seem to mind the mud-caked bottom or the crowded, tiny beach.

"Let's go." Aunt Hattie hustled her two children around the back porch to the path leading to their home.

"Sometimes it takes a lifetime to be a family," Grandma said.

Uncle Walter rolled his eyes and tapped the table with his cards. "Who wants to deal?"

Grandma, Uncle Walter, and Ivy played cards at the wobbly table until the Iowa twilight drew down the sun. A few anxious fireflies turned on their lanterns early, and the birds serenaded them from the woods behind the house. For one brief moment, Ivy felt content to be an only child.

Suddenly, the sound of a loud tractor engine and a pressurized spray startled Ivy.

"Sounds like the fogger," Uncle Walter said, referring to the tractor emitting a gray dusty cloud of chemicals that helped eliminate the bugs that killed the trees and ate the gardens. Like every summer, when the fogger sprayed its pesticides at dusk, everyone hurried inside and shut their doors and windows before the spray blurred their vision and choked their lungs. This summer, the citizens of Coffey also had to avoid Howard Decker's erratic driving. He was usually in a drunken stupor so the random path of the fogger's spray was quite unpredictable.

Ivy covered her nose with her hand and rushed inside to close the windows. At the window in Grandma's bedroom, she looked outside and watched the tractor as it bellowed smoky fog. Howard drove the tractor down the street, releasing an enormous expanse of bug spray.

Ivy saw something in the fogger spray. It was Weston Thrasher, Conrad's son, running in the middle of the hovering gray cloud. It looked unreal, like a hazy dream, as the thirteen-year-old boy vanished and reappeared in the heavy smoke like a vaporizing ghost.

Ivy shivered, remembering her escape from Conrad Thrasher's cold menace when she had fled into the cornfield. She pushed her hands deep in the front pockets of her shorts and touched the envelope she had taken from the glove box of her parents' wrecked car. She had forgotten all about it. She pulled out the envelope, then carefully extracted the torn slip of paper that was all that remained of its contents. She read the few handwritten words still visible.

have to get away.
No time left to
She's yours
Barbara

Where was her mother going? Who was the note to? It didn't make any sense. Ivy ran into her room and pulled off the back of the frame that held the photo of her parents. She hid the small scrap of paper inside. It was just another unexplained piece connecting her to her parents.

PART II

FINDING HER WAY HOME

(1970-1971)

Chapter 9

THE GARDEN HOE

Iowa summers were hot and humid. Everything slowed down and eased into a gentle lull. The air was thick like cotton candy, choking everyone's lungs with each smothering breath. The waves of heat shimmered in ghostly patterns on the sidewalks. Even the dogs lay in the shade with their tongues hanging out, waiting for the heat to pass.

The kids spent a lot of the summer at Hawks Bluff Park. They swam in the muddy lake or played baseball. Everybody watched the games from the rickety gray-metal bleachers lined up behind the broken chain-link fence.

That muggy summer afternoon, the muddy lake was crowded with swimmers, and the baseball bleachers filled with spectators for Coffey's championship game against the Stilton first place team, their rivals from a much bigger city a few miles away. As she splashed in the waters of Hawks Bluff Lake, twelve-year-old Ivy saw Angela talking to Coffey's baseball players as they gathered, including eighteen-year-old Ben, Miss Shirley's son, who played right field.

The short expanse of beach was created from sand trucked in from the local quarry. The soft sand stopped at the water's edge. The muddy bottom of the lake oozed between Ivy's toes, reminding her of the fearful grasp of Conrad Thrasher's pond. She shook the memory away.

Her cousin Russell lay on the beach nearby, resting after hours of swimming. Ivy knew that the concentration and rhythm of swimming kept Russell's mind focused and uncluttered, at least for a while.

Weston Thrasher, now seventeen, and a baseball player from the Stilton team sauntered over to the lake from the baseball field. The pimply faced boy with fat cheeks barely fit in his Stilton team uniform. The shirt stopped short of his protruding belly, and his pants hung low in the back. Weston Thrasher wore a thin leather headband around his head which held back his long, greasy hair. He didn't play baseball or any other sport that required him to be part of a team.

"Watch this. I'm going to make him dance," Weston said to the fat boy as he slapped him on the back. Weston pulled a firecracker from his pocket, lit it with a match, and threw it at Russell as he lay on the shore with his eyes closed. The explosion startled Russell and he jumped up, frightened. Weston laughed and lit another one, which landed close to Russell's foot. Russell hopped away from it and stood uncertainly on the beach, patting his wet hair and staring at his two tormentors.

"Hey, Patty-Cake Boy, don't you like fireworks?" said Weston. A few people on the beach began picking up their stuff and leaving. They knew Weston usually meant trouble.

Ben, a senior in high school with wavy hair and light brown eyes, walked over from where he was warming up for the game. Ivy got out of the water and headed toward Russell.

"Weston, stop. He wasn't bothering you," Ivy said.

Ben stopped next to Russell. "Why don't you guys leave Russell alone?"

Weston lit another firecracker and threw it at Ben. It exploded at his feet, but Ben didn't flinch. "Don't you guys have anything better to do?"

"No." The fat boy lit another firecracker. "Not a thing." He threw it on Russell's towel, which started to smoke and burn. Russell ran and dove into the lake, moving through the water with barely a ripple until he emerged on the other side. Ivy knew he wouldn't return, and she wouldn't have anyone to walk home with after the game.

With their prey gone, Weston and the Stilton boy glared at Ben and Ivy before slinking back over to the baseball field. Ivy looked at Ben. "Thank you, Ben."

"Any time." He smiled and trotted off to the baseball field for his game.

Ivy went to the bathroom and changed into pink culottes and a puffy-sleeved peasant shirt, stuffing her wet bathing suit and towel into her beach bag.

She sat with Raven and watched the baseball game stretch on until Ben scored the winning run. Ivy cheered as the Coffey team won. It served the fat Stilton firecracker boy right. By the time the game was over, the hot summer sun was hanging low in the sky.

Angela got into a car with Ben and some other friends from high school without offering Ivy a ride. Russell was long gone. She hadn't seen Nick all day and Raven didn't need to go home yet, so Ivy hurried to leave Hawks Bluff Park alone. She needed to get home for supper and cards with Grandma and Uncle Walter. The early evening arrived sullen and moist, ushering in the period of the day when time slows down, and the earth relaxes. The crickets warmed up for their nightly concert. Their incessant chirping sounded like the needle at the end of a record, clicking over and over as a reminder of the song's end. Grandma expected Ivy to be home before it got dark, but dusk was quickly approaching.

Ivy took the shortcut home, following the railroad tracks past the row of small, tidy homes along Mulberry Street. Ivy liked the way the clothes hung in a row on the clotheslines, flapping in the warm breeze like they were waving hello. Most of the back porches faced the railroad tracks and although Burlington Northern trains only ran a few times a day, it still seemed to Ivy like a bad place to watch the sunset.

When Ivy had asked Grandma why the black people of Coffey all lived on Mulberry Street, Violet told her there was no law saying that black people couldn't buy land beyond Mulberry Street. It was just the way it had always been, a socially enforced exclusion. An unseen line. A subtle, ugly racism, usually enforced by bankers who loaned money to pay for homes and Conrad Thrasher was Coffey's banker. So, the black families lived in these small homes on Mulberry Street, their back porches facing the railroad tracks where trains loudly sped past.

Ivy's friend Maggie Norton lived somewhere on Mulberry Street. They played together at school, but Maggie was always busy when Ivy invited her over to her house, and Ivy often wondered why she wasn't welcome on Mulberry Street.

The air smelled of fresh-cut grass and sweet clover. Ivy's sandals stuck against the patches of tar on the railroad ties, still sticky from the day's hot sun as she hopped from one railroad tie to the next. Ivy heard a car's wheels spinning on the gravel of Willow Drive beside the railroad tracks and turned toward the screeching tires and spraying gravel. Weston Thrasher and the firecracker Stilton boy pulled up alongside her in Conrad's big white Lincoln, which they'd nicknamed Moby Dick. They threw an empty bottle of grain alcohol out of the car as they hooted, whistled, and panted like dogs in the summer heat.

"Leave me alone, Weston. Haven't you caused enough trouble today?"

Ivy continued walking, head down, watching the railroad ties. Her heart pounded. She glanced toward the cluster of homes alongside the tracks. If only she knew where Maggie lived, but she knew she wasn't welcome there.

A tall man came out on his back porch in one of the homes.

Weston pulled off the road and drove alongside the tracks. The Stilton boy reached out and tried to lift up Ivy's shirt with a baseball bat. She jumped out of his reach.

"Poison Ivy," Weston taunted.

Ivy turned and glared at the boys. "Go away, Weston. Go far, far away."

Weston laughed and spat a big glob of brown chewing tobacco at her. "Like your mother did?"

She clenched her fists at her side. "Something's seriously wrong with you."

The man on the porch walked into his yard and picked up a garden hoe. A few moments passed. When Ivy glanced up, he was walking toward her. She recognized the lanky man as Maggie's father, Otis Norton.

The boys hollered louder and banged their hands on the sides of the car as they continued to follow her along the tracks and spat chewed tobacco out the window.

When Otis reached her, she saw the steel-cold anger in his dark brown eyes. Ivy and the tall black man stood together side by side. The pair stared at the threatening white boys, who got out of their car and lumbered toward them.

Otis held up his hand with his palm out and his long fingers spread apart and the hoe in his other hand.

"Now, you go on home. Fun's over, boys."

The Stilton boy shook his head. "I don't think so. Hey, wait, you're the trash guy at Warner College, ain't you?"

Although Otis worked for the maintenance department at Warner College in Stilton, he ignored the boy's question. He took a deep breath and shifted his weight. "I'm only going to ask you nicely once."

The chubby boy pulled a knife from his back pocket and waved it at Ivy. He imitated Otis's tone. "I'm only going to ask you nicely once to take off your clothes and lie face down on the ground, butt-naked, Sunshine."

Weston laughed and slapped the Stilton boy on the back. "Good one."

"She's just a child," Otis said. "No need to bother her with your nonsense."

The Stilton boy spat at Otis. The thick brown splatter from the chewing tobacco landed on the side of Otis's face and slid down. Ivy gasped. Otis's expression turned furious.

"Looks like we made the big black man mad," the Stilton boy said in a child's sing-song voice.

Ivy watched Otis clench the worn red handle of the garden hoe. Working maintenance kept his lean body in shape. His muscles flexed taut as he held the hoe, normally used to weed his garden and kill an occasional pesky snake.

Otis tilted his head back and swung the garden hoe cutting back and forth through the air, making a swishing sound. The hoe danced in the air in a blur, just a whisper from the boys' faces. Otis used the edge of the hoe to cut the leather headband around Weston's head. He knocked the Stilton boy's knife to the ground. The boys froze. They turned and jumped into the huge white car and sped off.

A whippoorwill called from a weathered fence post as if announcing Otis the victor of the standoff. "Looks like you got yourself in a bad fix," Otis said, rubbing his chin.

Ivy's hands trembled as she nodded at Maggie's father. "They had no right to spit at you and treat you like that."

Otis smiled at her. "Thank you, Ivy."

Otis had learned to survive by making concessions in a town where the railroad tracks were the best view a black man could get. He rubbed his pencil-thin mustache. "They're just ignorant white boys. Bold as you please on the outside, but scared as chickens in a strong wind on the inside." His hand rose to touch her shoulder, but he hesitated and let it fall back down at his side.

"Too bad your hoe wasn't a little longer."

Otis's shoulders shook and a great bellow of laughter escaped from the tall man. "You're a piece of work, Ivy, indeed you are."

Otis and Ivy walked along the railroad tracks, the tall weeds brushing against their legs. Grasshoppers jumped in surprise from their camouflage hiding places in the field. Several of Otis's neighbors were now standing on their porches watching them, their hands perched on their foreheads, blocking the last haze of the setting sun. None of them had come to help her, except Otis. She looked up at him.

"Maggie's lucky. I wish I had a father like you, Mr. Norton." Ivy reached out and linked her arm through his. He flinched when her fingers touched his arm. But Otis didn't pull away.

Maggie and her mother, Pinky, who had been watching anxiously from the safety of their home, hurried over to meet them. Maggie, who already stood as tall as her mother, hugged

Ivy. Pinky, a petite woman with tight, curly hair, patted Ivy's shoulder.

"Are you all right, child?"

Ivy nodded.

"Let me give you a ride home, little miss," Otis said.

Ivy nodded. "Okay. Thank you."

Ivy and Maggie walked to the Nortons' house and climbed into the back seat of their old Buick. Maggie's dog, King, tore out of the kitchen doggie door and jumped into the car at the last minute with his tail thumping. Ivy laughed at his enthusiasm. "Maggie, what's wrong with your dog? He's purple."

Maggie laughed and her face scrunched up. "I know, doesn't he look funny? King likes to roll in the mulberries. We have lots of mulberry trees." She flipped back her thick, shoulder-length braids. "That's why they call it Mulberry Street."

"What kind of dog is he?"

The dog jumped across their laps.

"Oh, just a big purple dog, I guess," said Maggie.

Ivy petted the friendly, mulberry-stained dog. "Maybe I could come over to your house sometime?"

Maggie looked down at her hands. "I'm not allowed to have friends over."

Ivy cocked her head to the side. "Why?"

Maggie blushed and glanced at her father in the front seat whose head almost touched the car's roof. Then she looked back at Ivy. "Well . . ."

"Oh, you mean white friends, don't you?"

Otis adjusted his brown plaid cap and glanced at Ivy through the rearview mirror. "Well, Ivy, it's kind of hard to explain. When you're black, you have to try and protect your children from situations that could be, well, misunderstood. We have a rule in our family that no white children are allowed to play at our house. Just to avoid any problems that might arise. I hope you understand; it has nothing to do with you."

Ivy looked at Otis's brown eyes in the rearview mirror. "Oh, it's okay, I understand. My Uncle Tommy's got that same rule about black people."

Otis turned the corner onto Meadowlark Lane. The muscles in his arms flexed as he turned the big steering wheel. He paused and rubbed his chin. "Maggie, what do you say we make an exception for Ivy?"

The girls clapped. King jumped up on Ivy. She glanced out the window and although King was in the way, she thought she saw Angela and Ben walking past Beecher Pond.

Otis drove the car up the driveway of 4120.

"You know where I live?" Ivy asked.

"Everyone knows your grandmother," Otis said.

Ivy smiled and opened the car door but turned back quickly. "Mr. Norton, do you remember when that goldfinch rested on your shoulder at the dump?"

Otis took off his brown plaid cap and ran his hand over his hair. He looked at her from the rearview mirror. "Yes, I do. I surely do."

"That bird knew, didn't it?"

Otis turned around, resting his long arm on the back of the car seat. "Knew what, child?"

"That you would bring me good luck."

Otis smiled. "Well, I'm sure glad it worked out that way, little lady. But next time a boy means you harm, fly like a bird, Ivy. Fly like a bird."

"Yes sir, I will. Bye, Maggie. Bye, purple dog. See you on Mulberry Street."

Ivy jumped out of the sputtering Buick and the purple dog barked.

Chapter 10

THE DOLL BABY ON
MULBERRY STREET

The next weekend, twelve-year-old Maggie pedaled her bike standing up, while Ivy sat on the seat behind her. Ivy held her feet away from the tires as they rode up and down Mulberry Street. Maggie's braids swayed as she pumped the pedals. The playing cards clothes-pinned to the spokes click-clacked as the wheels turned on the gravel road. The bike wobbled from the unbalanced awkwardness of the additional passenger and almost tumbled over. Ivy screamed. Curtains moved, and faces peered at them from the neighbors' windows.

A trim man in his early fifties wearing a sleeveless white undershirt, pressed black pants, and a hat with a stingy brim watched them from his front lawn.

Maggie waved at him, letting go of the handlebars. "Hello, Mr. Jackson."

The bike lurched to the right and almost fell over but Maggie's skinny arms were strong, and she pulled the bike upright again. The girls laughed as their feet dragged along the gravel road. King, the big brown dog covered with mulberry stains, barked.

Mr. Jackson smiled and waved back. "Hello, Doll Baby."

Ivy pointed with her chin as she held on to Maggie's waist. "Who's that?"

"That's Virgil Jackson. He's our neighbor. He paints houses."

"He call you 'Doll Baby'?"

King trotted beside the bike with his purple tongue hanging out. Maggie whipped her head around to glance back at Ivy. Ivy leaned back to avoid being hit by a swinging braid. "He calls everybody 'Doll Baby,' if he likes you."

Ivy looked back and saw Virgil Jackson lift the mail out of the mailbox and stroll back across his lawn to his little white house. It looked like the Nortons' house except for a homemade red-and-white painted pole near the front door. In fact, she noticed all the houses on Mulberry Street looked fresh from Virgil's house painting.

Ivy stuck her lower lip out in an exaggerated pout. "I wish he'd call me 'Doll Baby'. I feel left out."

Maggie turned the bike around and stopped in front of Mr. Jackson's house, her long legs keeping it upright. "Mr. Jackson, this is my friend, Ivy Taylor. She wants you to call her Doll Baby, too."

She pointed at Ivy, wiggling on the seat behind her. Ivy blushed and peered out from behind Maggie who leaned over the handlebars and laughed into her hands. Ivy reached over and pulled Maggie's braids.

Mr. Jackson surveyed Ivy. He shook his head without answering and walked into his house, closing the door behind him.

Maggie pumped the bike pedals and they wobbled down Mulberry Street again. She shook her head. "Mr. Jackson won't ever call you Doll Baby."

"How come?"

Ivy's foot dragged along the gravel road as they made

a sharp turn. Maggie stopped the bike in front of her house. They hopped off and Maggie set the bike down on her front lawn. The wheels spun on its side. King lay down beside it, panting.

"My dad says Virgil Jackson is from the old school. Mr. Jackson says white people have been messing things up since the world began. He says white folks can get away with murder, and he doesn't want it to be his."

"What does that mean?"

"Well, I'm not supposed to tell anybody this. Cross your heart and promise you'll never tell?"

Ivy drew two intersecting lines across her chest.

Maggie looked around and cupped her hand to the side of her mouth. "Well, Virgil Jackson was out at Deadman's Woods when he saw Conrad Thrasher throw his wife's body in that pond out back behind his house."

"How could he see the pond through the woods?"

"He says there's a clearing just past the cemetery where he was chopping wood."

"Why didn't he tell the sheriff?"

"The sheriff wouldn't have believed him. Mr. Jackson says a black man's word isn't enough to charge a white man with murder. He said it was best to keep his mouth shut. But don't tell anyone I told you."

Ivy stared blankly at the Jackson's house, thinking of the pond and the darkness that must live inside Conrad Thrasher. She shuddered. "Okay."

King yawned and rolled over on his back. Maggie looked carefully at the ground before sitting down next to King and scratching his purple belly. "I don't think Mr. Jackson will ever call you Doll Baby, because, well, you know, you're white."

"Grandma says a bird can't change the color of its feathers."

Maggie nodded and pointed at the ground. "Watch out for mulberries if you're going to sit down."

Ivy examined the ground for the purple berries and sat down. She stuck a blade of grass in her mouth and chewed on it as it dangled from her mouth.

Maggie laughed. "Well, I'll call you Doll Baby if you want."

Ivy took the grass out of her mouth. "Okay, Doll Baby." Ivy looked across the lawn to the Jacksons' house. "What's with the barber's pole on his house?"

"His wife, Ruth, works at the courthouse during the week, but on Saturdays, she does everybody's hair."

A train blew its whistle and raced by so close that everything, even the ground, seemed to shake. Ivy covered her ears. The train roared like the thundering of a tornado ripping through the neighborhood. When the caboose passed, the noise evaporated into the distance.

Maggie's mother, Pinky, opened the window and called them to supper. Maggie stood up and held out her hand, pulling Ivy up.

"Next time I come, let's invite Jesse and Nick," Ivy said.

"That would be pushing it."

Ivy shrugged. "What're you having for supper?"

Maggie opened the front door and King rushed inside. "Yard bird, yams, and greens."

Ivy followed her into the house. "I don't think Grandma cooks that stuff."

They walked into the kitchen.

"Yes, she does." Maggie laughed and pointed to the steaming food on the counter and the stove.

"Oh. You mean chicken, sweet potatoes, and spinach."

Pinky smiled at Ivy. "Those are collard greens, but you're

right about the rest." Pinky grabbed a dish towel and took a big pan of cornbread out of the oven. "And a meal wouldn't be complete without cornbread."

Maggie and Ivy washed their hands and helped Pinky bring the heaping plates of food to the two tables Otis pushed together. The Nortons had invited their neighbors, Miss Shirley and Ben, who had stood up for Russell at the park, over for supper, too.

Miss Shirley, almost forty, had raised Ben by herself in a small house across the street. Bertha Tuttle spread the rumor that Miss Shirley was not married when Ben was born, but none of the white people had the guts to ask Miss Shirley if it was true. They mostly just talked behind her back.

She cleaned the homes of several of the more well-to-do families in Coffey. Although the hard work hurt her back, at lunchtime she could watch the soap opera, *As the World Turns*, her 'story' as she called it.

That night, Miss Shirley had brought over her famous mashed potatoes with skins and wild morel mushroom gravy. She hunted the wild mushrooms in the woods around Coffey during a few weeks in the spring. Then she froze a plentiful supply, so she could use them all year long, just like Grandma Violet.

Ivy set a big bowl of the brown mushroom gravy on the table. Otis rubbed his stomach as everyone sat down. "Now, this sure is fine dining."

Ben smiled at Ivy. "Hey, Ivy. What's Angela doing today?"

"I don't know. She doesn't really talk to me much."

They all sat down around the table. Ivy noticed the bottom of her shoes were stained purple from the mulberries in the yard. She bowed her head as Otis prayed. When she raised her head, Ben rubbed his hands together.

"Hey, what are we waiting for? Let's grease on some yard bird, huh, Ivy?" He smiled his Hollywood smile.

The fried chicken smelled good. She picked up a leg and put it on her plate. "Yard bird sounds funny."

Ben laughed and flapped his arms. "They're birds that run around the yard, aren't they?"

Ivy laughed. She liked Ben. He didn't seem to notice that she was white. King sat down on the floor between Maggie and Ivy. Maggie slipped him a piece of cornbread under the table.

Otis took a bite of his chicken leg and waved it in the air. "Hey, that reminds me, did you all hear what Max Black was saying over at the Jacksons' this morning?"

Miss Shirley rolled her eyes, but a slow blush spread across her face. "Oh, Good Lord, there's no telling with that fool."

Otis rubbed his pencil-thin mustache and smiled. "Well, he said once there was this chicken at his old man's farm that got so scared during a tornado, all its feathers fell out."

Pinky laughed. "That can't be true, and you know it."

"I'm just telling you what Max said."

Ben picked up a chicken wing and stared at it. "Chickens can't live without feathers. It's unnatural."

"Max said it wasn't pretty, but he said that darn chicken sure could run when the wind kicked up, and it come up a dark cloud. It was the only chicken to ever live to old age—no one had the heart to kill it after it lived through a tornado and lost all its feathers, too."

Miss Shirley laughed and rocked in her chair. She wiped the sweat from her face with a paper napkin. "That Max can come up with some good ones." She turned to Ivy. "So, Miss Ivy Taylor, do you think that could happen?"

The room hushed except for the whir of the electric fan, which kept the stifling summer heat away. They all turned to

Ivy to hear her answer. Ivy looked around the table and then at the crispy chicken leg on her plate.

"Well, a tornado's pretty scary. So, yeah, a naked yard bird could happen."

Miss Shirley laughed suddenly. A piece of food flew out of her mouth and onto the floor. King, waiting for just such a moment, jumped up and gobbled it down.

Otis slapped the table. "Well, there you have it. Thank you, Pinky, for the naked yard bird, yams, and greens."

Ivy held up her finger. "And a meal wouldn't be complete without cornbread."

Miss Shirley threw her hands in the air. "Lord-a-mercy. There might be hope for white people, yet."

The purple dog barked.

As the months passed and the cool fall winds blew across the Iowa prairie, the black families grew accustomed to Ivy's presence on Mulberry Street. By early December, Maggie's neighbors even waved to Ivy every now and then.

One chilly winter night, Ivy, Maggie, and King were spread out on the Nortons' floor in front of the console TV, ready to watch *Soul Train*. The girls planted their elbows on the carpet, resting their chins in their palms. They crisscrossed their feet in the air behind them. The dog of dubious heritage stretched out beside them. As mulberry season was over, King had lost his purple hue and was back to his original light brown.

When *Soul Train* came on, the picture flipped from time to time. Pinky went into the kitchen to clean up and Otis and Miss Shirley settled in on the couch.

Ivy leaned over to Maggie. "Did you ask your mother if you could join the Chickadee Girls with me?"

"Yeah. She said I could."

"All right! You can help me with our community service project next month. It's Rosie Buckley, that old hermit lady."

"She's scary," Maggie said. "But her dogs are scarier."

"I know."

"Now hush up, you two," said Miss Shirley.

Ivy looked up at Miss Shirley. "Hey, where's Ben?"

"Hasn't been home much lately. Must be some girl. It always is."

Otis laughed. "Now you talking big trouble."

Pinky came out of the kitchen with tall glasses of iced tea, a favorite in the Nortons' house despite the cold weather. After she passed out the iced tea, she sat down on the couch to work on her latest quilt. Ivy loved Pinky's quilts. Grandma's house boasted many colorful quilts made by Pinky. They were spread out on every bed and couch. There was no excuse for being cold in Grandma Violet's house.

Ivy pointed to the TV. "Who is that guy that screams when he sings? He dances all crazy." Ivy knew who it was, but she liked to tease Miss Shirley. He was Miss Shirley's favorite singer.

Otis stared at Ivy and pointed to the TV. "You don't know who that is?"

"Otis, she's white. You know, snowflake white," Miss Shirley said.

Pinky smiled at Ivy as she set her piles of quilt squares on the floor. "That's Leon Wilson, dear."

"My Aunt Hattie thinks he's possessed by the devil."

Leon Wilson sang and danced, wearing a top hat. "Dig down deep until you find . . ."

Miss Shirley swayed on the couch and waved her arms in the air. She snapped her fingers. "The fight in your soul."

Her singing startled the dog and King jumped up and barked.

Ivy pointed at the singer's thick hair. "He's wearing a wig, isn't he? His hair looks like a helmet."

Miss Shirley shook her head. "No, that's his very own processed hair."

Ivy stared at the singer as he jumped in the air and threw off his top hat. "It sure looks like a wig to me."

Miss Shirley put her iced tea down on the end table. "Listen to her. I'm telling you, girl, that ain't no wig-hat. Edna Jean Whittaker's hair—now that's a wig-hat."

Ivy laughed. She loved to get Miss Shirley going. "But where'd Leon Wilson get the Mr. Peanut hat?"

Miss Shirley swayed back and forth. Her big body shook as she laughed. She slapped her legs. "Oh, you go on, child. You just messed up."

Maggie laughed and flipped back her thick braids. She grabbed Ivy's arm. "Ivy, you'd better stop or Miss Shirley's going to have a heart attack."

Ivy jumped up and imitated Leon Wilson's dance moves.

Miss Shirley groaned and covered her eyes. "Stop, girl. You can't dance. You too white."

Ivy laughed and sang, "I'm snowflake white. But I got the fight in my soul."

She pretended to throw off a pretend top hat. Miss Shirley pushed her big body off the couch. The dog whined and scurried out the swinging dog door that Otis had cut in the kitchen door.

"Look. King knows what's coming. He was nearly squashed years ago when Miss Shirley was dancing to Leon Wilson and broke through the porch floor," Otis said.

Miss Shirley shook her head. "I swear to God, can't a woman

fall through a floor one time without people making a big deal of it? Now, watch me, Ivy. Let me show you how it's properly done."

Miss Shirley moved to the center of the room to demonstrate her Leon Wilson moves and the floorboards held.

Chapter 11

ANOTHER HOLIDAY TAINTED
BY DISCORD

Snow covered the frozen ground on Christmas Eve and crystal-pointed icicles hung menacingly from the porch roof. The bare trees in the backwoods looked like icy skeletons.

Despite their long-standing conflicts, the Taylor family always celebrated Christmas together. Uncle Tommy, Aunt Hattie, and their two children joined Uncle Walter, Grandma, and Ivy at 4120 on Christmas Eve, like every year.

Grandma supervised as Uncle Walter carried the tree base and Ivy held the evergreen's top. The rest of the family watched as they ceremoniously marched the fully decorated white-flocked tree down the attic stairs. They unwrapped the white bed sheet covering the tree. It was already fully decorated, with bird ornaments dangling from the branches. They plugged in the lights, already strung on the boughs, and the tree was done. Then they all gathered on Grandma's back porch because it wouldn't be Christmas without taking care of the winter birds in the backyard, including the chickadees, nuthatches, finches, sparrows, cardinals, and goldfinches.

Russell's stocking cap, pulled down low, hid his hair except for a few rebellious curly strands. His tall frame made it easy for him to hang the suet for the birds in the branches of the trees in the backyard. Ivy used the kitchen broom to sweep the snow off the feeders. Then Uncle Tommy added extra birdseed for the birds and inevitably, the uninvited, thieving squirrels.

Ivy and her family breathed the cold December air, searching the Iowa skies for signs of more snow.

Angela shivered. "This is ridiculous. I'm cold." She marched back into the warm house which gave the rest of the family a reason to go inside.

Ivy leaned the broom against the family room wall. She climbed onto the kitchen stool and handed the punchbowl to Uncle Walter. He wiped the big bowl and set it on the counter. "Bring on the eggnog. Let the festivities begin."

Grandma sang Bing Crosby's "White Christmas" as she poured the fresh eggnog from the Coffey Dairy into the large white punch bowl. Uncle Tommy pulled out his flask and splashed whiskey into his mug.

"Got to give the nog a little Christmas spirit."

Aunt Hattie shook her finger at him. "Thomas Taylor, you've already had too many spirits."

Uncle Tommy raised his cup. "Reuben's house is the only thing I know that has too many spirits." He laughed and slapped his son on the back. Eggnog flew out of Russell's mouth and he coughed and regained his balance from his father's blow.

Angela smoothed the sides of her straight, long hair that almost reached the middle of her back. Then she took a sip of eggnog and spat it back in the cup.

"Eggnog makes me sick."

"Everything makes you sick," Russell said. "You eat like a bird."

Angela pushed the mug across the counter, knocking over a china bird. She winced and rubbed the perfect thin arch of her plucked eyebrows. "Sorry, Grandma."

"No harm done."

Russell set the fallen bird on the windowsill. "So, Grandma, how many new birds will you get this Christmas?"

Grandma smiled and shrugged. "One can only hope."

People who knew about Grandma's love for birds gave her small glass and china birds. Over the years, her collection had expanded until it took over her window sills, shelves, and cupboards.

"Your kitchen is so cluttered with all these birds perched everywhere. How many more can you even fit?" Aunt Hattie asked.

Grandma patted Aunt Hattie's arm. "You know there's no such thing as too many birds."

Russell fidgeted. "Grandma, did you know you have 257 birds, if you include the owls?"

Grandma smiled at Russell. "I wouldn't have imagined it was so many, and I'm glad you included the owls. Judy gave me a new one for Christmas."

Uncle Tommy stumbled a little. "It's lucky those 257 birds aren't real because the bird splat would fill up this kitchen."

He punched Russell hard on the arm. Russell rubbed it and started counting each of his shirt buttons, starting at the cuffs and working his way up the shirt, fingering each button. Ivy didn't even notice Russell's rhythmic button-counting. She accepted Russell's quirks just as she did all the strange oddities in her family. She knew things weren't going to change.

After they finished their eggnog they gathered in the living room in front of the Christmas tree. Every year since Ivy could remember, Uncle Walter dressed in his Santa suit. But before Uncle Walter could put it on, Uncle Tommy took another swig of whiskey from his pocket flask. Then Uncle Tommy took out the fake beard from the Santa costume box on the fireplace hearth.

"Ivy, tell him he's a sorry excuse for a Santa," Uncle Tommy said.

"Uncle Tommy says you're a lousy Santa."

Uncle Walter straightened the sleeves of his red argyle sweater. "What would the Grinch know about being a good Santa?"

Ivy shrugged and turned to Uncle Tommy. Her uncles' squabbling amused her. "He says you're the Grinch."

"That's a big pile of Whoville crap. Ivy, tell him it's my turn to be Santa this year," Uncle Tommy said as Jack Daniels' holiday greeting floated on his breath.

Ivy turned back to Uncle Walter. "Uncle Tommy wants to be Santa this year."

Uncle Tommy opened the Santa box and took out the red-and-white coat. Uncle Walter snatched it out of Uncle Tommy's hands. "It's not his costume, and there's no such thing as cranky old St. Nick."

"He says it's his costume and you're too grumpy," Ivy said.

Uncle Tommy grabbed the Santa suit back. He put two fingers in his mouth and whistled his shrill bird call. "That's bird-talk for ho, ho, ho. I don't give a rat's butt what he says. I'm going to be Santa this year."

Uncle Tommy took the Santa pants out of the old Yonkers Department Store box. Uncle Walter yanked the pants back and the uncles struggled. Holding on to opposite ends of the costume, they stumbled around Grandma's living room.

Grandma shook her head. "Boys, stop fighting. That's enough. Someone's going to get hurt."

They lost their footing and fell over backward into the fake white pine boughs, knocking over the artificial Christmas tree. The bird ornaments flew through the air.

"Daddy!" Angela said as she ran over and helped Uncle Tommy get up.

Uncle Tommy breathed heavily from the skirmish. He staggered to the bathroom, dragging the costume with him, having emerged victorious in the Santa coup d'état.

Ivy and Russell untangled Uncle Walter from the tree branches. His bad knee made it hard to get him upright. Uncle Tommy put on the red suit and sat on the hearth with a river of whiskey running through his Santa Clause veins. The crooked beard made him look even more inebriated.

"The North Pole is hot as hell. Santa doesn't need his pants!" Uncle Tommy said as the newly self-appointed Santa took off his red pants and dropped them beside him on the brick fireplace. Santa sat on the hearth, wearing his coat and beard, sagging brown socks, black cowboy boots, and white boxer shorts.

Uncle Walter shook his finger. "Ivy, tell Santa he's sitting too close to the fire."

Ivy motioned Uncle Tommy away from the burning logs. "Move away from the fire, Uncle Tommy."

Uncle Tommy's white-trimmed Santa hat tilted precariously on his head. Santa's blood-shot eyes twinkled merrily, but he ignored Ivy's warning. "What does he know? He's a mailman." He grabbed Ivy's arm, but she pulled away. "What do you want for Christmas, Barbara? Ho. Ho. Ho."

Ivy hated it when Uncle Tommy drank too much. "I'm not Barbara. I'm Ivy."

Aunt Hattie's face turned red. She shook her finger around the room. "No one's sitting on Santa's lap tonight." She pointed to Santa's boxer shorts. "Santa's a fraud."

"Are you sure you're not Barbara?" Uncle Tommy asked Ivy.

Russell, used to his father's drunken scenes, rolled his eyes. "She's dead, Dad."

"What'd you say?" Uncle Tommy looked confused.

"I said Aunt Barbara's dead. A long time ago," Russell said.

Uncle Tommy's face dropped. "Oh, yeah, Barbara's gone. So is Robert." His Christmas spirit disappeared. "It wasn't my fault. I didn't know it would happen. Can't undo it now." He closed his eyes.

"That's enough, Tommy," Grandma said.

A spark from the fire ignited the fluffy trim on Santa's pants, which were lying on the hearth, next to Uncle Tommy.

"Ivy, tell the fake Santa his pants are on fire," Uncle Walter said.

"Daddy," Angela said. "Watch out."

"Tommy, be careful," Grandma said.

Santa's coat caught on fire from the pants and the white trim blazed.

"Help, save Santa!" Uncle Tommy said. "Or Christmas will be ruined!"

Aunt Hattie jumped up and grabbed the broom resting against the wall. She began beating the burning Santa. Uncle Tommy danced around the room trying to get away from the fire and Aunt Hattie, who continued whacking him with the broom.

"I'm burning up. For God's sake, somebody do something," said the fake Santa Claus as he dodged Aunt Hattie's strikes. "Stop beating me!"

Russell jumped up off the couch and dashed into the kitchen. He grabbed the big punch bowl of eggnog on the counter and staggered into the family room. With a mighty fling, he heaved the remaining holiday drink on his flaming Yuletide father. The thick eggnog extinguished the fire of his Santa suit and Uncle

Tommy's eyes blinked through the creamy, dripping eggnog. "First, the mailman tried to burn me, my wife beat me with a broom, and then my son, Opie here, tried to drown me with the Christmas nog."

The Santa fire ended the Taylors' Christmas Eve celebration. Uncle Tommy threw the eggnog-soaked, charred remains of St. Nick outside in the snow and his family went home with an un- christmasy spirit.

The old Victorian house stood dark, except for the blinking Christmas lights on the front porch.

Ivy sat on the window seat in her bedroom and looked at the singed Santa suit lying in the snow. The snow clung to the trees and the wind blew restlessly through the woods. Her heart drooped heavy with the emptiness of having no parents and no brothers or sisters. Christmas was a time for family and that night she yearned for her mother and father. She lifted her silver heart necklace engraved with a rose and kissed it. It was all that remained of her beautiful mother and the Christmases that might have been.

She watched the streaks of moonlight shine into her room until exhaustion overtook her and her need for sleep became stronger than her heartache. She pulled one of Pinky's quilts around her and fell asleep curled up on the window seat a few hours before Christmas day dawned.

The next day when Uncle Tommy and his family arrived to spend Christmas afternoon, the burned Santa suit still lay crumpled on the snow as if Santa had mysteriously disintegrated on the lawn. Uncle Tommy's bloodshot eyes looked swollen. He headed straight for the kitchen to get a beer. Angela curled up on the couch and soon fell asleep with her shiny hair cascading down her back. Uncle Walter, Russell, and Ivy gazed out the window at the hastily discarded Santa suit.

"Looks like Santa was highly combustible this year," Russell said.

Uncle Walter shrugged. "Guess Santa got Raptured."

Aunt Hattie overhead them and folded her hands in prayer, shaking them back and forth. "That's right. Santa and all his little tiny elves will burn in eternal hell because they stole Christmas from the Christ child."

"Hey, speaking of stealing the Christ child, did you hear that someone stole baby Jesus right out of the manager at church last Sunday?" asked Russell.

Ivy looked at Uncle Walter. "Luther?" asked Ivy. Uncle Walter nodded as they laughed, but Ivy stopped abruptly when she saw Aunt Hattie's glare.

"Don't make fun of the Christ child." The tiny silver bells sewn on Aunt Hattie's Christmas sweater jingled softly as she trembled with anger. "None of you will receive anything of mine when the Rapture comes."

Uncle Walter chuckled to himself as he went into the kitchen to start frying the wild mushrooms. On the way, he leaned over to Ivy and pointed to Aunt Hattie, whispering, "Aunt Haughty."

Ivy followed him into the kitchen and watched him prepare the mushrooms. Uncle Tommy crowded around the stove, too. His glasses slid down his nose as he leaned over the morel mushrooms to examine them. The mushrooms had been frozen after one of Grandma's mushroom hunts last spring. Uncle Walter cut the thawed mushrooms in half and rolled them in a seasoned-flour coating. Then he placed the mushrooms side-by-side, lined up like little tin soldiers, in a frying pan bubbling with butter. Uncle Tommy sneered as he watched the sizzling mushrooms.

"Ivy, tell Postal-Boy he made the coating too thin."

Ivy could almost taste the delicious wild mushrooms. She smiled at Uncle Walter. "Uncle Tommy thinks the mushroom coating is too thin." She looked into the pan of morel mushrooms as they sizzled and popped, turning crispy brown. "But they look good to me."

Tommy scowled. "What would you know? Traitor. You're always on the mailman's side anyway."

"Tell him his hair is too thin. But my mushroom coating is just right," Uncle Walter said. "And it's letter carrier."

Uncle Tommy spat chewed-up sunflower shells into Grandma's sink and stomped out of the kitchen. Ivy patted Uncle Walter's arm. "Good comeback, Uncle Walter."

Ivy pulled off a piece of turkey from underneath the tinfoil and popped it in her mouth. She held her mouth open to avoid burning her tongue. Miss Shirley's pies sat on the counter. Grandma no longer made her own pies. She said Miss Shirley's pies were just as good as hers, so she traded them for morel mushrooms she found in the woods in the spring.

Uncle Walter flipped over the frying mushrooms and set the spatula down. He pointed at Aunt Hattie in the hallway. "Tis the season of the divide and Rapture." He made a circling motion with his finger at the side of his head and then clasped his hands together in prayer.

"Yeah. I know I'm not getting anything when she's Raptured," Ivy said as they both laughed.

Aunt Hattie cornered Grandma in front of the linen closet as Grandma searched for the holly berry tablecloth. Ivy wandered toward them to see what crazy thing Aunt Hattie was preaching now.

"What I'm saying is that a miracle is about to happen, a miracle, just you wait and see, Violet." Aunt Hattie's hands gestured wildly. "The Lord's wrath will be visited upon the whoremongers, drug addicts, and government lawyers. It's too late for Tommy. The Lord can't forgive him for his sin; but it's not too late for you to be cleansed, Violet. You need to purify your soul for hiding the evil truth." Aunt Hattie stared at Ivy as she approached. "If you don't, you'll be left behind like the rest of your family."

Her gloomy predictions scared Ivy, but Grandma just sighed.

"Hattie, I'm not sure where I fit in that list of sinners, unless God doesn't like fat old women. I'm afraid my soul is as pure as it's ever going to be." Her knowing gray-blue eyes gazed at Aunt Hattie. "And you need to watch what you say."

"The Lord's on my side." Aunt Hattie carried her religion like a turtle's shell, using it for protection whenever she was challenged.

"The Lord isn't that confused. If you will excuse us, Hattie, I need to check on the hot rolls." Grandma put her arm around Ivy as they escaped Aunt Hattie's biblical orations.

"What did she mean? What did Uncle Tommy do?" Ivy asked.

"Oh, who knows what she's talking about?" Grandma gave Ivy's shoulder a gentle squeeze on the way back into the kitchen. "She's a dandy, isn't she? But you know, I've always tried to be kind to the crackpots because I always figured I might end up being one."

Ivy smiled as she observed her family, an odd assortment of mismatched characters with brooding secrets and peculiar eccentricities. She drifted in and out of all their worlds, adapting to their uniqueness and finding their strangeness ordinary. Her family's holiday bickering never ruined Christmas for Ivy. She accepted the certainty of an argument and waited for the show.

When the food was ready, Grandma and Ivy set the table and carried the food out. Violet gathered her family around Christmas dinner, having so far escaped the inevitable family fight.

"Maybe this year we'll finish the entire Christmas dinner without feelings being hurt. At least, I hope so."

"Grandma, you say that every year," said Ivy.

Grandma's mouth twitched into a smile. "An old woman can dream, can't she? If we ever do get through a family dinner without a skirmish, I'll probably just keel over and die, right then and there."

"Then I hope there's a fight, and it's a pretty sure thing because Uncle Tommy's still here," said Ivy.

Grandma called the family together. She sat at the head of the big oak table and said a prayer to bless her grudge-bearing family. Then the dishing of the holiday feast began. The huge platters and bowls of food soon stalled next to Russell's place. He stared at his plate, his mouth silently forming numbers.

Uncle Tommy pounded the table. "What in God's name are you doing?"

Russell looked up, startled. "Counting my peas."

Uncle Tommy pushed his glasses up on his nose and shook his hand. "Stop being a fruit loop and pass the food before we all starve."

Russell patted his hair and stared at the serving bowls and platters stalled around him. He quickly scooped mashed potatoes and turkey onto his plate, quarantining them by food types. Russell glanced up. Everyone watched him.

"Russell," Angela whined impatiently.

"You know I don't like my food to touch."

Russell continued to manipulate the little piles of food on Grandma's holiday china plate. Scrape. Scrape. Scrape. Russell contained every creamed pea, lettuce leaf, mushroom, Jell-O salad wiggle, turkey slice, and gravy spillage until he felt comfortable enough to take a bite. Then his rearranging, patting, and pushing started all over again.

Uncle Tommy stared at his fidgety son and waved his fist in the air. "Leave those dadgum piles of food alone. Eat your dinner before we all grow old and die from hunger."

"Yes, Russell, stop pitty-patting your food. Control yourself. It's embarrassing," Aunt Hattie said.

Russell didn't even look up as his hands pushed and dragged the heaps of food around as if pulled like the strings of a marionette. Uncle Tommy gritted his teeth and his face turned red.

"I said stop fiddling with your dadgum food. I can't take it anymore."

Uncle Tommy jumped out of his chair, grabbed a serving spoon from the bowl of creamed peas, and lunged at Russell's holiday plate, stirring all of Russell's neatly piled food together. "There. Now eat."

The dining room shuddered into silence except for Uncle Tommy's angry, exerted breathing. He sat back down. "You do what I say. I brought you into this world, and I can take you out."

Russell stared at his jumbled Christmas dinner stirred into a lump of inedible torment. He stood up, knocking over his dining room chair and placed his hands on either side of his head. "I'm sorry, Grandma. I've got to go." He stumbled away from the table in anguish and ran out the front door.

"Another holiday tainted by discord," Uncle Walter said.

Grandma slapped her lap and turned to Uncle Tommy next to her. "Honestly, leave that poor boy alone."

Uncle Tommy's face fell for a second. "Mother, he's getting worse all the time."

"Maybe Russell just can't help it. Ivy, ask Tommy if he ever thought of that," said Uncle Walter.

Uncle Tommy ignored him and jabbed the serving spoon in the air. A clump of mashed potatoes flew off the spoon and landed on Grandma's holly berry tablecloth. "Mother, you don't know what it's like to live with someone who counts everything. His food can't touch! You just don't know what it's like to live with a crazy lunatic like that."

Ivy and Uncle Walter exchanged knowing glances.

"Now, now. I've always been of the notion that we're all a little touched. But most of us maintain pretty well with our oddities and imperfections," Grandma said.

"Are you saying we're all off our rockers?" said Uncle Tommy.

Grandma pinched her fingers together. "The difference is only a smidgen here or there."

Uncle Tommy pushed his chair away from the table. "Well, that's just hogwash. There's nothing wrong with me. I'm the only one in this family that hasn't completely lost his noodle."

Uncle Walter picked up his spoon and tapped it against the side of his glass, making a loud pinging noise. "Let's see, who eats the same thing for breakfast every day?"

Uncle Tommy held his spoon in the air. He looked at Ivy. "Has the mailman ever heard of a food preference?"

"Letter carrier," Ivy said, anticipating Uncle Walter's response.

Then Uncle Tommy started tapping his glass with the

serving spoon at a faster pace than Uncle Walter's tapping as the sounds of the uncles' dueling spoons got louder.

"Oh, Poppycock," Uncle Walter shouted to Ivy. "There's nothing wrong with Russell, except for an overbearing father."

Uncle Tommy threw his spoon on the table. "I'm not going to sit here and listen to this bull anymore."

Uncle Tommy shook his fists in the air as he headed toward the door. "You people are as crazy as he is." The heavy front door slammed behind him.

Uncle Walter took his spoon and scooped mashed potatoes onto his plate. "Well, I'm glad that's settled. Now the rest of us can enjoy our food."

Angela awkwardly stood up, her hand across her stomach. "Grandma, I'm sorry but I've got to go, too. I think I'm going to be sick." She covered her mouth with her hands and bent over as she rushed out of the room. The front door slammed again.

An awkward silence flooded the dining room. Only Aunt Hattie remained from Uncle Tommy's family. "The Lord sees all the sins of this family." Aunt Hattie stood up and folded her holly berry napkin. "May Santa and his elves burn in hell for all of eternity." Her head bobbed a short nod. Her frizzy curls danced as she hurried out of Grandma's house and followed the rest of her testy family home. Another holiday gathering gone awry.

The silent night hushed over the evacuated holiday dining room.

"And Uncle Tommy thinks *we're* crazy?" said Ivy.

Uncle Walter clapped his hands. "You're right, Ivy. They're all nuttier than one of Miss Shirley's fruitcakes."

Their laughter echoed through the empty dining room. Ivy realized Grandma's dream had not come true. The fragile

Taylor family harmony had not made it through the Christmas festivities unscathed and Miss Shirley's pies still sat on the kitchen counter uneaten.

Chapter 12

THE BARBERSHOP

Soon after Christmas, Ivy felt the unspoken tension in her family increase. Her uncertain internal world made her sensitive to the undercurrents of her moody family. Something had changed, but she didn't know what.

Suddenly, without Ivy knowing anything about it, Angela came over to say goodbye. Uncle Tommy was sending her to London for her final semester of high school. She didn't seem excited to go and that made Ivy mad because although she was only twelve, she longed to visit the cities and countries she read about in books. Angela hugged Grandma and even gave Ivy a quick side-hug before she left. When the door closed, Grandma's eyes were wet with tears. From the window, Ivy watched Angela trudge down the sidewalk toward her house.

"What's wrong with Angela?"

"It's always sad to leave your family."

"Well, I don't think it's fair. Why does she get to go to London?" Ivy stomped loudly up the stairs, just to make a point. "I should be the world traveler."

Ivy sat in her room and sulked. She was so different from Angela. Angela acted withdrawn, like she was too good for Ivy, and the four-year age difference always kept Ivy at a distance. It was almost as if they were not a part of the same family.

One snowy afternoon in late December, Ivy and Maggie went to visit Miss Shirley, Maggie's flamboyant neighbor and zealous Leon Wilson fan. The girls sat with Miss Shirley on her worn, brown tweed couch, eating tuna fish sandwiches with sweet pickles on plastic, flowered plates and watching *As the World Turns*. Ivy looked around.

"Hey, where's Ben?"

"Over at the Jacksons'," Miss Shirley said.

"It seems like he's always over there lately," Maggie said.

"Hush up now. I'm watching my story," Miss Shirley said as she pointed at the old console TV.

"My Aunt Hattie says soap operas fickle the mind."

Miss Shirley looked sideways at Ivy. "Then your Aunt Hattie's seen her share, hasn't she?"

The girls shrieked with laughter. Miss Shirley put her finger to her lips. "Now hush up, I said. One of my Stewarts has amnesia, and Lisa Hughes is going to tell somebody off."

"Miss Shirley acts like she knows those people," Maggie whispered to Ivy.

The girls giggled as they slumped on the couch. Miss Shirley shook her head and clicked her tongue. "I do know those people. They live right here in Coffey." Miss Shirley stuck out her bottom lip. "Mm-hmm. If this town could talk, it could tell some crazy mixed-up tales. And I bet your Grandma knows a few of them her own self. Your father's own tragedy was crazier than my TV story."

Ivy sat up and adjusted the white belt in her bell-bottom jeans. "Why?" she asked.

"Oh, no particular reason, I guess. I'm just rambling."

"How come nobody talks about that night? It's like the whole town has amnesia."

"See what I'm saying. My story's not so crazy, when you think about it."

"Miss Shirley, tell me. Nobody else will."

"Nothing much to tell. After all the brouhaha of that horrible night was over, everyone wanted to forget it, I guess. Too painful."

What sounded like footsteps from the upstairs bedroom interrupted Miss Shirley.

Ivy gripped the arm of the couch. "What was that?" She looked sideways at Maggie, who sat stiffly as if straining for the next noise.

"My cat, Mr. Tibbs." Miss Shirley moved her hand through the air, dismissing the startling sound with a joke. "Or Reuben Smith's spooks might be visiting." She got up and adjusted the rabbit ears antenna to get a better signal.

After Miss Shirley's story ended, Maggie looked at the clock. "Hey, Ivy, why don't you come over to the Jacksons' with me. I'm getting my hair straightened. I'm sick of these heavy braids."

Ivy jumped off the couch. "The Jacksons' barbershop? Sure thing, Doll Baby."

Miss Shirley stood up and grabbed her coat from the coat rack. "Wait a minute, girls. I'm going with you." She shook her head. "This I got to see."

For the residents of Mulberry Street, Ruth Jackson served as the unofficial and unlicensed beautician and barber. She worked at the records office of the county courthouse during the week, but

she did hair in her living room on Saturdays. Many neighbors
went over to the barbershop to just exchange the weekly news
and gossip of the neighborhood and give their opinions of
politics and the world.

"I wish I had good hair," Maggie said to Miss Shirley as
they crossed the street, the wind whipping the hems of their
coats.

"Maggie girl, there's nothing wrong with your hair." Miss
Shirley fluffed up her own curly hair. "Curls drive men crazy.
You just wait. You'll be glad for those curls someday."

Ivy hurried behind them, fighting against the strong wind.
Ivy's straight, shoulder-length hair blew across her face. Miss
Shirley turned around. "Hurry up, Snowflake, or you might
blend in with the snow drifts."

When they reached the Jacksons' house, Maggie opened
the door without knocking. The warmth and laughter of the
neighborhood barbershop washed over them as they came in
from the cold Iowa wind.

Maxwell Black sat on a step stool in the center of the room
while Ruth shaved his head. Wearing a dark blue uniform shirt
with Mobil's flying red horse on the sleeve, his large body
seemed to dwarf the stool. He pointed both index fingers at
Maggie as she stepped into the house.

"Ladies and gentlemen, put your hands together for the
Supremes."

Maggie waved and Miss Shirley followed her into the noisy
makeshift shop. Max whistled. "And Miss Diana Ross, her own
self."

Virgil Jackson put his hands on his waist. "Well, if it ain't
two of my favorite Doll Babies."

Miss Shirley held the door open and Ivy stepped into the
Jacksons' living room. Their lively chatter stopped. Ivy blushed,

and her eyes darted around the hushed living room, searching for a welcoming face.

Although they knew her, Ivy knew the black community did not easily welcome white people into their world. The Jacksons' makeshift barbershop was one of only a few places in Coffey where black people could be themselves outside the white world. A place where they could tell the truth and not worry about what others thought. Ivy's presence put a strain on that easy comfort.

Ben saw Ivy from across the living room and a smile spread across his handsome face. "This is going to be good."

Miss Shirley put her arm around Ivy's shoulders and faced the stunned silence of her neighbors. "What? None of you brothers and sisters ever seen a white person before?"

Vigil shook his head. "Nope. Not here. Ain't never seen any white folks up in my house. Uninvited visitor."

Ruth waved the shaver at her husband. "Now you hush, Virgil. Ivy's welcome." She went back to shaving Max Black's head. "Did you come to watch Maggie get her hair straightened?"

Ivy felt the discomfort of the people in the barbershop, but she was used to the tension in her own family. She learned to pretend it wasn't there. Being funny always helped.

"Yeah, but I don't know why she wants it straight. Miss Shirley says curls drive men crazy."

Max looked at Miss Shirley and smiled. "They do indeed. She ought to know."

Max Black, a mechanic at the Mobil Station, was the only man bigger and stronger than Miss Shirley. "Nothing finer than a real natural black woman."

Miss Shirley swayed her hips and nodded her head. "You got that right, Mr. Maxwell Black."

Ruth rubbed a towel over his smooth dome and removed the short cape.

Virgil grumped into the kitchen and brought out another pot of coffee and a plate of peanut butter cookies. "Caucasians don't know their place no more."

"Ivy, don't pay no never mind to that old fool," Ruth said. She pointed to the kitchen step stool used as their barber chair. "Okay, Maggie, have a seat and let's see what we can do."

Ruth untied Maggie's braids and smeared Pomade grease in Maggie's hair. She wiped her hands on a towel. "Virgil, get me that pressing comb, would you?"

Virgil picked up the wooden handle of the long metal comb heating up on the gas flame of the kitchen stove. He handed it to Ruth, who pulled the straightening comb through Maggie's hair. It smoked and sizzled from the heat and the grease. "Did you know we went to all this trouble to straighten our hair?"

Ivy shook her head as she watched the straightening process. It looked like Maggie's hair would just disintegrate into nothing.

Ben leaned against the wall with his arms crossed. "What do you think of all this, Ivy?"

Ivy stared at the hot comb smoking in Ruth's hand. "I think I'd be a natural black woman."

The barbershop regulars looked at each other. Max slapped his muscled thigh and his loud, honking laugh joined the others. Even Virgil chuckled. Ivy laughed with them, relieved that the tension was broken. Then she picked up the broom resting in the corner of the living room and began to sweep up the hair on the floor, just like she did at Judy's Beauty Shop.

The door to the Jacksons' house opened and a tiny woman who lived a couple of houses down the street, walked in holding a four-year-old girl's hand. The woman, standing less than five feet tall, stared in disbelief at Ivy sweeping the floor. Ivy stared back because the woman looked just like the garden gnome riding the mushroom in Uncle Walter's yard—the evil pixie.

Ivy nudged Maggie. "Who's that?"

Maggie whispered behind her hand. "That's Thelma Sampson and Remmie, her daughter. Thelma works at the old folks' home. I feel sorry for the old people there." The dark hair above Thelma's lip made her face look angry, almost menacing. The tiny woman made a disapproving guttural noise in her throat and wheeled around.

The little girl protested, but the door slammed behind them just as a train rumbled down the tracks behind the row of tidy houses. The dishes in the cupboards rattled so loudly Ivy was sure they would tumble from their shelves and shatter. The roar of the locomotive drowned out all conversation until it passed and the relative quiet of Mulberry Street returned. Conversation resumed, and the quick departure of Thelma was never mentioned.

Chapter 13

THE ROSIE PROJECT

The community service project for the Chickadee Girls troop was Rosie Buckley, the old hermit lady. This meant that each week, one of the Chickadee Girls took Rosie some food and a piece of warm clothing. Because Rosie's dogs barked so ferociously and sometimes chased them, the girls usually left the items on an old tree stump in front of Rosie's home. The Chickadee Girls often delivered their contributions on the run.

After the holidays, Ivy took her turn at Rosie-duty. She had avoided going past Rosie's place since the wild dogs attacked her on her bike. She asked Raven to come but Raven was too scared of Rosie. Raven said Rosie kidnapped children and turned them into dogs and cats.

Ivy talked Maggie into going, but her eyes grew wide as they approached Rosie's broken-down shack. Maggie pulled her stocking cap down tighter over her shiny flattened hair. She gritted her teeth. "Weston Thrasher says Rosie's a witch."

Ivy shook her head. "Don't believe a word Weston tells you."

Ivy carried a steaming Tupperware container of Grandma's beef stew and some biscuits wrapped in tin foil. Maggie held a pair of woolen socks and a bag of dog biscuits. They hurried past the snowy stump to place the items on Rosie's filthy doorstep, when suddenly the door flew open.

Rosie stood in her doorway with barking dogs jumping and snarling behind her. She wore an old pair of men's pants and a well-worn flannel shirt. Her hair looked disheveled with bits of straw twisted among the dirty strands. Rosie cocked her head back and forth like a little Chihuahua dog and her ears twitched. "What do you want?"

Ivy froze. Her eyes widened, and her hands turned sweaty inside her thick woolen gloves. "We just wanted to bring you some food and stuff."

She felt relieved that they had left King at home—the wild dogs would have ripped him to shreds by now just by their sheer numbers and excessive determination.

Rosie looked at the girls with a sideways glance. "Why didn't you just leave your filthy charity on the stump like all those other do-gooder girls?"

Ivy held out the Tupperware bowl and biscuits, her hands shaking. "We wanted to make sure you got them."

Maggie extended the rolled-up socks and the bag of dog biscuits. The dogs sniffed the bag and barked excitedly. Rosie reached out her gnarled hands and took the items. Ivy stood stunned at all of the clutter visible through the open doorway.

"Well, don't just stand there like two bumps on a log. Come on in," Rosie said.

Ivy looked at Maggie. The dogs scared her. She still remembered how they had tried to attack her on the summer day she had escaped from Conrad Thrasher through the cornfield and across Rosie's yard.

Rosie waved her hand in the air like a magic wand. "Quiet down, my babies."

The dogs stopped barking.

Despite her fear of the dogs, Ivy's curiosity won out. No

one knew what the inside of Rosie's house looked like. She reluctantly stepped in, and Maggie followed, ducking her head to get inside the tiny door.

As soon as they entered the house, a putrid odor burned their nostrils. Piles of rank trash and animal feces covered the floor. Ivy immediately regretted her Chickadee goodwill. Rosie waved her crooked hand in the air, motioning to the other side of the stagnant room. "Have a seat, girls."

Maggie looked like she wanted to throw up, but she followed Ivy to Rosie's couch, exploding with white stuffing. The girls sat between broken springs and garbage. Ivy wondered if the decaying smell would soak into their clothes, like Uncle Tommy's aftershave sometimes did.

Rosie's wrinkled lips twitched. "So, who in tarnation are you?"

"I'm Maggie Norton."

Ivy lifted her feet off the piles of trash, trying to find a clear spot to set them down.

"I'm Ivy Taylor."

Rosie sniffed and jerked her head back. "You Violet Taylor's granddaughter?"

"Yeah."

"As I remember, your mother never liked this town much. Sad what happened to her. I remember it was the worst rain. My dogs and I were walking home from town when we saw her on the Coffey Shop bench, waiting for the Greyhound bus. Guess she wasn't meant to leave."

The old lady's mind was definitely gone. Ivy's mother hadn't been waiting for the bus. She was with her father in their new Bonneville car that night.

Rosie scratched her wrinkled chin and sighed. "You know,

you and I have a lot in common. We lost our mothers early. Got trapped in a life we didn't ask for, in a place we couldn't get out of." Rosie sighed.

She poked her fingers into her hair and a small twig fell out. "I used to be a schoolteacher. I bet you didn't know that. I quit teaching school when my mother took sick. Tuberculosis is a very bad thing. We didn't have a doctor in Coffey back then. We traveled twenty-three miles to Stilton to see the doctor. But he rotated to other towns further away and was only there on Mondays."

Rosie prodded her tangled hair with her thick fingers that looked more like miniature toes. Her stubby thumb looked like a deformed big toe and her nails turned up slightly at the ends.

"My mother suddenly took a turn for the worse and died before the next Monday came. Can't stand Mondays. Never could go back to work after that. Couldn't see the need with her gone and all. Nothing I could do would bring her back. I couldn't save my mother."

She waved her stubby hands at the dancing dogs and tiptoeing cats that filled the house. "But I saved all the strays. These sweet babies need me now. Don't you, my honeys? And we get along just fine. Don't need any charity from sweetie-sweet Chickadee girls."

Ivy stood up, trying to avoid the garbage and debris, and the animals. "Well, there's some treats for the dogs and some socks for you. Hope you enjoy the stew and biscuits. Keep the Tupperware. We've got to go now."

She motioned for Maggie to stand up and they cautiously walked back toward the door. But Ivy's snow boot hit the side of an empty cat food can on top of a pile of wet dog poop and her foot slipped out from under her. As she fell, she instinctively reached out for Maggie, who was standing on a rotten slimy rag. They both landed on Rosie's decomposing trash-heap of a living room floor.

Maggie held up a gloved hand covered with stinky, brown goo. Stuck to the gunk, hung a remnant of a chewed bone and some stuffing from the armrest of the couch. Maggie vigorously tried to shake it off, but the waste hung on.

Ivy got up from the poop-covered floor and hurried for the door, dodging the mangy dogs and matted cats as she negotiated the piles of rubbish. Maggie followed, holding her soiled gloved-hand in front of her. Rosie remained in her chair, petting a black-and-white cat that had curled up in her lap. When they reached the door, Ivy turned and looked at Rosie. "Sorry, we couldn't stay."

"So, go. Cats are better company anyway."

"I'm sorry about your mother," Ivy said.

"Yeah. Same here." Rosie smiled, revealing missing teeth. "I bet you wish you had that bike of yours now. Never seen a girl ride so fast." Rosie cackled as the door closed.

Once outside, the girls gulped fresh winter air. They ran until they were far away from Rosie's house and slowed to a stop when they reached an empty field.

A giant snow owl flew over their heads, an unusual sight during the day. They watched it soar, its huge wingspan commanding until it blended in with the white sky and snow of the landscape.

Ivy looked at Maggie. "We'd better earn our Chickadee badge for this one."

"Ivy, there's poop on you," Maggie said.

"Oh my gosh, how sick." Ivy turned in a circle. "Where?"

"Right there."

Maggie pointed to the dark smear on Ivy's cheek, but her own glove was covered in squished dog excrement.

"Oh, my gosh," she screamed. "This is the grossest thing that has ever happened to us."

Ivy wrinkled up her nose and turned around like a runway model. "Do I have any doggy doo-doo or kitty poo-poo on my coat?"

"Both. Ivy, there's poop all over you."

Ivy looked at her coat and laughed. She imitated George Kelsey, the town doctor, speaking with precise medical terms. "Bowel movement, Miss Norton. We are covered in animal bowel movement."

Maggie laughed, spraying spit. "My good doctor, do you mean a BM?"

Ivy laughed and fell in the snowy field. Maggie joined her on the ground and they lay down on their backs, rubbing handfuls of snow on themselves to get the poop off. Ivy brushed the snow from her mittens and scrambled up. She reached out her hand to help Maggie up and imitated Rosie's welcome. "Don't just sit there like a bump on a log. Come on in."

Their laughter billowed in hazy puffs, floating on the winter air as they strolled arm in arm toward the gravel road which was covered with a new frosting of snow.

"I can't wait to tell Nick," said Ivy.

Maggie's cheeks turned red from the cold wind. "Do you think your Grandma's heard about our great poop adventure yet?"

"If those stinking dogs and cats told the nosey birds, Grandma knows already." Ivy threw a snowball at a telephone pole. "Man, sometimes it's hard to be a do-gooder."

Chapter 14

MUSHROOM HUNTING

In spring, the light rain refreshed the land and a lush green spread over the gentle hills of Iowa. The trees leafed and the flowers bloomed, like a child's crayons bringing brilliant colors to the drab landscape of winter.

It was the time of year that Grandma Violet and Matilda Kelsey turned into a devoted pair of mushroom warriors for the few weeks of mushroom season. Ivy often joined them.

Matilda Kelsey helped her husband, the doctor and county coroner, run the only medical clinic in town. Despite a twenty-six-year age difference, Grandma and Matilda Kelsey developed a great friendship that grew from their love of mushrooms.

One May morning, as the wild plum trees flowered and the redbud trees bloomed purple, Ivy was hunting for morel mushrooms with Grandma and Matilda in Luther Matthew's woods. Luther didn't like mushrooms, so he let Grandma, Matilda, and Miss Shirley hunt in the woods behind his house whenever they wanted. Miss Shirley said she didn't have the time or the energy for mushroom hunting anymore, so Grandma gave Miss Shirley huge bags of mushrooms that she froze to use in her famous gravy. In exchange, Miss Shirley gave her pies.

Most people were scared to hunt for mushrooms in Luther's woods after his father died of mushroom poisoning when Luther was still in high school. But that never stopped Grandma,

Matilda, and Ivy because they could identify the edible morels from the poisonous fakes.

The morning brought dampness and the woods bloomed with dogtooth violet, mayapples, and Dutchman's breeches. The birds watched them and occasionally called to them from the trees. Ivy breathed in the smell of leaves and damp earth as they tramped through the trees behind Luther's house, looking for mushrooms.

"I smell mushrooms," Ivy said, searching the ground. The pits and ridges of morels looked like Christmas trees made out of sponges or honeycombs. The brown, gray, yellow, or almost white mushrooms grew from less than an inch to almost a foot tall.

"You've got to think like a mushroom," said Grandma.

Ivy stopped and leaned on a maple tree, pulling off the burrs stuck to her sweatpants. A flash of white metal caught her eye through the trees. "Looks like Conrad Thrasher's car over there."

Matilda looked over at the parked big white whale of a car and shook her head. "Really? Who's he trying to fool?"

Grandma picked up a sturdy branch for a walking stick and snapped off the smaller twigs. "Why doesn't he hunt his own woods? That old coot's been trying to steal our mushroom territory for years. But Luther won't let him step foot on his property."

Ivy pulled off the last bur and threw it into the weeds.

Grandma rubbed the extra skin hanging under her chin. "No-good mushroom thief."

Matilda shook her head. A few strands of her jet-black hair fell loose from the two combs that swept her hair up on her head. "If we're lucky, he'll get a poisonous one."

Ivy knew that mushroom hunting could be a dangerous

hobby for the careless or uninformed. Grandma had carefully explained how the false morels looked similar to morels and contained a toxic chemical called monomethyl hydrazine that caused diarrhea, vomiting, severe headaches, and sometimes even death.

"It takes sharp eyes and years of experience to find mushrooms—" Grandma started.

"And not get poisoned," Matilda finished with a smile.

Grandma leaned against her walking stick. "Is the good doctor still nervous about mushrooms?"

"He won't touch them," Matilda said.

Ivy picked her way carefully across a wet gully, choosing her path carefully. "Why doesn't he like them?"

Matilda cupped her hand to the side of her mouth and whispered, "Afraid of getting poisoned."

Grandma leaned on her stick, breathing heavily. "He's never forgotten Luther's father's death. It must have been horrible. But I figure, what the heck, all the more mushrooms for us." She pointed to a cluster of dead maple trees at the top of a sunny, steep rise. "If I was a mushroom, that's where I'd be. Got to outsmart the fungus. Ivy, you run on up there and see if I'm right. Matilda and I will wait right here."

Ivy's muddy shoes made the short climb difficult. A lone hawk at the top of a dead maple tree watched her approach. When Ivy reached the crest of the hill she smiled and turned back toward Grandma and Matilda, raising her arms in victory. "Mushrooms!"

The hawk screeched and swooped down. Ivy turned to watch his rapid descent.

A shot rang out in the woods. Branches shattered nearby. Ivy covered her head and stumbled back as twigs rained down around her. The hawk dropped from the sky, dead.

Ivy's slipped on a protruding root and twisted her ankle. She tumbled backward. The underbrush crunched like a fleeing animal as she fell down the short incline. At the bottom, she sat up, leaves and mud clinging to her. A cold chill ran down her back. She felt evil in the air. She had felt it before at Thrasher's pond.

"You all right there, Ivy?" Grandma called.

"Twisted my ankle," Ivy said as she got up and limped down the hill to them.

"Let's get the doc to check you out," said Grandma. "But don't tell him what we were doing."

Matilda laughed. "Oh, he'll know."

Dr. Kelsey, wearing his usual brightly-colored Hawaiian shirt and open-toe sandals, examined Ivy's ankle and wrapped a bandage around it. "Just a bad sprain. It'll be tender, but you'll be fine in a few days. Mushroom hunting can be dangerous."

Ivy nodded, glancing at Grandma and Matilda, who laughed.

When they came out of the examining room, Ivy froze. Conrad Thrasher was slumped in one of the orange vinyl chairs. Matilda straightened her shoulders. "What are you doing here?"

"Tetanus shot. Tangled with some rusty barbed wire when I was in my fields," Conrad said.

Grandma thumped over to Conrad, reminding Ivy of Grandma's determined attacks on her perpetual enemies, the pesky backyard squirrels. Violet stuck her face close to his, speaking just loud enough for Ivy and Matilda to hear. "I know exactly where you were today, and it wasn't in your fields."

Conrad smiled, showing his tobacco-stained teeth. "What?" He flapped his arms. "Did your birds tell you that?"

Grandma shook her finger at him, the flab of her arm swaying. "Let me tell you this. If you ever come near my granddaughter again, I'll see to it that seed corn isn't the only thing planted in your fields. That's a promise from this old lady who knows all your secrets."

His face lost its color, but he stared back defiantly. "And I know yours."

The door opened, and Miss Shirley and her new baby entered the clinic. "Hello, good people. Saved any lives today, Dr. Kelsey?" Her voice filled the waiting room.

Miss Shirley, unmarried and entering her forties, was a large woman, both tall and voluminous. The birth of her baby had surprised everyone in town. No one even knew she was pregnant. Miss Shirley's son, Justin, was a beautiful baby with soft curly hair, light brown skin, and penetrating light gray eyes. She wouldn't say who the baby's father was, but most of the people on Mulberry Street thought it was Max Black, who was three years younger than Miss Shirley, and Max did nothing to deny it. Grandma took a liking to Justin from the beginning, buying him gifts and looking forward to the times when Miss Shirley, baby Justin, and Grandma would sit on the back porch for a while, after she had brought over the pies.

"No, but I plan to save some lives before the day is out. I'll be right with you, Miss Shirley," said Dr. Kelsey, standing in the doorway behind Ivy, Grandma, and Matilda. "Conrad, you can come with me."

Conrad glanced at Grandma and then sauntered toward the doctor. "Aloha, Doc. Looks like Miss Shirley's got a who's-the-daddy baby. She needs to figure out what's causing that, don't you think, Doc?"

Conrad's deep laugh boomed throughout the clinic even after he shut the door. Ivy could tell by Miss Shirley's scrunched-up eyes that she was contemplating storming the examining room and rearranging the mayor's face. She'd seen that look before when Miss Shirley watched the villains in her soap opera story.

Chapter 15

THE SUPREME COURT SAID
YOU COULD

Once Ivy's ankle felt good enough, she, Nick, and Maggie spent the afternoon riding their bikes around town. King, the great purple dog, trotted beside them as they circled the familiar streets of Coffey. They stopped by Judy's Beauty Shop and made faces at Judy through the shop window. Judy laughed and pretended to chase them away. Judy was thirty-one and Ivy wondered why she had never remarried. Judy told her she would never rely on a man again.

The Iowa sky remained blue and cloudless. The spring sun warmed their faces as they rode around the town square before parking their bikes and sitting outside the Coffey Shop. King curled up on the sidewalk next to them.

After Bertha Tuttle, the official town snoop, whispered to everyone about the disgrace of Miss Shirley's unexpected son, Miss Shirley lost her cleaning jobs. But she didn't care.

"A child is worth losing a job over. A hardworking woman like me can always find a job," Miss Shirley told Ivy and Maggie. And she did. Miss Shirley started working as the new cook at the Coffey Shop only a few weeks after her second son was born, but now she could only watch her soap opera on her one day off a week. Her neighbors loved the baby and took turns watching the little boy while Miss Shirley worked.

The corner restaurant filled up as soon as the word got out that Miss Shirley was cooking. People flocked to the restaurant for her special chili, chicken dumplings, mashed potatoes with skins and wild morel mushroom gravy, and most of all, her homemade pies, now available to everyone, not just her friends.

Ivy loved to eat at the Coffey Shop, especially after Miss Shirley started working there. But Maggie, along with all the other black families, didn't frequent the Coffey Shop because the bank was across the street and Conrad Thrasher was often there for lunch or coffee with the guys.

Ivy, Nick, and Maggie watched people in the square going about their daily business. Ivy's ankle throbbed, and her throat felt dry.

"Let's just go inside. It's way after lunch, so, he won't be there," Ivy said.

Maggie shook her head, her brown eyes wide. "I can't go in there."

"Miss Shirley's in there," said Nick.

"Yeah, but she works there. That's a whole other thing."

Ivy frowned. "Okay, listen. I'll look in the window. If it's empty, we'll go in, all right? Come on."

Maggie glanced around. "I don't know. I guess. If you're sure there's nobody there."

Ivy tucked her hair behind her ears and tiptoed up to the window. She cupped her hands around her eyes as she peered inside. "It's empty. Let's go in. I'm thirsty and tired, and besides, Nick's dad says the Supreme Court said you can. Right, Nick?"

"Yeah."

"That's easy for you to say," Maggie said.

Ivy opened the creaking screen door. She stepped into the restaurant and the smell of French fries filled the room. Miss Shirley looked out from the kitchen and wiggled her hands high in the air. "Glory be, let the sun shine in."

"Hi, Miss Shirley," Ivy said.

Nick followed Ivy, blocking Maggie. "How is the best cook in Coffey?"

"Pretty darn fantastic," Miss Shirley said.

Kitty, the waitress, waved from the kitchen. "Hi, kids."

Maggie took a deep breath and followed Nick into the restaurant. Miss Shirley froze when she saw her, and her eyes darted to the restroom. The kids walked toward the red stools by the grill as the restroom door opened, and Conrad Thrasher stepped out. He glared at them as they sat down.

Conrad Thrasher pointed at Maggie's stool. "That seat's taken."

Maggie's face went pale. She looked at the stool and slid over to the next one.

"They're all taken," Conrad barked.

Quiet tension filled the Coffey Shop. Miss Shirley was still frozen and Kitty peered fearfully from the kitchen. Ivy's hands trembled at her side as she turned to face Conrad Thrasher. Beads of sweat broke out on her forehead, and her heart pounded. She could feel his hatred oozing from the holes in his cold heart. "We just want to sit down."

Conrad's blue eyes shone cold beneath his bushy eyebrows. "Her kind don't come in here."

Ivy swallowed, trying to get rid of the huge lump stuck in her throat. She glanced back at Maggie and Nick. "Well, the Supreme Court said she can."

Conrad pointed at the kids with his chin. "Don't see no

Supreme Court in Coffey. Hate uppity people like you. Your grandmother may have everyone else in town shut up, but I know what really happened and I know who you really are."

Miss Shirley dropped a pan, and it clattered to the floor, echoing in the empty restaurant. Conrad's eyes narrowed as he glared at Ivy.

Nick moved to stand next to Ivy as she took a deep breath.

"What do you mean?" she asked.

"Just what I said."

Ivy absently pulled her mother's necklace back and forth along the chain. Conrad's steel eyes followed her every movement.

Ivy looked straight ahead. She wanted to run away from this hateful, frightening man, but she stayed because she could not move. A few empty seconds ticked by.

"Miss Shirley, we'd like three Green Rivers, please," Nick said politely.

Miss Shirley squirted lime syrup in the carbonated water and set the glasses down on the counter. Conrad Thrasher glared at Miss Shirley.

"You'll all regret this." He stomped across the restaurant's wooden floor without paying for his three cups of coffee and piece of apple pie. "And you got no business wearing that necklace," he mumbled, as the creaky screen door bounced shut behind him. King's barks and growls turned into a yelp as Conrad kicked him as he passed.

Ivy let out a shaky breath as Miss Shirley nodded to the vacant stools. "Looks like a few seats just opened up, folks. Old man Thrasher can go to hell. He's halfway there already. Somebody ought to have the guts to take him the rest of the way."

The three friends sat down on the stools, and Ivy took a sip of her Green River. The cold carbonated liquid felt good. Ivy grabbed Maggie's trembling hand. "I'm sorry. I didn't know—"

Maggie sat quietly beside her, straining under the weight of her skin. "You didn't know what it was like to be black? I know, Ivy."

Ivy's eyebrows wrinkled. "I wonder if Conrad Thrasher thinks I'm black."

Miss Shirley laughed and leaned against the counter. "Now Ivy, that's the best one you've come up with yet. You ain't black, sister, you just an inconvenience to him."

Miss Shirley reached into the glass pie-keeper and set down three pieces of her homemade strawberry-rhubarb pie on the counter. "How about a slice of pie? My treat."

Ivy nodded. Miss Shirley wiped the sweat off her forehead with a napkin. "Oh, Lordy. What gave you the all-mighty gumption to come in here, Maggie girl?"

"Well, we were thirsty . . ." Maggie shrugged and smiled. "And the Supreme Court said I could."

Miss Shirley slapped her thighs and laughed. "You tell them, girl."

Ivy's smile disappeared. "Do you think you'll get fired for this, Miss Shirley?"

"Who cares? I can always get another job. It's not like this one is making me rich. It was worth it just to see his face. The old fool banker." She threw her head back and yelled like Leon Wilson. "Find the fight in your soul." Her throaty laugh filled the restaurant.

The kids laughed in relief and Ivy tapped her pie plate with her fork and her face grew solemn. "What did he mean when he said he knew what really happened and who I really was?"

Miss Shirley shook her head. "Don't pay no mind to him. He's full of spit and vinegar. He never makes sense. Some white peoples is just strange." She turned away, humming a Leon Wilson tune, and finished cleaning the grill.

When Ivy arrived home for supper a few hours later, she found Salisbury steak, mashed potatoes, lime Jell-O with pears, and fried morel mushrooms waiting for her.

"Grandma, that smells good."

Ivy scooped her finger in the bowl of mashed potatoes and put it in her mouth.

"Wait for supper," Grandma scolded.

Ivy kissed Grandma and Uncle Walter, who often came over to eat with them. "Hey, you guys won't believe what happened to Maggie and me and Nick today."

Grandma pointed her finger at the kitchen sink. "Before you say another word, go wash up. Lord knows where those hands have been. I hope you washed your hands before you ate Miss Shirley's strawberry-rhubarb pie this afternoon." Grandma winked at Uncle Walter, who smiled as he set the plates on the table.

"You already heard what happened?" Ivy said in disbelief.

Grandma nodded. "Yes, I did, little missy."

Ivy washed her hands and wiped them on a tea towel. "You should have seen Conrad Thrasher's face. He looked like one of Rosie Buckley's bulldogs, all dirty and snarly and ready to bite."

Grandma put the silverware on the table. "Some people's hearts are cold as ice, and nothing you do can warm them up. What did he say?"

"He said Maggie couldn't eat in the Coffey Shop. He said we'd all regret it. Oh, and he said he knew what really happened and who I really was, like I wasn't your granddaughter or something. What's he talking about?"

Grandma clicked her tongue and shoveled Salisbury steak onto the plates. "Oh, *pshaw*. That's just folderol. The old goat is probably still mad at us for outsmarting him mushroom hunting in Luther's woods. He's a bitter, angry man."

"Why is he like that?"

"He blames everyone."

"For what?"

"For his unhappiness."

Ivy sat down at her place at the table. Her hands trembled when she lifted her glass to take a sip of water. "How did you know about what happened at the Coffey Shop, Grandma?"

"The birds told me."

Grandma's clairvoyance proved so astounding that Ivy believed the birds told Grandma everyone's secrets. It wasn't hard to imagine because Grandma loved the birds. And the birds trusted Grandma.

Every day, Grandma had Ivy pour birdseed in all the bird feeders in the backyard. Grandma loved to sit in her old pine rocker on the back porch and watch the birds. She placed birdseed in her hands, and they flocked around her. Their tiny feet hopped along her hands and fingers as they ate out of her palms.

When Grandma sat quietly in her porch rocking chair, the birds often landed on her shoulder or head, resting for a moment from their busy bird day. Grandma knew each bird's character and she named the distinctive personalities of the feathered fowl. She called one frequent shoulder-percher, "Sweetie Pie." The little gray and white chickadee, with a black cap and a black stripe over its eyes, often rested on Grandma's shoulder and sang in her ear.

After they finished supper that night, Ivy gazed out the kitchen window as she washed the dishes and saw the squirrels invading the bird feeder. She sounded the alarm. "Squirrel alert! Squirrel alert! Grandma, get the broom."

Grandma's bulky frame lumbered through the house. She grabbed the broom and charged out the back door to force the pesky squirrels into retreat. Ivy giggled as Grandma waved the broom in the air.

When Grandma came back triumphantly, she huffed, "Don't know why God wasted his time making squirrels. The little thieves."

Uncle Walter raised his eyebrows and clicked his tongue. "Those squirrels will be the last creatures alive on earth."

Ivy imitated Aunt Hattie's haughty preaching voice. "All that'll be left after the Rapture will be all the faithless sinners and a few squirrels."

The bushes along the path moved and Uncle Tommy marched up to the porch from the yard. "Squirrels aren't that tough, if you know what you're doing."

Uncle Tommy raised his thumb and extended his index finger in the shape of a gun. "I could use a little target practice on the nasty rodents." He jerked his hand back as if he'd fired the gun. "Got to get ready for duck hunting season."

Ivy shuddered.

When hunting season opened, Uncle Tommy and Reuben could often be found at their duck blind on Beecher Pond. As a child, Ivy would sometimes tag along, but she considered killing unarmed ducks an inexcusable crime and refused to bear witness to the duck assassinations. But during the off-season, Uncle Tommy used cats for shooting practice. "The best way to stop a pesky varmint is to shoot him in the head before he knows what hit him," he used to say.

"I don't want you killing them, I just wish they'd find another home," Grandma said.

"Cats don't come through my backyard anymore," Uncle Tommy said.

"Cats are smarter than Tommy," Uncle Walter said to Ivy.

Uncle Tommy ignored his brother. "Hey, I just stopped by to see if you got any extra mushrooms."

Grandma gestured to Walter. "Get Tommy a bag of mushrooms."

Uncle Walter went into the kitchen and brought out the smallest bag and handed it to Ivy, who handed it to Uncle Tommy. He dropped his handful of sunflower seeds to grab it.

"I'm out of here. Had enough family time for one day," Uncle Walter said as he headed home to his trailer. Ivy knew too much time around his brother made Uncle Walter stressed.

After Uncle Tommy left with his mushrooms, Grandma and Ivy went to bed. They forgot to turn off the porch light, so from Ivy's bedroom window, she watched the stealthy squirrels celebrate their cunning victory as they ate the sunflower seeds Uncle Tommy spilled on the porch.

PART III

MISCHIEF, TRICKERY, AND DISAPPOINTMENT

(1975-1976)

Chapter 16

THE COFFEY SHOP

Iowa is an orderly state. The rows of crops run straight and long. Tightly strung barbed-wire fences surround the livestock yards and fields. The many unmarked country roads crisscross the rolling hills, farmlands, and small towns. There is nothing haphazard about Iowa farming. There is, by necessity, a distinctive rhythm to rural life. Growing crops and raising livestock takes precise tending: the planting, the harvesting, the feeding, and the selling. Farmers cannot afford to guess. They plan and measure, and nature does the rest.

In early fall, the farmers delivered mountains of yellow corn to the Coffey Farmer's Co-op for sale. Trails of golden corn spilled from the wagons as the tractors pulled the harvest to the co-op silos in town, while the Hy-Vee grocery store stacked pumpkins and squash on the sidewalk outside the store. Breezy sunny days alternated with cool, windy ones.

That September Saturday turned crisp and cool. A welcome change and a new season blew into Coffey. Seventeen-year-old Ivy would graduate from high school that year. Although she'd briefly been to Des Moines, Kansas City, and Omaha, soon she could finally leave Coffey for good and see other places and be a part of other worlds.

Luther Matthews came out to 4120 to replace Grandma's storm windows and check her furnace. Ivy, Raven, Nick, and

Jesse—now Ivy's boyfriend, the one who never planned to stay long in Coffey—helped Luther unload two cords of split wood for Grandma's fireplace. When they finished stacking the logs on the side of the house, their cheeks flushed the color of Macintosh apples and their breath floated like steamy clouds in the cold autumn air. Luther got in his old beat-up truck and leaned out the window. "Tell your Grandma, no charge." With a wave, he drove off, leaving a trail of smoky exhaust behind.

The friends stepped inside Grandma's kitchen from the cold back porch. The tangy smell of hot apple cider filled the house.

Nick hugged Grandma Violet. "Hi, Grandma V. What's new with the great all-knowing being?"

Grandma often demonstrated her legendary powers of knowledge and skill when she cooked without a recipe, sewed without a pattern, and plucked her few chin hairs without a mirror. She knew when snow would fall and where to find morel mushrooms. Her many years of experience had taught her a lot, as well as what the birds told her.

Nick's hands pointed in front then back as he danced and bobbed his head. "I bet you didn't know I was going to do my dog dance." Nick tilted his head up and howled, making an "oh, no!" sound mimicking Reuben's dog.

Grandma threw her hands in the air and slapped her big thighs. "No, your dog dance is definitely one of the few surprises left in life."

Jesse rolled his eyes and smoothed down his blow-dried hair. "Nicko, don't embarrass yourself, mutt."

Jesse reached over to give him a push, but Nick turned and danced toward Grandma. He put his arm around her and kissed her peach-soft cheek that always smelled of lilacs. Grandma pinched Nick's cheek, still pink from the cold.

"Now stop this foolishness and drive Ivy on down to the

Coffey Shop to pick up my pies. Go on. You kids, get out of here with your crazy nonsense." She shooed them out of the house, still laughing.

The kids piled into Nick's newly purchased vehicle. He had bought Howard Decker's strangely built truck-camper. Driving the fogger during the summer didn't pay much. Howard had run low on beer money, and Kitty, his hardworking waitress wife, refused to give him any more, so Nick had bought the Monstrosity for next to nothing. Nick's father said that's exactly what it was worth. But Nick, like Howard, saw its potential, and although Nick didn't want anyone else driving it, Ivy and her friends now had transportation.

Nick pulled the smoking and sputtering truck into a parking spot on the town square. Ivy, Jesse, Raven, and Nick entered the Coffey Shop. Kitty led the four kids to an open table to wait for Grandma's pie order. Kitty didn't wear any makeup. She didn't have the time or the energy to try to please others. She was too busy trying to make a living for herself and her drunken husband.

Ivy waved to Miss Shirley as they passed the kitchen. Nick blew Miss Shirley a kiss and she pretended to catch it. Ivy laughed. Everyone liked Nick. He fit in so well among the strange personalities of Coffey. He was such a small-town kind of guy.

Kitty sat them at a booth next to Uncle Tommy and his friends. "Ignore them if you can, kids."

Ivy waved to Russell as he ate his dinner while Uncle Tommy, Reuben, and Charlie, the sheriff, sipped their coffee. They often stayed there for hours on the weekends, nursing their cups of coffee and joking with the other customers.

Russell had graduated high school several years back and Uncle Walter got him a job at the Post Office, which Uncle Tommy despised. But Russell paid attention to detail and he was good with numbers. Those were qualities the post office admired. He had moved into the apartment above the Coffey Shop and since he hated the unorganized stress of cooking, he ate most of his meals at the restaurant. He often joined his father and his friends, not because he wanted to, but because it would be awkward not to.

"Hey, Ivy, do you know what the Blue Plate Special is today?" Uncle Tommy asked.

Ivy shook her head.

Uncle Tommy pretended to put a finger down his throat. "Whatever didn't sell yesterday."

Kitty frowned and rocked her head from side to side. "Very funny. You ought to know. You're here every day." Kitty mimed stabbing Uncle Tommy with a fork behind his back.

Charlie wagged his finger at the good-natured waitress. "Watch out there, Miss Kitty. That's assault, and I'm a sworn officer of the law.

"Actually, the special today is Miss Shirley's poison mushroom gravy," Uncle Tommy teased.

"And I consider that an aggravated assault," said Charlie.

The men laughed that deep kind of laugh they used when they thought they were funny at someone else's expense. Uncle Tommy, sitting at the end of the booth, stood up.

"Hey, what's taking so long with those burgers?"

Miss Shirley waved her spatula from the grill across the room. "Oh, pipe down over there, or I'll poison your food."

"See, I told you," Charlie said.

The men howled with laughter again.

Kitty brought their burgers and turned to Ivy and her friends at the next table. "You kids want something to drink while you wait?"

"No, thanks," Ivy said.

"A glass of water? It's city water," Kitty said.

Charlie hit the table. "Hey, that reminds me. Did you hear our mighty mayor talked the town council into running city water out to his place? So now Thrasher won't have to use that giant cistern in his backyard for water."

Reuben cocked his head back. "Hey, my place is closer to town than Conrad's, and I don't remember getting any city water. Must be nice."

Russell stared down at his freckled hands as he buttoned and unbuttoned his Izod shirt, counting under his breath. "Did you know the Coffey Shop has eight stools, seven booths, nine tables, and forty-three items on the menu?"

Uncle Tommy shook his head as he chewed his burger. "Oh Lord, my son, the nerdy bean counter. Both of my kids are embarrassments. Angela's traveling around the country trying to find herself. Haven't seen her in years. Guess she hasn't found herself, yet." Ivy envied Angela. After London, she had never returned to Coffey. She was lucky.

"Sometimes I think you were lucky, Reuben, that you didn't have kids," Uncle Tommy said.

Charlie strained to rest his ankle on his knee. His tan uniform was stretched tight and the buttons looked like they were going to pop. The white streak in his stiff crew cut grew wider over the years. He hit Uncle Tommy on the arm. "Hey, maybe Russell knows how many ghosts Reuben has over at his place?"

Russell pushed back his chair, its legs scraping along the old floorboards. He stood up, his face red. He turned and hurried out of the restaurant, his freckled face pinched, and his long arms twitching awkwardly.

"Shoot. He don't know. He won't step foot in Reuben's house. Neither of my kids would. Just Ivy," Uncle Tommy said.

Uncle Tommy picked his teeth with the edge of a matchbook. Then he tapped his empty coffee cup with his spoon. Kitty understood Uncle Tommy's signal and came over to refill his coffee.

"So, Reuben, have you seen any of your ghosts lately?" Charlie asked.

Reuben sat back against the padded, red booth and rested his thumbs under the straps of his overalls. "Yes, as a matter of fact, do you know what one of those dadburn ghosts did? Busted my furnace. Took all day for Luther to get it going again."

Kitty refilled the rest of their coffee cups. Jesse looked at his Timex watch. He was always in a hurry. That was one of the reasons Ivy liked him. He would never be satisfied to stay in such a slow, boring town. It was just one more guarantee that he would help her get out of Coffey.

Miss Shirley put the two apple pies in white boxes and handed them to Ivy. "Tell your grandmother I hope she enjoys the pies."

Ivy could feel the warmth emanating from the pies as they filled the air with the smell of sweet apples and cinnamon. "Thank you. Grandma says a piece of your pie can solve any problem."

Uncle Tommy jerked his chin at Miss Shirley. "Speaking of pies, you people are supposed to be good at cooking, aren't you?"

Miss Shirley didn't answer, but instead stared at Uncle Tommy with a stern look that stopped many stronger and smarter men, but Uncle Tommy continued. "Well, some of your pies are passable, but if you made that angel pie of yours, then there'd really be something to talk about." Tommy patted his belly. "Wouldn't there, Reuben?"

Reuben nodded. "Mm-hmm."

Miss Shirley put her hands on her wide hips. "My angel pie takes too long to make, especially for the likes of you. You know I only make it for funeral potlucks. I guess you'll just have to wait for someone to die."

She turned to go back to the kitchen. Uncle Tommy clutched at his throat and stuck out his tongue, pretending to fall off the end of the booth. "Yeah, your cooking probably sent them to their grave in the first place."

Miss Shirley swaggered back to the grill, swishing her big hips. "You'll never know." Her deep laughter rang through the small restaurant. Ivy and Nick looked at each other and laughed. Jesse stared out the window. The old wooden ceiling fan spun in an endless rhythmic circle.

Kitty set the lunch bill on the table. "When you're done, boys, why don't you go on home? You've stirred up enough trouble for one day," said Kitty. "You know, I see you guys more than my own husband."

Uncle Tommy laughed and slapped the top of the table. "You mean the fogger man? This summer I saw him driving down the church alley on that bug tractor. Don't think he knew where he was going. Nearly ran over the preacher and a little old lady."

Ivy picked up the pies and her friends got up to leave.

"Ivy, will you take these clowns with you?" Kitty asked, pointing to Uncle Tommy and his buddies.

"Sorry, they're all yours. But thanks for the pies."

Ivy never paid for Miss Shirley's pies because Grandma's deal with Miss Shirley to supply wild morel mushrooms for her special gravy extended to the Coffey Shop.

Chapter 17

THE DUSTY LIBRARY

After leaving the Coffey Shop, Jesse and Raven headed to the high school gym that was open on the weekends for workouts. Jesse's only goal was to get out of Coffey and be a football coach for a Division 1 college. He despised unranked college teams and small towns.

Nick waited with Ivy outside the Coffey Shop and a few minutes later, Uncle Walter pulled up in front of the library, driving Grandma's Dodge Dart with the window rolled down. "I'm looking for some pies. Miss Shirley's bartered pastries are the best, don't you think?"

Ivy smiled and nodded as she put the pies in the back of the car. The cool fall air blew Ivy's hair. The breeze felt good, like a fresh breath after the stifling summer heat.

Uncle Walter got out of the car carrying a stack of books to return. "Come with me to the library. I may need backup with Edna Jean."

Ivy and Nick laughed and followed him into the library.

Although it was her job, Edna Jean Whittaker did not like to loan books. She inspected each returned book with a high-powered magnifying glass to check for reading crimes; bent corners, smudged pages, or small tears. She accused patrons of taking advantage of her failing eyesight.

Ivy and Nick waited with Uncle Walter while he returned his books.

Edna Jean's very pale vampire-like skin showed almost translucent, because she never saw the sun. Edna Jean took off her glasses, and cleaned the lenses with a tissue as if using them as a prop.

"Walter, I must say, I hear the shenanigans that go on over at your place are absolutely appalling." Her high-pitched whisper echoed around the almost empty library. "No self-respecting man would let his brother rampage through his trailer, doing only God-knows-what-all."

Uncle Walter frowned and shuffled his penny loafers. "Edna Jean, for your information—and your gossip friend Bertha's—I don't let Tommy rampage through my trailer. He breaks in. He picks my locks. I have several."

Edna Jean straightened out the tangled chain connecting the earpieces of her thick glasses and she put them back on her long, pointed nose. "Tommy Taylor's been bothering people his whole life. For years, he told people that he put my precious pretties up the library flagpole in high school." Her hand grabbed at the air. "Lies, all of it. No, indeed, I sure wouldn't let him pillage my private things, if I were you."

Uncle Walter ran his fingers through his thick dark hair and sighed. "Right, Edna Jean. Thanks for the advice."

Edna Jean bent down to examine Uncle Walter's returned books with the magnifying glass. She gasped and straightened up, pointing to a victimized page.

"What's this? There's a tear on page 143."

Uncle Walter shrugged.

"It looks like a tiny, little rip. I don't even know how you could see it, it's so small."

Edna Jean wore no makeup. She didn't have the eyesight for that kind of detail. She stared at Uncle Walter with her mouth pulled to the side. "What? Do you think I'm blind?"

Ivy and Nick exchanged a glance.

Uncle Walter's well-manicured hands gestured in the air. "No, Edna Jean, the tear is just so small. It was just an accident."

Edna Jean's eyes narrowed until they were two little slits in her glasses.

"There are no accidents, only careless readers." Her high-pitched voice rose even sharper. "There is no excuse for book abuse."

Ivy looked at Nick who pursed his lips and shook his finger, imitating Edna Jean behind her back. Afraid she would laugh, Ivy covered her mouth and turned away.

"Really, Edna Jean. Books are supposed to be read." Uncle Walter shook his head and turned to go. "Ivy, do you want a ride home?"

Ivy glanced around the library. "As long as I'm here, I think I'll get some more travel books and maybe look up something for school. You want to help me, Nick?"

"Not really."

She nudged him.

"Sure," he said.

Uncle Walter winked. "Well, make sure you don't turn the pages."

Edna Jean sniffed loudly. She shushed a group of little kids in the children's section and turned back to her desk to stamp Uncle Walter's books.

Nick leaned over to Uncle Walter. "You have to cut her some slack. She's a member of the library police."

Ivy and Uncle Walter laughed.

Edna Jean turned around and glared at Nick. Her tiny bat ears twitched. "I heard that. I have a very keen sense of hearing, you know."

Uncle Walter waved to them as he left the library, still chuckling to himself.

Ivy turned to Edna Jean. "I need to go through some old copies of the *Coffey Gazette* for a school project."

Nick cocked his head to the side and gave her a questioning look, but didn't say anything.

The floorboards creaked as Edna Jean slowly crept around the stacks with a pencil sticking out of her stiff wig. The dust-phobic librarian led them to the back stairs that went down to the lower level of the library where the periodicals and damaged books she considered unreadable or needed protecting were kept.

Edna Jean avoided going down to the basement because everything was dusty. The place smelled old and forgotten, like the Rose Hill Nursing Home. "I find the smell of dust overwhelmingly distressful and problematic," Edna Jean coughed. She pointed to a bookshelf at the far end of the dark room. "I think you'll find the old papers over there somewhere. Don't mess with the stuff down here." Edna Jean put her hand over her nose and mouth and hurried up the dingy stairs.

"What? Can she hear us turning the pages down here?" Nick asked.

"Probably."

Ivy found a dusty pile of oversized folders filled with the yellowed pages of the *Coffey Gazette*. Nick leafed through huge books that contained the weekly paper from over the years. "What are we doing here?"

"I'm trying to find my parents' obituaries or something about their crash." She opened the cover of the big book resting on top of the pile. She gingerly turned the brittle pages filled with Coffey's news. The date was July 7, 1944. She turned the page. "Hey, look. Isn't that Reuben?"

The picture showed the young Reuben Smith, a member of the Future Farmers of America, winning a blue ribbon for his oversized tomatoes at the McKinley County Fair.

Nick leaned in closely to look at the yellowed picture. "Oh, my gosh. That's Patty next to him."

"Let me see."

Ivy stared at the thin, smiling girl standing beside Reuben. She ran her finger over the old picture. Her heart sank. If only someone could have warned this young, pretty girl about the heartaches that would someday haunt her.

Ivy sighed and turned the page to the obituaries and wedding announcements. A newly engaged young woman peered out of her thick glasses, looking happy and hopeful. The name under the picture read Edna Jean Whittaker.

Nick looked at Ivy. "Oh my God! Edna Jean used to have real hair." Nick exaggeratedly threw himself against a bookshelf. "And someone was actually going to marry her."

"Uncle Tommy says Edna Jean's boyfriend ran off with her best friend."

"She had a best friend?"

Ivy hit Nick's arm. "Stop, Nick. She'll hear you. She has keen hearing. Help me find the papers from 1959."

They neatly rearranged the stacks until they found the newspapers from the year her parents died. Ivy flipped through the papers until she found December 14. She tucked her hair behind her ears and read each yellowed page, searching for reports of her parents' accident. But she found no mention of the deadly car wreck. Why wouldn't a fatal car crash be in the local paper?

On the front page of the newspaper from December 21, 1959, the week after her parents died, there was a big article about the search and tragic discovery of Conrad's wife in the pond behind his house. But the obituaries of Ivy's parents had not been published in the paper. It was as if the accident had never happened.

Ivy and Nick climbed the stairs out of the dark basement filled with discarded books and forgotten periodicals. Ivy felt dusty and discouraged. When they reached the main floor of the library, they saw Edna Jean hunched over a book with a magnifying glass. She straightened up when she heard them coming. She pushed her glasses up and leaned forward to within inches of Ivy's face. "Oh, it's you." She covered her nose. "You smell dusty. What do you want now?"

Ivy stepped back and swallowed hard. "Miss Whittaker, I was wondering. Do you remember the night my parents died?"

Edna Jean pushed her glasses up. "Sure. I can still smell the rain. It pounded that night, nearly broke my eardrums."

Ivy shifted nervously. "Do you remember seeing my mother that night?"

Edna Jean looked around the library, her tiny bat eyes squinting. "Well, sort of. I left here late that night. You wouldn't believe how dirty this place can get. Lord knows I try to keep it clean. Anyway, I heard your mother talking to somebody down the street. I recognized her voice." She tapped her ears. "Keen. But I couldn't see who she was talking to. My eyesight's not the best, you know. But I could tell it was a man. I could smell a man's smell." Edna Jean tapped her long, pointed nose.

"Like aftershave?"

Edna nodded. "Maybe. Definitely a musty man smell."

Ivy thought about how much Uncle Tommy's Old Sage aftershave stunk. "But what happened after that?"

Edna Jean leaned forward to within an inch of Ivy's face. Her voice turned to a scratchy, high-pitched whisper. "You know, sometimes you can't see what's right in front of you." She moved her hand up and down in front of her eyes.

Ivy glanced at Nick, who stood behind Edna and squeezed his eyes shut, groping the air in front of him. Ivy suppressed her laughter and looked at Edna Jean, nodding. "I know what you mean."

With her back to Nick's antics, Edna Jean continued her advice. "Just be forewarned. I've learned that the truth is often disappointing. Ask Bertha. She's never been the same after her husband ran away with that dime-store floozy. Some of us don't survive the betrayals."

Ivy nodded, absently reaching up to touch the silver heart necklace around her neck.

Nick grabbed Ivy's arm and gently steered her out of the library. She looked up and saw Russell staring out of his apartment window above the Coffey Shop. She waved but he didn't see her. She could tell his mouth was moving as he counted the bricks in the street.

Chapter 18

THE CORN QUICKSAND

The Iowa woods dressed up in their best reds, oranges, and yellows, in a fall foliage fashion show. The brisk breeze of autumn brought the clean and earthy smell of Mother Nature.

On a windy but warm Sunday in September, Ivy wandered around the old Victorian house, restlessly pacing like a polar bear confined at the zoo.

After going to church with Grandma and Uncle Walter in the morning, Ivy had spent the afternoon putting up travel posters of New York City, London, Paris, and Athens on her bedroom walls. But when she finished, she had nothing to do. "Grandma, I'm going to call Jesse and see if he wants to go for a run. I should be back in an hour or so if Nick or Maggie call."

Grandma looked up from reading the *Des Moines Register* in front of the big windows facing the backyard. "Okay, dear. Watch out for cars."

Ivy laughed. "Grandma, it's Sunday. Nobody goes out after church. Everything's closed except for the Coffey Shop. It's a ghost town."

"Still. Danger can strike at the oddest times. Believe you me."

Ivy pulled her shoulder-length hair back in a ponytail and put on a pair of old gray sweats and her red with a white-stripe running shoes. She met Jesse at his house and they went for a run down the deserted streets of Coffey toward the high school gym. Jesse had planned to meet the coach for a workout.

As they jogged by the train station, the silos behind the Farmer's Co-op loomed high in the air like silver skyscrapers, a silhouette of the farmer's harvest. The birds soared against a clear, blue sky and the air smelled sweet. Down the block, a lawn mower whined, cutting the grass one last time before the cold weather blew in.

"So, I saw my Dad last weekend," Jesse said.

"Really? How'd it go?"

"He's married. Got another kid. Said we'd get together soon."

"That's good. You're lucky."

"Yeah, lucky. Lucky Strikes were the cigarettes he went to buy the night he never came back. I probably won't see him again."

The lawn mower turned off as they passed the grain elevator of the Farmers Co-op. Suddenly, a muffled voice echoed through the quiet afternoon.

"Help! Help me!"

Ivy listened, then sprinted across the street toward the Co-op, glancing over her shoulder at Jesse. She motioned to him and he followed her down the hill and around the corner to the grain silos, as they ran toward the faint cries. Pausing outside the towering silos, she turned in a circle, listening for the voice.

"Where are you?" Ivy yelled.

The cry, unclear but desperate, came from inside the silver cylinder closest to her. "The corn! In the silo!"

The grain bin door of the silo remained slightly open, some yellow corn spilling out. Ivy went in, stepping knee deep in the corn spread out by the door. Jesse followed. The large mountain of corn inside almost reached halfway up the silo. Shafts of sunlight squeezed in from the short door.

The face of a young girl peeked out of the huge pile of corn. It was Remmie, Thelma Sampson's nine-year-old girl from Mulberry Street. Ivy scooped away the corn with her hands and pulled her out of the suffocating, deadly corn trap.

The round-faced girl pointed to the heap of yellow corn next to her. "The corn ate Justin."

"Justin Roberts?"

Remmie nodded. The quicksand of grain had swallowed Miss Shirley's little boy without a trace. Ivy could see the corn dust swirling around the few shafts of light. She could feel it in her lungs as she breathed heavily from her run. She quickly climbed onto the bank of corn, her legs sinking into the grain and trapping her movements.

She remembered playing "king of the mountain" in the corn when she was little. She had scaled the corn mountain by flattening her body against the pile, and crawling along like a spider on a web.

Jesse grabbed her arm. "Ivy, don't do that. You know how dangerous it is. It's too late for that boy. Do you want to die, too? There's no need to risk your life."

Ivy looked back at Jesse. "I've got to try."

"Seriously, get down. He's a goner."

She shook her head and dug through the pile, throwing the kernels in every direction. She pushed her arm into the corn, frantically grasping for any sign of five-year-old Justin. She didn't know where to dig or how far down he had sunk. But she had to try to save Miss Shirley's little boy.

Behind her, Remmie jumped up and down, repeating Jesse's words. "He's a goner. He's a goner."

Ivy climbed up the pile of grain, pressing her limbs against the mound and clawing at the yellow mass. "Justin! Justin! It's Ivy. I'm going to get you out. Move your arm! Move anything, so I can find you."

She desperately dug, pushed, and kicked at the corn. Breathing hard, she scrambled further up the mound and continued searching through the pile. Terrifying seconds passed. Remmie flailed her short arms around and spit flew out of her mouth. "He's a goner. He's a goner."

"Remmie, be quiet. Move your arms, Justin. Do it now!" Ivy's frantic words echoed up the silo's tall chamber, like a ghost rattling around in an empty barn.

The corn sank in a little funnel toward the back of the round, metal cocoon of the silo. She carefully scooted over, pulling out her legs as they slipped into the grip of the corn. She pushed her arms deep into the mound. A few tiny fingers broke through the corn hill and a little hand swayed weakly. Ivy scrambled toward the hand.

"Justin, I got you!" She grabbed his hand but she couldn't free the boy from the corn's grasp. He sank down further and Ivy knew there was precious little time to save Miss Shirley's son. She quickly burrowed through the corn, the kernels flying in a yellow snowstorm. "Please be okay."

She dug until the corn released his little body, and dragged him out by his arms. Once the corn let go, Justin's little body felt amazingly light. Ivy held him in her lap as they slid down the grain heap together. The solid ground felt good under her feet.

Jesse carried Justin across the corn floor and out the little door at the bottom of the silo. Remmie and Ivy followed.

The afternoon light shone unbearably bright as Jesse lay the little boy on the ground. Ivy sat beside him and held up his head.

"Justin?"

Justin's corn-dusty eyes fluttered open and he gulped for air, his lungs hungry for life. Ivy held him in her arms and brushed the dust off his little face. Corn dust coated every part of his body. Justin looked like an old piece of furniture, forgotten in the attic for years.

Ivy glanced at the empty streets around the town square. The shops were all closed, but she needed to get help. "Justin, you're going to be okay."

Justin's eyes blinked open, squinting in the bright sunshine. He coughed, and his thin lips quivered. He closed his eyes again.

"Jesse, can you carry him to the Coffey Shop? It's the only place that's open and it closes pretty soon." She looked up, still panting after her furious dig.

Jesse shook his head. "Ivy, he's breathing. He's fine now."

"I can't leave him."

Jesse looked toward the high school. "Listen, I've got to go. I'm supposed to meet Coach at the gym. You shouldn't get involved in everybody's problems. It's not your responsibility. It'll suck you in. I've seen it happen to my mom. It's going to smother you and you can't get away." Jesse turned, avoiding Ivy's gaze. "I've got to go." He jogged away and didn't look back.

Ivy looked down at Justin and picked him up. "Come on, Remmie. We've got to get help."

Ivy jogged toward the Coffey Shop three blocks away, carrying Justin. Remmie trotted beside her. All three were covered in corn dust, looking like ghosts.

Kitty's long, thin face appeared at the restaurant window as they approached. She hurried out the back door to meet Ivy. "Is that Miss Shirley's boy?"

Ivy nodded as she tried to catch her breath. "Trapped in the corn. Miss Shirley here?"

"No. She went home. We're closing pretty soon. I'll call Dr. Kelsey and tell him to meet you at the clinic. Your Uncle Tommy's here. He can drive you over. I'll get him."

Ivy nodded. Sunday was the only day the clinic was closed. It stayed open late on Fridays and Mondays to allow the farmers to finish their chores and come in from the fields, but Dr. Kelsey and Matilda always came in for emergencies, even on Sundays.

Kitty hurried back inside. She returned after in a few seconds, with Reuben following behind her.

Ivy narrowed her eyes. "Uncle Tommy couldn't pull himself away from his coffee to help, huh?"

Reuben adjusted his John Deere cap, his big ears sticking out. "You know Tommy. Loves his coffee. Come on, I'll give you a lift."

Ivy cradled Justin in her lap and held Remmie's hand as they rode to the clinic across town in Reuben's truck.

"You're going to be okay, Justin. We're almost at Dr. Kelsey's."

Justin's eyes fluttered open for a moment. His clear eyes shone like a cat in the dark.

Wearing white pants and an aloha shirt, Dr. Kelsey, waited for them at the front of the clinic. The weather didn't affect his wardrobe until the temperature dropped below freezing. He took the little boy from Ivy. The doctor's sandals flopped against his heels as he hurried inside the clinic.

Ivy helped Remmie out of the truck. "Thanks, Reuben."

Reuben tipped his John Deere cap. "You bet. Hope the little fella's okay. He's about the age of my brother when he died."

Ivy nodded. "That must have been hard." She took Remmie's hand and went inside the clinic.

Ivy and Remmie walked down the clinic's hallway. "Do you need any help?" Ivy asked the doctor as she pushed open the door of the exam room.

Dr. Kelsey checked Justin's vitals. "No, Ivy. Just rest. Miss Shirley and Thelma will be here soon. You saved his life." He looked at Remmie. "And Remmie's too, from the looks of it. Come on, I want to check you out, too." The corn-dusty girl stepped into the exam room and the heavy door closed behind them.

Ivy went back to the waiting room and collapsed on an orange, vinyl-coated chair. She took a deep breath, trying to calm herself. Her hands shook, sprinkling tiny particles of corn dust on the carpet.

A few minutes later, Miss Shirley's old station wagon squealed into the parking lot with tiny Thelma in the passenger seat, her head barely visible above the dash.

Ivy watched from the waiting room as Miss Shirley struggled to get her big body out of the car and bolted to the clinic door. Tiny Thelma trailed behind, sprinting to keep up with Miss Shirley's long strides. Ivy held the door open as Miss Shirley and Thelma dashed past her into the waiting room. Miss Shirley wheezed as she tried to catch her breath.

"Where's my boy?"

Dr. Kelsey opened the door of the examining room. "In here ladies."

They hurried into the room and the door shut. Miss Shirley's booming voice, muffled but cracking with emotion, yelled from inside the room, "God bless you, Ivy. God bless you, my child. You saved my boy's life."

Ivy smiled. She sat down in Matilda's chair at the receptionist's desk, the tension in her body easing up.

A few minutes later, Thelma came scurrying out with

Remmie in tow, rushing past Ivy at the receptionist's desk. Thelma's fuzzy mustache twitched. "Don't expect me to thank you. You're just a white do-gooder."

Remmie reached up to hold Ivy's hand. "We were goners."

Ivy smiled and reached out to touch the little girl's hand but Thelma, the evil pixie, grabbed Remmie's hand and dragged her out the clinic.

"Bye, Ivy," Remmie said.

After the door slammed shut, Ivy used the receptionist's phone to call Grandma and tell her what happened. Ivy picked up a pen lying on Matilda's desk and doodled as she talked.

"Thank God you saved that sweet boy," Grandma said as tiny sobs escaped between her words.

Ivy doodled a flower on a pad of paper. "I'm going to stay here for a few more minutes, and then I'm going to jog home. I think I need to run some of the adrenaline out of me."

Still shaking, Ivy fumbled to hang up the phone and dropped the pen. It fell into a file drawer that was partly open. Ivy opened the drawer to retrieve the pen, but it had fallen between the patient files. She started pushing them aside one by one, when she saw the names of her parents on files. Without thinking, she pulled out the two files. Scrawled in big letters across the top of the old medical files, it read: "Confidential." An official-looking note was stapled to it: "Not to be opened without the written consent of Violet Taylor."

Ivy's hands sweated and her heart pounded in her ears. Why all the secrecy? What were they trying to hide? She glanced down the hall. The door to the examination room remained shut. She opened her father's medical file. She knew she couldn't just take the files because someone might notice they were missing, but she could make a copy. No one would know.

She turned on the copying machine behind her and freed

the old medical pages from the long metal clips. The machine hummed as she fed in the sheets. After the first two copies, the machine jammed. She opened the copying machine. Her dusty hands trembled as she freed the stuck paper. She finished copying her father's file and returned it to the drawer. Then she opened her mother's file. The folder contained only three pages.

Down the hall, the door to the examination room opened. Ivy pulled the pages out of the metal clips and stuffed them in her gray sweatpants along with the copy of her father's records. She put the files under a pile of papers on the desk.

Dr. Kelsey's sandals clicked and his aloha shirt flashed bright colors as he came down the corridor. "Ivy, you still here? I thought I heard something. You okay?"

Ivy felt the medical records pressing on her leg. "Yeah, I just wanted to make sure Justin was okay."

Dr. Kelsey patted Ivy's shoulder. "He's going to be just fine, Ivy. You can go on home. Those kids were lucky you came along when you did."

When the doctor's door closed again, Ivy pulled out her mother's records. She quickly made a copy, put the originals back in the file, and closed the drawer.

Ivy tucked the copies in her sweatpants, along with the others, and left the clinic. Her legs wobbled as she jogged down Coffey's empty streets. Her parents' medical records settled at the bottom of her sweatpants. She could feel the papers brushing against her leg as she ran.

Instead of going home, Ivy jogged to Beecher Pond. Her aching muscles and ragged breath were a reminder that Justin and Remmie were alive. Drowning in corn would have been an unbearable tragedy and it reminded her how unexpectedly life could end, just like it did for her parents.

She hiked around the pond toward Uncle Tommy's and Reuben's duck blind, pushing past the pussy willows that grew silky gray catkins resembling tiny cat tails. It had been a long time since she'd visited Uncle Tommy's duck blind. Ivy opened the rickety plywood door, making sure the hinged boards that passed as windows were closed.

She sat in Uncle Tommy's broken recliner and pulled out the medical records stuffed down her sweats. What was in these files that required permission from Grandma to examine them? Having copied the confidential records, she would never be able to ask Grandma or Uncle Walter about them. She wished Nick was with her. He was good at taking risks.

Her father's records showed the usual illnesses, vaccination records, and allergies. It also contained a copy of his death certificate, signed by Dr. Kelsey, who had recorded the time of Robert's death at 9:22 p.m. It listed the cause of death as extensive hemorrhaging from severe head injuries due to a car accident that threw him through the windshield.

Ivy felt queasy. The loss of her father swept over her. A loving father she never knew. The tragic ending to her family before it barely began. She ran her fingers over the papers, smoothing them out. Her hands trembled as she picked up the file belonging to her mother. Barbara Taylor's medical records only contained information regarding her pregnancy, nothing more. There was no mention of the cause or time of her death. The good doctor had forgotten to include her mother's death certificate in her files, as if her tragic passing was uneventful. As if her life was insignificant.

Ivy folded the papers and leaned back in the old recliner. On the opposite wall of the blind, Uncle Tommy had taped up newspaper clippings of his bowling triumphs and hunting feats. A picture from the *Coffey Gazette* hung in the center of the wall. It showed Uncle Tommy proudly displaying a dead buck beside him. The once powerful stag slumped exhausted and empty, its life extinguished for a trophy. A thick line of dark blood oozed from the deer's temple. Unfortunately for the once mighty buck, Uncle Tommy was a very good shot. Ivy shivered.

At the end of the wall, almost buried by the other taped-up news stories, was a small black-and-white snapshot she had never noticed. Ivy pulled the old picture off the wall, recognizing Grandma's handwriting below the photo. "Robert and Barbara." She stared at the young couple, strangers bound to her with the interwoven strings of family. Ivy kissed the picture and added it to the folded pile of medical records. She stuffed them back down her pant leg. With all this stealing, she thought, maybe she and Luther had more in common than she knew.

She shut the door to the duck blind. It was time to go home. Grandma and Uncle Walter would be waiting.

Chapter 19

WHERE THE BUFFALO ROAM

Every October, the high school seniors collected the dead wood from Hawks Bluff Park and made an enormous bonfire for the pep rally the night before the homecoming football game. Then they ceremoniously burned an effigy of the Stilton Buffaloes, their rival team.

The day before the pep rally, Ivy and her friends loaded branches onto a lowboy wagon pulled by Reuben's tractor. When it was full, they drove it to an empty lot next to the football field at Hawks Bluff Park and dumped it.

Nick threw a huge branch on the growing pile of wood. "I've decided we're not making a dummy this year. We're going to get Luther Matthews to steal the Stilton Buffalo for us."

The Stilton mascot, a real stuffed buffalo, stood on the stage in the Stilton school gym. The huge beast with matted brown fur was the pride of the school.

Ivy brushed the bits of wood and bark off her Coffey High School sweatshirt and looked skeptically at Nick. His wild antics and fearless view of life sometimes scared her. He always seemed so close to the edge which made her feel uncertain and off balance, like she was going to fall. She needed someone more stable and secure; a sure thing like Jesse.

That night, a little before nine o'clock, Ivy, Maggie, Nick, Raven, and Jesse arrived at the Blue Moon Bowling Alley and Bar. They waited in the snack bar for Luther Matthews to show up like he usually did on Friday nights.

Nick, Maggie, and Raven ate nachos while Ivy and Jesse walked over to watch Uncle Tommy and Reuben bowl. The jukebox played "Love Will Keep Us Together" by Captain and Tennille. Reuben swung his blue bowling ball into position and performed his elaborate wind-up dance. He brought the ball up to his chin to aim and crooked his leg high in the air like a major league baseball pitcher. He shook his body, bent down, and released the spinning ball down the lane.

"It's just a blue streak of lightning," he said, jerking his arm back with his fist clenched. "STEE-RIKE!" The ball hit the pins dead center.

Ivy clapped. Reuben turned around and bowed. "Thank you very much, ma'am."

The bell above the door to the Blue Moon rang, and Ivy turned to see Luther saunter in. Nick quietly spoke into his fist like a megaphone. "Ladies and gentlemen, the handyman is in the building."

Ivy laughed. Jesse rolled his eyes and pulled her toward him. They followed Nick to an empty pool table beside the snack bar. Nick picked up a pool cue.

Luther set his beer on the table and slung his ragged brown bomber jacket across the back of an orange plastic chair near the pool tables. Ivy waved. "Hi, Luther. How're you doing?"

Luther straddled the chair backward. "Okay. Little tired." He jerked his head toward Reuben. "Fixed Reuben's furnace today. His ghosts did a number on it. Screwed it up pretty bad. Poor Reuben. Those dang ghosts make me a lot of money."

Ivy's friends joined her at Luther's table. Luther took another gulp of beer, and unsuccessfully tried to lick off the white foam from his whiskery upper lip.

Raven wrinkled her nose and ran her fingers with bright red nail polish down her tight jeans as if she was wiping something away. She leaned over to Nick and spoke in a loud whisper. "He's gross."

Ivy glared at her.

Luther looked at them suspiciously out of the corner of his eyes. "Okay. So, what's up?"

Nick slid a bowl of peanuts over to Luther and waved the pool cue in the air. "Nothing, Luth. Just hanging out and playing a little pool."

The kids all walked over to the pool table next to Luther's table. Nick turned to Ivy. "Hey, you know what, Ivy? I think we ought to try and steal that ugly buffalo mascot from Stilton for the pep rally."

Ivy picked up a pool cue and hit a striped ball in the side pocket. "Nah, nobody could steal that thing. It's huge."

Nick thumped the side of the pool table. "How hard could it be? It's on the stage in their gym. In and out the side door. Gone."

Ivy glanced over to see if Luther was listening. Luther threw peanuts into the air, catching them in his mouth. Jesse pushed up the sleeves of his letter jacket and folded his muscled arms across his chest.

Maggie gestured. "Wouldn't it be great to have that buffalo at the homecoming bonfire?"

Nick nodded. "Yeah, it'd be cool to steal that wily beast."

Maggie walked over and stood next to Nick at the pool table. "But nobody could do that."

Luther looked over at the kids and smiled. Ivy could see Luther wasn't fooled. He lobbed another peanut toward his mouth but it missed and bounced off his chin. He ignored it and took another drink. Some of the beer dribbled down his unshaven chin.

"He's disgusting," Raven said under her breath as she moved away from Luther and huddled against Jesse. Her blue eye shadow made a deep hazy arch over her brown eyes.

Maggie handed Nick the pool cue chalk. "Nobody's got the guts to steal that thing."

Nick chalked his cue stick and lined up his shot. "You're right. That would take a genius." He hit a ball in the corner pocket. "Too bad. It would have been the greatest prank since someone took Stilton's plastic Holstein cow from their Ag class and put it in with Conrad Thrasher's herd."

Luther dropped his handful of peanuts back into the bowl. "Hey, how'd you know about that? I was in high school."

"Some legends never die," said Nick.

Luther took a long drink of beer and wiped off the white-foam mustache with the back of his hand. His shoulders heaved up and down in a big sigh. "There's so few challenges anymore."

The next night, an hour before the bonfire, Jesse, Raven, Maggie, and Maggie's dog King, crowded together on the benches in the back of Nick's Monstrosity to check out the bonfire woodpile. Ivy sat up front next to Nick on their way to Hawks Bluff Park. Nick kissed his fingers and touched the dashboard.

As they rounded the corner towards the football field. Ivy saw Ellen, Nick's mother, walking aimlessly. "Look, Nick, it's your mom. Should we give her a ride?"

"She likes to walk. She says it helps the sadness evaporate."

He sighed. "But it doesn't really. Even when I'm with her, she's sad."

Ivy nodded. "She can't really help it, can she?"

"No. It's her life's curse." Nick said as he made a sharp turn toward the football field. "She's sort of like a ghost mother."

"So's mine," Ivy said.

The Monstrosity peeled to a stop in the gravel parking lot at the back entrance to the field. The kids stared out the crooked windows of the camper, squinting at the strange sight in front of them. A huge, hairy animal grazed by the pile of bonfire wood.

Jesse shook his head in confusion. His hair bounced and fell exactly back in place. "What the heck?"

They opened the doors of the camper and jumped out. Nick threw his arms in the air. "It's the wily beast!"

King ran toward the huge animal, barking and growling. "Get him, King," Nick said.

The kids looked at each other with their mouths open and eyes wide. Ivy laughed and clapped her hands. "He did it! He really did it. Luther stole the buffalo."

"Man, are we in trouble," said Jesse. "I want nothing to do with this creepy thing, and I mean Luther." He stayed back to help Raven, who was wobbling across the gravel parking lot in her tight jeans and high heels. The others rushed down to where the Stilton's stuffed buffalo mascot majestically guarded the wood for the bonfire. Nick tipped his head back, howling "oh, no" like Reuben's dog Buckshot. King joined him, howling at the beast.

Ivy stared at the buffalo in awe. "Luther must've snatched the thing right from under their noses."

"That's really weird. Why would he want to steal this thing for us?" Jesse asked.

"Because he's a thief," Raven said with a shrug, flipping back her dark hair.

"He's not weird, and he's not a thief. He likes the challenge. It's kind of like a game to him," said Ivy.

"Well, he's gross if you ask me. Real creepy." Raven scrunched up her face.

Maggie rubbed the matted fur of the huge buffalo, patting the solid mass of the beast. "How did Luther lift this thing? Even Max couldn't pick this up by himself."

"Don't ask. All bow to the great and powerful Luther," Nick said as he danced around the buffalo, pretending to shoot arrows into its side. King ran beside him and both of them barked.

Jesse examined the mangy brown buffalo. "It's so ugly."

Ivy touched the wooly fur of the rival school's mascot. "Yeah, if it were alive, it would probably have fleas."

"It's disgusting," said Raven as she backed away and stood beside Jesse. "I'm not touching that prehistoric thing."

To keep it hidden from the others, Ivy and Maggie draped the buffalo with a green plastic tarp from the back of the camper. Nick tied the tarp to the ground with rope and rocks. He smiled. "I love this town."

Later that night at the pep rally, Nick, as co-captain of the football team, ceremoniously lit the bonfire with a torch. A few hundred students gathered around the leaping flames. Ivy stood between the green-tarped object and the fire, warming herself from the chill of the brisk October night.

Nick gave a short pep talk while excitedly pounding a football between his hands. "We are the masters of the football field. We will destroy the Stilton Buffaloes! They will no longer roam the earth. The Buffaloes will be our captives." Nick pointed the football in his hand at Ivy, who dramatically pulled off the tarp to reveal the massive beast of the prairie, placidly staring back at the Coffey students. The crowd screamed and cheered as sparks from the fire danced in the air.

Jesse and Raven sat on the outskirts of the crowd, watching as the bonfire roared hot on that cold, fall night. The students took turns riding on top of the Stilton mascot. The sky remained clear, but the stars seemed dim compared to the bright light of the fire.

In the nearby gravel parking lot, Ivy noticed a dark figure lurking among the shadows of the cars. She left the bonfire's heat and walked over to see who it was. It was Luther.

"Hey, Luth. I thought that was you. Why don't you come on over?"

Luther shook his head. His hair jutted out in all directions as if it couldn't decide which way to go. He backed up a step. "No, that's okay."

"Luther, I can't believe you took that buffalo."

"Who said I did it?"

"Nobody else has the skills."

Luther kicked the gravel but smiled. "It's been a long time since people have really appreciated my talents. I haven't even had a real challenge since I took baby Jesus during the Christmas pageant."

"Yeah, I heard about that." She pointed to the Stilton buffalo. "How'd you move that thing? It must weigh a ton."

Luther pinched his lips together. Then he smiled, his crooked teeth peering out of his mouth. "I never tell my secrets. That's why I'm still alive. But check out the old buffalo at tomorrow's game."

Ivy smiled. She liked Luther. "I will." She paused. "Luther, have you always lived in Coffey?"

"Mostly." Luther scratched his stomach under his brown bomber jacket. "I moved here when I was just a little kid. Never knew my mother. I was a baby when she took off. My old man died when I was in high school, and I've been on my own since then."

"Do you ever think about getting out of here?"

"Nah. I'd never leave now. This is my home."

Ivy glanced over at the raging flames of the bonfire. "I'm not going to live in Coffey all my life. I'm leaving as soon as I graduate."

Luther looked at his feet and then shrugged. "I figure Coffey's as good as any other place. They know me here. A person can only take so much uncertainty."

Ivy put her hands in the back pockets of her bell-bottom jeans. "Poison mushrooms killed your father, right?"

Luther nodded and rubbed his unshaven chin. The whisker stubble sounded scratchy like a tree branch rubbing against a fence.

Ivy sighed. "I'm sorry." A comfortable silence settled between them. Ivy tucked her shoulder-length hair behind her ears. "Not having parents stinks, doesn't it?"

Luther sniffed. "Only if you had good ones. You got a good grandma. Sometimes things work out for the best."

"Luther, you aren't scared of anything, are you?"

"You're not so scared if you got nothing to lose."

Ivy cleared her throat. "Remember when you told me that my mother used to go over to the Thrasher farm?"

Luther nodded and shuffled his feet, moving the gravel around.

"Did you see her out at his place on the night she died?"

Luther looked away. "Don't remember. That was a long time ago."

Several seconds passed before Luther released a deep breath. "You know, there's two ways dead people can talk to you. Through their gravestones and through their death records at the courthouse." He smiled. "Well, three, if you count the ghosts at Reuben's place. But I'll tell you something I've learned from fixing things all my life. What's not there is as important as what's there."

Sometimes Luther didn't make any sense, but she nodded as if she understood.

"Hey, you did good with the buffalo. They'll be talking about that for years." Then she left the buffalo outlaw alone to watch the celebration of his larceny from his shadowy hiding spot among the parked cars.

Around midnight when the fire died down, the kids covered the buffalo with the green tarp, put the coals out, and went home.

The next day, Ivy arrived at the football field a few minutes before the game started. Edna Jean Whittaker took Ivy's ticket at the back entrance to the stadium. The librarian held the ticket about an inch away from her tiny bat eyes before waving Ivy in.

Ivy looked over at the vacant lot next to the field. The buffalo was gone. It no longer stood bravely by the burned remnants of the bonfire. Ivy looked around. Then she saw it. The stuffed buffalo, dressed in a pink-flannel nightgown, grazed on the fifty-yard line of the football field. The huge flannel nightgown seemed oddly familiar.

Nick, Jesse, and the rest of the football team, dressed and ready to play, milled around the sidelines, waiting for the game to start. Next to them, a group of men, including Uncle Tommy and Reuben, huddled together, trying to decide what to do with the uninvited buffalo. Some kids played Frisbee on the sidelines.

Ivy walked over to Jesse and Nick. She pointed to the buffalo dressed in a nightie, standing in the middle of the field. "What happened? Change of wardrobe?"

Nick exaggeratedly sighed. His shoulders heaved up and down like Luther did at the Blue Moon, and he imitated Luther's voice. "There's so few challenges anymore."

Ivy laughed. Nick always made her laugh, but his mischief also made her nervous. Uncle Tommy and Reuben overheard Nick and looked over at him. Buckshot, Reuben's dog, sniffed the ground. Uncle Tommy shook his head and clicked his tongue. "Good Lord. You boys did it, didn't you?"

Reuben rested his hands on the waist of his overalls. "It must weigh a ton of bricks."

"Believe me, we didn't have anything to do with it." Jesse held up his hands. "I swear."

A smile spread across Nick's face. "He's right. We didn't do it."

Uncle Tommy shook his head. "Bull. Where'd you get that huge nightgown? I didn't even know they made them that big."

Reuben turned and stared at the buffalo's gigantic sleeping attire. He tugged at his huge ears and his cheeks blushed.

Ivy reached down and petted Buckshot. The dog sniffed the air and watched the referees struggling to get the buffalo off the field. Buckshot barked and ran onto the field, growling at the unfamiliar animal. Reuben darted after him but nothing could distract Buckshot's attention until a Frisbee zoomed across the field. Buckshot howled "oh, no" and took off after the flying disk.

Edna Jean Whittaker left her ticket-taking post to get a better look at what was causing such a commotion. She didn't see the white lines and stumbled onto the field. Reuben's dog shot between Edna Jean's legs and knocked her over. She landed with her legs straight up in the air, showing her precious pretties. The crowd gasped.

The dog scrambled across the field, chasing the Frisbee at full speed, with Reuben running behind him. The growing Coffey crowd cheered at the spectacle. The referees tried to drag the giant buffalo off the field, but the heavy animal refused to budge. Luther stood at the top of the bleachers and surveyed the commotion he had created.

Ivy left the boys and climbed the stairs to join Luther. "Looks like they're having a hard time getting that thing off the field."

They watched in silence as the officials wrestled with the huge stuffed buffalo.

"They don't know what they're doing."

Ivy laughed. "Luther, how come you like to take things?"

Luther rubbed his neck and adjusted the grease-streaked ball cap on his head. "Just for kicks. I don't really plan it. I guess I've just got a talent for it."

Ivy pointed to the buffalo dressed in nightclothes. "That's Patty's nightgown, isn't it?"

"Yeah. Patty gave it to me when I went back to fix the furnace at Reuben's yesterday. I needed something that would fit the buffalo. It was her idea."

Ivy laughed. Underneath Patty's sadness, humor still lurked.

Luther pulled up his jeans but they slid back low on his hips. He put his hands in his pockets and pointed across the football field with his bristly chin. "Look." His lips parted in a smile that revealed crooked teeth, black from chewing tobacco.

The Stilton football squad had arrived and the angry, red-faced captain sprinted across the field. He ripped the pink nightgown off the mascot's back and the defenseless buffalo stood naked.

The horn section of Coffey's high school band started playing the stripper song. The Coffey crowd cheered and whistled and the people in the stadium stomped their feet. They pounded the bleachers until it sounded like a herd of buffaloes stampeding across the Iowa prairie.

Chapter 20

DEADMAN'S WOODS

The first snow fell on Halloween. When night descended, the spooky dark clouds veiled the full moon like black lace on a lantern. Only a soft glow illuminated the snowy earth.

Ivy and her friends, dressed in costumes, piled into Nick's misfit camper and King joined them for their Halloween romp. Nick kissed his fingers and touched the dashboard, then pounded the truck's huge steering wheel. "Ride the Monstrosity-atrocity, if you dare. Let's tame this wily beast."

Raven, dressed like a nurse, pinned a nurse's cap to her long dark hair. A toy stethoscope hung around the revealing neckline of her very short uniform. Ivy looked like Raggedy Ann with red yarn hair and a white pinafore. Maggie dressed like Merlin the Wizard. She converted last year's witch's hat into a magician's cap and pinned white moons and stars on Ruth Jackson's black barber smock. Maggie touched Ivy's yarn hair with her magic wand, which was an old ruler covered with silver glitter. "Hey, rag head."

"Don't mess with my wig-hat, man. Leon Wilson would be jealous," Ivy said.

"Don't let Miss Shirley hear you say that," Maggie said.

Nick and Jesse had dressed as ghosts with tattered white sheets and white paint covering any skin that showed.

As they drove down the streets of Coffey, Nick and Jesse sat in the front cab. Nick pushed in his Merle Haggard eight-track tape. "Now we can officially cruise."

"If We Make It Through December" blared out of the speakers.

They stopped at Judy's Beauty Shop for the hot cocoa and cinnamon rolls that Judy was giving out just before she closed for the day, then piled back into the Monstrosity.

"Let's have some fun," Nick said as he took a sharp corner, and everyone fell off the benches, spilling together in the back of the camper. Maggie grabbed the edge of the bench and pulled herself up. Nick jerked the steering wheel, hollering like a rodeo cowboy.

"Yee-haw!" The camper tilted, and the tires screeched on the path cleared by the snowplow. "I'm going to make this wily beast squeal."

Jesse put his hands over Nick's eyes. Nick pushed Jesse away with one hand on the steering wheel. The camper lumbered over a bump, jarring the riders. "What was that? Did we just run over somebody, or what?" Ivy asked.

"Probably crazy Rosie on her way home from town with her stupid dogs," said Jesse.

Holding her head, Ivy crawled onto the bench and looked out the smudged back window to see the camper careening erratically over Edna Jean Whittaker's wide expanse of lawn. "Hey, slow down, Nick."

"If Edna Jean sees us, she'll call the sheriff," said Maggie.

"She can barely see. What's she going to tell him?" Nick said.

"That a UFO flew across her front yard, just like she always says. But this time, she'll be right," said Maggie.

"It's Halloween. What does she expect?" Nick said.

Edna Jean's front door swung open. The librarian squinted into the dark night like a frightened rodent. The camper reeled across the yard in front of her.

Nick let go of the steering wheel and pounded the dash. "Look, there's Edna Jean!"

Edna Jean's white miniature poodle, Tiny Fifi, yapped as the camper zigzagged past the door. Her high-pitched bark had the same pitch as Edna Jean's voice—high and shrill.

King barked and jumped up on the bench to see what was making such a hideous yapping. Maggie braced her hands on the roof and bench. "She probably thinks we're dog-nappers."

"Hey, man, look, she's not wearing her wig," said Nick.

Fuzzy clumps of matted hair stuck out all over Edna Jean's head. Ivy had heard that in her anger and grief over losing her barber boyfriend, Edna Jean had taken the barber's clippers, the only thing he had left behind, and shaved her head. Her defiant lovesick revenge had backfired. Her hair never grew back and she was forced to wear wigs for the rest of her life.

The Monstrosity swerved in the icy snow and Nick barely missed Edna Jean's azalea bushes. The front tire hit her picket fence, obscured by the falling snow. The short fence collapsed like an evenly-placed row of dominoes.

As the camper lurched, Ivy spoke to Jesse through the open window to the cab. "Jesse, you've got to get me out of Coffey fast, or I'll start to think this place is normal."

Jesse held Ivy's hand through the window as the camper bounced over the curb and wobbled back onto the road. "This town could never be normal. I've got it all planned. We're getting out of here this summer. We'll go to Europe and leave this jerk town."

Ivy looked at Jesse's handsome face, arrogant with confidence. Jesse planned everything. He never took risks or left anything to chance, and she knew that Jesse would never be satisfied in Coffey. "Yeah, I hate this place," she said.

"I love this place," Nick said as he banged on the steering wheel. "Let's go check out the cemetery and see what our fellow spooks are doing."

They drove by Luther Matthew's place and Rosie's old shack. Just past the Thrasher farm, they turned onto the overgrown dirt road to Deadman's Woods. Nick pulled into the Weeping Willow Cemetery about a quarter mile north of Reuben's farm and got out. Maggie told King to stay in the truck.

The boys turned on their flashlights and crept through the shadowy graves. The wind picked up, and the cemetery's old gate squeaked and groaned in the dark. Maggie shuddered at every sound. "The woods are creepy at night. You could lose your mind out here."

"No wonder that old Rosie lady is so crazy," said Raven.

Ivy had never felt scared at the cemetery because her father's gravestone was there, lying right next to Grandpa Sam. In a strange way, it comforted her to know she could be that close to her father. She walked over the second hill to her father's grave and brushed the snow off his marker. She had read the words so many times, she had it memorized.

Robert Taylor, Born September 2, 1933. Died December 14, 1959. A loving son, brother, and father.

She remembered what Luther had said about dead people talking to her through their gravestones. What could her father's gravestone tell her? She wished she knew where her mother was buried but she'd never even met her other grandparents, so she couldn't ask them.

Jesse yelled to Ivy and she walked back down the hill to

join her friends. Nick flapped his white sheet and turned to his fellow ghost. "Okay, Mr. Heebie-Jeebies, are you ready for Operation Spook?"

"I still think it's a bad idea. We'd better not get caught," Jesse said. "I don't want to get thrown off the football team for trespassing."

Nick waved his sheet in the breeze. It billowed and snapped in the cold wind. "We aren't trespassing. We're going over to Reuben's to commune with our fellow ghosts."

Raven adjusted her nurse's hat. "You're going to scare that old Reuben guy, aren't you?"

Ivy looked across the field to Reuben's farmhouse, which sat across the creek from Deadman's Woods, about a quarter of a mile as the crow flies. The graveyard guarded the border of Reuben's fertile fields.

Nick touched Ivy's arm. "Don't worry. Reuben's used to ghosts."

"Well, I guess he deserves it for all the things he and Uncle Tommy have done to Uncle Walter. But we're not staying behind. We're going with you," said Ivy.

"You can't come. You're mere mortals. This is for ghosts only," Jesse said.

"Shut up. Ghosts don't talk," Nick said. "You guys can come."

Raven flipped back her long black hair. She exhaled white puffs of cold air from her pink lipsticked mouth and rubbed up against Jesse like a cat on a scratching post. "That old Reuben guy is creepy, with all his ghosts and stuff."

Jesse laughed and flicked Raven's nurse's hat with his finger. "They're not real, you know."

"Hey, let's go," said Nick.

Ivy looked at her watch. "All right. Patty should be asleep by now. She doesn't need any more ghosts in her life."

Nick spread his arms and flapped his sheet. "Let's go talk to the dead."

"I'm not staying here by myself," Raven said, hurrying to catch up as King barked from inside the camper.

The cemetery dumped out into Reuben's back pasture. The creek, although low for that time of year, still flowed beneath the frozen patches of ice. They forged across the creek with their flashlights illuminating the slippery ground. They crossed the wide expanse of flat land known for its high yield and crept inside Reuben's drafty old barn. Stale hay on the dirt floor emitted a musty smell, and the wind whistled through the holes in the roof. A few chickens huddled in a corner.

"Okay, you guys stay here," Jesse said, his voice barely audible against the wind. He hit Nick's shoulder. "You go first."

Ivy watched the two ghosts float away toward the farmhouse. Nick danced, throwing back his head and howling like a dog as he led the way in his white sheet while Jesse followed, skulking around the side of the house.

Several minutes passed. The wind howled, muffling any sounds coming from the farmhouse. The old barn creaked and groaned, sounding like a ghost trapped in its weathered wood.

"What was that?" Raven asked.

"Ghosts," Ivy said, straining to decipher the noises in the wind. She closed her Raggedy Ann eyes for a second as the wind whipped her red-yarn hair. Something was wrong. "Wait. I know what they're doing. Those guys aren't coming back for us."

Raven held on to her nurse's hat, so the wind wouldn't blow it away. "What do you mean?"

"They set us up," Ivy said. "Like a snipe hunt when they take you out hunting for snipe. But there's no such thing as snipe. Time to go." Ivy headed to the barn door, with Maggie right behind her.

"What?" Raven said.

Maggie turned and flicked her glittery wand at Raven. A few sparkles blew away in the wind. "We've been tricked. We've been snookered, Nursie-poo."

Raven frowned, and her white nurse's coat flapped in the air as she stomped her high heels. "I'm cold. I don't have time for this."

"Let's get out of here. I don't want to be stranded out here with Reuben's ghosts," said Maggie.

"I'm pretty sure Nick left the keys in the Monstrosity," Ivy called over the wind as they trekked across the field.

The moon and stars on Maggie's magic robe danced in the blustery wind as the tall outline of Merlin led them across Reuben's pasture back to Deadman's Woods. They maneuvered around the hard stubble of the corn stalks still left in the ground after harvest. Raven tiptoed across the field so her high heels wouldn't sink into the snow and ground. "Wait for me."

They crossed the creek, higher this time, and arrived at the graveyard a few minutes later. The dark clouds pulled away from the moon, and its light lit up the graveyard. The snow began to ease up.

Maggie pointed. "At least the camper's still there."

The girls hurried toward the Monstrosity, dodging the gravestones. The snowy ground hid icy patches and Ivy's foot slipped out from under her. The other girls didn't see her fall and kept walking.

Ivy gingerly got up, glancing at the stone marker near her.

It was Mildred Thrasher's grave. She shivered and looked around. Her friends were almost at the camper. She cleared the snow from the grave marker. It read, "Mildred Darlene Thrasher. Born June 10, 1937. Died December 14, 1959. May she rest in peace."

Ivy read the words again. The date wasn't right. That was the night her parents died. The night Mildred went missing. She remembered from the old newspapers that Mildred's body wasn't found until a few days before Christmas.

Why would Conrad inscribe on her grave that she died a week before her body was found? Unless Conrad knew she died a week earlier because he had killed her! She jerked, as if a thousand cold needles had stabbed her. She looked toward the Thrasher place, obscured by the trees at the edge of the cemetery. Luther was right. The dead could talk.

The girls called to Ivy from the camper. She shook the snow off her Raggedy Ann pinafore and ran to the truck. Jumping into the driver's seat, she started the engine.

"What's wrong?" Maggie asked from the passenger's seat.

"I think I saw a ghost," said Ivy.

"Then let's get out of here," Maggie said.

Ivy tapped the big steering wheel. "The Monstrosity-atrocity never looked prettier."

King barked. He jumped into the front seat from the back of the camper and licked Maggie's cold face. Raven sat on the bench in the back by herself, but scooching as far to the truck cab window as she could get. They locked the doors. Ivy drove the Monstrosity out of Deadman's Woods as the moon illuminated the cemetery, leaving the ghosts behind.

Through a small clearing, she saw Thrasher's pond glistening as it reflected the eerie moon's glow on its surface.

Ivy's heart pounded. She stopped the camper and leaned forward to get a better look. She pointed out the windshield. "Look, Maggie. Without the leaves, you can see right through to Conrad's pond."

They stared at each other. Goosebumps crept up and down Ivy's back. Maggie's neighbor, Virgil Jackson, was right. He could have seen Thrasher's pond from Deadman's Woods. Even on a snowy night, the clearing offered an unobstructed view of the deadly pond.

Ivy drove on through the cemetery. Suddenly, they heard a muffled yell and the sound of running footsteps.

"What was that?" Raven whispered hoarsely.

Maggie put her hand over Raven's mouth through the open cab window. "I don't know. But if you'd be quiet, maybe we could hear."

Raven pulled Maggie's hand away from her mouth. "You're going to ruin my lipstick."

Ivy pulled the truck behind a clump of trees. "It's probably the guys coming back to get the Monstrosity."

The girls looked out the camper windows. Two men dressed in black ran down the hill, dodging the old gravestones and scurrying past the girls in the half-hidden camper.

Maggie tapped her magic wand against the window. Glitter sprinkled down and stuck to the cold windowpane. "That's your Uncle Tommy and Reuben Smith, isn't it, Ivy?"

Ivy wiped the icy window with her Raggedy Ann sleeve and peered outside. "Yeah, it is. What are they doing?"

"Look, they painted their faces black," Maggie said, pointing. "Why would they do that?"

"Who knows? It's Uncle Tommy, remember?"

Sprinting down the snowy slope, Reuben got tangled in

some low willow branches. He slipped and rolled down the hill, bowling Uncle Tommy over like a pin at the Blue Moon Bowling Alley.

Maggie sat back in her seat. "Good Lord, you guys. Reuben isn't even at home for the ghost-boys to scare. Where are they then? This is getting too strange. Let's get out of here. They deserve it for leaving us in the barn."

Ivy drove out of the snowy Deadman's Woods, leaving the ghosts to reappear on their own. The headlights of the old camper lit up the falling snow. As they passed Rosie's house, the Thrashers' car, Moby Dick, pulled onto the road behind them. The huge white whale of a car followed the camper into town. Although Weston had graduated high school several years ago and worked with his father on the farm when he felt like it, he had never really grown up.

When they reached town, Moby Dick pulled up beside the camper, forcing Ivy into the oncoming lane. The Monstrosity and the whale rode side-by-side down Main Street.

"I really wish this night would end soon. Weston Thrasher is giving me the creeps," Maggie said.

Ivy motioned for Maggie to roll down the passenger window.

"What do you want?" Ivy yelled at Weston.

Weston leaned out the car. His long greasy hair blew across his face. "I wanted to show you this." He held up a dead, black and white cat. He gripped it by the tail and dangled it from the car window. It bounced against the door and left splotches of blood and bits of fur against the paint of the white whale. "Rosie won't miss this one, do you think?"

King leaned out the passenger window, barking and growling.

"Maybe Maggie's mutt will be next. Crown the King," said Weston.

Raven closed her eyes and groaned. "That's so sick. I think I'm going to throw up."

Ivy glanced over at Weston and the dead cat. She took a sharp left turn and the Monstrosity wobbled down the alley by the Coffey Shop. Moby Dick couldn't react in time, and the huge car drove on, its bloody torment smeared on its white door. Ivy stopped the camper in the alley by the back door of the Coffey Shop.

Raven's face turned as white as her nurse's cap. "I'm tired of spooks and dead cats. I really don't feel very well. I want to go home."

The wind whistled outside, and the unstable camper swayed on the truck bed. Snow stuck to the windshield and caked the blades. After they dropped Raven at her house, Raggedy Ann and Merlin sat in the Monstrosity for a minute to clear the icy windshield.

"He's the stuff of horror movies," Maggie said.

"Growing up with his father, you know he wouldn't turn out good," Ivy said.

Because of the raging snowstorm, Ivy and Maggie drove back to Deadman's Woods to rescue Nick and Jesse. The bald tires slid on the icy road and snow fell in heavy clumps. The clouds drifted over the moon and blocked its hazy light. As they drove around the corner past Rosie's house, Ivy sighed. "Poor Rosie. She'll miss that cat. Those animals are all she has."

"I know. Remember when she said her cats were better company than us?" Maggie said.

They both laughed. "She was right," Ivy said.

As they approached Deadman's Woods, the snow swirled all around them like in a child's snow globe. Then, through the twisting white flakes, they saw them. Two hazy white figures floated in the dark of the country road. It was the ghosts.

Ivy stopped the camper and leaned out the window to get a better view of the apparitions flying toward them. Their sheets flapped behind them in the howling wind. Their painted white skin blended in with the swirling snow.

Nick opened the back of the camper and jumped inside. King scampered over and licked Nick's face. Jesse pushed Nick and King out of the way and dove onto the camper floor, twisted in his ghost sheets. His usually perfect hair was wet from the snow and plastered to his head. The door blew shut behind them.

Ivy stared at her friends. "What in the heck happened to you guys? You look like you saw a ghost." She laughed.

Nick shivered as he sat down on the bench in the back of the camper. "We did."

The girls laughed at the shivering boys, whose wide eyes were glazed with blank expressions. Jesse's sheet bunched around his arms. Nobody said anything for a few seconds.

"You know the spooks Reuben is always talking about?" Nick asked.

The girls looked at each other and nodded.

"Well, we saw them," Nick said.

"What exactly did you see?" Ivy asked.

"It's kind of hard to describe," Nick said. "It was like dark, floating kind of people. There were two of them."

"They were like these smoky shadows with dark, sunken faces," said Jesse. Snowflakes clung to his eyelashes. "I told you it was a bad idea."

Nick wiggled his hand through the air. "Evil, black cloud beasts."

"Woo," Ivy said in a quaking ghost voice. She put her hand up to her mouth and whispered to Maggie. "Uncle Tommy and Reuben?"

Maggie nodded and smiled.

Ivy turned around from the driver's seat. "So, Nick, you want to drive now?" She knew Nick never let anyone else drive the Monstrosity.

"No, you're doing fine."

They got back into town after ten o'clock. The town's Halloween pranksters had been busy. Toilet paper flapped in the branches of the trees like unraveling mummies in a haunted house. Ivory bar soap mingled with the frost on the windows. An abandoned outhouse lay on its side, surrounded by burning hay bundles.

Ivy drove the camper around the town square past the library. Maggie grabbed Ivy's arm. "Wait, Ivy. Stop."

Ivy pulled the camper to a stop and Maggie pointed to the flagpole outside the library. "Look, someone tied a pair of old-lady underwear to the top of the library flagpole."

Ivy stared at what she was sure was Edna Jean Whittaker's precious pretties snapping in the wind in ghostly surrender. Uncle Tommy and Reuben had struck again.

But the boys, in a zombie trance in the back of the camper, didn't even notice.

Chapter 21

THE LAWN CREATURES

Late the next morning, Ivy stopped by Uncle Walter's trailer to deliver some of Grandma's homemade cinnamon rolls. When Uncle Walter unlocked the door, Ivy pointed to his small yard.

"Hey, Uncle Walter, what happened to your lawn creatures?"

Uncle Walter ran his fingers through his brown hair with a hint of silver showing on the sides.

"What'd you mean?"

"They're gone."

"Gone?"

Uncle Walter stepped outside and looked around. His snowy yard was empty, his lawn creatures kidnapped. "How do you like that? An art heist on Halloween night."

When Uncle Walter and Ivy entered the sheriff's office in the basement of the county courthouse to report the theft, Edna Jean Whittaker gestured wildly at Charlie. Her high-pitched voice screeched. "A UFO landed on my lawn, and you tell me you can't find it. Someone defamed the public library's flagpole with some poor soul's unmentionables, and you don't know who did it. And my Tiny Fifi was dog-napped."

Charlie remained seated at his desk. "Who?"

Edna Jean adjusted her slightly crooked wig. Her expression looked wild behind her thick glasses. "Tiny Fifi. You know, my canine companion. It was Luther who did it."

Charlie tapped his pencil against his desk. "Oh, yeah. Your poodle. Now Edna Jean, why do you suspect that Luther is the perpetrator?"

Edna Jean pushed her glasses up on her nose. "After the UFO destroyed my fence last night, Luther came early this morning to fix it. After he left, I couldn't find Tiny Fifi. She wasn't in her little princess bed or anywhere."

"All right, Edna Jean. I'll check it out."

He turned to Uncle Walter and Ivy standing on the other side of his desk. "Now what can I do for you, Walter?"

Uncle Walter shifted his weight off his aching knee. "Well, Charlie. Someone stole my lawn art last night."

"Run that by me again?" Charlie said, trying not to laugh.

"You know, my lawn creatures."

"That junk in your yard?"

"It's not junk," said Uncle Walter.

"I didn't mean it that way."

Uncle Walter sat down. "Someone took them last night while I was passing out candy over at my mother's house."

Charlie cleared his throat. "Could be another Luther Matthews deal."

Uncle Walter tapped his fingers on the table. "I don't think so. Can't imagine why he would want them. It's more like a Tommy deal."

"No. Trust me, it's a Luther Matthews offense," said Charlie.

Uncle Walter shook his head. "I really doubt it. I—"

"Listen, we'll run out to Luther's place and see what he's got to say for himself."

Uncle Walter stood up. "I don't think that's necessary. You need to—"

Charlie clicked the padlock closed on his file cabinet and stood up. "Humor me." He rubbed the white patch in the middle of his bristly crew cut, which over the years, had widened. "Edna Jean and I are headed to Luther's place on a similar investigation anyway. Why don't you come along?"

Charlie drove out to Luther's house with Edna Jean in the front seat and Ivy and Uncle Walter in the back. He parked in Luther's driveway and they all walked up to Luther's snow-covered porch. Ivy heard the sound of a basketball hitting a backboard. It was Weston shooting baskets at the barn over at the Thrasher place. How could Luther stand to live so close to them?

Charlie hiked his pants up over his big belly and knocked on Luther's door. The screen door bounced and hit the huge stacks of wood Luther chopped from the woods behind his house. The door, hanging only by the bottom hinge, smacked Charlie's head.

"Luther, Deputy Sheriff Carter here. Your danged door just accosted me. Open up."

Luther answered from inside his dilapidated home. "I'm kind of busy, Charlie. What do you want?"

Charlie leaned his hand against the side of Luther's house and paint flaked from the wood. "I want to know if you absconded with Edna Jean Whittaker's canine."

Edna Jean held her hand to her ear. "She's in there. I can hear my precious baby. He's got her." She cupped her hands around her mouth, calling to her dog. "Tiny Fifi."

A muffled yapping came from inside the house. Charlie nodded to Edna Jean. "Looks like he's got the poodle hostage."

Edna Jean's eyebrows wrinkled and a few strands of hair hung down from her unkempt wig. The faint, high-pitched yapping grew louder. Edna Jean adjusted her glasses, which magnified her beady eyes. "Tiny Fifi. Mommy's here."

Charlie held up his hand, gesturing for Edna Jean to be quiet. "Luther, we can hear the dog. Hand me Fifi."

The rickety front door opened and they carefully stepped inside Luther's broken-down house. The pungent smell of wet campfire mixed with dirty socks permeated the air.

Ivy smiled and waved at Luther. He winked back. She knew he had not taken the lawn art, it was too easy a heist.

Luther opened a cupboard door, picked up the yapping dog, and handed the wiggling poodle to Charlie, nearly knocking over a purple cookie jar sitting on the edge of his cluttered counter. Ivy's mouth dropped open, and she pointed to the counter. "Hey, Uncle Walter, that looks just like your eggplant cookie jar."

Uncle Walter stared at the ceramic jar that was missing from his collection. "It is."

Luther picked it up and handed the missing eggplant to Uncle Walter. "Sorry, Walter. I fixed the broken lid for you."

Uncle Walter rubbed his hand over his long-lost cookie jar. "Thanks, I appreciate that, Luther. It's hard to find a purple vegetable, you know."

Charlie shook his head and clicked his tongue. "Luther, you've got to stop pilfering things that don't belong to you or I'm going to have to lock you up for good this time."

Luther scratched his hair, which stood stiffly on end like a frantic game of pick-up sticks. He stared at Charlie as if looking through him to something more important.

Charlie took a step toward Luther. "Did you wrongfully appropriate the objects on Walter Taylor's lawn last night?"

Luther shook his head and a fly flew out of his hair. "No, they don't interest me. There's no challenge."

Ivy knew it. Luther looked at Ivy and smiled, showing

his chewing-tobacco-stained teeth. "Besides, that mushroom gnome is a little too creepy, even for me. The evil pixie."

Ivy giggled but Charlie narrowed his eyes and tilted his chin down, adding another roll of skin on his neck. "Well, I don't see it on your property. I better not find out differently."

"Are you questioning my honesty?" asked Luther, frowning at Charlie.

"Wouldn't think of it, Luth. Hey, you need to get that door repaired. It nearly killed me. You could use a handyman around this place."

Luther kicked a broken tile on the floor. "Hard to find a good one anymore."

Ivy and Uncle Walter looked at each other and smiled. Charlie adjusted his belt and sniffed. "Well, try to keep your nose clean, Luther. I'd hate to have to arrest you." He looked around Luther's dirty, cluttered home. "But then, maybe you'd enjoy our fine incarceration accommodations."

Luther scratched the seat of his jeans and pointed to Charlie's head. "Charlie, you'd better have Judy down at the beauty shop do something about that white patch in your hair or the skunks'll think you're one of them."

"They're friends of yours, I'm sure."

Charlie held Fifi out in front of him like a dripping sack of week-old garbage as she paddled her paws in the air. He handed the poodle to Edna Jean. "Here."

Edna Jean snuggled her face in the dog's curly white fur. "My poor baby will probably never get over this trauma."

"Her yapping nearly drove me crazy anyway," Luther said, yawning as if tired from the whole dog-napping ordeal.

"Why'd you take her?" asked Charlie.

"She seemed lonely," said Luther.

Tiny Fifi began her high-pitched barking. Edna Jean pushed up her thick glasses on her long, pointed nose. "You're already crazy, you dog thief." Her own shrieking voice sounded like Tiny Fifi's yapping.

Charlie shook his head as the group walked to the car. The poodle investigation was closed. He opened the car door. "Edna Jean, make sure that canine doesn't relieve himself on the seats."

"Him? She's a refined lady. Tiny Fifi would never dream of such a thing."

Edna Jean and the poodle slid into the front seat. Tiny Fifi wagged her curly tail and snuggled close to Edna Jean. "Now that you've found Tiny Fifi, you can start working on finding that UFO that landed on my lawn."

Charlie nodded and backed the car out of Luther's dirt driveway. Ivy soon noticed a growing wet spot on the front seat next to Fifi.

The next day, Uncle Walter and Ivy stopped by the sheriff's office to see if any more suspects had been rounded up now that Luther wasn't under investigation for Uncle Walter's looted lawn art. Charlie sauntered toward them as they entered the office.

"Walter, I'm glad you're here. I just tried to call you. We found your lawn things." He pointed to the ceramic creatures placed against the far wall like a police lineup. "And we've got the two perpetrators in custody. We also got a witness." He beckoned to them with a flip of his hand. "Come over here. You're going to want to hear this."

He led them to his office where Weston Thrasher sat with his ratty high-top sneakers resting on the handle of the padlocked file cabinet drawer. Charlie pushed Weston's shoes off the drawer. "Get down, boy. Now, tell Walter Taylor what you observed."

Weston stood up, his baggy bell-bottom jeans dragging to the floor. "Last night, I saw these two black guys running away from the cemetery."

Charlie nodded at Weston. "Tell them who the thieves are."

"Ben Roberts and Otis Norton." Weston smirked.

"That's a lie," Ivy gasped. "You made that up!"

"I saw them. You can thank me any time." Weston glared at her. His long greasy hair fell over his eyes.

Charlie's hands rested on his wide, black leather belt. He stuck out his lip. "Thanks, Weston. You can go. I've got your statement. I'll let you know if we need you further."

Weston tapped his foot on the floor. "Whatever." His shoulder bumped into Ivy as he sauntered out.

"Uncle Walter, you're not going to believe Weston, are you?"

"No."

"Walter, we found your lawn things in a circle around your brother's grave."

"Charlie, that doesn't make any sense. Why would Ben and Otis want to do that?"

He shrugged and rubbed his hand over the top of his bristly crew cut. His silver streak rippled like corn stalks in a stiff wind.

Uncle Walter shook his head. "I want to talk to them."

"There's no need for that. Listen, you can take your things home now. We just need you to sign the paperwork."

"Well, I'd feel much better if I could talk to them. Won't take a minute." Walter brushed past Charlie and headed toward to the cells.

Ivy grabbed his arm. "Uncle Walter, last night we were on the back road to the cemetery. We saw Uncle Tommy and

Reuben out there. They were dressed in black, with their faces painted black."

"Now that makes more sense," said Uncle Walter.

Charlie followed them to where Ben, twenty-three, and Otis sat on a metal bench inside the cell. Otis seemed embarrassed as he rested his head in his hands. Ben looked scared and bewildered.

Uncle Walter looked over at the deputy sheriff. "Hey, Charlie, you have no business putting them in a cell."

He shrugged his shoulders. "Precautionary measures. You never know."

Ivy took a deep breath, trying to control her anger. She tucked her straight hair behind her ear. "Never know what?"

Charlie pointed to Otis and Ben and whispered behind his hand. "Unpredictable."

Uncle Walter shook his head and turned back to the accused men. "You didn't take my lawn art, did you?"

Otis stood up, his head almost touching the low ceiling of the cell. "No, Mr. Taylor. I've told the sheriff I don't know what he's talking about. I mean, I know your lawn things. I get a kick out of them. But I didn't take them."

"I knew you didn't, but I had to ask," Uncle Walter said. "What about you, Ben?"

Ben shook his head. "No, sir. My mom would kick my butt if I did anything like that."

Ivy knew Ben was right.

Charlie shook his head. "Don't take their word for it. I have a witness."

Uncle Walter raised his eyebrows and scratched the side of his face. "Charlie, if they said they didn't do it, then they didn't do it. I'm not going to press charges against them. If I was you, I'd let them go before Miss Shirley gets wind of this."

Ivy thought she saw Charlie shudder.

Otis nodded. "Thanks, Mr. Taylor."

"Call me Walter."

Ben rose to his feet. "Yeah, thanks. I don't want any trouble with the law. Mr. Norton just got me a maintenance job at Warner College until I can save enough money to go to EMT training."

Uncle Walter shook Ben's hand through the bars. "Well, congratulations, Ben. I'm sure Miss Shirley is very proud."

Charlie's arms gestured erratically in the air. "What is this, a kissy-face party? Walter, based on my substantial law enforcement experience, I think releasing them is a mistake. You can't let these boys get away with dangerous pranks. It just leads to violent crimes. I think the situation warrants further investigation."

Uncle Walter shook his head. "Charlie, they didn't do it. Let them go."

Ivy looked up at Charlie. "The ones you're looking for are Uncle Tommy and Reuben. They'll probably tell you all about it at the Blue Moon tonight."

"Ivy's right. This is Tommy's kind of caper. Remember the time they broke into my home and destroyed my cookie jar?"

Charlie bit his lip to stop smiling. "Yeah, I remember the zucchini incident." He rubbed the extra skin under his chin. "Well, at least your lawn figures were returned unharmed."

"Yeah, I figured you wouldn't want to look into Tommy and Reuben," said Uncle Walter.

Charlie let the two men out of the cell. "Okay. Go on home, you two."

Otis stepped out of his cell. He shook Uncle Walter's hand and pointed to the lawn creatures in a row against the wall near the entrance. "Can we help you carry your things to your car?"

Uncle Walter put his hand on Otis' shoulder. "Well, thank you, Mr. Norton. That's mighty nice of you."

"Please call me, Otis." Otis turned to Ben. "Grab a . . . animal, son."

Ben picked up a deer. "It looks like the ear got a little chipped, but you can't hardly tell."

They carried Uncle Walter's ceramic figures to his car. Otis held the brown mushroom and he stared in astonishment at the tiny pixie face of the gnome. "Good Lord, this gnome looks just like Thelma Sampson!"

Ivy smiled. "Right?" She examined the lawn art as each piece was carefully placed in Uncle Walter's trunk. "Hey, Uncle Walter. Look, there's a sunflower seed stuck to the gnome's hat."

Uncle Walter bent over the trunk and flicked the sunflower seed off the gnome with his finger. "There's your conclusive evidence."

"Mr. Taylor and Mr. Smith ought to find another hobby, don't you think?" Otis asked.

"Yeah, this is getting real old," Uncle Walter said as he closed the trunk. "A lifetime of pranks can wear a person down."

Chapter 22

THE GREAT PURPLE DOG

The strong winds in late spring bent the green stalks of the tulips until the colorful blooms almost touched the ground. April's warmth coaxed the buds on the trees to grow. Life returned to Iowa's black soil. With the end of the school year nearing, Ivy's escape from Coffey had almost arrived. She and Jesse had planned to backpack across Europe right after they graduated high school.

Ivy picked up a passport application from Uncle Walter at the post office, but it required a birth certificate. Grandma said she couldn't remember where Ivy's birth certificate was, so as soon as school let out that day, Ivy went to the courthouse records office to get a certified copy.

Maggie's neighbor, Ruth Jackson, still worked as a clerk for the county. She greeted Ivy at the records counter. "Hi, Ivy. What's up?"

"Hey, Ruth. Grandma can't find my birth certificate. I need to get one for my passport."

"Finally going to Europe, huh?"

Ivy smiled and nodded.

"I'll just need your birth date and full name," said Ruth as she handed Ivy a slip of paper.

Ivy wrote down her details and passed the paper back to Ruth.

"So, you're finally getting out of Coffey, huh?"

"Yeah, as soon as I graduate."

"Well, good for you. I can't even get Virgil to go to Des Moines with me. Says he's got everything he needs here, and you never know where you might not be welcome. I'll be right back."

Ruth disappeared into a room filled with white file cabinets lined up against the walls like giant teeth. She emerged several minutes later with a certified copy of Ivy's birth certificate. "Here you go, Ivy. So, when you're gallivanting around Europe, who's going to take care of your Uncle Walter after his knee surgery?"

"What are you talking about? No one told me anything about knee surgery." Anger surged through Ivy. Why were they always keeping stuff from her? She wasn't a child anymore.

"Oh gosh, Ivy, I'm sorry. Shouldn't have said anything. Miss Shirley mentioned it and . . ."

"No, I'm glad you did. Thank you for the birth certificate." She looked down at the certificate and froze. Her birth certificate did not include her father's name. She set the document on the counter and pointed to the empty space. "Hey, Ruth, how come my dad's name isn't on this?"

Ruth glanced down to where Ivy was pointing. "Probably just the hospital's mistake. You wouldn't believe the sloppy record keeping I've seen."

"Seems weird," Ivy said.

"It's sort of unusual. But it'll still get you a passport."

Ivy nodded slowly. "Okay, thanks, Ruth. See you around."

She walked out of the building, her mind whirling in confusion. No father on her birth certificate and no one had bothered to tell her about Uncle Walter's knee surgery.

Grandma had stopped driving as soon as Ivy got her driver's license a few years back. Her arthritis made it very painful to drive and even getting into a car took a major effort. Uncle Walter wouldn't be able to drive after having knee surgery. So, who would get him to the doctor and run errands while he recovered? She knew Uncle Tommy wouldn't do a thing to help. Her heart sunk. As much as she wanted to get away, Uncle Walter needed her help after his knee operation and during his recovery. She knew she and Jesse could go to Europe a little later, maybe at the end of the summer, but she felt as if the ground had turned to quicksand and the sinking feeling pulled her down until she felt like she couldn't breathe.

After her graduation ceremonies and parties were over, Ivy and Jesse sat on the glider on the back porch, enjoying the quiet. She had already told him about postponing their trip until after Uncle Walter's knee surgery and recovery. Although it would delay their departure, their future stretched out before them, finally within reach. She had her passport and in just a few weeks, they'd be together, far away from Coffey.

It was almost midnight. The locusts hummed, their shrill vibrating sounds amplified in the warm night. Ivy slapped a mosquito on her leg. The mosquitoes and gnats were bad. It was time for Howard Decker to start spraying the fogger pesticide.

Jesse cleared his throat and scratched his head. "Ivy, I didn't want to tell you and ruin graduation because I know you have to stay here and help your uncle, but I've decided to go to Europe anyway."

"What?"

Jesse looked into the woods, his voice was soft. "I'm leaving tomorrow."

Ivy put her feet down, suddenly stopping the glider. "To-morrow? Why?"

"There's nothing for me here." Jesse shrugged. "I don't want to be a porch-sitter. I've got to get out of here."

Ivy grabbed Jesse's arm, trying to understand. "What about me? Jesse, don't leave. We'll be out of here soon. We're so close."

Jesse looked down at his hands. "If I don't leave now, I'm afraid something will happen, and I'll never get out of here. I mean, look at you." He licked his lips and took a deep breath as if preparing to dive underwater. "I'm leaving tomorrow morning. And Raven's coming with me."

Ivy let go of Jesse's arm and shrunk back. "Raven? Jesse, don't do this. You know what she's like. She just does what she wants."

"Ivy, sometimes I wish you were more like that. I'm not good at waiting."

The locusts stilled, and quiet filled the air.

"Yeah, I see that."

He'd found his way out, just like she knew he would. But he wouldn't be taking her with him.

"I love you, Ivy, but there's nothing for me here."

Jesse tried to kiss her, but she turned away before he could see her tears. She waved her hand. "Yeah, you're right. Just go."

He walked off the porch and started down the path. He turned around. "I'll be back soon."

Ivy didn't respond. She sat down and rocked the glider with her feet, staring into the dark woods. A squirrel chattered from its hiding place in the trees. A summer in Coffey without Jesse was an eternity, a death sentence. As soon as Jesse disappeared around the side of the house, Ivy's tears came in torrents. Raven had shoved her way in like she always did.

As Ivy sat on her porch, fearful of losing Jesse and her dreams of freedom, intruders infiltrated Mulberry Street.

Miss Shirley later told Ivy that the smell of meat must have roused the mighty King from his sleep. She imagined he got up from his usual spot near the kitchen stove and went out the swinging dog door. Outside, King probably yawned and stretched his paws, sniffing the air. He must have known the mulberries would be ripening soon. Miss Shirley figured that King circled the piece of steak on the ground, then gorged himself on the tasty and unexpectedly deadly midnight snack.

The next morning, as the sun rose over the railroad tracks, Maggie called Ivy and told her through tears about the brutal murder of King, hung from his beloved mulberry tree with a rope around his neck. The great purple dog had met an undignified death.

Ivy called Nick and they hurried over to Maggie's house.

Otis reported King's murder to the deputy sheriff, but Charlie refused to investigate the dog's death. Charlie said that if no one saw it, nothing could be done.

"Weston Thrasher did it. There's no doubt about it. No one else could be that mean," said Ivy as they all sat around the Norton's kitchen table.

"You're right. We've got to do something. We can't let him get away with this." Nick said with his head in his hands.

"I understand how you feel." Otis rubbed his chin. "Uh huh. I certainly do. But the death of an old dog belonging to a black family will never stand as an excuse for revenge against the banker's son. I understand the helpless feeling. But if you do something to Weston, it'll be blamed on us. Our family will suffer even more. The score'll never be even,"

"But it's not right," said Maggie.

Nick pounded the yellow Formica kitchen table. "It's time somebody taught him a lesson."

Pinky wrung her hands like a dishrag. "That Thrasher boy is dangerous. He's got no limits."

Otis put his arm around his petite wife.

Nick gritted his teeth. "What we need is some dog justice. Someday all the dogs and cats in Coffey are going to turn on Weston."

Otis shook his head. "King was a good dog, and we loved him for a long time. But I don't want anybody getting hurt over this. This can't go any farther. King's gone and there's nothing we can do about that. Why don't you kids go dig a grave in the field by the railroad tracks and bury him? Then go on home and try to forget this happened."

Ivy knew they would never be able to forget. Maggie's shoulders slumped as she walked out the kitchen door and kneeled beside the lifeless dog. Ivy and Nick followed her. Maggie stroked the dog's head and buried her face in his fur.

"King never cared what color anybody's skin was," Maggie sobbed.

Ivy put her arm around Maggie.

Nick dug a hole down by the railroad tracks. Then he picked up King and carried him to his final resting place. When he had finished shoveling dirt on King's grave, Nick threw back his head and raised his arms. He howled like a dog in mortal anguish, a final tribute to the great purple dog.

When she got home, Ivy' anger expanded until she thought she would explode. She borrowed Grandma's old Dodge Dart and drove out to the Thrasher's farm. Her knuckles turned white as she gripped the steering wheel. Her head pounded, like hail on a roof during an unexpected spring storm.

She found Weston sitting in the big white car in the barn next to the farmhouse with smoke wafting out the window. Weston used to spend his afternoons fiddling with the old car or playing basketball on the hoop nailed to the barn, but all he did now was smoke weed that he grew in a secret spot in the woods.

Ivy marched toward Weston. She kicked a basketball lying on the barn floor and it hit the wheel of the car. Weston sat up in the front seat and turned to her.

"What do you want?"

She fingered her heart necklace with one hand, while the other made a fist at her side. "Listen, Weston. Don't think you got away with killing King. I know you did it."

Weston shifted his weight. His long hair hung down in front of his face. "Prove it. Nobody saw me."

Ivy took a step toward him. "Why do you hate Maggie so much?"

Weston took another drag. "I didn't do it because I hate Maggie and her stupid mutt. I did it because I hate you. But you don't have a dog."

A cold charge swept through Ivy. "Me?" She swallowed hard and took a deep breath. "You killed King because of me?"

Weston rolled his eyes. "Duh."

"What have I ever done to you?" Her fingernails dug into her palms. "How would you feel if someone killed something you loved?"

For a moment Ivy recognized some trace of human feeling in Weston's eyes, but then it dimmed and flickered out. Nothing could ever touch Weston Thrasher's heart.

"There's nothing left to take." Weston's eyes narrowed accusingly at Ivy. He stared at her with vacant, hazy eyes as the smoke swirled around his head. Grandma was right. Weston's soul floated somewhere outside the boundaries of this world. "There's something seriously wrong with you," Ivy said.

Weston got out of the car. "You always act like you're so special, but you're not. Your mother left you behind."

Ivy put her hands on her hips. A torrent of anger surged inside her. "My mother didn't have a choice. She died, just like your mother."

Weston spat on the ground with hatred in his eyes. "Ivy, you're so stupid. People have been lying to you all your life. Your mother's not dead. She just didn't want you."

Blood rushed to Ivy's head, and the tempest brewing in her heart for years began to rage. "That's not true. Anyway, your mother didn't drown. Your father murdered her." Ivy stood stunned for a moment by her own cruelty. Then she turned and fled out of the barn.

Weston's words echoed inside Ivy's head, like words shouted in a rock quarry. Could he be right? Her mother's death notification was missing from Dr. Kelsey's medical files and Grandma didn't know where she was buried. Could her mother still be alive?

Luther had been right about the dead talking through their gravestones. Maybe he was right about the death records at the county courthouse, too.

Chapter 23

THE RAIN STOPPED

The late afternoon sun felt good on her face as Ivy crossed Main Street and entered the county courthouse on the town square. Ruth waved to Ivy as she entered.

"Hey, Ivy, what's going on?"

"I need copies of my parents' death records."

Ruth tapped her hands on the counter. "Sure. Listen, Ivy, I'm sorry you didn't get to go to Europe. I should have kept my big mouth shut about your uncle's knee surgery."

"It's okay. There's plenty of time. What's a few weeks?"

Ruth patted Ivy's hand. "I'll be right back."

A few minutes later, Ruth returned, shaking her head. Her heels clicked against the black and white tile floor. "Here's your father's file, but I couldn't find one for your mother."

Ivy's heart raced. She broke out in a cold sweat. "How come?"

"I don't know. Could be misfiled. Particularly since it was so long ago."

"She died in the accident with my father, and you've got his." Ivy played with her silver heart necklace, running it back and forth along its chain. Goosebumps crept along her skin. Luther was right—sometimes what was missing was more important than what was there.

"This whole thing doesn't make any sense."

Ivy glanced at the death certificate, signed by Dr. Kelsey. It was the same as the one in her father's medical file at the clinic. Ruth looked around.

"You know, accident reports are filed in the sheriff's office."

"That's a good idea. Thanks, Ruth," said Ivy, but she knew Charlie would never show her the report. She'd seen his padlocked file cabinet.

Ivy walked out of the courthouse and paused for a moment at the top of the steps. Across the street, Bertha and Edna Jean stood close together talking outside the library. Bertha knew everybody's business. She loved to talk. Ivy stopped at the bottom of the step. Bertha. She'd ask Bertha. Bertha would know what happened the night of the accident and if her mother was still alive.

Early the next morning as Uncle Walter was delivering his Saturday mail route, Ivy knocked on the door of Bertha Tuttle's trailer. The town gossip opened her door wearing a leopard-print robe and black bristly curlers in her hair. The angle of the plastic picks in the curlers gave the illusion that they were sticking straight into her head.

"What do you want? Did you come by to see my nose stuck to the window?"

Ivy couldn't help but glance at Bertha's round nose. "I just wanted to talk to you for a minute."

Bertha opened the door and waved Ivy toward a chair. "Since you're here, you might as well come in. I could use the company."

Ivy sat down. "Bertha, I need to know what happened the night of my parents' accident. I know you know something."

Without her usual mask of makeup, Bertha's face had lost its clownish-plastic severity and almost looked pleasant. She took out her curlers and lined them up in a neat row on the table next to the couch.

"Well, that was a long time ago," she said, running her fingers through her dyed red hair.

Ivy took a deep breath. "There was no obituary in the paper and there's no death record for my mother at the courthouse." She fingered the lace doily on the arm of the chair and noticed her hands trembled. "What really happened to my mother?"

Bertha sighed deeply. She leaned back in her chair. "There wasn't an obituary or a death record for your mother because your father was alone in that car when it crashed. Your mother didn't die."

Ivy jumped up. "I knew it!"

Bertha held up her hands. "Now, I wasn't supposed to tell you that. But I figure you should know. Don't tell anyone or I'll be run out of town."

Ivy sat back down on the edge of the chair. "My family's good at keeping secrets. I won't tell." Her mind raced with questions. "So, what really happened?"

Bertha adjusted her cat-eye glasses. "It was a rainy night. You know the kind of cold when the rain freezes as it hits the ground. Your mother was on the bench outside the Coffey Shop, waiting for the 9:18 Greyhound bus going north."

Ivy gasped. "Rosie was right."

"What?"

"Nothing. How do you know all this?"

"I lived in the apartment above the Coffey Shop with my husband before he left me for that dime-store tramp. The same apartment Russell lives in now that overlooks the street. It was a really dark night with the heavy rain and all. We could hear your mother hollering when your father pulled up. She said that she needed to get out of Coffey that night. It was a matter of life or death."

Ivy gripped the arms of the well-worn chair. "So, my mother got on the bus?"

Bertha pulled at the stiff round humps of hair left from the curlers. "When the Greyhound came, she left your father standing there in the rain without so much as a howdy-do. She followed another passenger on board. Your father got back in his car and sped after the bus. But that's all I know."

"Why won't anyone talk about it?"

Bertha leaned forward. "Your grandma knows a lot of secrets around here. She can be very persuasive." Her voice changed to a whisper, and she put a finger to her mouth. "It was all very hush-hush. I guess she thought she was protecting you."

"From what?"

"Well, from your mother, I guess."

"Why?"

"I don't know."

Ivy pushed her hair behind her ears. "Why are you telling me now?"

Bertha bit her lip and looked over the top of her cat-eye glasses. "I guess because, although you were a sassy little girl, I know what it's like to be left behind."

Ivy stood up, and her legs quivered. Bertha had given Ivy back her mother. Ivy hesitated, then she hugged Bertha. Her robe smelled faintly of cheap perfume and pancakes.

Bertha grabbed Ivy's shoulders. "Listen, Ivy, if you've got a notion to try and find your mother, you'd better think twice. I've seen what it can do when you hang onto useless hope.

Edna Jean's hair never grew back after her boyfriend ran away with her best friend. Your mother's been gone a long time. People usually leave for a reason. Some people don't want to be found."

"She'll want to see me, I know. She may not be perfect but she's my mother. Nothing can change that." Ivy reached out and held Bertha's hands. "Thanks, Bertha. Listen, I'm really sorry about the nose thing."

Bertha cleared her throat. "That's okay. I'm by myself a lot and sometimes I'm just curious."

"Yeah, me, too."

Grandma was sitting on the back porch when Ivy got home.

"I'm glad you're here. Luther needs you to help him unload Rosie's winter wood."

"Isn't it time you stopped bossing me around and let me make my own decisions? You don't always know what's best for me."

Ivy stomped off with Grandma looking after her with a confused expression on her face. Ivy paced her room in agitated frustration for a while, then she put on her sweats and jogged out to the old hermit lady's place to meet Luther like Grandma had asked. The run calmed her down and she thought maybe that was what the fast night-walking did for Nick's mother, Ellen.

As Ivy jogged toward Rosie's house, she saw a dark cloud of smoke. Why would she have a fire in the summer? As she got closer, she saw smoke billowing out of Rosie's tiny windows. Ivy sprinted to the front door and pounded on it.

"Miss Rosie, are you in there? Rosie?"

A flash of movement caught her eye. She turned around to see Weston creeping around the back of Rosie's ramshackle house. Rosie suddenly opened her door and the wild dogs ran out of the shack, growling and slinking low to the ground. They knew Weston's smell.

He stepped back as the dogs approached. In his hand was a twisted rag wrapped around a large stick. He flicked his lighter under the rag until it blazed. The dogs stopped their pursuit, barking at the flames in front of them.

Ivy came up behind them. "You did this, didn't you?"

The smell of gasoline and rotting trash filled the air.

"No. I was just trying to help but these dogs wouldn't let me." Weston turned around and pointed the homemade torch at Ivy's face. "I wonder if Poison Ivy burns." Weston laughed and taunted her with the burning rag.

Luther's truck sputtered into Rosie's overgrown driveway with the back filled with winter wood. The truck door slammed.

"Luther, it's Weston! I think he set Miss Rosie's house on fire," Ivy said.

Luther's footsteps crunched the dry leaves and brush as he ran across the yard. He grabbed his hammer, Old Dan Tucker, from his tool belt. "Put that down, Weston."

"Right, Gomer."

Luther threw the hammer. It sailed in a spinning arc and knocked Weston's burning torch to the ground. Ivy kicked dirt on the torch and it went out. Behind them, the trash in Rosie's house fueled the smoldering fire and another blaze ignited. Standing in the doorway, Rosie's raggedy skirt caught on fire. She rushed out of the house beating the flames with her hands. A few of Rosie's dogs circled her, barking at the fire but unable to help.

Weston froze for a second before he sprinted through the woods toward his house and the safety of his father.

Luther took off his brown leather bomber jacket and flung it over Rosie as he pushed her to the ground.

"Roll, Rosie. Roll."

Rosie rolled across her dirt yard, scratched bare from her animals. Ivy and Luther ran beside her. Rosie rolled to a stop when she hit the old tree stump. With a dazed look in her eyes, she lay panting as her clothing smoked.

Ivy reached out and pulled Rosie to her feet. She was remarkably light. Rosie swayed, still disoriented and bewildered. She poked her tangled hair with her stubby fingers.

"My family needs me."

She turned and ran back into the burning shack to rescue her remaining dogs and cats from the fire blocking their escape.

"No, Miss Rosie!" Ivy called, as she reached out to stop her but Rosie, surprisingly agile, headed straight into the smoke and flames of her house. She appeared at the doorway every few seconds with another dog or cat in her arms. Luther and Ivy helped pull the animals to safety. But Rosie's rescue attempt seemed endless.

Luther cupped his hands and yelled. "Rosie, come on out of there. You've done all you can."

"I've got to save my babies," she insisted and the fire raged behind her.

The town of Coffey didn't have enough funds or enough fires to warrant a full-time paid fire department. But when a fire was reported, a low-pitched constant horn echoed across town, different in tone and pattern from the tornado siren.

The volunteer firefighters gathered at the fire station in response to the alarm. The location of the fire was written on a large blackboard hanging outside the station. Anyone could just check the blackboard to find out where the fire burned.

Ivy greeted the volunteer fire brigade at Rosie's shack. They told her that Reuben had called in the fire, but by the time they got there, it was too late to save Rosie.

Charlie eventually showed up to investigate the arson, but Ivy knew Weston would not be prosecuted. There were, after all, no witnesses to speak against Weston's lies and she hadn't actually seen him light Rosie's house on fire.

The firemen's heavy spray of water put the fire out. They checked the smoldering remains of Rosie's shack and then went home.

Luther stared at the charred house. "Everyone should have the right to die the way they want, I reckon." He bent down and picked up his bomber jacket burned through in places from Rosie's flames. He shook it and held it up, peering through a charred hole in the back. He shrugged and put it back on.

Dr. Kelsey arrived in his station wagon to place Rosie's burned remains in a black zippered body bag and take her back to the clinic to make his coroner's report.

Ivy helped Luther lift Rosie's dogs and cats into the back of his pickup. The animals rode on top of the stacks of wood that Luther never got to unload.

"Get in. I'll give you a lift home," Luther said to Ivy.

His rusted pickup sputtered to a stop in Ivy's driveway as the dogs barked frantically in the back of the truck. Ivy got out and walked around to Luther's door. "You did good tonight."

Luther tapped the steering wheel. "Not good enough. That poor old lady never bothered anyone."

"Well, I'm glad you were there."

Rosie's dogs and cats meowed and barked in the back of the

pickup. Ivy pointed at the anxious animals. "I guess it won't be so quiet around your place anymore."

Luther smiled. "I reckon wild dogs are better than bratty little poodles any day."

Ivy sighed. She knew that although Rosie had died inside her burning, ramshackle home, that finally in death, her tormented mind was at peace, something she hadn't found in life, and her sweet babies "she'd saved" had found a good home.

Chapter 24

LEAVING COFFEY

The hot summer days, filled with the smell of hay and the sounds of birds, could quickly turn into gusty storms with the possibility of tornadoes. The twisting winds might suddenly threaten to erupt into a powerful funnel of destructive fury.

Ivy watched the dark sky with fear until the menacing clouds passed across the prairie and calm returned to the heavens. Knowing her mother was still alive increased Ivy's unrest. But she held her twisting secret inside. Her season was about to change. It would be her turn to leave. Ivy couldn't wait to get out of Coffey, to escape the town forced to betray her by the silent threat of Violet Taylor. She had been robbed of her mother. Grandma had no right. Grandmas were grandmas. She needed a real mother.

Ivy didn't blame her mother for leaving and not coming back. It just strengthened her connection to the image she had of her mother. Ivy knew that Coffey's brick-tiled streets and gently rolling farmland offered a strong, sturdy life, but she considered her mother breaking free an act of courage. She understood her unrest. Leaving Coffey was the smartest thing her mother could have done. But why did her mother leave her behind?

Ivy would take cover until her swirling emotions calmed,

then she would venture into the unknown. But she didn't even really know where to begin.

Eighteen-year-old Ivy remained in Coffey through the summer, helping Uncle Walter while his knee healed. The years of walking his mail route had taken their toll. He was only forty-seven, so now with his knee repaired, he could continue working a few more years before he retired. Ivy didn't understand why Russell couldn't help him sometimes, but he worked most days at the post office and kept to himself, eating his meals at the Coffey Shop.

Although she begrudgingly stayed busy taking care of Uncle Walter and Grandma, Ivy resented the demands made on her from the very people who had kept her mother away from her. They had no right to make those decisions for her.

Accepting the loss of the years without a mother was magnified by all the people in her life who were leaving. Maggie had already moved to Kansas City, a few hours away, where she worked at a dive restaurant and bar near her apartment. Shortly after King was killed, Maggie told Ivy it was time for her to leave. She would never find happiness in Coffey. "I already know everybody here. I need something new."

Ivy wished she could go to Kansas City with Maggie but her responsibilities were too controlling. Instead, she went with Maggie to say goodbye to her parents and her Mulberry Street community.

Virgil was the last to hug Maggie. "Now you be careful, Doll Baby. The city can swallow you up."

Tears streamed down her cheeks as Ivy drove her to the bus stop outside the Coffey Shop.

Ivy put her arm around Maggie as they waited for the bus with Maggie's one suitcase sitting at their feet. "I wish you weren't going. I'm going to be lonely in this town. It's bad enough that I didn't go to Europe this summer."

The whoosh of brakes sounded as the big Greyhound bus came around the corner and pulled up in front of the Coffey Shop. Maggie pulled away from her friend. "Ivy, just stop feeling so sorry for yourself. I'll never get to go to Europe or college. I've never had a boyfriend and some maniac just killed my dog for no reason."

"Maggie, I know. I was just . . ." Ivy hugged her.

Maggie nodded with tears in her eyes. She turned and shoved her suitcase into the bus luggage compartment before getting onto the southbound Greyhound to Kansas City without a glance at Ivy.

As the bus took off, Nick flew out of the door to his father's law office and ran beside the bus, waving and making faces as it pulled away down Main Street. "Bye, Maggie! Remember, the Supreme Court said you could!"

Maggie smiled and waved at Nick and then she looked back and waved at Ivy with tears running down her cheeks.

Nick worked full-time at his father's law office that summer. The only time Ivy saw him was at night when he played baseball at the park. He had been accepted into New York University and would be leaving soon. Everyone was leaving her.

Ivy felt relieved as the final weeks of summer passed and her escape grew closer. Uncle Walter's knee healed and her obligations at home were almost over. She would soon be free.

Nick told her that Raven and Jesse were back from their

trip to Europe. He'd seen them at the ballpark. As much as Ivy didn't want to see either of them, she kept an eye out for them just so she could make sure to ignore them.

On her nightly run to Beecher Pond, Ivy could smell honeysuckle in the muggy summer air. She wondered if every town had its own smell. As she rounded the second hill on the gravel road, the weeds beside the road moved in front of her and Jesse walked into the road. She jogged past him. He jogged up beside her.

"I'm back."

"So, I see."

"Raven and I aren't together. All I could think about was you the whole time."

Ivy stopped running and stared at Jesse. Then she melted into his arms. He was home and she could start her life.

A few days before she planned to leave for the University of Iowa in Iowa City, over four hours from Coffey, Ivy ate a late supper with Grandma and Uncle Walter. It wasn't far enough away for Ivy, but Jesse had convinced her it was a fun college town with a great football team, so Ivy agreed to go.

"I can't wait to get out of here," she said.

Grandma reached over and gently put her hand on top of Ivy's. "I've watched many young people leave, but most of them come back home, at least in their hearts. Someday, you'll realize that Coffey is more a part of you than you know. Wherever you go, your future is always right in front of you."

But Ivy knew that living somewhere else would ease her restlessness. She pulled her hand away from Grandma's touch. "Well, not me. There's nothing here for me. I'm leaving and never coming back."

Grandma's face grimaced, as if someone had struck her. Uncle Walter shook his finger at Ivy. "Don't be so ungrateful. You're just upset because Nick's leaving for New York tomorrow."

"No. I just want to get on with my life. Nothing's real here," Ivy said, taking a deep breath. "I know my mother's alive. You've lied to me my whole life. Why? Why didn't you tell me the truth? I trusted you."

Grandma stared at Ivy, taken aback. "I did what I thought was best."

"Well, it wasn't."

Uncle Walter took a step toward Ivy. "Ivy . . ."

"No, just stop. You lied to me, too," said Ivy, pointing her finger at him.

Grandma sighed. "Maybe I was wrong, but we have to make decisions for our children. Your road may lead you out of here, but this town is filled with many good people and good things. Who's to say that the people who leave have better lives than the ones who stay? I think I made the right decision for you but . . ."

"Well, I need something I can't get here—the truth. I want my life to make sense. I've got to try and find out who I really am."

Grandma cleared her throat and used the kitchen chair to grab onto as she stood up. "Of course." She shuffled to the back porch and sank into the comfort of her old wooden rocking chair.

Ivy went up to her room and started packing for school, although her long-awaited departure from Coffey was still a few days away. Her clothes were in piles around her room.

Uncle Walter entered and started neatly refolding Ivy's clothes with perfect creases. "Looks like you're ready to go."

"More than ready. I'm going to die if I have to stay here."

Uncle Walter paused as he folded a pair of jeans along the seams. "Ivy."

"I'm not going to apologize. It's how I feel."

"It's not that." Uncle Walter leaned against the end of Ivy's sleigh bed, taking the strain off his newly mended knee. He sank down on the edge of the mattress.

"You're right about telling the truth. So, I'm going to tell you something that's been weighing heavily on me."

Ivy looked up briefly from sorting her clothes. "What?"

Uncle Walter glanced at the door and then back at Ivy. "The doctor found a lump in her other breast. Her cancer's back."

Ivy broke out in a cold sweat. The clothes in her hand fell to the floor. "No. No! She said she wouldn't die till I was ready."

"She's not going to die, yet. She's going to fight it like she did before. She's getting surgery and doing chemo. But I thought you should know." Uncle Walter slowly stood up. He put his hand on her shoulder. "Her chances are good. She caught it early."

"Why does this always happen to me? Why can't I get a break?" Ivy said.

"It's not all about you, Ivy. She didn't want me to tell you because she knows how much it means to you to get out of Coffey. But maybe you're right, the truth has a power of its own."

Ivy's hands trembled and she felt faint. Time stopped and the motion of the earth stilled. Her mind surged with anger at her Grandmother for keeping her mother from her, but her heart froze with the overwhelming dread of Grandma dying, the crushing fear of losing herself, and the dark disappointment of life's circumstances. Her escape waited for her just a few days away. But plans change and that pulled her into a deep sadness.

Ivy slumped into Uncle Walter's comforting embrace. "I'm so sorry. I didn't mean it."

He patted her. "I know."

She stared over his comforting shoulder and out the window. The clouds covered the moonlight, and Ivy's world turned gray.

The next day, although Uncle Walter tried to talk her out of it, Ivy unpacked her carefully folded clothes and enrolled at nearby Warner College. Her future elsewhere would have to wait. Grandma's cancer was back, and chemo would be rough.

Ivy drove to Jesse's house to say goodbye. She had called him that morning to tell him that she couldn't go to college away from Coffey. She knew he wouldn't stay, so, she didn't even ask him. She turned onto his block and saw Jesse loading his stuff into Judy's car. As he shut the trunk, she spotted Raven getting into the back seat. Ivy caught Jesse's eye, but she drove on by without stopping. There was nothing left to say.

In the evening, Ivy said goodbye to Nick, the last of her friends to leave. They sat on the Coffey Shop bench near his father's law office on the town square, waiting for the bus to take him to New York City. His father was worried about his wife and had decided to remain at home to comfort Nick's mother. It was not easy for her to let go of her only child.

Ivy told Nick that Grandma's cancer was back, and that she had decided to stay in Coffey and go to Warner College. Nick's face flashed to worry. "I'm so sorry. Why didn't you tell me? I told her goodbye yesterday and she didn't say anything about it."

"I just found out."

They could see the bus approaching a few blocks away.

Nick reached into his pocket. "Hold out your hand."

Ivy opened her palm and Nick dropped the keys to the poorly-built camper into her hand. "Take care of the Monstrosity-atrocity for me? She wouldn't get the respect she deserves from anyone else."

Ivy smiled. "Sure, Nick. You can't let a wily beast like her go to waste."

She couldn't remember a time without Nick. Their lives were intertwined, and for a moment she felt her future slip from her fingers, as if she was falling from a sheer cliff. She never did like to stand on the edge. To be stuck in Coffey without Nick would be unbearable. She wrapped her arms around her friend in desperation. "Nick, stay here and go to college with me."

Nick hugged her back. "I can't. Things are set."

"Please don't leave me."

"You left me the day Jesse got here on that bus."

"Oh, Nick. I'm sorry. You know I love you."

She leaned in to kiss him on the lips. He turned his head and kissed her cheek.

"Yeah, but not enough."

She kissed his cheek as the 9:18 Greyhound bus pulled up to the Coffey Shop curb. Black diesel exhaust filled the air. The headlights of the bus flashed like fireflies in the woods.

Ivy stared at Nick as he stood up, like she was seeing him for the first time. He gave his bags to the driver, who threw them in the huge open belly of the bus that would take Nick away from Coffey.

Nick stood at the top of the steps, just like Jesse did when he had arrived in Coffey so many years ago.

"Don't worry. I'll be back."

Then he threw back his head and howled like Buckshot's "oh, no." Nick's voice echoed across the empty Main Street. Then he ducked his head and entered the lighted bus. Everything else turned dark for Ivy.

Ivy smiled and waved, but then the sadness flooded in and the tears fell. She stood in the middle of the deserted street as the huge bus drove off. She felt a strong urge to get in the Monstrosity and chase after the bus; to follow Nick no matter what happened. But her feet wouldn't move. Grandma needed her. She watched the bright tail lights of the bus disappear around the town square. Then it was gone and she was alone. Coffey was her life's curse.

She thought it was weird that Nick headed toward a different path and a future far away, when she was the one who desperately wanted to leave. His departure ripped the last piece of security from her.

When the loud engine of the bus could no longer be heard, she walked back down the sidewalk. She looked up and saw Russell waving to her from his apartment above the Coffey Shop, Bertha's old home.

Although the Coffey Shop was closed, Ivy knew it was unlocked. She went in through the alley to get one of Miss Shirley's pies waiting for her on the counter. She would need a little rhubarb pie to get her through her heartache. By the time Ivy reached the back door to the restaurant, Russell was there.

"Getting some pie?" he asked as he held the door open for her and followed her in.

She nodded. "Rhubarb."

"Nice choice. Nick left, huh?"

"Yeah."

"You know, Ivy, since you don't have any friends left and I never had any, maybe we could be friends now."

Ivy looked at her cousin. He was right. They shared so much

in common, including an unexplainable family. She nodded and smiled. "Want a piece of pie?"

"Sure."

They sat down at a table in the empty restaurant. Ivy cut into the pie and they talked and made fun of Uncle Tommy.

When they were done, Ivy drove the Monstrosity through the deserted streets of Coffey toward home, where Grandma and Uncle Walter waited for her. Maggie was gone. Jesse was gone. Nick was gone. Old people and Russell were all she had left.

That night, Ivy watched TV with Grandma and Uncle Walter until they fell asleep upright in their chairs. Uncle Walter snorted as his chin bobbed down on his chest in slumber. Grandma's head tipped back; her mouth fell open and her snoring filled the room. It was strange, because Grandma never slept.

Ivy could no longer hear the TV over their sleep noises. Feeling trapped like a caged bird, she got up to have another piece of pie. Slipping outside to the back porch for some air, she slumped in the glider with her feet resting on the porch railing. She ate the last slice of pie and realized how Patty felt. Food was the only pleasure she had left to fill her empty heart.

The darkness coaxed a bat out into the night. Dark wings flapped and the bat swooped down to eat mosquitoes and other insects, inspecting each bug closely as if examining it for imperfections. The bat flew in the darkness by some inner radar, circling low and flying close to the ground. Ivy sat up, afraid it would not be able to make it, but the shadowy mammal regained its height and disappeared into the night, blending in with the dark sky.

The last few birds pecked at the seeds in the feeder as

night settled over the hills of the Iowa prairie. Ivy's aloneness consumed the evening air. "It's just you and me now," she said to the birds.

But they flew away, startled by the sound of her voice. "Oh, so you're leaving me, too? Why not? Everyone else has."

The glider swayed. Ivy's shoulders slumped as she gazed into the darkening woods. The squirrels chattered somewhere hidden among the trees where they spied on her and laughed. Her life had reached an all-time low. Perhaps it was time to find her mother and find out the truth. Maybe somewhere along the way, she would find herself and escape the shackles of Coffey. Maybe that hope was all she had left.

PART IV

HEARTS HAVE NO SKIN COLOR

(1979-1980)

Chapter 25

LOSING TOUCH

In the autumn, the bright hues of the fall leaves swirled in colorful twisters of wind and dust, hurrying to go nowhere, just enjoying the dance. After leaving Coffey, Ivy's friends had found new lives and seldom returned home. Ivy didn't stop thinking about Jesse but she was still mad at him for betraying her again. Like her uncles, she found it hard to let go of deep-seated resentment. After all, holding a grudge was a family tradition.

Ivy was twenty-one and a senior at Warner College. She would graduate that spring. Grandma's other breast had been removed, the chemo was declared successful, and her hair was slowly growing back. Violet Taylor had fought cancer again and won. With Grandma's recovery, Ivy's world would open up after graduation. She didn't need Jesse. She didn't need anyone. She would strike out on her own.

Since she had found out that her mother was alive, Ivy had searched the phone books, calling or writing to anyone with a similar name. But everything was a dead end, as if her mother had fallen into a secret world hidden from the little girl she left behind. Ivy's life was such a strange puzzle and she was determined to find the missing piece.

Although Maggie moved to Kansas City right after King died, Ivy thought she would still see her a lot. But as the years passed, Maggie came home less and less. Ivy felt her pulling away. Miles Jones, Maggie's new boyfriend she'd met at the restaurant and bar where she worked, consumed most of her time. But she came home to Coffey for a visit as the fall winds of change blew in, pushing away the warm air of summer.

Ivy parked the Monstrosity and she and Maggie went into the Coffey Shop for lunch. Miss Shirley put her hands on her wide hips and stared at Maggie. "Well, if it isn't the big city girl. I haven't seen you in a month of Sundays. How are you, Miss It?"

Maggie looked around the restaurant as if expecting Conrad Thrasher to be lurking on a nearby stool, challenging her right to be there. "Good."

"What's this?" Miss Shirley said as she touched Maggie's hair. Maggie stopped straightening her hair and let her natural curls grow into a small afro. "I told you, girl, curls drive men crazy."

Ivy laughed. She remembered her first visit to the Jacksons' barbershop. "Nothing finer than a real natural black woman."

"Mm-hmm. Now you talking some sense." Miss Shirley turned back to cleaning the grill.

Ivy looked in the rotating glass pastry keeper to see which pies were left. A fly landed on the glass. Ivy flicked it away. "So, what's your new boyfriend's name again? Leon Wilson?" Ivy swung her leg over a red stool and sat down. She smiled and ran her hands slowly down her hair.

Miss Shirley wiggled her finger in the air. "Stop. Don't say it."

Ivy smiled. "Wig."

Miss Shirley scowled and then bent over with laughter. She

flipped her white apron at Ivy. "Oh, go away." She turned to Maggie. "Now seriously, City Girl. Is that Miles guy still your main squeeze?"

Maggie blushed and patted her hair. "Yes. Going natural was his idea. He's teaching me to be black."

Miss Shirley scraped the grill with a big metal spatula. "Girl, you was born like that. There ain't nothing he can teach you about that."

"He says that some black people, like my mom and dad, have forgotten how to be black. He doesn't really like white people very much."

"Neither does Virgil Jackson, but he likes me," Ivy said.

Maggie shook her head. "But you're not a Doll Baby, are you?"

"Not yet, but someday I'll be the first Caucasian Doll Baby."

A fly buzzed by Ivy's ear.

Maggie rolled her eyes. "Don't hold your breath."

Ivy exaggeratedly took a deep breath, puffing out her cheeks. Maggie reached out with two fingers and pushed in Ivy's cheeks. They both laughed. For a moment, Ivy felt like everything was the same.

Ivy and Maggie ordered tenderloins, French fries, and Green Rivers, their favorite drink since they were little girls. Some things hadn't changed.

Miss Shirley pulled the wax paper off the tenderloin patties and tossed the meat in the fryer. They sizzled and popped as they bobbed in the hot grease.

Ivy took a drink of her Green River. "So when will we finally get to meet your white-people-hating boyfriend?"

"See, that's why you meeting Miles isn't a good idea."

Ivy reached over and hugged Maggie. "I'm sorry. I was just kidding."

Maggie pulled away.

Miss Shirley slid a red plastic basket with a tenderloin sandwich and fries in front of Maggie. The pork tenderloin hung out beyond the sides of the bun. "Here's your food, my soul sister."

Ivy pouted. "What about me?"

Miss Shirley gave a little bow and set Ivy's basket down. "Here's your food, Snowflake."

"And future Doll Baby," Ivy said as she took a bite of the steaming sandwich and set it back down to cool. "Hey, Maggie, maybe I could drive the Monstrosity down and see you some weekend."

The fly buzzed in front of Ivy's face. She swatted at it, waving her hand close to Maggie's face. Maggie flinched, raising her arms to protect herself. She cleared her throat. "Well, I don't know. I'm pretty busy right now." She took a bite of a fry and dipped it in the ketchup. "I'm moving to a new place and you've got college."

Ivy glanced at Miss Shirley who raised her eyebrows and clicked her tongue. Ivy picked up her sandwich and nibbled around the edges. "But I'll see you at Christmas, right?"

Maggie kept eating her fries with her head down and she didn't answer. Things had definitely changed. Ivy set her sandwich back in the basket. She no longer felt hungry.

Shortly after her visit to Coffey, Maggie stopped returning Ivy's phone calls. The loneliness of not having Maggie to talk to overwhelmed her. The months passed.

Max, still working as a mechanic at the Mobil Station, overhauled the Monstrosity's engine and tuned it up. It still ran well. So, one weekend, out of loneliness and frustration, Ivy climbed into the truck with the homemade camper and drove to Kansas City without telling Maggie.

Ivy honked as she pulled up outside Maggie's two-story apartment building at the new address Pinky had given her. Maggie appeared at the front window of the second floor.

Ivy got out of the truck. She jumped up and down and waved, puckering her lips and blowing Maggie exaggerated kisses. The front door to the building was open and Ivy dashed up to Maggie's apartment, taking two steps at a time. Maggie stood in the doorway, her face swollen and her eyes puffy. Her hunched shoulders seemed to be pulled down by many layers of clothes.

At the doorway, the apartment smelled like burned toast and Ivy could see stacks of dishes piled high in the sink of the tiny kitchen. Huge metal support posts were inconveniently situated in the middle of the open room.

"Maggie, what's going on?"

"Ivy, why are you here? You shouldn't have come." Maggie's matted hair stuck out at strange angles. Her skin flaked ashy. Maggie looked over her shoulder down the hallway leading to the other room. Her fingers danced nervously in her palms.

"You don't answer my calls. Are you okay?" Ivy asked, grabbing Maggie's arm.

Maggie grimaced at Ivy's touch. "Yeah. Everything's okay." Dark rims circled her eyes.

"Maggie, have you looked in the mirror lately?" Ivy reached out to touch Maggie's face.

Maggie flinched and pulled away.

"You look like Rosie Buckley."

Maggie looked away and Ivy's smile faded. "What's wrong? It's your boyfriend, isn't it?"

Maggie took a step back. "No. You will just never understand what it's like to be black." She glanced behind her down the hallway of the dark and dirty apartment.

"You're right about that, but I know what it's like to be your friend."

"I wasn't your friend. I was your lifetime Chickadee community service project."

For a moment Ivy stood still, stunned by the accusation. "Are you out of your mind? Have you forgotten who we are?"

Maggie shook her head. "You don't know who I am. I'm just beginning to know who I am." She leaned against the door frame.

Ivy grabbed Maggie's arm, but Maggie pulled away. Ivy swallowed hard, and her eyes filled with tears. "I miss you, Maggie. Everyone's gone."

Maggie tossed her head back and looked at Ivy. "Well, I'm glad I'm gone. I'm sick of living in your world. Mulberry Street. Sectioned off like we don't belong."

A door opened and heavy footsteps thudded down the hallway. A tall, good-looking black man with dreadlocks pulled back in a ponytail came up behind Maggie who still blocked the doorway. He yawned. His brown eyes rimmed with dark circles were hazy and distant. Ivy felt a sudden rush of fear and a desperate desire to flee. She turned to Maggie.

"I agree with you."

Maggie suddenly cringed and clutched her stomach, doubling over.

"Maggie, what's wrong?" Ivy stepped protectively toward her friend, but Miles stuck out his arm in front of Maggie. His forearm showed a tattoo of a hammer dripping blood. The words "Alliance" circled the hammer. He leaned menacingly toward Ivy.

"Listen, Ellie May, why don't you get back in that Beverly

Hillbillies truck of yours and get on out of here before something real bad happens to you."

Still holding her stomach, Maggie looked up. "Please just go away, Ivy."

Miles jerked Maggie back inside the apartment by her hair. Then he stepped out in the hall, pushed Ivy against the wall and leaned in close. The vein in his neck bulged. "You heard her. Get out."

He stepped back into the apartment and slammed the door. Ivy leaned against the wall and breathed deeply. She tentatively took a few steps forward, resting her hands and her forehead on Maggie's apartment door, unable to leave. Maggie was in danger. She took a deep breath and pounded on the door with her fists. "Maggie! Maggie, please. Fly like a bird!"

Inside footsteps pounded and then the door locked, shutting out all hope for Maggie's flight. Cold loneliness swept through Ivy like an icy winter rain. The same kind of bone-chilling emptiness she felt when she thought about her mother and father.

Ivy waited in the cab of the truck outside Maggie's apartment in case she changed her mind. The curtain in Maggie's apartment moved once. But when it got dark, Ivy gave up and drove home.

Later that night, back in Coffey, Ivy stopped by Russell's apartment as she drove back into town. She needed someone to complain to who wouldn't give her wise sayings, just sympathy.

They sat at Russell's round kitchen table, drinking Dr. Pepper and eating strawberry Twizzlers. The hollow ache of losing her friends and the frustration of being stuck in a town that wouldn't let go, overwhelmed her. She pulled the heart on her necklace along the chain from side to side. If only she could find her mother. Her mother would understand.

"Have you ever heard your dad or mom talk about my mother?"

"Sure."

Ivy gently touched Russell's arm. "What'd they say?"

"Just that they had to get married. She was pregnant. My mom called her a harlot and my dad said being with Barbara came at a high price."

"How come you never told me that?"

"You never asked."

When Ivy got home that night, Grandma shuffled down the hall. Her Keds tennis shoes with the holes flopped untied and she used them like slippers now. Her soft magenta robe billowed over her body. She had lost some weight.

"What's wrong?" Grandma asked as she motioned Ivy into the kitchen where the tea kettle was on the stove.

Ivy sat down at the table and pushed a strand of her hair out of her eyes. "My life isn't working out like I planned."

Grandma sat down and patted Ivy's back. "It never does, my dear. It never does. But believe it or not, that's what keeps life interesting."

The tea kettle whistled. Ivy got up and poured the water for Grandma's tea. "There's no place for me anymore. The world's moved on without me. I feel like I'm just sort of fading away."

She set the steaming mug in front of Grandma, who added a little milk and stirred. "Everyone finds their own path through life. But it's not where you end up that's important, but how you got there."

Grandma dunked the tea bag in the water and then twisted the bag around the spoon. Ivy sat down again. She traced her fingers in a circle on the table. "My path is a circle around

Coffey. There's like an undertow that keeps me from leaving. It's dragging me under."

"Sometimes things don't work out like we planned," said Grandma, watching the steam rising from the teacup. "But sometimes what we want can be disappointing when we get it. And other times, life's disappointments turn out to be blessings. Those are the seasons of life."

"I need to ask you a question, Grandma. Was my mother pregnant when she married my dad?"

Grandma looked at Ivy, stirring her tea. "Yes. But having you was the best thing to ever happen to Robert. It gave him a purpose he never had. He grew up for you."

Grandma sipped her tea. "Ivy, I've been thinking. I'm feeling fine nowadays. I'm back to my old surly self. You go ahead and get out of Coffey for good. There's no reason for you to stay around here anymore. I'm good. Really."

Ivy hugged her Grandmother and snuggled in the folds of Grandma's soft robe. Maybe she could get out of Coffey after all. "Are you sure?"

"Indeedy."

Later that night, Ivy stared out her bedroom window in 4120, which had been her home for her entire life. She grieved for the comfort of childhood and her friendships with Jesse, Nick, and Maggie. But her heart filled with hope that a new world waited for her just a few months away. She would be free of Coffey. And soon, she hoped, she would find her mother.

Chapter 26

THE WOMAN AT THE WINDOW

The December wind blew the snow in chaotic patterns, dancing like ghosts across Mulberry Street. The mulberry trees shivered as the cold gale whispered through their bare branches.

Ivy stopped by the weekend barbershop on Mulberry Street. She opened the door to the cozy living room of the Jacksons' house where most of the neighborhood had gathered. "Hey, everybody."

Max made the sound of an alarm into his closed fist as he flapped his long fingers. "Honkey in the house."

Virgil pointed at Ivy. "Look out, it's the Caucasian invasion."

Miss Shirley motioned to Ivy. "Hey, Snowflake. Come on in."

Ivy laughed and handed Miss Shirley an envelope. "Special Christmas delivery from Grandma."

"Bless her heart," said Miss Shirley as she slipped the envelope into her pocket.

Ivy hung her coat on the coat rack as if she was a regular at the Mulberry Street barbershop. Otis sat on the stool in the middle of the room getting his hair cut. "Come tell us a story, Ivy."

Nine-year-old Justin smiled at Ivy. Justin was turning into a handsome boy. He reminded her of his big brother, Ben.

Thelma Sampson sat on the end of the couch, her feet dangling above the floor, but when Ivy entered, she scooted off the couch and stomped out of the house, slamming the door behind her.

"I'm guessing she still doesn't like me," Ivy said as she watched Thelma's dramatic exit.

Ruth rolled her eyes and swished her hand through the air. "She doesn't like anyone."

Virgil raised his eyebrows. "But she especially doesn't like you."

"Why?" said Ivy.

"Because white peoples get away with stuff," Virgil said. "That don't seem right. A white man can kill his wife and get away with it, but Otis and Ben get arrested for something your uncle and his friend did."

Ivy remembered when Otis and Ben were locked up because of Weston's made-up charges.

"Walter and Ivy were the ones that sprung us," said Otis.

"Our freedom shouldn't depend on the charity of white people," Virgil said.

Ivy agreed. She thought that life shouldn't rely on other people's consciousness but on the community of truth. She sat down on the couch beside Virgil. "You said a white man can kill his wife and get away with it. Were you talking about Conrad Thrasher? Did you really see him throw his wife's body in his pond?"

All the conversations in the barbershop stopped.

"Where'd you hear that?" Virgil asked. "I told your Grandmother not to tell anyone."

"Grandma didn't tell me. Maggie did, when we were little."

"She shouldn't have told you that."

"Grandma knew?"

"She can keep a secret. That man has too much power in this town."

"So, is it true?"

Virgil didn't answer.

Ruth finished cutting Otis's hair. She brushed the tiny curls of hair off the cape on his shoulders. The clips of hair landed on the floor in dark half-moons. "Course it's true," she said.

Ivy looked at Virgil. "Did anybody else see him do it?"

"Doubt it. Except the other person in the house," Virgil said. "I was out chopping wood at Deadman's Woods near that clearing at the cemetery, but there was somebody at the window."

Ivy's eyes grew wide and her mouth dropped open. "Who?"

"Couldn't tell."

Ivy shivered. The barbershop hushed, but the wind whistled around the corners of the house, blowing its power across the Iowa prairie.

Otis finally broke the silence as he stood up. "Conrad Thrasher used to be a pretty decent guy. That's how he first got elected mayor." He brushed a few hairs from his neck.

"Yeah, but something changed after he killed his wife," Miss Shirley said.

"That's what I'm saying. He never was right in the head after that," said Max.

Ruth shook her black smock. "Let's talk about something else."

Just then, a train barreled behind the house. Virgil grabbed the coffeepot so it wouldn't fall off the table from the rattling vibrations. The screeching howl of the train faded as it raced on into the distance. Otis moved his toothpick to the other corner of his mouth and cleared his throat. "Well, Ivy, have you heard? Maggie isn't coming home for Christmas."

"Not surprised," Ivy said.

"I guess we're not good enough for her no more. She be acting mighty uppity," Virgil said.

Ivy shook her head. "No. It's her Alliance boyfriend. He's—"

"He's in the Alliance?" Otis asked. "How do you know?"

"He has a tattoo on his arm with a hammer dripping blood."

"Maggie's got herself into a real bad fix," Ruth said.

Ivy picked up the broom resting against the wall and began sweeping up the hair on the floor. Maybe she shouldn't have said anything.

The wind howled outside the barbershop, wailing in agony from its strength. Otis looked down at his long, callused hands. His smile went flat. "Maggie's pregnant."

Ivy let the broom drop to the floor. Her heart pounded wildly. Now there were two people who might be in danger.

That night after supper, Grandma sent Ivy back to Mulberry Street to give the Nortons one of Grandma's sweet pumpkin pastry rolls, a bottle of Haig & Haig scotch for Otis, and a pair of electric sewing scissors for Pinky. Ivy stood outside their house feeling fearful for Maggie.

The front door opened and Pinky appeared in an apron smudged with flour and molasses. Her eyes had dark circles under them, but her smile was bright when she saw Ivy. She held out her arms. "Ivy dear. Come on in," Pinky said as she coughed.

Ivy walked into her embrace. She followed Pinky into the living room and sat on the same couch that she'd sat on with Maggie and Miss Shirley to watch Leon Wilson sing and dance.

"Otis. Ivy's here," Pinky called.

Ivy sat next to her on the couch and handed her the gifts. "Merry Christmas from Grandma and me."

Otis came down the stairs as Pinky unwrapped the electric sewing scissors. "Oh, my goodness. Won't these come in handy for making my quilts?" She hugged Ivy again. "I don't make as many as I used to. I get so tired nowadays."

Otis saw the bottle of scotch with a ribbon around its neck. "I hope that has my name on it for my poker nights. In fact, I could use a little pinch right now."

Pinky leaned forward. "So, how you really doing, Ivy?"

"Grandma says she's feeling fine now. I can finally make some plans."

"Sounds wonderful," Pinky said.

"But I really miss Maggie," Ivy said.

Pinky patted Ivy's arm. "Don't worry, Ivy. She'll come back to us." Pinky gazed at the pictures of her daughter hanging on the wall, showing happier days. Pinky told Ivy she and Otis had wanted a child for over fifteen years. When she found out she was pregnant with Maggie at the age of thirty-five, she knew it might be their only chance. Although they were older parents, Pinky said Maggie gave them a new life, a new purpose. To lose her now was devastating. Maggie was their everything.

Otis rubbed his thin mustache and jabbed his finger in the air. "It's that Miles. He's a street rat. I've tried to get her to come home. I even went up there one time, but she won't leave him."

"I know," Ivy said as she shuddered, remembering Miles' cold, angry eyes. "I don't understand the Alliance and why he thinks he can tell her what to do."

"Society doesn't give young black men any control, so, they try to take it. But in the end, it takes them." Otis stood up and paced around his small family room. His hand patted the flat waves against his head. "The Alliance's got our girl."

Dark circles hung under Pinky's eyes from her worrying and sleepless nights. "Well, let's talk about something else. After all, it's almost Christmas."

"Grandma says it's been hard for you to walk," Ivy said.

Pinky sighed, rubbing her swollen ankles. "Yes. I saw your Grandma over at Miss Shirley's the other day. I'm not as young as I used to be."

"Grandma was at Miss Shirley's?"

"Miss Shirley goes and picks her up. She's been over there a lot."

Ivy looked puzzled. "With those two, you know they're up to no good."

"Poor Ivy, you got stuck here with all us old folks," Otis said.

"Well, do you feel like playing a little cards tonight? We'll just pretend it's game night down at the Rose Hill Nursing Home." Ivy laughed.

Otis pulled out the cards from the side table. "I hope my life never gets that bad. They've put Thelma in charge over there. But I'd love the chance to beat a highfalutin college girl like you."

"We need another player," said Pinky as she picked up the phone. "Let me see if Miss Shirley wants to play a couple of hands."

A few minutes later, Miss Shirley burst through the Nortons' front door without knocking. Her commanding stature filled the doorway. "Empty your pockets, suckers. I feel lucky tonight."

Ivy jumped up and waved her arm in the air. "Miss Shirley's my partner."

"Smart girl, Snowflake," said Miss Shirley, holding out her

arms. Ivy hugged her and she smelled of fresh laundry and French fries.

"Ready, girl?" Miss Shirley pretended to throw off a top hat. Then they both yelled at the same time, "Find the fight in your soul!"

They danced a few steps to the Leon Wilson groove.

Pinky laughed as she brought in a plate of gingerbread cookies. "You two."

Miss Shirley snatched a cookie off the tray as Pinky went by. "Hey. Look at this little gingerbread brother-man. He's got an afro." Miss Shirley nibbled at his head. "Oops. He just got a haircut. Now he looks like Max." Miss Shirley took another bite and held up the headless gingerbread man. "Ruth's clippers must have cut it a little too close this time."

They all laughed, and for a few hours Ivy forgot about being stuck in Coffey while the rest of the world went on without her.

When Ivy stepped out of the Nortons' house to go home, the December wind blew cold, slushy rain against her face. The freezing rain triggered an icy panic, an internal loneliness that something wasn't right.

She looked back at the warmth and safety of the Nortons' house. Miss Shirley's laugh bellowed inside. Ivy got into the Monstrosity, hoping the fear would subside but knowing it would never leave her until she left Coffey.

Nick's Merle Haggard eight-track sat in the open tape player, and she pushed it in, wishing Nick was driving and she and her friends were tumbling over each other in the back.

Chapter 27

THE BETRAYAL

A few days before Christmas, Ivy stopped in to see Judy at the Beauty Shop. Silver tinsel hung from Judy's pale pink smock. She wore the dangling Santa earrings that Ivy had given her and snapped her Doublemint gum.

"Jingle Bell Rock" played on the radio. Ivy took off her coat and grabbed Judy's hands. They danced around the shop like when Ivy was a little girl.

Judy suddenly stopped twirling, and her smile disappeared. "I wanted to tell you. They got in last night, and—"

The back door to the shop opened and Jesse and Raven entered without seeing Ivy. Jesse's arm was circled around Raven's waist as he leaned over and kissed her.

Ivy's face turned ashen.

The pair froze when they saw Ivy. Jesse's mouth fell open and Raven's usual perfect complexion, blushed a deep red. Judy looked at the floor as her Santa earrings swayed.

Ivy grabbed the edge of the pink sink to steady herself. Her mind raced. She couldn't catch her breath.

Jesse cleared his throat and smoothed out his hair. "Listen, Ivy, I've been meaning to . . . I didn't plan it."

Waves of shock shook her. She felt as if a train was rushing by her, pounding in her eardrums. Her legs wobbled. "You always plan everything."

Raven flipped her long dark hair out of her fur coat collar. "Ivy, plans change. You were here. We moved on. We didn't mean to hurt you."

Ivy took a deep breath.

"You're never leaving here. You have this weird sense of family responsibility that's going to suck you in every time. I think you're even starting to like Coffey," Jesse said.

Ivy took a deep breath, trying to contain her anger. "Yeah, I guess I have a sense of family responsibility. But I will leave here someday, and when I do, I'll know I didn't leave someone behind uncared for. Life isn't where you end up—it's how you got there."

She picked up her coat and put it on, feeling like her legs wouldn't hold her. Judy's eyes filled with tears as she followed Ivy to the front of the store.

"Ivy, I'm so sorry. Jesse never really had a father, you know."

"Neither did I." Ivy kissed Judy's cheek. "Merry Christmas, Judy."

"Merry Christmas, Ivy." Tears ran down Judy's cheeks, smearing her usually perfect makeup.

The bells jingled as the heavy shop door shut behind her. Ivy stepped outside and stared at the blinking Christmas lights, tracing the outline of the store roofs and doorways. But the color drained from her world.

Ivy finally understood that her chance for a future with Jesse had blown away on the winter wind like the last dead leaves of autumn. Not everyone you love will love you back the way you want. The older Ivy got, the more Grandma was right. She took a deep breath and tramped down the sidewalk as Christmas carols filled the air through the town's loudspeakers. She struggled with the loss of everything she'd ever hoped for, while her destiny flickered like the blinking holiday lights strung along Coffey's town square.

She glanced in the library window, bare of any holiday decorations, not even a snowman. Edna Jean said the holiday hoopla seemed unnecessary folderol and Ivy began to understand her point. She could see Edna Jean inside the dark library, spraying lemon polish on the tables. No matter how Edna Jean tried, she could not stop the unending dust.

Ivy trudged down the sidewalk and opened the door to the Coffey Shop. Bertha Tuttle sat by herself at the front table, with her lipstick smudged, sipping her coffee and staring into space. Ivy turned around and walked out. The cool wind hit her. She understood Edna Jean and Bertha now. Despite Ivy's determination to get out of Coffey, she remained trapped, betrayed, and abandoned just like them. She turned around and hurried up the stairs to Russell's apartment before anyone could see her tears and humiliation, and feel pity for her.

Chapter 28

THE DEATH GRIP OF LOVE

The farmers detasseled their corn, walked their beans, and baled their hay. The end of the summer brought hope for good crops and cooler days, and for Ivy, a chance to get out of Coffey. She was twenty-two and had graduated from Warner College in the spring. Her plan was to leave Coffey. But where should she go?

Grandma began to sleep all night and sometimes during the day. Despite what Grandma and Uncle Walter said, Ivy could tell she was slowing down.

Ivy spent the summer working at the alumni office at Warner College. One humid August evening, she played cards with Grandma and Uncle Walter until they went to bed. But it was still early, so she sat by herself under the covered back porch. It began to rain, cooling off the summer heat. A cat's distant meow sounded like a baby crying. Ivy sighed. Maggie must have already given birth to her baby. Ivy tried to put it out of her mind. Maggie was just one more missing piece in her life. There were so many now. The phone rang inside the house.

She turned out the porch light and hurried to answer it, so it wouldn't wake Grandma.

"Ivy, it's me. You've got to help me," Maggie, out of breath, whispered.

"Maggie, what's wrong?"

"Miles is on a rampage. You've got to come and help me. I'm at the restaurant where I work. I wouldn't ask you after what I said and everything, but I'm all alone and I'm scared. I've called everyone on Mulberry Street and nobody answered."

"I'm on my way. I'll be there as soon as I can. Sit tight. Are you okay?"

Maggie's voice trembled. "Yes, but Ivy, please hurry. He's got my baby."

Ivy gasped. Miles had the baby. Fear took hold of her and she couldn't breathe.

It was still drizzling, so Ivy grabbed Uncle Walter's old tan trench coat. She got in the Monstrosity and sped down Interstate 35. The truck's headlights cut through the dark night as she hurried to reach Maggie, not knowing what to expect when she got there.

After an hour and half of driving, it began pouring rain a few miles outside of Kansas City. A Greyhound bus passed Ivy's camper, splashing her windshield and obscuring her vision. When the wipers pushed the water away, she could see the passengers peering out into the dark from the lighted bus windows. Ivy stared at the bus through the rain. Her mother, Maggie, and Nick had all left on a bus and cold goosebumps crept over her as the bus roared past in a blinding splash.

It was the middle of the night when Ivy pulled into the empty parking lot of the restaurant and bar not too far from Maggie's apartment. She hoped she wasn't too late. Maggie was huddled in a corner of a phone booth by the closed bar as the rain fell.

She looked up. "Ivy, you came."

"Of course I came." Ivy opened the truck door and Maggie

got in. She stared at her friend's swollen eye and the dried blood on her cut lip. "Hey, you okay?"

Maggie nodded, and they hugged each other. "What happened?"

"I told Miles I was leaving him, and he went crazy. I've never seen him this bad. He wouldn't let me have Carly. He said he would kill us both if I took her. And he would have, so I left to let him cool down."

"Let's get out of here and call the police. They'll help us."

Maggie didn't move. "No, you don't know Miles. If he sees the police, he'll hurt her. I know he will. He hates the police."

Ivy shook her head. "I've got a real bad feeling about this."

"Please, Ivy. She's just a baby. I've got to get her back. Miles usually goes to his friend's house in the evenings to get high. He probably just left Carly in her crib. If we go get her now, we'll be gone by the time he gets back."

Ivy rested her head in her hands for a moment. The cold goosebumps of icy dread returned, but a baby should not be left behind. Ivy raised her head and nodded. "Okay."

Maggie's hands trembled. "Thanks, Ivy. I knew you would help me."

"Sure, Doll Baby." Ivy hugged Maggie, relieved to have her back.

The darkness added to the eerie emptiness as they drove to Maggie's rundown Kansas City neighborhood. They pulled up at the side of the apartment building, which loomed shadowy and quiet. A few broken children's toys lay abandoned in the yard.

They opened the front door and crept up the stairs. Maggie's hand shook as she tried to put the key in the lock. She dropped the key. A door closed inside an apartment. Ivy froze for a moment before silently picking up the key. She unlocked the door and slowly pushed it open.

The dark apartment's only light glowed from a night light in the baby's room in the back, casting a hazy glow over the dreary furnishings. Dirty dishes, silverware, and days-old food covered the kitchen sink and counters. It smelled like the rotting garbage mounds of Coffey's town dump.

Maggie motioned for Ivy to leave the lights off. They walked around the steel poles inconveniently placed in the middle of the room and crept along the hallway toward Carly's room. Each footstep and floor creak echoed in the depths of the still apartment. When they reached Carly's eerily lit room, Ivy's heart stopped. She gasped in horror. The baby's wrists were tied to the bars of the crib with dirty sweat socks. Silver duct tape covered the baby's mouth. But somehow the baby still slept, as if she was used to this cruel restraint.

Maggie carefully released Carly's wrists and gently pulled the silver tape off of her mouth. A red square mark was left after she removed the tape, but she didn't seem too surprised to find her daughter restrained that way.

Maggie wrapped the baby in an old hooded sweatshirt she found on the floor. Carly stirred and her sleepy eyes fluttered open. They hurried out of the room and made their way back down the long hall. A muffled thud, like the ghostly sounds of Reuben's farmhouse, sounded behind them.

A closet door in the hallway suddenly swung open, hitting Ivy from behind and knocking her to the floor. Miles jumped out and grabbed the baby out of Maggie's arms.

"Don't take Carly. Please, Miles."

Miles dangled the baby by her arm and she began to scream. His unruly dreadlocks added to his wild appearance and his drug-hazed green eyes seemed to glow in the dim hallway.

Maggie lunged at him. "Don't hurt my baby."

He raised his fist and punched Maggie in the face. She crumpled to the floor, unconscious, but the blow's force made him drop the baby. Before she could reach Carly, Miles grabbed the terrified baby off the floor. Ivy wanted to cover her ears. The baby's cries and Maggie's silence were unbearable. Ivy looked around and grabbed a serrated kitchen knife off of the cluttered kitchen counter. She pointed the knife at Miles, her hand trembling. "Give me the baby and let Maggie go."

He laughed, and his cold eyes shone like a stray alley cat in the night. "No one leaves me. Maggie's not going anywhere. Neither is this baby." Without warning, he flung Carly at the wall. Ivy dropped the knife and dove to catch the baby, hitting her head hard against the wall. Dizzy and terrified, Ivy wrapped her arms around the screaming baby. Ivy lay on the floor for a second, feeling the warm wet blood dripping down her face from the impact.

Maggie's eyes fluttered open as Miles jerked her back by her hair. She groaned.

The vein in his neck throbbed and his dreadlocks swayed as he struggled to drag Maggie over to where Ivy and the baby were huddled. Maggie wrapped her legs and arms around one of the posts in the middle of the room. "Give me the baby, or Maggie dies."

Maggie looked at Ivy and shook her head. "Fly like a bird, Ivy. Fly like a bird." Her voice sounded faint, as if she was calling from a distant world. Ivy gazed down at the crying baby in her arms. She struggled off of the floor and ran toward the door, still dizzy from hitting her head on the wall.

Miles grabbed her foot as she ran past. Ivy fell and landed on her side, protecting Carly. She kicked Miles with her legs and scooted across the floor out of his reach.

He couldn't get to Ivy and the baby without letting go of Maggie. It was just a matter of who he hated more.

Ivy scrambled to her feet. The room swirled as she tried to focus. Her head hurt. She stumbled toward the apartment door holding the baby tightly, but she hesitated at the threshold, unsure what to do.

"Go, Ivy! Save my baby," Maggie pleaded. "Fly."

As she sprinted out of the apartment, Ivy heard a dull thud against the wooden floor. She held Carly against her chest and staggered to the truck before Miles could get to them, too.

She pulled herself into the driver's seat and pulled the door shut just as Miles stumbled towards the truck. Ivy gunned it in reverse, still holding the baby tightly with one arm. Miles grabbed the door and it swung open.

But the Monstrosity squealed and sped backward out of the parking lot, dropping Miles to the pavement. Ivy put it in drive and pulled onto the street, leaving Miles on the ground and the baby saved, but Maggie was doomed.

Ivy called the police from the pay phone by the bar. When Ivy led them into the apartment, Maggie was barely alive; and Miles was long gone.

At six o'clock in the morning, Ivy left Maggie's room at St. Joseph Medical Center. She needed to stretch her legs and get a hot cup of tea. The few stitches in her head hurt. Carly lay sleeping in a crib that the hospital staff brought down from the children's floor. Ivy left Carly and Maggie in the care of the nurses and the hospital security officer who stood outside their room.

She rode the elevator to the cafeteria in the basement. The elevator door wobbled open and Ivy saw Miles standing in the hall. He spotted Ivy and sprinted to the elevator, panting and seething like a pit bull attacking. He wore a dirty, blood-stained T-shirt and his dreadlocks dripped with sweat. Ivy pounded the elevator buttons but Miles slammed his hand in between the closing doors and they opened back up.

"It's over," he said.

Ivy trembled with rage and fear. She knew Miles was capable of murder. "No, it's not. How did you find us?"

"I called the hospitals." Miles lunged at Ivy, grabbing her around the neck. He pulled her out of the elevator and forced her into the empty passageway. "If you hadn't butted in, Maggie wouldn't be hurt right now. This is all your fault."

A door opened down the hall and a big man pushing a mop in a silver rolling bucket emerged from a swinging gray metal door. Miles released Ivy, shoving her into the wall. Ivy sucked in air and grabbed the wall for support. Miles turned his back to the cleaning man who had interrupted his plan.

Miles pressed one hand against the wall by Ivy's face and the vein in his neck pulsed. "I told you no one leaves me. I'll get what belongs to me. You can count on that."

The cleaning man stepped closer to Ivy. "Miss, you okay?"

Miles turned and pushed past the man, almost knocking over the silver bucket, and dashed down the hall.

Maggie was in critical condition, floating in and out of consciousness when Otis and Pinky arrived at the hospital after their drive from Coffey.

Ivy sat by the bed, holding her hand. "Your parents are here," she whispered to Maggie.

Maggie stirred and opened her eyes.

Pinky sat down and stroked her daughter's face. Her eyes

were red and ringed with dark circles. "We're here. Don't worry."

Bandages wrapped most of Maggie's head, but some blood had soaked through, the red stains a horrifying contrast to the white bandage. She looked up at her mother and father. "I'm sorry."

"It's okay. Everything's going to be fine," Pinky said as she coughed and tried to clear her throat.

Maggie barely shook her head. "I'm not going to make it." Her breathing slowed from the effort of speaking. She grabbed Ivy's arm. "Don't let Miles get her. I want you to raise her."

Ivy's heart pounded. "Me?" She couldn't take care of Maggie's child. A baby was too much responsibility, too heavy a burden. Ivy looked at Otis and Pinky. "What about your mom and dad? They're her grandparents."

Maggie shook her head. "Everyone deserves a mother, too. You know that. She needs you."

Ivy's breathing grew shallow. "Maggie, I don't know. I don't think I can."

Maggie gazed at Ivy with her brown eyes. Ivy shook her head, feeling trapped. She searched for another way out. "I'm white, remember?"

Maggie closed her eyes for a moment, then opened them and reached out her hand. Her voice sounded faint as if she was speaking from a distance. "Hearts have no skin color. I want you to be her mother. Please promise me."

Ivy shook her head. She looked at Otis and Pinky put her arm around her. "We'll help you. You won't be alone."

Ivy sighed. There was no escaping. She touched her mother's heart necklace. Carly needed somebody; and Grandma didn't seem completely well.

"All right, Maggie. I promise. I'll never let anything bad

happen to her." But fear raced through her. Now she'd be trapped in Coffey forever. She'd need help raising the baby and she couldn't take Carly away from Otis and Pinky, the only biological family Carly had left.

Maggie died that night from head wounds inflicted by the man she loved. Ivy, at twenty-two, the same age as Barbara when she had Ivy, became Carly's new mother.

Chapter 29

EVERY ENDING CREATES A BEGINNING

The next night, Ivy found Grandma on the couch with one of Pinky's handmade quilts pulled up to her neck, although the house was stifling hot. Grandma raised her head, her eyes wide, looking surprised. "Oh, my, it's just you, Ivy, dear."

Ivy lay the sleeping baby next to Grandma on the couch. She sat down and hugged Grandma, breathing in her lilac smell. "You okay?"

Grandma patted Ivy's arm. "Sure enough. You just looked so much like your mother standing there, it startled me for a second." Grandma looked intensely at Ivy as if trying to distinguish Ivy's features from Barbara's. "I'm just a little tired. Would you like something to eat?"

"I'm not hungry, but I could go for a cold Dr. Pepper. I went to the Baker Funeral Home with Otis to make the funeral arrangements for tomorrow. I'm going to put Carly to bed, and then let's go sit on the porch and watch the night settle in."

"That sounds good." Grandma sat up slowly. She kissed the sleeping baby and looked up at Ivy. "She's beautiful isn't she?"

Ivy nodded with tears in her eyes.

Grandma patted her cheek. "I'm sorry for all your troubles."

Ivy touched the bandage covering the stitches on her head. "Thanks, Grandma," she said, kissing her on the cheek.

She trudged upstairs and lay the baby on her bed. She

surrounded Carly with piles of pillows. She would have to buy a crib soon.

Then she met Grandma in the kitchen and poured cold pop into two glasses. "So, Grandma, can we talk about something other than death for a little while?"

"Of course."

When her hair had grown back after the chemo, Grandma let it go back to its natural color, a glossy silver-gray, like the silky pussy willows growing at Beecher Pond. Grandma put her hand on Ivy's arm.

"What did the birds have to say today?" Ivy asked.

"Well, I think Sir Lancelot and Miss Susie are in love." Grandma was talking about two thrushes she had named. "My goodness, the silly love games they play. She's so standoffish whenever he ruffles his feathers. Neither one knows the other feels the same. Some people are like that too, you know." Grandma rocked back in her chair.

Ivy smiled. "Did you outsmart the squirrels today?"

Grandma's lifetime rivalry with the squirrels had only intensified over the years. "No, but I'm determined to be rid of those bushy-tailed rodents if it's the last thing I do. Those crafty squirrels know exactly what they're doing. They dug up my potted nasturtiums this morning just to spite me."

Ivy laughed at the devious squirrels, plotting their retribution against Grandma. It felt good to think about something else besides tragedy.

They walked out to the back porch carrying their drinks. Grandma pointed to the trees. "Sometimes I see the squirrels spying on me from the woods, their beady little eyes just daring me to try and stop them. One day I looked out and one of those nasty squirrels was rocking in my chair, just having a good old time. I couldn't believe the audacity of the loathsome little fellow." She sat down in her old pine rocker.

Ivy sank into the green metal glider next to Grandma and sipped the cold Dr. Pepper, listening to the hushed night sounds. Ivy breathed in the fresh Iowa night air. She loved how the smell of the air changed as summer ended and autumn approached. The fragrance became more earthy and somewhat musty, like the smell of dry leaves crushed in the palm of a hand.

Grandma tapped the wooden floorboards with her tennis shoe. "A good porch can cure a lot of ills."

Ivy pulled up her legs and hugged her knees. "All my life I've been trying to get away from here. But leaving Coffey will have to wait. I've got Carly now."

"Yes, but you know, maybe life is what you make it. I've found it's not so much where you live, but who you share it with. You have to find your joy in the people around you."

The fireflies flickered like tiny lanterns floating on the summer breeze. Ivy slapped a mosquito on her arm, never stopping the glider's movement. "Grandma, have you had a happy life?"

"Mostly, and that's all you can ask for. But we'll both have to face the fact that my life is nearing an end." Grandma stopped rocking and she reached out her hand to Ivy. "I've always believed that every ending creates a beginning. When I die, you'll have to find another beginning. You'll be just fine. As for me, death is only a door to another world."

"I thought we weren't going to talk about death."

Grandma squeezed Ivy's hand. Her eyes grew teary and she cleared her throat. "It was a good thing you did for that baby. Children are a blessing, that's for sure." Grandma sipped her pop. "So much of life is just the willingness to take a risk and accept the consequences. Being able to make the right choice at the right time isn't always easy to do. Most of the time we just try and survive the bad times in order to get to the good times. That's what life is all about, I've found."

Ivy's feet pushed off the porch floor and the glider swayed. "I just miss Maggie so much." Ivy sighed. "You know, I guess I didn't really ask you how you felt about Carly coming to live with us."

Grandma set her empty glass on the porch floor. "You know, as you get older, your family and friends start dying, leaving holes in your life where their souls used to be. That's why old people love babies so much. Because babies fill the spaces left by the souls that are gone. I need a baby in my life, to fill up some of my holes, and maybe you do too. Yes, indeedy, she's very welcome."

"I just don't think I can do it."

"Do what, dear?"

"Raise Carly."

"Of course you can. There's something about a heart that can't help but be touched by a child."

"But I don't know what to do. I don't know what to say to her. How to protect her."

"Yes, you will, the same way we all do. You muddle through. You do the best you can."

Ivy tapped her fingers on the metal arm of the glider. "You know Conrad Thrasher will probably have something to say about you having a great-grandchild with brown skin."

Grandma's eyes flashed with anger. Her hands danced in the air. "Land sakes, I do not concern myself with what Conrad Thrasher thinks or says. And for your information, little missy, I've loved my other great-grandchild for a long time."

Ivy planted her feet on the porch and the glider stopped in mid-swing. "What does that mean?"

"Oh, *pshaw*. For crying out loud." Grandma sighed and shook her head. "Well, you should know before I go, anyway."

The porch boards creaked under the rhythm of the old pine rocker. Grandma's eyes were watery and her voice filled with emotion. "Justin Roberts is my great-grandson."

"What are you talking about?"

Grandma slapped her knees. "Oh, fiddlesticks. Justin Roberts is Angela's son. There, I've said it. It's done."

"What? Does Uncle Tommy know?"

"Heavens, no. He's the one who made her give the baby away. She got pregnant during her senior year of high school and he told her to leave town. Didn't want anyone to know. Thinks the child is somewhere far away."

"I thought she went to Europe that year."

"That's what Tommy told everybody."

"But why did you let her give Justin away?"

"That wasn't my decision. Angela needed to make her own life choices. It wasn't easy for her. She was scared to death of her father. You know how long Tommy can hold a grudge."

Ivy stood up and the old porch boards creaked. "But what about Justin? Angela was his mother."

Grandma reached for the handkerchief tucked in her stuffed bra. "Believe me, I've cried many nights over that little boy." She wiped away her tears.

Ivy paced the porch. The night breeze rustled the leaves in the trees and the air still smelled faintly of freshly cut grass. "Why didn't you tell me?"

Grandma started rocking again.

"You weren't even a teenager yourself when Justin was

born. You were the last person Angela wanted to know about the baby. She was ashamed and she figured you'd ride your bike over there and bring him home. Everyone has a right to their own secrets."

Ivy stopped her frantic pacing. "But doesn't Justin have a right to not have secrets? Doesn't he have a right to grow up with his mother?"

"We make choices for children based on what we think is best for them. Sometimes you look back and realize you were wrong, but at the time, you did the best you could. I know I've made mistakes. We all do. But Justin is with the other side of his family. Ben is his father. Miss Shirley is his grandmother and one of the best mothers on this earth. Justin grew up in good hands and I did the best I could to send Miss Shirley a little money and check up on him from time to time."

A hoot owl called from the woods and Ivy sat back down on the glider. "I can't believe no one ever told me."

"Ivy, not everything you know to be true will stay that way. But be kind when that happens. Time can change your perspective." Grandma rubbed the well-worn arms of her rocker and looked into the woods. A dog barked in the distance. "Some secrets can weigh a person down. My heart feels much lighter having told you about Justin. I'm glad you know now."

She sighed, as if releasing a heavy load. "Ivy, I'm too old now to change anything, but when I die, I want you to bring Justin home. He belongs here, too. Help Angela find her way back to him. You know you're the only one that can do it. Will you do that for me?"

"Yes, Grandma. I will do that for you and for Justin."

The owl's lonesome hooting began again.

"I know Angela was never very nice to you, but she didn't

have an easy life growing up. She didn't want to give Justin away, but her father left her no choice."

Ivy shivered, not from the cool night breeze, but from something inside her. "I know. I wouldn't want him to be my father, but Angela still had a choice. She chose Uncle Tommy over her own child."

Grandma's silvery thin hair moved with the night breeze. "What we did was wrong. For Angela and for Justin. You have to make it right. My soul will not rest until Justin is accepted as part of this family. Do you hear me?"

"I hear you. Lord knows we can't have another restless soul in Coffey. I'd probably find you floating around with the other spooks over at Reuben's place."

"There may not be enough room for me over there."

That week's *Coffey Gazette* printed Maggie's obituary, announcing her funeral would take place at six o'clock on Monday evening at the Baker Funeral Home.

On the day of the funeral, Otis and Ivy carrying Carly went to the sheriff's office in the basement of the county courthouse. Otis took off his brown plaid cap and cleared his throat. "Sheriff Carter, we're here because we're afraid Maggie's boyfriend—his name is Miles Jones—will show up at her funeral today. He murdered my daughter." His voice choked, and his eyes filled with tears.

Ivy shifted Carly high on her hip. "We think he might try and take Maggie's baby."

Charlie pointed to the baby. "Is this his biological offspring?"

Otis nodded and Ivy hugged the curly-haired baby. "There's a warrant for his arrest in Kansas City and I got emergency custody this morning." She handed him the legal papers.

Charlie sniffed and wiggled his nose. "I'll call the authorities down there and get a read on this Miles Jones guy. If it warrants protection, I'll swing by the church."

Otis twisted his cap in his hands. "Thanks, sheriff. I appreciate it."

Charlie tipped his head in a short nod. "Sorry about your girl."

"Thank you." Otis walked to the door. "I need to check on Pinky. I'll see you at the church, Ivy."

"I'll be there early," Ivy said as she waved goodbye.

Once Otis had left, Charlie turned and scowled at Ivy. "Ivy, you're not really going to keep that baby, are you? Don't you have enough to worry about with Violet so sick and all?"

She kissed the baby's soft cheek. "I'm going to keep her. Children are the best medicine for Grandma. Fills up her holes."

Charlie's radio screeched. His deputy needed help removing some runaway cows that were blocking traffic on old Highway 69. "Got to extract some bovine. I'll call about that Miles Jones situation when I get back."

Charlie adjusted his gun belt, put on his hat, and headed out the door to the urgent herding of unruly cows. Carly let out a short cry. Her baby sounds seemed out of place in the empty sheriff's office. Ivy rubbed the little girl's cheeks. "Yeah, I know. But you'll get used to him."

On her way out, Ivy noticed the unlocked padlock dangling from the file cabinet. She looked around. Charlie wouldn't be back for a while. The cells in the back were empty. The clerks were at lunch. She put Carly on her hip and opened the file cabinet. She rummaged through the top drawer and the middle drawer, looking for the accident reports.

The phone rang and Ivy jumped. She looked around and quickly opened the bottom drawer. In the back, she found an accident report dated December 14, 1959. She pulled the file out and opened it. It was the sheriff's report on her father's accident. She scanned the report and read the last sentence. "Accident found to be due to ice. Witness Tommy Taylor reported his brother's car was going too fast to stop when it hit a patch of black ice at an intersection. He was hit by an 18-wheeler. The car spun around and careened into the back of the Greyhound bus he had been following."

Bertha was right. Her father had died chasing the bus, trying to get his wife back. Ivy placed the file back in the cabinet and started to shut the drawer when she saw a file marked "Mildred Thrasher." She pulled it out and opened it. The sheriff's report simply stated, "Death due to drowning. Case closed." But behind the report was Dr. Kelsey's coroner's report. She scanned the document quickly. "The body suffered a contusion to the head but the cause of death was drowning," she read on the final page.

Footsteps sounded outside and Ivy put the report in the drawer and closed it. She adjusted Carly on her hip and hurried out of the sheriff's office with the confirmation that the lake had killed Conrad Thrasher's wife. But how did she get there?

Chapter 30

PATTY'S DAY OUT

Grandma and Uncle Walter would arrive later, but Ivy decided to get to the church early for Maggie's funeral, so she could make sure they set it up the right way. She wanted Maggie's funeral to be a perfect final tribute to her best friend, who forced her acceptance on the Mulberry Street residents.

The sun sank low in the Iowa sky and dusk began to settle gently on the horizon. When Ivy drove up to the church, she saw Charlie sitting in his car at the far end of the front parking lot.

Ivy drove to the small parking lot behind the church by the alley. She wanted to slip in the side door and avoid any trouble in case Miles showed up. Carrying Carly and the diaper bag, she hurried up the path to the church, avoiding the muddy puddles from the recent rain.

A twig snapped on the ground behind her. Ivy startled and turned toward the sound. Miles jumped out from behind the corner of the church and pressed a gun to Ivy's head. "Give me that baby. I told you I'd come to get what belongs to me."

Ivy could feel the cold barrel of the gun against her temple. The pressure made her stitches throb. A cold wind of fear turned her mind into a kaleidoscope of thoughts tumbling over each other. But there was only one possible answer. After all, she had promised Maggie. "No, Miles. I can't do that."

Out of the corner of her eye, Ivy saw Reuben slowly driving his truck down the church alley toward them. Ivy could see Patty—too large to fit comfortably in the cab of the truck—sitting in the back of the pickup eating a hamburger. She wore her long pink nightgown under an old blue sweater. Buckshot's tongue hung out as he circled Patty in the back.

Ivy hoped that they would notice that she was in trouble, but Reuben turned into the parking lot.

Miles grabbed Ivy's hair. "Give me that baby."

"No."

A tractor loudly sputtered and popped as it turned down the alley. The noise drowned out Ivy's words. Howard Decker in a sleeveless white T-shirt, shorts, and his Kansas City Chiefs ball cap, erratically drove the fogger, spewing thick gray smoke down the alley behind the church. A blanket of smelly fog enveloped them. Ivy could barely breathe and the baby coughed between her cries.

Suddenly, a whizzing object cut through the smoky air. The Frisbee hit Miles in the back. Buckshot howled his "oh, no" and chasing the Frisbee at full speed but unable to see his target, slammed into Miles. The dog's impact knocked Miles to the ground and the gun flew from his hand, skimming along the ground. Buckshot lay beside Miles, stunned from the impact.

Howard Decker, driving in a drunken stupor, adjusted his Kansas City Chiefs hat and drove the fogger past the church, oblivious to the unfolding danger.

Ivy breathed bug spray as she ran through the hazy fog with the crying baby bouncing in her arms.

Miles scrambled up. His dreadlocks bounced like the legs of a spider as he ran after Ivy and Carly.

From the back of the truck in the parking lot, Patty saw Miles chasing Ivy and Carly. The ground still swirled in a smoky bug spray haze and he slipped on a muddy patch and stumbled around to the front of the church. Patty scooted off the truck bed and ran toward Miles like a slow-motion replay. Buckshot joined the chase. When Patty reached Miles, she pulled him down like he was a calf at ear-tagging time. Miles hit the ground unaware of what struck him. Buckshot barked and growled.

When the pesticide-fog lifted, Patty sat on top of Miles, flattening him like a rolled-up newspaper on an annoying bug.

Ivy and the baby, along with Reuben rushed to Patty who adjusted her weight and breathed heavily from her short run. "This ought to hold him."

Miles struggled underneath Patty, who smiled in victory. Reuben put his hand on his wife's shoulder. "Now that's the gal I know." He turned to Ivy. "You guys all right?"

Ivy hugged Reuben. "Yeah."

Reuben gestured, demonstrating the Frisbee's path. "Did you see my Frisbee?"

Ivy nodded. "Yeah. Perfect aim or what?" She kneeled down and patted Buckshot. The dog sniffed Carly and nudged her little hand with his muddy nose.

Reacting slowly to the bodies tumbling out of the bug fog, Charlie Carter, the big-bellied deputy sheriff, waddled out of his car and strutted across the church lawn to the man squirming under the massive weight of Patty. He ran his fingers through his silver streak, now a wide strip extending almost to the back of his head. "I reckon I'll take over from here." He rested his hands on his belt, spread his feet apart, and bent down to look at Miles. "Is this the murdering malcontent?" Ivy nodded. Miles's green eyes were bloodshot and puffy as he glared at Charlie through his dreadlocks.

Many of the funeral-goers gathered around Patty. The growing crowd stared at the trapped man. Luther Matthews, the tool-belted handyman, stepped to the front of the crowd. "I'm here to help," he said. Luther looked at the hammer tattoo on Miles's forearm and tapped his own hammer in the palm of his hand. "I'd like you to meet my hammer, Old Dan Tucker."

Miles stared at Luther, whose hair stood on end like a salute to wild unruliness. Luther's face was covered in weeks-old stubble and grease stains streaked his shirt. Miles blinked his bloodshot eyes as if trying to focus.

"What is this place, 'Deliverance' or something?"

Ivy ignored Miles. "Thanks, Luther, but I think Patty's got it under control."

Patty shifted her weight and Miles coughed as he tried to catch his breath. Carly stopped crying and watched the strange sight, her little tongue darting in and out of her mouth. Ivy glanced toward the road in front of the church. Conrad Thrasher watched the commotion from his big white car idling in the street. His face lay partly in shadow, but she could see him smile as he pulled at his bushy eyebrows.

The church door opened and Virgil Jackson and Max Black emerged. Max's large frame filled up the doorway. He wore his dark blue gas station uniform with the flying red horse on the sleeve because he came directly from work for the funeral. Virgil wrinkled up his nose. "Smells like the damn fogger's been by."

Max pointed to the crowd gathered around the squished intruder whose arms and legs stuck out beneath the beefy form of Patty Smith. "That ain't all that's been by."

Miss Shirley marched up the sidewalk toward Max and Virgil. "Is that the good-for-nothing Miles Jones?"

Virgil held his black hat in his hand. "Maybe what's left of him." He opened the heavy wooden door of the church and called inside. "Hey, Otis, hurry up and get out here. Miles showed up and Patty Smith's got him dead to rights."

Virgil adjusted his hat on his head. Otis hurried out of the church and stared at the strange scene. "Don't let the murderer go!" Otis yelled, cupping his hands around his mouth.

Max's dipped his chin down to his chest. "It don't look to me like that cat can even breathe." Max ran his hand over his shiny bald head. "He ain't going nowhere."

Otis looked at Virgil and Max. "What's Patty Smith doing out of the house?"

Max shrugged his massive shoulders. The flying red horse on his sleeve seemed to leap into the air.

Virgil took a deep breath and shook his head. "Wished we'd been here earlier."

They all hurried over to where Miles was sprawled on the church lawn. Miss Shirley put her hands on her big hips. "Well, Lord. I can't wait to hear how this happened. Nice to see you, Patty. If you need a break, let me know. I can take over for a while."

Patty wiped the sweat from her forehead with the sleeve of her tattered blue sweater. "Thanks, Miss Shirley, but this is the most fun I've had in a long time."

Miles looked up at the faces staring down at him. "My brothers and sisters, don't you care about the fact that that she stole my daughter?"

"She saved that child's life," Miss Shirley said. She pointed across the road. "Look, Sheriff, a jay-walker." Charlie looked up to where she pointed as Miss Shirley kicked Miles in the side.

Miles glared up at Miss Shirley. "Ow. Why are you protecting her? She's a white girl."

"You killed our girl," Miss Shirley hissed through clenched teeth. "You ain't taking another one of ours, black or white."

Miles spat on the ground near Max's huge feet. "Your man needs to teach you a lesson."

Max took a step forward and twisted the wet spot with his work boot, grinding Mile's spit into the ground. He glared down at the flattened man. "I'm trying to restrain myself here, but you better shut your mouth, my brother, or you won't be talking out of it again."

Otis bent down to look Miles in the eyes. "Why'd you do it? Why'd you kill my daughter?"

"She had it coming, old man. It's a new generation. Black men are due some respect."

Otis jumped down on the man squirming beneath Patty's bulk and put his hands around Miles's neck.

Charlie stepped forward. "That's enough, Otis. I got this."

Max and Virgil pulled Otis away.

Miss Shirley stepped closer to Miles. "Are you saying it was her duty as a black woman to take a beating because you're a new generation brother?" She tilted her head to the side as she spoke.

Buckshot growled. "Do not go down that road if you want to go on living," Max warned Miles.

Miss Shirley pulled her leg back for another kick. "I'll give your narrow behind a little respect myself." But before Miss Shirley could kick the downed man again, the dog got there first. Buckshot gripped Miles's leg, biting and snarling until Reuben pulled him off.

Charlie pulled out the handcuffs wedged in his back pocket. "All right. We've had enough fun. Release him, Patty. It's time to handcuff the disruptive element."

Patty awkwardly rolled off the murderer. Charlie shoved his knee in Miles's back, handcuffed him, and jerked him to a standing position. It took four men to haul Patty to her feet. When she was upright, Ivy hugged Patty tightly. "You saved Carly."

Patty held the baby's hand and breathed heavily. "No one should mess with a child. They're too hard to come by." She kissed the top of Carly's soft curls.

"You a good woman, Patty Smith," Miss Shirley said.

"Okay, show's over." Charlie waved for the small crowd to move into the church for the service. He leaned in and whispered to Miles. "Looks like your luck finally ran out when you came up against the deputy sheriff of McKinley County."

Miles glassy eyes squinted, and a shadow crossed his face. "You had nothing to do with it, Skunkhead. That stink bomb blinded me and then a ton of fatback fell on top of me."

"Shut up!" Reuben and Charlie shouted at the same time.

"I'm hauling you down to jail," said Charlie, pushing Miles toward his vehicle. "You're going to enjoy our fine accommodations. The rest of you need to come down to the station and give me your statements after the funeral."

The crowd dispersed and headed into the church. Rueben shook Otis' hand. "Came to pay our respects but looks like we need to head home now to clean up."

"We're awfully grateful to you and Patty," Otis said.

Conrad Thrasher's car still idled in the road. He shook his head and drove off.

Reuben put his arm around Patty. Her long, pink flannel nightgown hung muddied and ripped beneath her stretched-out sweater. Buckshot circled them with the Frisbee in his mouth, ready for another romp. They headed back to the pickup. Reuben would have something to talk about down at the Blue Moon that night.

Max turned to Ivy and offered her his muscled arm. "Let's go."

Ivy nodded as the smell of the fogger spray dissipated and she could breathe easily again. She took his arm and held the baby close to her.

Max escorted Ivy and Carly to the top of the church steps. At the entrance, Virgil held the heavy church door open for Ivy and tipped his hat. "You go right in, Doll Baby. You go right in."

Ivy's eyes filled with tears, but she managed to whisper, "Thank you." If only Maggie were here to see the longed-for moment when she had officially become a "Doll Baby."

Ivy hesitated for a moment as her eyes adjusted to the sanctuary's darkness. Organ music filled the church with the tune of "Amazing Grace." Carly scrunched up her face and tears fell from her brown eyes as if she understood the sadness of the day.

Uncertain about where she should sit, Ivy held the little girl as she entered the space filled with mourners. People turned and watched Ivy and the baby as they made their way down the aisle. Ivy saw Jesse and Raven sitting in the back. Seeing them together was still painful. Ivy searched for a seat away from them.

At the front of the church, Otis rose from his pew. He clapped his hands in a slow, rhythmic beat. The sound echoed off the church's ceiling. Then Pinky stood up beside him and applauded as well.

Across the crowded church, people rose to their feet as Ivy walked down the aisle with Carly in her arms and Max guiding her. The congregation joined the applause until it sounded like thunder coming from heaven during an Iowa rainstorm. For once, Ivy welcomed the rain as tears fell down her cheeks. She cried for the loss of Maggie, but also for the grateful support of the people she shared her life with, the people of Coffey, and the people of Mulberry Street who had reluctantly learned to love her.

The sounds of sorrowful weeping filled the little church as

sadness whispered down the aisles and flew through the church rafters. Maggie was gone and life had changed.

Ivy later found out that while the pallbearers escorted Margaret Louise Norton to her grave on the third hill at the Weeping Willow Cemetery, a strange coalition had formed down at the jail. After Charlie went home from his shift and another deputy took over at the jail, Conrad Thrasher brought Miles Jones a tenderloin and fries from the Coffey Shop.

At the funeral reception at the Nortons' house on Mulberry Street, Ivy hugged Otis and Pinky. Miss Shirley wrapped up a slice of her special Angel Pie to take home to Grandma who had gone home early.

"Death can drain your spirit," Grandma had explained before she left.

That night, Miles slipped out of jail. Miss Shirley told Ivy she overheard a conversation at the Coffey Shop about how Miles had escaped when his cell was left unlocked after Conrad brought him his supper and the deputy received an anonymous call about teenagers drag racing on old Highway 69, which turned out to be a ruse.

Ivy wondered if Miles had fled out of town on foot or if he had help from a big white whale of a car, but she figured either way, he was back with the Alliance in Kansas City and in hiding again.

PART V

THE GREAT HEREAFTER

(1984-1985)

Chapter 31

PREPARING FOR DEATH

Iowa's rich, dark soil offered a fertile land with plentiful crops stretching for acres in its glorious abundant growth. The small farming community of Coffey grew accustomed to the cycle of growth and harvest, death and rebirth. Yet every change required adjustments. As the fall ended, the dead leaves tumbled along the sidewalk. The Iowa weather could change suddenly.

Twenty-six-year-old Ivy hurried across the Warner College campus where she worked as the assistant director of the college alumni office. The college students strolled back from their classes with backpacks slung across their shoulders, oblivious to the blustery weather. But Ivy looked at the sky and sensed a change in the autumn wind.

Although Grandma denied it, and Uncle Walter refused to talk about it, Ivy knew Grandma's cancer had returned. Its unrelenting persistence had come to claim her. There was a translucence to her skin and she had become thinner. The fire in her eyes had dimmed. Ivy knew fate had allowed Grandma to raise her, but Grandma's time was running out. The cancer now sought its revenge for death's delay and Violet Taylor could no longer put up a fight.

The shocking news tumbled along with the strong prairie winds and Ivy listened to the wild birds chattering to each other, all a-twitter as she crossed the campus to go pick up four-year-old Carly from Patty's house. She figured the birds were spreading the news from Coffey that Violet Taylor was preparing for death.

Only two months after Maggie's murder, Pinky had unexpectedly died of heart failure. Ivy suspected her grief over Maggie's death and her guilt for not protecting her only child had sent her to an early grave. Ivy understood that sometimes life's devastation could be unbearable. Sometimes a heart can only take so much.

Uncle Walter, Otis, and Patty took turns babysitting Carly while Ivy was at work. When Ivy arrived to pick up Carly from Patty's that day, she noticed the child's cheeks were slightly red as if wind-burned. Ivy raised her eyebrows in surprise. "Patty, have you guys been outside today?"

"Yeah, we played in the back."

Carly nodded and smiled. "Played house in the barn and climbed on the roof like a squirrel."

"Nearly scared me half to death," Patty said.

"Chased the chickens," Carly said.

Ivy stared at them both. Patty never stepped outside the house if she could avoid it.

"Well, stay off the roof next time, little girl."

"Ivy, I was wondering if you could buy me some regular, you know, outside clothes?" asked Patty.

"I'd be glad to."

"I'm not even sure what size I am anymore."

"We'll figure it out."

Something inside Patty had changed. Her sadness faded. Having Carly in her life had coaxed Patty out of her pink flannel nightgowns and was bringing her out into the sun again.

When Ivy and Carly got home, they found Grandma sitting on the living room couch leafing through the *Coffey Gazette*. At seventy-nine, Grandma had watched all her contemporaries die, and she now relied on the subsequent generations to fill her life.

"Everyone my age is long gone. You know, I read the obituaries every day to see who's left this world. I figure, if I'm reading them, then I'm still here." Grandma's chuckle led to a coughing spell. Ivy sat down next to her on the couch and gently rubbed Grandma's back. Her bony shoulders felt so unfamiliar. "You're still here, Grandma."

Ivy wasn't used to Grandma's gradual thinness. The cancer had taken both her breasts, and now it slowly stole the rest of her body. Grandma patted her stomach.

"Yeah, I'm here, but I get a lot colder now without as much padding to insulate me."

"Well, it's good you have a quilt or two around here," Ivy teased with a smile.

Carly snuggled on the other side of Grandma, who pulled one of Pinky's homemade quilts across their laps. Ivy held Grandma's hand and played with her wedding ring like she did as a child. The ring spun loosely now. "Grandma, do you really think there's another world after death?"

Grandma nodded. "Yes, my dear. I'm sure of it. Robert and Sam Taylor will meet me in the Great Hereafter."

"What do you think it looks like?"

"I don't know, dear. But I'll tell you when I get there."

"Okay. Just send me a sign when you're all settled on your back porch in the Great Hereafter."

Grandma coughed. "Sure enough. What kind of a sign?"

"I don't know. Something that I'll know is you."

Carly clapped her hands. "The birds. The birds."

Grandma chuckled. "The birds. You like them, too?"

Carly nodded. "You talk to them."

"Yeah, that's perfect," Ivy said. "Send a sign with the birds. Then I'll finally know if they really talked to you or if you've been teasing me all these years."

"Okay, I'll do that and don't forget to feed them when I'm gone." She hugged Carly.

"All right, Grandma," Carly said. "But they'll miss you."

"And I'll miss them and you, very, very much."

Ivy tapped Grandma's arm. "Did I tell you Nick passed the bar exam and is working for a big law firm in New York? His dad told me."

Grandma smiled. "Really? Sir Lancelot makes it big, huh, Miss Susie? But is he happy? I've always been of the mind that the best marriages are made with your best friend. Nick's my favorite, always was." Grandma patted Ivy's hand. "You know it's not too late for you two."

"Did your birds tell you that, too?"

"No, I didn't live seventy-nine years for nothing. I'm the all-knowing being. Ask Nick."

"I don't think he'll ever forgive me for choosing Jesse over him. I don't think I'll forgive myself."

"Sometimes things are meant to be." Grandma's chuckle led into a coughing spell. She lay back on the couch and closed her eyes.

Grandma, the woman who never slept, began to doze for long stretches with Pinky's quilts pulled up to her chin.

The next day, when Ivy peeked into Grandma's bedroom, she

saw Carly curled up beside Grandma, basking in the comfort of her great-grandmother's presence. Grandma sleepily looked up. "Ivy, come on in, dear." Grandma's voice sounded husky and deep.

Ivy pushed open the door. "I'm sorry, Grandma, I didn't mean to wake you. I was just checking on you."

Carly sat up and Grandma patted her face. "Carly, thanks for keeping me company. Why don't you go play for a while? I need to talk to your mother for a few minutes."

Carly kissed her Grandma's cheek. "Okay, Grandma. I check on you."

"Thank you, my love."

Carly ran out of the room and shut the door. Grandma motioned Ivy over, and she sat down on the mahogany four-poster bed. "Ivy, I'm going to need to go soon."

"Go where?" Grandma wasn't strong enough for any long trips.

She pointed skyward and smiled. "To the Great Hereafter, to join my Sam Taylor and Robert."

"I know. But what about me and Carly?"

Grandma shifted on the bed. "Ivy dear, I've kept this old rattle-trap of a body alive all these years for you. But I'm tired, and you don't need me like you used to."

Ivy shook her head. "Grandma . . ."

Grandma shook her finger. "You hush up. You're strong enough without me and that's a great comfort to me. I'm plum worn out. It's time for me to rest in peace."

Grandma struggled to sit up. "I've lived to see you grown. Having you beside me has truly been my life's blessing. You've kept me alive all these years since your father's death. You put laughter back in my life. But Ivy, my child, I'm not long for this world."

Ivy shook her head. "Grandma, I don't want to think about that. I don't know how to live without you."

Grandma clasped Ivy's hand. "Well, child, I won't live forever. When I die, you will have to fill your heart with your love for Carly, like I did with you. Having you here helped me get through my unbearable grief. I had the boys to love when Sam Taylor died, and I had you when my sweet Robert died. I knew when Carly came into your life that it would soon be safe for me to leave. She will carry you through all of life's sorrows, like you and the boys did for me. Now it's your turn to be strong for your little girl. Now it's your turn to be the great surly one."

Ivy cried, and warm tears fell down her cheeks. "I'll try, Grandma, but I'm not as strong as you." Ivy stroked Grandma's hand and it felt cool.

"Yes, you are. You are my child and my kindred spirit. I've known too much in my days. It's been a heavy burden on my heart and mind." Grandma paused, smoothing the quilt on the bed. Her tongue circled her lips. "My mouth is dry. Could you get me some ice water, please?"

Ivy's hands trembled as she poured cool water from the pitcher next to Grandma's bed. Grandma took a few small sips and settled back against the pillows. "There's something I should have told you a long time ago, but I didn't know how. Now my time has run out."

Ivy's heart pounded loudly. Grandma shook her head. "I'm too old for fancy words." Grandma took a deep breath. "Ivy, your mother lives on Beckman Street in Des Moines."

Ivy gasped, and tears welled up in her eyes. She hugged Grandma. "Thank you."

"I don't remember the number. But who told you she was alive?"

"You've got your secrets, and I've got mine."

Grandma patted Ivy's hand. "All these years, I've been so afraid that you would hate me when you found out."

"I was pretty mad. But I know you were doing what you thought was best. I know it's weird, but I think I felt more alone after I found out she was still alive and out there somewhere."

"All of us are alone in this world. Our only true connection to others is through love."

The lilting songs of the birds in the backyard floated through the window.

"What was my mother really like?"

Grandma rubbed the edge of the quilt. "Well Ivy, she was empty and lonely. No matter how much she had, she was never satisfied. I don't think she knew what she wanted and it was hurtful. She couldn't wait to get out of Coffey."

"Like me."

Grandma shook her head vigorously. "No, you're nothing like her."

Ivy winced.

"You're you. We all have to choose our own path. You sacrificed a lot for the people you love, but your mother sacrificed the people who loved her." Grandma looked out the window for a moment. "Robert was twenty-six when they married and Barbara was only twenty-two when you were born. She was still a newlywed. They hadn't been married very long when you came along. She wasn't finished growing up. She wasn't prepared to take care of you. She still wanted someone to take care of her and I think she resented Robert for loving you so much.

"No matter what Robert did, it was never good enough. The poor boy worked double shifts at the packing plant to buy her that new car. She just had to have a red Pontiac Bonneville. And he got it for her. " Grandma coughed and cleared her throat.

"She worked out there too, but she quit when you were born. Then she complained so much about having to take care of you that Robert asked me to watch you during the day. So, I went over one morning to pick you up."

Grandma rubbed her arms. "It still gives me shivers to think about that day. Your mother was sitting at the kitchen table drinking coffee, smoking a cigarette, and painting her long nails while you cried hysterically in your crib. When I rushed to you, your foot was caught in the crib railing and your diaper needed changing. You had nothing on but a dirty undershirt. From that day on, I picked you up every morning and Robert came to get you after he got off of work. She did nothing and was fine with it."

Ivy felt pity for her mother. She understood the overwhelming responsibility of taking care of a child. She, too, had felt reluctant about being Carly's mother. The responsibility of a baby must have been too heavy and too restricting for someone so young. Barbara sounded depressed.

"There was a terrible storm the night your father died. When your father came home from work, he found a note from your mother, telling him she was leaving. He was angry. He said he couldn't live without her. I guess he didn't."

Ivy wondered if it was the same letter she had found in the glovebox at the dump. Grandma reached over and patted Ivy's hand.

"But he couldn't stop her, and she got on the bus. I have to tell you I wanted her gone. Robert must have been distraught because he pulled through the intersection without stopping. An 18-wheeler hit his car and he was killed instantly. Your mother talked to the sheriff and then got back on the bus to Des Moines."

Grandma patted her lap as she remembered that night. "Some rainy nights can change a generation. Uncle Walter went out there with Charlie that night. He came back a different man. Never seemed to be able to trust anyone again. I never told you all this because I wanted you to believe you are worth everything. I hope you'll forgive me."

Ivy kissed her Grandmother and stroked her face. The sweet smell of lilacs still hovered around Grandma. "There's nothing to forgive."

Uncle Walter had retired from the Post Office a few years earlier and his life had slowed to a crawl. That night when he walked from his trailer for supper at Grandma's house, Ivy pulled him into the kitchen. "Grandma and I talked about my mother today. Grandma says she thinks she lives on Beckman Street in Des Moines. I need to find her."

He shook his head. "I'm not so sure that's such a good idea. Barbara tends to tilt the world her way."

"What do you mean?"

"She uses people to get what she wants."

"I don't think I have anything she wants."

He glanced around the room, as if making sure no one else was listening. "You know, you can find anyone's address through the postal service's address management records. Russell can check Beckman Street for you."

Ivy hugged him. Uncle Walter had softened over the years. Perhaps he would someday be able to forgive her mother. "Thanks. I'll ask him."

"She might not be what you expect. It's been a long time, you know."

"Maybe. But I need to find her. She's my mother."

He sighed. "Yes, I guess you're right. Secrets grow heavier over time."

A tragic twist of fate gave her a wise and loving grandmother instead of a misunderstood and confused mother, but she also lost the father who loved her and her dream of a perfect mother. How could her mother be as bad as Grandma described if her father loved her so much? Maybe her uncles weren't the only members of the Taylor family who held a family grudge.

Ivy went upstairs to check on Grandma and bring her a glass of water. "Grandma, here's some ice water. Can I get you anything else?"

"Could you put that other quilt over me? I've got a chill in my bones."

"Sure, Grandma." Ivy pulled another one of Pinky's beautiful quilts over her. "Is there anything else you need?"

"When I go, I want to be buried in that blue dress with the white pearl buttons. It's the only good dress I have that won't fall off me. Not that I'd have to worry about that in a casket. Don't bother with hose. I haven't worn hose for decades and a bra seems unnecessary without breasts." She continued to list her burial clothing as if reciting a grocery list. Ivy was shocked at her casualness. There was so much about death that Ivy didn't understand.

"I won't need any shoes." Grandma raised her finger. "And will you bury me with one of Pinky's quilts? The one with all the children of the world holding hands in a circle? I don't want to feel the chilly draft on the way to the Great Hereafter."

"Okay."

Sadness washed over Ivy like a cold prairie wind. She stood up quickly, so Grandma would not see her tears. When she turned back, Grandma had pushed all the quilts off the bed. She lay sweating as her eyelids closed into sleep.

The next afternoon, Ivy helped Grandma get dressed. "Justin Roberts just called. He's coming over with some of Miss Shirley's homemade soup."

Grandma waved her hands. "Help me get downstairs so I can watch the birds while I wait for him."

Ivy guided Grandma down the stairs and onto the porch. Although the weather had turned cold, the birds still flocked to Grandma's backyard. Justin, now a sophomore in high school, came up the back porch with a steaming pot of Miss Shirley's potato soup and a cherry pie. Each year Justin looked more like, Ben, who was now an EMT for the ambulance service.

Grandma tried to stand to greet him, but the strain was too much. "My, my. That soup smells delicious."

Justin sat down next to Grandma as Ivy took the soup and the pie into the kitchen. She knew Grandma wouldn't taste Miss Shirley's food. Grandma rarely ate anymore.

Ivy joined them on the porch. "Miss Shirley sent us one of her cherry pies."

"Well, Justin, if your Mother didn't send an angel pie, I must not be dead yet."

"My mom says your spirit will fill up the heavens, and the Lord doesn't have enough room for you yet."

Grandma laughed and cupped her hand to her ear. "I think I hear them rearranging the furniture right now. My time is coming. You can count on that." Grandma looked into the gray eyes of the great-grandson she never got to claim. "You've had a good life haven't you, Justin?"

"Yes, Ma'am. What about you?"

"Some years were better than others, with a few surprises along the way and a few regrets. You'll probably find that yourself." Grandma's eyes glazed over and her hands pulled at the tissue in her lap. "But all in all, I've taken a happy path." She shook her head slightly and sighed. "It was mighty kind of you to bring me the soup and the pie."

"Yes, Ma'am."

She reached over and hugged the grandson who had been wrapped in secrets and excluded from their family acceptance. "Goodbye, my dear."

When Justin disappeared around the backyard path, Grandma slumped in her chair, hanging her head as great drops of regret fell from her all-knowing eyes.

Chapter 32

IVY VISITS HER PAST

Russell found Barbara's address in the Des Moines post office records. He told Ivy her mother lived at 609 Beckman Street, apartment 4. Her need to go to Des Moines and find her mother gnawed at Ivy until it floated in the back of her mind every waking moment and plagued her dreams at night. The chance to have the mother she yearned for all her life, even if she was imperfect, kept her thinking about how close she was to meeting Barbara Taylor. Ivy understood her mother because she knew all too well the fear of being trapped in Coffey, in a disappointing life she didn't choose.

She couldn't wait any longer to find her mother. It was time.

One morning, Ivy dropped Carly off at Patty's and got in the Monstrosity. The rattle-trap sounds of the old camper truck remained her only connection to Nick. They hadn't spoken in a long time. He was busy practicing law in New York. His father said he was doing well, but his heavy caseload prevented him from coming home. It was weird how Nick, the risk-taker, had ended up with a plan.

Ivy put Nick's Merle Haggard tape in the old eight-track player. She turned up the volume and drove through the gravel back roads of Coffey and onto Interstate 35 to Des Moines with the music blaring, to meet her mother. Her world was about to open up.

When she reached Des Moines, she parked outside the rundown apartment building on 609 Beckman Street and took a deep breath as she got out. Anxious to face this ghost from her past, she hurried up the cracked sidewalk, dodging the broken concrete jutting up at all angles. The winter wind blew trash across the apartment's small yard. The building looked almost abandoned.

The warped front steps creaked and the railing wobbled as Ivy approached the front door of the building. She pushed open the peeling door and stepped into the tiny, dusty entryway. Ivy carefully climbed the rickety stairs, afraid that any minute the entire building would collapse on her like a house of cards.

Ivy found her mother's apartment. The number four hung upside down, holding on desperately to the door by a single, rusty nail. She hesitated. Her mother was hopefully behind the door and Ivy would finally meet her. A lifetime of dreaming of this moment was about to come true. She fingered her mother's silver heart necklace around her neck, took a deep breath, and knocked on the door.

Footsteps thudded inside the apartment. The door opened a crack, but was secured by a chain lock. A woman's bloodshot eyes peered through the opening.

"What'd you want?" she said as if Ivy had interrupted something important.

"Are you Barbara Taylor?"

"What's it to you?"

Ivy's dry throat felt like it was being poked by a million tiny needles. She had waited twenty-six years for this moment. She swallowed hard. "I'm Ivy Taylor, your daughter. Can I come in?"

"No need." The suspicious eyes disappeared as the door slammed shut and the dead bolt clicked.

Ivy stared uncertainly at the banged-up apartment door, but she couldn't give up. She knocked again, a little louder. She waited in the empty hallway that reeked of urine and rotten apples. Ivy cleared her throat and spoke loudly through the closed door. "I'm not leaving. I've spent my whole life without you. I don't blame you for leaving. Can you just talk to me for a minute?"

There was silence. Then the chain rattled and the dead bolt unlocked. The door opened. Her mother stepped into the dingy light of the filthy hallway, pulling the door shut behind her. "All right. You got one minute."

Although she was only forty-seven years old, only a hint of Barbara Taylor's famed beauty remained. A cigarette dangled from her chapped lips and dark shadows circled her bloodshot eyes. Leaving Coffey hadn't protected her mother from the reality of a disappointing life.

Barbara flicked her cigarette and the ashes floated down like gray snowflakes on Ivy's shoes. The woman looked Ivy up and down, like someone examining damaged merchandise. Her chin jutted forward and she bit her lip. "I wondered when you'd show up." She put her little finger in her ear and wiggled it. "You sure got my good looks."

Ivy smiled. "That's what Grandma says. Can I come in? I won't stay long. I've wanted a mother all my life, but I thought you died with my father in the car crash."

Her mother's dirty robe fell off her shoulder, revealing a yellowed slip and needle marks on her arm. Barbara quickly wrapped the ratty robe around her. "You should keep on thinking that. I left a long time ago."

"Believe me, I understand why you left. I can't wait to get out of there," Ivy said as her heart pounded. "I've been wondering, do I have any brothers or sisters?"

"Heavens no. You think I'd want to go through that hell again? I never wanted to be pregnant in the first place."

"Do I have grandparents?"

She bent forward. "Don't go near them. My father did things to me that no little girl should know about. He's a monster. I left Stilton as soon as I could." Barbara's breath smelled like alcohol as she leaned in and spoke in a whisper. "Men are pigs. Use them before they use you."

Ivy shuddered and took a step back.

Barbara's face scrunched up like she had tasted something sour and flipped back her tangled hair. Her lips slid over her yellow teeth in a smile. "You should have seen me. I was a beauty in my day but I was wasting my time with Robert and the others. Now, Conrad Thrasher, we spoke the same language." She ran her hands over her breasts and swaying hips.

Ivy shuddered as chills rolled up and down her body. "You had an affair with Conrad Thrasher?"

Barbara pulled her tangled hair back in a messy ponytail and let it drop. "Why not? Don't act so surprised. Conrad was furious at me for leaving, but he knew Violet, the old witch, was forcing me to go."

Ivy felt a lump in her throat that left her gasping for air.

"That was a long time ago. I never looked back. You shouldn't either," Barbara said. "There's nothing there."

Ivy leaned against the wall. Time seemed to slow. Nothing existed outside the hallway. She tried to swallow but her mouth felt rusted.

Barbara raised her eyebrows and scratched the back of her neck. "So, is that old woman dead yet?"

Ivy shook her head.

Barbara coughed and spat into a wadded-up tissue she pulled from the torn pocket of her robe. She sniffed. "That nasty old woman raise you?"

Ivy nodded, unable to speak.

"She drove me crazy. Telling me what to do. Always fussing over you. I didn't want anything to do with the whole worthless lot of you, and I still don't. I thought I made that clear when I left. That old bossy woman never could mind her own business."

Ivy clenched her sweaty, shaking hands and somehow found her voice. "You have no right to talk like that. Grandma was the best thing that ever happened to me. You're the one who ran away."

Barbara wiped the corners of her mouth. "I didn't run away. Violet forced me to leave. She threatened me, more like it and I was more than happy to oblige the old biddy. Is Tommy still married to that little troll?"

"Hattie? Yeah."

"Shame." Barbara scratched her hip, her robe riding up and down with each rub. "Couldn't stand one more minute of that place. Thought it would be better than Stilton, but nothing good ever came out of that dirt-ball town." She shivered, as if remembering a chilling nightmare.

Ivy stared at Barbara. She hadn't expected such raw hatred. She didn't want to believe that such an angry, spiteful woman could be her mother. "What about me?"

Barbara pulled something off the tip of her tongue with her fingers and spat on the dirty hall floor. "I don't even know you."

Ivy's anger burst to the surface. "Look at this place! Look at you." Ivy shook off the ashes from her shoe, dropped there from Barbara's cigarette. As the ashes disappeared, so did her little girl dreams of her mother, and she suddenly realized that she had not grown up motherless after all. Luther was right, sometimes things work out for the best.

"We might look alike, but we have nothing in common. You're not my mother. Grandma Violet is. Being a mother isn't just giving birth. It's giving a child a life."

Ivy ripped the heart necklace from around her neck and held it out to her mother. "I think this is yours. I don't want it anymore."

Barbara cupped her tobacco-stained fingers and caught the necklace as Ivy let it go.

"Where'd you get this?"

Ivy's chin quivered, but she held back her tears. "I found it in a small box of your stuff. It's all I had left of you. I've worn it every day of my life."

Barbara dangled the old silver chain up in the air. Her husky laugh cackled in the empty hallway. "Conrad gave me this necklace."

An icy wave of betrayal traveled down Ivy's body. She had to get out of there. "I've got to go home." She turned and hurried down the stairs, feeling dazed. The stairs blurred in front of her as she gripped the wobbly handrail, feeling as if she were going to plunge headlong down the uneven stairs. Ivy looked back as Barbara threw the necklace down the stairwell at Ivy. "Tell your stinking family, thanks for nothing."

Ivy ran the rest of the way down the stairs, no longer afraid of falling. She hesitated when she reached the silver heart necklace lying on the landing and stared for a second at the once-cherished keepsake, laying on the floor, discarded and unwanted. Then she ran on. Opening the door, she felt the cold Iowa air blast across her face, blowing away all her unrealistic dreams. She finally felt free from the ghost of her mother.

Ivy drove home down Interstate 35, her heart beating fast as if nearly missing a catastrophe. She realized a cold, unfeeling mother could have raised her instead of her strong and loving Grandma. She could have lived in a broken-down neighborhood in Des Moines instead of the comforting, close-knit community of Coffey.

A light snow started to fall, swirling around the headlights of the Monstrosity. The snow slowly painted the Iowa countryside white, covering the fields and the roofs of the barns and farmhouses as she passed.

She played the confrontation with her mother over and over in her mind; going over each sentence, reliving each painful disclosure, hoping it would all make sense. Her mother had had an affair with Conrad Thrasher, the snake.

A prickly fear rose on the back of her neck and spread down her body. The horror of it seeped into her reality. Could Conrad Thrasher be her father? Is that why he hated her so? Is that why he said she wasn't who she thought she was? Ivy slammed the brakes and pulled over to the side of the road as the nausea hit. She opened her door and hunched over a nearby ditch, vomiting until there was nothing left inside her.

That night, when Ivy pulled into the driveway at 4120, she saw Grandma staring out the upstairs window, waiting for her to return. She ran into the house.

"Ivy?" Grandma called. "You're home?"

"Yes." Ivy ran up the stairs and burst into the bedroom. She hugged Grandma tightly. "I love you, Grandma. You know that, right?"

"Of course, my child."

"I went to see my mother, Grandma. You were right. She was not what I expected and she's everything you feared. Thank you for taking care of me. I wouldn't have made it without you."

Grandma smiled. "I did my best and God did the rest."

Ivy kissed the woman who had manipulated the truth and saved her life. Then she turned out the light and went to check on Carly. Uncle Walter had picked her up from Patty's.

Carly was looking at an illustrated book of "Hansel and Gretel" with a flashlight. When she saw Ivy at her door, she quickly turned off the light and pretended to be asleep. Ivy smiled and sat down on the bed beside the fake-sleeping child. Carly fluttered her eyes, pretending to wake up. Ivy smiled and hugged her.

"Hey, Carly. How was your day?"

"Good."

"I missed you. What did you do at Patty's?"

"Went to the dump with Reuben and Uncle Tommy."

"Ah. That's always fun."

"There's a lake where a lady died."

"Uncle Tommy told you that?"

"Yeah. Why was the lady dead under the dock?"

"I don't know, but there's nothing to be afraid of. I was there once, under the dock. There's room under it to breathe." Ivy cleared her throat. "The lake is calm now. So, no more talking about dead ladies in lakes, and no more looking at witch stories with a flashlight."

Carly's eyes got big, realizing she had been caught. She nodded. "The witch takes the kids."

"It's only a pretend story. I would fight the witch and come save you." Carly laughed as Ivy hugged her. "I love you, Carly. You know that, right?"

"Of course. You're my mom."
"Yes, I am."

Chapter 33

A CHILD IS WORTH SOME TROUBLE

Spring arrived wet and windy, and the flowers and trees eagerly drank up the moisture and were enticed above ground by the warm sun. Life returned to the Iowa prairie. Like the rebirth of spring, Ivy, now twenty-seven, found a way to embrace life. But the hole left by her mother's rejection filled up with other worries and fears.

Ivy was concerned about Otis, who never recovered from the deaths of his wife and daughter. He withdrew into himself and sank into listless despair; even his friends on Mulberry Street could not bring him out of his depression. Only Carly, his granddaughter, kept him from giving in completely to his deep hopelessness.

Carly was also the reason that Patty emerged from her years of household exile. Every day Patty got dressed in the regular street clothes Ivy bought her and was often seen outside playing with Carly. There had even been a few Patty-sightings in town.

Early one May morning, Ivy dropped Carly off at Patty's house on her way to work at Warner College. The rain poured and the sun crept behind the storm clouds as if afraid to show its bright face. The horror that unfolded next was relayed to Ivy later that day by Patty.

Patty had long since said goodbye to Reuben as he left to meet Uncle Tommy at the Coffey Shop when she looked out the window and saw two cars slowing on the gravel road a short way from her farmhouse. A light-colored car stopped down the road while the other pulled up outside Patty's house. A man wearing sunglasses, a gray sweatshirt and a hat tilted low over his face got out. Patty told Ivy she thought it was probably a mushroom hunter who had lost his way. The other car continued along the gravel road.

Carly was playing in the living room and Patty was in the kitchen when she heard footsteps and the unlocked door opened. When Carly screamed, Patty came pounding out. The man with the hat shielding his face, stood in the middle of her living room. None of Reuben's ghosts from the world beyond would ever be as scary as what haunted Patty's living room that morning. It was Miles, Maggie's murderer. He held his daughter against his chest as Carly screamed and kicked, trying to get free. Patty froze in horror at the unexpected disaster that stood before her.

He pressed a gun in Carly's curly hair and laughed at Patty. "Not so fast on your feet this time huh, you raggedy-butt cow."

"Don't hurt her. Please. She's a good little girl."

Miles gripped five-year-old Carly's arm so tightly his fingers made dents in her skin. "Just taking back what's mine." A drop of rainwater rolled off his hat and trickled down his face like an artificial tear. He wiped it away with the back of his hand, still holding the gun.

Patty edged toward Miles as if propelled by some force that allowed her to move despite her paralyzing fear. "Don't hurt her. Please."

Miles waved the gun in the air. "Don't be stepping up on me."

Patty kept moving toward him with a glazed look in her eyes.

Miles placed the gun barrel back against the little girl's head. "Slow your roll. I mean it. Watch this." He grinned and pulled the trigger. The hollow click of an empty chamber echoed in the silence. Miles laughed. "That was just a warning. Next one's loaded or maybe not. You want to take the chance?"

Patty stood rooted to her living room floor as if her feet were stuck in concrete. Miles backed out the door, taking Carly with him.

"Patty! Patty! Help me! Don't let him take me." Carly's little hands reached out for Patty. "I want to stay with you. I don't want to go."

Miles pinned her arms down. "Shut up. I'm your father. Those people ain't nothing to you."

Patty closed her eyes and covered her ears, unable to bear the cries of the child she loved, the little girl who had brought her back to life. "I'm sorry, Carly. I'm so sorry." Patty's legs buckled, and she fell against the screen door, which broke from its rusty hinges. She landed on the floor with a resounding thud, but she reached out her arms. "I love you, Carly."

"Patty!" Carly cried and kicked as Miles stuffed the little girl into his trunk. "I'm scared!"

"Carly. I'm sorry. I'm sorry. I wasn't meant to have children."

Then Patty told Ivy of the horror that came next. As she lay sobbing on the floor, Buckshot came running from the barn, growling and charging at Miles. The man kicked Buckshot. "Where's your Frisbee now, mutt?"

The dog clenched his teeth around Miles's leg and Miles yelled in pain. Then he lowered his gun and shot Buckshot right in the head. The dog's blood splattered on Miles's gray sweatshirt, turning it into a bright mosaic of terror.

"Tell Ivy to meet me at the cemetery tonight at midnight,"

Miles said menacingly. "Leave the law out of it and tell her to come alone if she wants the kid to live."

Carly's muffled screams from inside the car trunk sounded like a tormented ghost of an unsettled passing. Patty passed out on top of the broken door in the old farmhouse, with Buckshot lying dead a few feet away and Carly ripped from her life.

It was still raining when Ivy burst into Grandma's house. Grandma and Uncle Walter were sitting on the couch.

"Carly's gone. Miles took her."

"Oh, dear God, no." Grandma buried her face in her hands. "Why didn't I know?"

Uncle Walter rose from the couch, supporting his knee with his hand. "What? What happened?"

Ivy took a deep breath. "Miles broke into Patty's house this afternoon and put a gun to Carly's head. Said he'd kill her. There was nothing Patty could do."

"What's Charlie going to do?" said Uncle Walter.

"I didn't tell him. Miles said to come alone to the cemetery at midnight if we want to see Carly alive. If we bring Charlie, I'm afraid of what Miles will do. He has nothing to lose."

Ivy's stomach twisted into a knot. Grandma's thin face lost all its color.

Uncle Walter's hands shook as he hugged Ivy. "What are you going to do?"

"Whatever I have to."

Grandma wiped her teary eyes with the handkerchief she always kept tucked in her stuffed bra along with all the other odd assortments of filing.

Ivy gazed out the windows overlooking the backyard. Then she paced the big house, counting each lonely, tormented minute without Carly, mourning the unbearable emptiness, and thinking about a way to get her back before midnight came. She needed to call Otis. He had the right to know.

The hours stretched into early evening. Tormented by her dark nightmare, Ivy startled when the phone rang. It was Luther, his voice low, almost whispering.

"Carly's over at the Thrasher place. Ellen told me she saw her when she was on her walkabout. What's going on?"

"Miles kidnapped her from Patty's. I'll meet you at your house."

"Okay."

"Luther, did Ellen actually talk to you?"

"She didn't stop walking, but she pointed to Conrad's house and she said, 'Tell Ivy the snake has her girl.'"

"I love that woman."

The moon fought its way through the clouds again and so did Ivy. The rain stopped. Ivy hung up the phone and walked over to Grandma, who was lying on the couch.

"Luther said Ellen saw Carly over at Conrad's. I'm going to go get Carly back, one way or the other. Luther says we need the element of surprise to get her before midnight."

"Be careful. Miles and Conrad both got a powerful hate."

"So do I." Ivy tied up her black boots and looked Violet in the eye. "Grandma, there may be some trouble over this."

Grandma patted Ivy's cheek. "A child is worth some trouble."

Ivy went the back way, so she wouldn't go past Conrad's place, and pulled into Luther's dirt driveway. His barking dogs, Rosie's old friends, announced her arrival.

Luther answered the door before she knocked, motioning

her inside the house without a word. The broken door banged shut behind them and the dogs jumped up and down like grasshoppers in a summer field. Ivy held out her hands for them to sniff. "Hey, wild dogs. It's just me."

The dogs licked her hands as she stood beside the worn-out couch covered with cat hair and pieces of dog food. There was a cat sleeping on the statue of baby Jesus lying on the floor, stolen from the church manger many years before.

"So, Luther, what happened?"

Luther's greasy hair stuck out in every direction like a scarecrow pecked by birds. "The dogs were barking like crazy and I went outside to see what in tarnation was going on this time. Ellen came skittering out of the woods, pointing to Conrad's place and ranting about how the snake's got your girl."

He nodded and lowered his voice. "So, I snuck over and looked in every one of his windows. Didn't see nothing. But there was a light on in that tiny window up top. I saw a shadow. I think they've got Carly in the attic."

"Let's go find out. I'll do anything you say. Anything."

Luther's face was expressionless. "We'll have to work fast. Get the jump on them before midnight. I don't trust neither of them."

"Let's do it."

Luther paced the small space inside his crowded house. His jeans rested low on his hips and his ripped T-shirt hung inside-out. He picked up a cat and petted it. "Haven't found nothing yet I can't fix. Sometimes it's hard to tell what tools'll come in handy." The corners of his eyes wrinkled in concentration. He raised his eyebrows.

"What?"

"I'm thinking."

"All right." Ivy pulled her hair back in a ponytail and let it drop. She paced with Luther as he rubbed his unshaven chin. After a few minutes, Ivy couldn't take it any longer. She grabbed Luther's arm. "What? What're you thinking?"

Luther nodded. "We're going to steal Carly back. We need some help but not from Charlie. Conrad's got Charlie by the short and curlies. Only way he'll arrest them all is if there are witnesses."

Ivy closed her eyes for a second before throwing her arms around Luther and hugging him. She breathed in his musty, dirty-sock smell, the smell of salvation. Luther looked down at his feet, blushing from Ivy's affection.

"No one's ever hugged me before." He cleared his throat. "Go into town and gather everyone that you trust one hundred percent. With witnesses, Charlie will have to do something this time."

"Almost everybody I know is pretty old."

"That's okay. If they can walk and they can see, we want them. Bring everyone here as soon as possible and tell them to wear something dark. I've got more thinking to do."

"Okay." She picked up the statue of the Christ child and handed it to Luther. "You really ought to give Baby Jesus back to the church. We're going to need all the help we can get."

Luther shrugged, showing his crooked teeth with bits of black chewing tobacco wedged in between. "Okay."

Ivy left Luther's house with rising hopes as the handyman plotted Carly's escape. Luther was good at fixing things. If he could move a stuffed buffalo by himself, surely he could extract a little girl from her kidnappers before midnight.

She drove the dilapidated camper to the Coffey Shop. Opening the heavy door, she breathed in the welcoming smell of fried chicken and gravy. She stopped by the kitchen and whispered to Miss Shirley. "Carly's been kidnapped by Miles. She's out at Conrad's place. We're mounting a rescue. If you can get Kitty to cover for you, meet me at Luther's place as soon as you can. Go the back way and wear black."

"I'll be there."

Just like Ivy thought, Uncle Tommy and Reuben were at their regular booth drinking their coffee and eating pie. Russell sat with them eating French fries. Ivy was relieved to see Charlie hadn't arrived yet.

Dark rings circled Reuben's eyes. He looked as if he had not taken the news of Carly's kidnapping very well. Ivy sat down beside him and patted his shoulder. "How's Patty doing?"

Reuben pursed his lips. "She hasn't spoken a word since Carly was snatched. It's like she's paralyzed. Never seen her this bad. Doc Kelsey says it's not good. I'm headed home in a minute. How you doing?"

"I'm going to be okay. You didn't tell Charlie, did you?"

"No, she told me not to."

"Good. Luther's planning a rescue. We need your help. But don't tell anyone—not anyone."

Reuben and Russell nodded. Russell dabbed a French fry in the ketchup. "You can count on me."

Uncle Tommy shook his head at Russell. "Well you're good at counting and you're just a dag-burn mailman so there's nothing you can do to help."

"Letter carrier, Dad," Russell said. He used his knife to push the ketchup into a perfect circle. "I'll be there, Ivy."

Ivy ignored Uncle Tommy. "Thanks, Russell. You're a good friend. Meet us at Luther's as soon as you can."

"Luther's?" Reuben asked.

"Yeah. I'll explain everything when you get there."

Uncle Tommy stuck out his lower lip and shook his head. "Reuben and I aren't taking part in any of crazy Luther's cockamamie schemes."

Ivy leaned toward him. Her voice was so low it was barely a whisper. "Carly's just a little girl."

Uncle Tommy sniffed and pushed his glasses up on his nose. "We're still not going to do it."

Reuben narrowed his eyes. "Speak for yourself. A child is never forgotten. My little brother died when he was about Carly's age. I still miss him. Don't even know where he's buried." Reuben pounded his fist the table and the coffee cups rattled in their saucers. "That man killed Buckshot. He's not going to get our Carly, too." He looked at Ivy and nodded. "I'm in."

Uncle Tommy stared at his buddy across their booth. "Reuben, have you lost your mind?"

Reuben rubbed his puffy, red eyes. "I can't take another thing haunting me."

Uncle Tommy looked over the top of his black-rimmed glasses at Reuben. "I guess I'm going to the Blue Moon by myself tonight."

Reuben took a sip of coffee, his hands shaking. "Yeah, I guess so."

Miss Shirley brought over a coffee refill. She slammed her hand down on the table. "Tommy Taylor, if you had any guts, you'd help your girl."

Uncle Tommy grunted and took a bite of his pie. "That little girl's got nothing to do with me."

"I meant Ivy." Miss Shirley frowned and thumped back to the kitchen.

Ivy glared at Uncle Tommy. "I suppose it doesn't matter to

you that Conrad Thrasher had an affair with my mother right before the accident?"

The three men stared at her.

Uncle Tommy's face turned white. "I didn't know that. Who says?"

"My mother. I saw her in Des Moines."

Reuben's jaw dropped and Russell patted his hair.

Ivy slid out of the booth and looked directly at Russell and Reuben. "Conrad's been doing what he wants for a long time. It stops today. I'll see you at Luther's place as soon as you can. Don't tell anyone. Wear black and come the back way." Ivy turned and strode to the door.

Ivy stopped by Peter's law office, but Bertha said he was taking care of Ellen who was in her crazy mind and had been ranting about a kidnapping. Ivy explained the situation to Bertha then went to find Otis, but no one answered at his house. She knew Otis shouldn't be alone. The deaths of Maggie and Pinky had sent him spiraling into sadness, and Carly was his only lifeline. When Ivy had called to tell him his little Carly was gone, he had broken down and cried. But Ivy didn't have time to look for him now. Carly needed her. She would find Otis later and make sure he was okay. She stopped and talked to Virgil and Max before she left.

Ivy didn't stop at Judy's Beauty Shop. It was closed for the day, which meant Judy was visiting her son. Jesse and Raven had been married for several years and now lived in nearby Stilton. Raven taught home economics and Jesse was the football coach for the Stilton Buffaloes, their old high school rivals. Despite all his plans, Jesse's life hadn't ended up that different from Ivy's after all.

Even though it was very late, Ivy made her stops around town and talked to everyone she trusted who might help her. Then she went to Luther's to wait for their arrival and the handyman-led rescue of Carly.

Chapter 34

THE RESCUE

Ivy paced Luther's cluttered living room. She paused and looked out the filthy, spiderweb-filled front window. "I hope they come."

Luther gazed over her shoulder. "Don't worry. They will. They're Iowans."

Ivy pointed to the headlights appearing out of the dark. "Look."

A line of cars and trucks came over the dark hill, the back way so as not to drive by Conrad's house. The vehicles, with their lights off, pulled into Luther's dirt driveway and Ivy held the porch door open. The consolation of living in a small town was the assurance, that despite the constant intrusions on privacy and the petty bickering, they could depend on each other. Ivy discovered great solace in knowing her community would offer support during life's crucial battles.

Luther stood beside Ivy as he checked out the chosen witnesses she had assembled. Edna Jean bumped her head on the car door as she got out of Bertha's car. Luther whispered to Ivy, "You asked Edna Jean? I said they had to be able to see."

"I know, but I couldn't leave her out," Ivy whispered back.

The ragtag rescuers filed into Luther's small house: the dust-phobic librarian Edna Jean Whittaker, the town gossip Bertha Tuttle, the suspicious defenders of Mulberry Street Virgil

Jackson and Max Black, the ghost-haunted Reuben Smith, the pitty-patter Russell, the maven of the Coffey Shop Miss Shirley, and the bullied ex-mail carrier Uncle Walter. Some sat down wherever they could find a seat in the unkempt room, but most of them stood.

"You could stand a little cleaning up around here, Luther," Miss Shirley said.

"No time for such luxuries," Luther said. "Now let's get busy."

"Let's just storm the place," said Max.

"What if Luther's wrong?" Bertha asked.

"I'm not wrong," Luther said, insulted. "We got to move fast. We need to disrupt his midnight cemetery plans. Keep your eyes open and your mouths shut."

"Shouldn't we notify law enforcement?" Edna Jean asked.

They all looked at her. "Have you met Charlie?" Uncle Walter asked.

Miss Shirley gestured. "He's so far up the mayor's—"

Reuben leaned against the wall near the door. "Okay, no sheriff. So, what do you want us to do?"

"All you need to do is watch. You're the witnesses. I'll figure things out as we go along," Luther said.

"That's your rescue plan, Luther? To figure it out as we go?" Virgil asked.

"You can't plan for the unexpected," Luther said. "I find it best to go on instinct. Don't worry, I've got enough for all of us."

Edna Jean frowned. "What? Do you think you're James Bond or something?"

"More like Jethro Bond," said Bertha.

Edna Jean adjusted her thick glasses and nodded, trying to follow the blur that was Luther. "Maybe your thieving skills can be used for something good instead of taking poor little innocent poodles."

"Let that go for now," Uncle Walter said. "Folks, we need to be together on this. Our little girl's life is at stake here."

"I trust Luther," Ivy said as she confidently put her arm around him. "We're going to do what he says."

Max balled up his fists. "I'd like to get my hands on that thug."

"Save a piece of him for me," said Miss Shirley. "I like to clean up."

Russell pointed at the moon outside the window. "It'll be midnight soon. We'd better go."

Luther picked up his tool belt. "Let's load up."

Ivy pointed to the split wood at the end of the handle by the hammer's head. "Old Dan Tucker's seen better days."

"Never let me down before."

The community of protection rose from the bouncing animals and the collected clutter to face an unplanned and perhaps dangerous rescue of Carly.

As midnight approached, they all piled into the Monstrosity and sat down on the sturdy benches in the back of the camper, like a misfit army troop being transported to battle.

Edna Jean yawned. "Haven't been out this late in years."

Ivy drove around to the cemetery and parked by the clearing at Deadman's Woods. They all got out and crept along the deepening shadows until they reached the border of Conrad Thrasher's farm. A night owl called mournfully from the top of a tree. Its hooting seemed to warn of the dangers that lurked before them.

Luther and Ivy left the others at the edge of the woods and headed toward the barn.

"I don't know about you, but I'm not staying here if Carly's in danger," whispered Max to the others.

Virgil nodded. "Well, if we're doing this, let's do it."

So instead of staying put as they were told, the community contingent followed Luther and Ivy in a strange shuffling line. When they rounded the barn, Reuben stumbled over a basketball left from one of Weston's solitary games. Luther and Ivy turned to discover the entire group right behind them.

"Get back where I told you!" Luther whispered.

"You want us to come to just stand in the woods?" Bertha asked.

"You might need us," said Miss Shirley.

"You'll ruin it," Luther scowled.

Ivy rested her hand on Luther's arm. "They just want to help. Let them come."

Luther pressed his finger to his lips. "Okay, but at least be quiet. Go wait in the barn while I go to the house."

"It's locked," Virgil said.

"Then just stay out of sight on the side," Luther said.

The witnesses collected on the side of the barn and Luther motioned for Ivy to follow him. "Look in the windows. See if you can see her."

But as they approached the house, they heard a frantic scuffling and shouting coming from inside.

"I told you to keep an eye on her!" Conrad's voice scolded.

"She was locked in!" Weston said.

"Obviously not. Where would she go?" Miles asked.

"Check everywhere in the house," said Conrad.

Ivy looked up at the small attic window. It was open. Ivy grabbed Luther's arm and pointed at it and they both ran back to join the group. Luther took his hammer from his tool belt to pry open the lock on the barn. As the lock opened, the head of his hammer broke off from the handle. Luther picked up the corpse of Old Dan Tucker and put it in the pocket of his tool belt.

Miss Shirley quietly opened the double doors of the barn and everyone squeezed inside.

"Carly's escaped. We need to find her before they do," Ivy said.

They searched the entire barn and hayloft but there was no sign of the girl. "She's not here." Luther scratched his head. "Let's try the cistern."

He led them back outside into the darkness and pointed to the cistern. They all headed to the old concrete tank in the ground, about fifty yards from the house. The top of the cistern was broken, but there was a hole big enough for a little girl to climb inside. A padlock and chain kept the rest of cistern lid shut.

Ivy tugged at the lock. Luther's broken hammer was useless. She looked at Reuben. "Can you do it?"

Reuben nodded confidently, and walked over.

"That shouldn't even be a challenge," said Uncle Walter. "He's picked harder locks on my trailer."

In the distance, a light flickered in the farmhouse kitchen. With the curtains open, they could see Conrad and Weston moving around inside.

"You know, they'll just get away with it," said Russell, vigorously patting his hair.

Miss Shirley shook her head. "Not this time. You don't hurt a child."

Luther gave Reuben the knife from his tool belt and he picked the lock in a few seconds. The rest of the group stood guard behind them. With the cistern open, Ivy nodded at Max. "Your turn, Max."

Max moved the lid, then jumped up on the edge of the open cistern. He descended into the concrete tank and, after a few seconds, emerged at the top shaking his head. His bald head glistened in the flashlight's beam. "It's dark down there but she's not there. It's empty."

Everyone turned and stared at Luther, their rescue leader. "What do your instincts say, Luther?" Ivy asked.

Luther looked at the ground. "I think she's hiding."

Ivy's confidence that they would steal Carley back crumbled. She looked around at the strange group of friends standing around her.

Rueben pushed through the group. "I'll go search the house. Conrad will let me in. Won't be suspicious."

Luther and Ivy looked at each other and then nodded to Reuben. He nodded back, then walked across to the farmhouse and knocked. Conrad let him in. The others watched from the shadows of the trees as the minutes ticked by. The door opened again and Reuben walked down to the road, before doubling back through the trees to the group.

"Miles is there," Reuben told the huddled group. "I saw him duck into the coat closet. They seem panicked. I looked everywhere I could. Told him I'd lost my wallet at the last card game. Didn't see any trace of Carly."

"Let's scatter around the house and watch the windows," Miss Shirley said.

"The first one to see Miles or Conrad can shoot them dead," Max said.

'We don't have any guns," Bertha said.

"And none of us are that good a shot," Uncle Walter said.

A splash sounded in the lake, startling them. They looked over as two more birds landed on the water with a splash.

"Shh," Edna Jean scolded, using her best librarian voice. "Shush now." The rescuers grew quiet, accustomed to obeying her shushing. "I hear her." Edna Jean turned and pointed in the direction of the pond. "Carly's under the dock."

"Oh, sweet Jesus," Miss Shirley said. "Lord have mercy."

Ivy's mouth dropped open. She grabbed Edna Jean's arm. "How do you know?"

Edna Jean concentrated hard, squinting her eyes as she listened. "I can hear the water rippling."

Ivy hugged Edna Jean. "You have exceptionally keen hearing. I'm glad you came." Ivy turned toward the pond. Then she put her arm around Russell. "Russell, do you feel like a swim?"

Russell stopped fidgeting and nodded curtly. He stripped off his shirt as he ran to the water's edge. He waded toward the old swimmers' dock, anchored in the middle of the pond. Russell took a breath and quietly dove under the muddy water, as if the lake had just quietly absorbed him.

Ivy watched from shore as her friends stood beside her. An owl hooted in the still night like a sentry for their rescue.

Russell broke the surface for a moment and dove back down beneath the dock. Ivy knew there was plenty of space under it, almost a foot. She'd been under the dock herself when she was little. But the seconds seemed to stretch endlessly.

With a quiet ripple that only Edna Jean could hear, Russell emerged from the dark underbelly of the old dock. His lanky arms rose out of the water, holding Carly's body above his head. Her little arms and legs hung limply.

A lump of terror stuck in Ivy's throat as she waited for

Russell and Carly to reach the edge of the water. Silence stretched on the shore where the citizen rescue crew waited. Men capable of despicable acts were still in the house only a short distance away. But Ivy knew she couldn't go on living if Carly was dead.

From the dark and murderous pond, Russell escorted the little girl to shore. The fireflies flashed their lights in the woods and an owl's hoot sounded like a solemn warning. As shock and grief overcame her, Ivy sank to her knees and the deadly water lapped around her legs.

"Don't leave me," she said, her voice barely above a whisper.

Max gently lifted Ivy up with his strong arms, keeping her on her feet. "No time to give up now," he said.

Ivy looked at Max and held her own weight. He was right. She must face the fate of her child no matter what. That's what all mothers were supposed to do.

When Russell arrived at the shore, Miss Shirley stomped her feet. "This atrocity will not be forgotten, by God or me."

Bertha reached over and gently moved the hair out of Carly's face.

Ivy grabbed her little girl and held Carly's cold body against her own.

Edna Jean Whittaker put her hand on Ivy's shoulder. "She's alive. I can hear her heart beating."

Carly's chest rose with a shuddering breath, like the fluttering wings of a dragonfly. Ivy's lips quivered, and she looked to the dark heavens in gratitude.

When Carly opened her eyes, a grateful moan escaped her blue lips. "I'm cold, Momma. I'm scared."

"Shh. Carly, we're here. Everything's okay now," Ivy said, glancing over at the house. The men could come out anytime.

"What were you doing in that lake, child?" Miss Shirley asked in a whisper.

"Hiding till morning. I couldn't see. But I flied like a bird, Momma. I did it. I flied out of the witch's house."

"Yes, you did." Ivy held back her tears as she looked up at the open attic window.

"Lord have mercy," Miss Shirley said.

"We all came to get you," Ivy whispered.

Carly looked around at the assembled rescuers and smiled. "Hi, guys."

A shrill bird call echoed eerily in the night. Everyone looked up. Ivy turned, expecting to see Uncle Tommy after all. But the birds flew up to the sky. The door of the farmhouse opened, and Miles came striding out. His dreadlocks careened back and forth as he walked across the backyard, heading straight toward them.

Ivy pointed to the woods. "Head for the trees, everybody. Run."

Everyone scattered for the edge of Conrad's property. Ivy grimaced when she saw Edna Jean blindly run into a bush and fall face-first on the ground. Virgil helped her up and with his guidance, she followed the dark blurs and the sound of footsteps, and for once ignored the dirt on her clothes.

Ivy ran to the end of the barn with Carly in her arms. Luther followed her without a sound as they sprinted toward the woods. But it all became too much for Carly and she started to cry.

Ivy looked back and saw Miles turn when he heard the little girl's cries. He dashed after them around the barn. Ivy saw Weston's forgotten basketball lying in the grass and looked back at Reuben.

"Lane's open," Ivy called.

Reuben stopped his loping retreat and picked up the ball. He wound up into his bowling stance, lifting the ball up to his chin to aim. Then he crooked his leg high in the air. He shook his body and threw the ball at Miles, who was running towards them. Ivy held her breath as the ball skimmed along the ground and hit Miles in the leg, making him stumble. He fell over like an unstable bowling pin. Reuben jerked his arm back with a clenched fist. "STEE-RIKE."

The distraction gave Ivy enough time to get Carly safely into the woods but she looked over her shoulder as she ran.

Miles rubbed the back of his head and looked up to see Reuben heading toward the barn. Picking himself up, Miles stumbled in the unfamiliar yard as he chased after Reuben. He grabbed the back of Reuben's shirt and pulled him to the ground. Reuben fell hard, twisting his ankle.

Ivy paused in the woods and strained to hear them.

"Who in the hell are you?" Miles yelled. He turned Reuben over to see his face. "You?" He twisted Reuben's arm behind his back and put a gun to the back of his neck. "I got the old man," Miles yelled into the empty night. "Do you hear me, Ivy? I know you're out there hiding in the trees. I'll kill him if I have to. I told you to come alone to the cemetery."

Ivy could see the shadows of her friends hiding behind the trees. Ivy took a deep breath and Luther stopped beside her near a dense clump of bushes. She looked back to see Miles looming over Reuben. Ivy kissed Carly's cheek and handed her to Luther. "You'll be okay now. I'll see you soon. Reuben's in trouble. I've got to go help him." She patted Luther on the arm. "Call Charlie. Then let the wild dogs run free."

Luther took off running toward his house with Carly in his arms.

Ivy watched as Miles pressed Reuben's face to the ground. Blood and dirt smeared Rueben's face. Then she hurried to her friends, who were huddled in the dark woods, catching their breath from their escape and watching the unfolding horror.

Virgil pointed to himself and Max. "Let us go. We know how to handle his kind."

"He's looking for me and he's got a gun," Ivy said. "This one's mine."

"We got your back. Just holler if you need us," Miss Shirley said. "Be careful, Ivy. Miles won't play by the rules."

"There are no rules for this," said Ivy.

Each of her friends held out their hands and touched Ivy as she hurried by, as if their touch could give her strength. And it did. She glanced back at the faces of the people who had helped her save her little girl. Then she darted out of the trees and into the dim light coming from the farmhouse kitchen.

"Miles, let him go," Ivy said walking towards him.

Miles pushed his dreadlocks out of his face. "You're a sucker for your old geezer friends." He shook his head. "I told you to meet me at midnight at the cemetery."

"Plans change."

"How does it feel to have someone messing with your family?" Miles asked.

The side door to the house opened and Conrad Thrasher stepped onto the back porch, watching them from the shadows.

Reuben stared at his buddy. "What're you doing, Conrad? Stop him."

"Not my doing." He turned to go back inside.

"Conrad, we're friends."

Conrad pulled at his bushy eyebrows. "You're on your own if you side with her and that child."

Ivy stepped forward. "Okay, Miles. Let's get this over with. I'm here. Let him go."

Miles pushed Reuben's face into the ground before releasing him. "Get out of here, old man."

Reuben rose to his knees. His face was contorted in pain as he tried to stand. Miles laughed and kicked Reuben's leg. Reuben groaned and fell over again.

"My ankle. I think it's broke."

Miles laughed. "Then I guess you'll have to crawl on out of here."

Ivy stepped toward Reuben to help him up, but Miles grabbed her arm. "Where's all your buddies now?"

"Right here." Uncle Walter and Max walked across the yard. When they reached Reuben, Walter bent down and put his arms around the man who helped Uncle Tommy torment him for over twenty years. Despite Uncle Walter's own weak knees, he and Max slowly helped Reuben to his feet. Then with Max helping Rueben and Walter limp off together, they vanished into the darkness of the nearby trees.

Miles waved his gun at Ivy. "I'm sick of messing with you and these grandpas." He spat at Ivy's feet and some of the saliva landed on his unshaven chin.

"You won't get Carly," Ivy said.

Miles shook his head. "I don't want the girl. I want my freedom. I'm tired of hiding." He pointed to his Alliance tattoo on his arm. "But if I get locked up, the Alliance will make sure you never get her."

Miles wiped the spit from his face. "I'm going to offer you a deal."

Leaves crunched in the darkness by the pond. Ivy and Miles looked around but couldn't see anyone.

"I'm tired of all those old folks popping up out of those

woods." With the barrel of the gun, he pushed Ivy toward the lit farmhouse. "Move."

Ivy could see the shadowy faces in the woods still watching them. Miles prodded Ivy through the back door of Conrad's farmhouse and into the kitchen. Ivy could see a pan of leftover fried mushrooms still sitting on the stove. Conrad and Weston stood against the kitchen counter filled with empty beer bottles. Conrad glared at Miles as Ivy entered the farmhouse. "Why you bringing her in here?"

Ivy stood behind one of the chairs around the kitchen table.

"Bunch of raggedy old people sneaking around in your woods, man," Miles said.

Conrad looked out into the dark. Worried, he turned to Ivy. "This has nothing to do with us. It's all him."

"You helped him kidnap a child. You won't get away with this one like you got away with killing your wife. There's witnesses this time," Ivy said.

Conrad's eyes flashed with anger. "I didn't kill Mildred. Your mother did."

Ivy gasped and jerked back, but Miles gripped her arm even tighter.

"Why would my mother kill Mildred?"

"Mildred found us together. She called your mother a 'small-town tramp' and Barbara pushed her down the stairs. Mildred hit her head and died from the fall. I put her body under the dock to protect your mother. A drowning was easier to explain."

He took a drink of his beer. "Your grandmother somehow found out. She told Barbara that if she didn't leave that night, she'd tell Charlie that I drowned Mildred. She said she had proof. Violet always was a liar. But Barbara left town to save me."

Ivy broke out in a sweat. "Grandma didn't lie. Mildred wasn't dead. The fall didn't kill her. She drowned after you put her in the water."

Conrad's face tightened. "No."

"I saw Dr. Kelsey's coroner's report. She died from drowning."

Conrad took a long drink of beer. He scrunched up his face, trying to hold back the tears. "I thought she was dead. I was trying to protect Barbara. Your grandma should have stayed out of it. Now you know what it feels like to have someone you love taken away."

"I've known that all my life."

"Barbara never wanted to be a mother. It cramped her style. Ruined her plans." Spit flew out of Conrad's mouth. "Barbara was looking for a way out."

"Why didn't you go with her?"

"I couldn't leave that night with Mildred dead. So Barbara found someone else to go with her."

"Who?"

Conrad shrugged.

Truth creates its own freedom. It was time for Ivy to know. "You're not my father, are you?" She closed her eyes and braced for the impact.

Conrad choked on his beer. "Heck, no. You were already born when I took up with Barbara."

Miles let go of Ivy and pushed his face inches from hers. His breath smelled like cigarettes and liquor. "Shut up. I don't know what's going on with you two, but stop talking. Here's the deal, I'll give you Carly and you forget you ever saw me and everything that happened the night Maggie died. Without a witness, they can't convict me."

Ivy stared back into his angry black eyes. "So, you'll trade Carly for your freedom?"

He took a couple of steps back and leaned against the refrigerator by the window. The gun rested across his chest. He nodded. "The Alliance needs me. I want my life back."

"So, does Maggie."

Miles smashed the butt of his gun against Ivy's face, knocking her to the floor. She touched her cheek and felt the warm wet blood. The ticking of the clock on the stove echoed in her head as it counted down the seconds. Anger surged through her.

Ivy thought of Carly, scared and wet, waiting for her at Luther's house. She knew she might not get out of this house alive and Carly could lose another mother, but she was going to stand and fight. It needed to be finished. This had to end.

She grabbed the corner of the stove and defiantly pulled herself up, glaring at Conrad and Miles. "There's no difference between you two. You're both thugs who killed the women who loved them. I hope you both rot in prison."

Miles lunged at Ivy and grabbed her around the neck. He pressed a gun against her head with his other hand. The vein in his forehead bulged. "That's not the way this is going to go down."

"Pull the trigger. Pull the trigger," Weston yelled.

Ivy reached for the iron frying pan of mushrooms and grabbed the handle that was still warm. She swung it at Miles but his hand with the gun blocked it. The impact broke his hand and stopped him from shooting. The greasy mushrooms spilled all over the floor. Ivy kicked him, and Miles slipped on the mushrooms, stumbling back against the stove, his broken hand dangling.

A shrill bird call pierced the deathly quiet night. Then a shot rang out, shattering the kitchen window and hitting Miles in the temple. He crumpled to the floor, dead. The purple hole in his head oozed blood. Ivy startled and ducked down.

Weston knocked over a chair. "There's a sniper in the woods."

Conrad threw down his beer bottle, which smashed as it hit the floor. Weston and Conrad ran ducking through the house and out the front door. Ivy stared at Miles splayed out on the kitchen floor, shot in the head like a varmint before he knew what hit him.

She backed away from the body but slipped from the greasy mushroom floor and landed in Miles's blood, which was spreading in a red pool on the kitchen floor. Ivy trembled as she crawled across the floor, littered with broken glass. She shook as she stood up and stumbled out the back door. She needed to get away from that house of death.

The sound of barking and growling dogs broke the stillness of the night. Luther's wild dogs had surrounded Weston and Conrad as they tried to escape and drove them toward the pond. Rosie's four-legged family had finally exacted their revenge against Weston, the fire-starter and town tormentor.

The sheriff pulled into the gravel driveway with his lights flashing. Charlie got out and hustled down toward the dark pond and the canine commotion. Conrad waved wildly at his old buddy.

"Charlie, thank God you're here. Shoot these vicious mutts before they kill us."

Charlie sniffed and pulled at the loose skin under his chin. "Conrad, I can't protect you and Weston any more. This time I've got to take you in. I got no choice." He turned and pointed to the woods. "Too many witnesses."

Out of the trees, Ivy's friends emerged, stepping into the brightness from the sheriff's headlights.

"I got you that job," Conrad said.

"And I've paid you back over and over for that. Now let's go, Conrad. You've gone too far this time."

Charlie scratched his white hair which stood on end in his stiff crew cut. "Luther, get these dang canines out of here. You made your point."

Luther was still carrying Carly, who was wrapped in Luther's old bomber jacket. "Wild dogs, cease," he said. They reluctantly came.

Ivy knew Ben and the other EMT's would be there soon. Then Dr. Kelsey, who still served as the county coroner, would come to examine Miles's body. Miles would be zipped into a black body bag for his final removal. Carly's father could never hurt her again.

Despite their protests, the deputy sheriff handcuffed Weston and Conrad. He looked at Ivy. "I don't suppose you know who shot Miles?"

Ivy shook her head. "I wish I did. I'd thank them."

Charlie nodded. "Okay. I need all of your statements tonight at the station." He put Conrad and Weston in the back seat of his car and took them to jail.

Ivy ran toward the people of Coffey who had risked their lives for her and her daughter, the little girl she couldn't live without. She threw her arms around them, trying to hug them all at once.

"Thank you. I love you all and especially whoever shot Miles."

"It wasn't one of us," Virgil said.

Ivy looked around in the darkness. "Then who was it?"

"Most probably one of my ghosts," Reuben said.

They all piled back in the Monstrosity. Ivy gave the keys to Luther and climbed into the back. She nuzzled her face in

Carly's hair which smelled like the murky lake, but also like hope. The lake didn't take her. It was a new chance.

Reuben turned to Uncle Walter. "Hey, listen, Walter. Sorry about the zucchini. I shouldn't have gone along with Tommy's pranks all these years. Guess I was just looking for a distraction from my dang ghosts."

"Don't worry about it. Tommy's always been good at getting people to do the wrong thing."

Luther turned into his dirt driveway with the dogs running behind the camper. Patty sat hunched on the front porch, exhausted from the walk from her house. Patty flung open her arms when she saw Ivy get out of the back with Carly.

"Carly!" Patty yelled.

Ivy put Carly down. Carly ran to Patty, dragging Luther's ragged bomber on the ground.

"God bless this child. And God bless you all for finding her." Patty held Carly and cried.

Miss Shirley grabbed Ivy's arm as if in a hurry. "I've got to get back to the restaurant. Got to clean up whatever's left over after tonight. No one messes with my Carly-girl. I've been cleaning up all my life. Believe you me, I know how to clean up. Yes, I do." Ivy hugged her, and Miss Shirley hustled away to her car.

One by one, Ivy watched her exhausted friends leave Luther's house. The fear and terror of the night had drained their strength, but they still had to give their statements as witnesses to Charlie before the night was over.

Ivy hugged Luther, who stood awkwardly in her embrace. "Thank you, Luther. You have good instincts."

"Told you."

"I love you and I love your wild dogs."

Luther didn't speak, but nodded and gave a little grunt as a tear ran down his cheek.

Chapter 35

PLAY THE HAND THAT'S DEALT

After talking to Charlie at the station, Ivy, Uncle Walter, and Carly pulled the Monstrosity into the driveway at 4120. The old maple tree swayed. Its branches looked like open arms welcoming them home. Grandma sat wrapped in a quilt by the front window, waiting for them. Ivy pointed to the eighty-year-old woman bathed in the warm light of the big house. "Hey, look, Carly. Grandma's still up waiting for you."

Grandma smiled and waved from inside the family's old Victorian house. Carly waved back. "Grandma's shrinking," she said quietly.

Ivy's heart jumped. Carly had noticed Violet slipping away, too. "Yes, she is. Go on inside. She's been worried about you."

Carly climbed out of the Monstrosity and rushed inside, followed by Ivy and Uncle Walter.

Grandma hugged Carly tightly. "Give me some loving, my precious girl." She kissed Carly's upturned face.

Ivy hugged Grandma as well, breathing in her lilac smell. They'd been gone an eternity in one night. She felt good to be home.

Carly twirled around the room. "I love this place. I'm never leaving here again."

"You're home," Ivy said, relieved to have her little girl back.

Dr. Kelsey came by soon after to make sure Carly was all right. He examined her and pronounced her fine. "Remarkable. She's a strong little girl." He planned to stop at Reuben's farm to check out his twisted ankle before going to the clinic to deal with Miles' body.

When Ivy tucked Carly in bed for the night, she turned on the cow-jumping-over-the-moon nightlight. "The witch took me," Carly said.

"But we found you. I told you we would."

"He hurt my first mom when I was a baby, but he didn't get me."

"No, he didn't get you," Ivy said with tears in her eyes.

It would take a while for Carly to get rid of the nightmares about her ordeal.

Ivy pulled up the blankets and looked down at the beautiful little girl who she had reluctantly agreed to raise. Now, she couldn't live without her. Ivy had learned from Carly that no one was ever alone as long as someone loved them.

After Ivy said good-night, Grandma shuffled into Carly's bedroom in her untied tennis shoes. Ivy watched them from the doorway. Grandma sat on the side of Carly's bed and kissed her good-night. Carly rubbed Grandma's velvety robe, now many sizes too big.

"Grandma, are you sick?" she asked.

Grandma clicked her tongue. "Yes, you know I'm pretty old. My parts are just beginning to wear out. When you get as old as me, you know you aren't going to live much longer. That's why I'm so happy for every day I have with you before the Good Lord calls me up to heaven." Grandma gently bounced the bed. "And why I'm so glad to have you home safely."

Carly's eyelids fluttered as drowsiness cascaded over her

like a waterfall. "It was scary in the lake, Grandma. I was afraid I would never see you again."

Grandma smiled as tears filled her eyes. "I love you, pumpkin." She spread her arms apart. "I love you more than the great blue sky."

Ivy swallowed the lump in her throat as she watched them.

Tears flooded Carly's brown eyes. "I was scared I was going to die."

"The Lord's not ready for you yet," Grandma said. "But he's almost ready for me."

Carly's finger traced the blue veins showing through Grandma's translucent skin. "But Grandma, aren't you scared?"

"No."

"But won't you miss us when you're up in heaven?"

"Of course, I will." Grandma tapped her tea-towel-stuffed bosom. "But I'll be watching you, my sweet girl, from my back porch in the Great Hereafter." The bed rocked as a tear ran down Grandma's wrinkled cheek. "Always believe in possibilities."

"I did," Carly said.

"Exactly. You're my strong girl."

Carly hugged her shrinking Grandma. "I wish I had a nice dad."

"Sometimes you get a nice father and sometimes you don't. It isn't fair. It's just like playing cards. Sometimes you get a good hand and sometimes you just have to make the best out of what you're dealt. It's the luck of the draw. But you got lucky in other ways. You've got Grandpa Otis and Miss Shirley. You got a good mother. And you've got Uncle Walter and me." Then Grandma sang "Red River Valley" until her little granddaughter drifted off to sleep.

Ivy sighed. She felt relieved that Conrad wasn't her father. She needed Robert's image to hang onto and it seemed silly that she'd ever thought someone else could be her father. Grandma always told her Robert loved her like only a father could.

Ivy watched Grandma go downstairs and lock all the doors, something she had never done before. Carly's dangerous night took a lot out of Grandma, at a time when she didn't have much left. Then Grandma shuffled into the kitchen and sunk down in a chair next to Uncle Walter.

Ivy put a bag of popcorn in the microwave and pushed the buttons. The popping in the microwave sounded like an Iowa spring rain on an old tin roof. Then Ivy joined Grandma and Uncle Walter at the round kitchen table.

Uncle Walter sighed. "Our little Carly-girl is safe."

Grandma leaned back in her kitchen chair. She clasped her hands and rocked them back and forth in the air in a thankful prayer as silent tears rolled down her cheeks. "Thank the Good Lord for bringing her home."

Then they all held hands around the table, grateful to have Carly back. The microwave dinged. Uncle Walter limped across the kitchen to get the popcorn. Ivy went down to the windowless canning room in the basement and got three Dr. Peppers from the darkest corner of the house that was so good at keeping the pop cold.

She set the Dr. Peppers down on the kitchen table. Grandma shuffled the deck as they got ready to play cards, as if nothing was different from any other night of their lives. Uncle Walter put the popcorn bowl on the table and sat down.

"Oh, my gosh, we need to call Otis and tell him Carly's safe," Ivy said.

"There's something I need to tell you about Otis," Grandma said.

"What?"

Grandma coughed and cleared her throat. "I heard Otis moved himself into the Rose Hill Nursing Home today."

"Rose Hill? Why? He hates that place. Thelma's there. That's why I couldn't find him this afternoon. What's wrong with him?"

"I don't know. Maybe he just gave up," Uncle Walter shuffled the cards. "Let's play some hearts."

"There's nothing wrong with Otis. He's still a young man," said Grandma.

Uncle Walter looked over at his mother. "Everyone's a young man to you, Mother."

Grandma swished her hand at him. "Too much sorrow robs the spirit."

Uncle Walter dealt the cards, placing them methodically in front of each person. Grandma and Uncle Walter picked up their cards and fanned them out, studying them. Ivy's cards lay on the table.

"Why don't the birds talk to me?" she asked.

"They do. It just takes a while to hear them," said Grandma.

"But how come I never know what's going on?" Ivy said.

Uncle Walter tapped his cards on the table. "Well, maybe Otis doesn't want to be a burden to you."

"Why would he think he's a burden to me?" Ivy said.

"Maybe he sees all the dreams you've sacrificed for me," Grandma said.

"What're you talking about? You gave me my dreams. Without you two, it would have been just nightmares." Ivy pulled her hair back in a ponytail and let it drop. She sighed. "Anyway, I'm going to go see Mr. Norton tomorrow. I've got to tell him about Carly and I'll find out what he's doing at Rose Hill." She picked up her cards and fanned them out. She was dealt all hearts and the Queen of Spades, which could be a very good hand, depending on how she played it.

Chapter 36

ROSE HILL

Although the ordeal was over, Ivy barely slept that night. She kept getting up to check on Carly. Finally, she just laid down beside her and slept. When the sun came up, she took a shower and got dressed. Then she drove to the Hy-Vee store on the town square to get some groceries.

The cool spring morning showed only a few clouds in the sky. The earth needed a rest before the intense heat of the coming summer. Ivy pulled into the parking lot across the street from the courthouse.

Charlie peered out the window, then hurried out of his office and down the steps. He beckoned to Ivy. "I need to relay some information that you might be interested in." Charlie rubbed the loose skin under his chin and spoke in a whisper. "Not too many people know yet, but Conrad and Weston were found deceased at 6:08 a.m. in their jail cells."

Ivy's mouth dropped open. "What happened?"

Charlie rocked back on his heels. He took a deep breath. "Suspected poison mushrooms."

Ivy grabbed his arm. "Poison mushrooms? You've got to be kidding."

"Nope. That's what Doc Kelsey says. He should know. He's seen it before with Luther's dad."

Ivy shook her head and put her hand to her mouth. She looked up at the cloudy spring sky then back to Charlie.

"Last night, I locked them up. They ate and went to sleep. By the time I came in this a.m., they were dead."

"What'd they eat?"

"Miss Shirley brought over some fried chicken after the Coffey Shop closed up," Charlie said.

Ivy's heart pounded but she quickly spoke up. "There was a pan of mushrooms on Conrad's stove." Maybe it was Conrad's mushroom greed that had finally taken him down or maybe that night the fried chicken and Miss Shirley's famous gravy had come with a side of false morel mushrooms. Didn't Miss Shirley say that's what she'd do? Maybe Miss Shirley had cleaned up.

"Yeah, I saw them all over the floor of Conrad's kitchen."

Ivy looked at Charlie. He nodded. "I'll tell the doctor he was right."

Ivy jingled the keys in her sweaty hand. "I better go tell Grandma."

"How's Violet doing, by the way?"

"Well, Grandma's been pretty sick lately. It's hard for her to do too much by herself. Dr. Kelsey says if she lives to see the new year, it'll be a miracle." Ivy kicked at the gravel in the parking lot. "To tell you the truth, I think she wants to go."

Charlie scratched the side of his face. "Hard to think of Coffey without her."

"Yeah. I know." Ivy wanted to get out of there. "Thanks for everything."

Charlie shook her hand and nodded quickly.

Ivy walked toward the car feeling a little lightheaded. Was it possible that the Thrashers were finally gone from her life?

She turned back to Charlie. "Do you think you'll have to investigate their deaths any further?"

"Doubt it. I think justice has been served, don't you?"

She nodded. Mushroom justice.

"What about Miles? Any ideas where the bullet came from?"

"Nobody saw a thing. It was like a shot from the dark. We combed the woods and couldn't find anything. Damnedest thing I ever saw," Charlie said. "Well, got to go meet the guys at the Coffey Shop. You take care, Ivy. Tell your grandma I said hello."

Charlie sauntered across the street.

Ivy couldn't say she was sad about Miles' death. In fact, all she felt was relief. And as for the Thrashers, it was a short journey to their final destination.

Grandma was right—their souls had drifted away when Mildred died. Many people in town sighed with relief. There would have to be a new election for mayor and perhaps now, bank loans would be given on merit instead of personal prejudice. But Ivy felt her mother was partially to blame for their demise. Her mother had used men and destroyed many lives because of her desperation to get out of Coffey and escape from the little baby she never wanted and the husband she didn't love.

That afternoon, Carly baked cookies with Uncle Walter as Grandma supervised from her chair in the kitchen.

Ivy bought a bottle of Haig & Haig scotch and went to visit the self-exiled Otis at the Rose Hill Nursing Home.

The big front desk of the nursing home engulfed tiny Thelma

Sampson. She tapped the chewed-up end of her pencil against the desk. "What do you want?" she said as Ivy approached.

"I want to see Otis. What room is he in?"

Thelma peered over her half-glasses at Ivy. "Is he expecting you?" She looked exactly like Uncle Walter's gnome riding the mushroom. The evil pixie.

"No, but I'm sure he'll want to see me."

"Are you planning on staying long?"

Ivy leaned over the desk toward Thelma. "Thelma, I don't have time for this. Tell me his room number, please."

Thelma glared and waved her stubby finger at Ivy. "8B, but don't you bother him none."

"I wouldn't dream of it."

Ivy hurried down a long hall that smelled of musty clothes locked in a trunk for many years. "Hey, wait. What you got in that sack?" Thelma asked from behind the desk.

Ivy ignored her and kept walking.

"We have strict rules at Rose Hill, you know," Thelma called after her.

Ivy quickened her pace down the dark corridor. She didn't want Thelma to see the top of the scotch bottle sticking out of the brown paper bag. As she walked down the hall, her shoe stuck to the floor. She stopped and examined the sole. A dead cockroach was smeared on the bottom of her shoe. Ivy scraped her shoe on the tile floor and continued on her way to Otis's room. She knocked on the door marked 8B, but there was no answer. She knocked harder.

"Mr. Norton? It's Ivy."

A muffled voice answered. "If it's bad news, don't tell me."

Ivy pushed the door open. Otis sat on the side of an unmade bed in a dark room.

"Did you find my Carly?" he asked.

Ivy nodded and sat down beside him on the bed. "Yes, she's safe at home."

Otis hung his head and his shoulders heaved with heavy sobs. Tears of relief fell in torrents. "I was afraid I'd lost her, too."

Ivy put her arm around him. A small TV blazed in the darkness with its volume turned off. Ivy's eyes adjusted to the darkness and the glow from the tiny screen. She patted his arm. "She's fine. I'll bring her by to see you tomorrow."

Ivy stood up and turned off the TV. Then she felt for the switch on the wall and flicked on the light. Otis's eyes drooped heavy and dark. His wrinkled and stained clothes hung on his lanky frame and his unshaven face looked slack and ashy. His hair, usually so tidy, stuck up in places. She'd never seen the dapper man looking so awful.

"Everything's going to be okay." Ivy pulled out the bottle of scotch. "I brought you something to wash away your troubles."

"Thank you," Otis sobbed, "but I think I've got too many troubles for that one bottle."

"Well, it's a start." Ivy held his hand until the tears stopped.

"Had a little run-in with Thelma, your prison guard. Thought I was going to need a garden hoe."

He smiled and Ivy recognized the old Otis. "Yeah, Thelma's an old battle-ax, but she's harmless."

Ivy sat down beside him on the bed. "What are you doing here, Mr. Norton? If I'd known, I never would have let this happen to you."

He put his head down and shifted on the bed. "That's why I didn't tell you."

Ivy tried to look into his downcast face. "Why wouldn't you want me to help you?"

Otis didn't look up. "Because if you have me to worry about, you'll never get out of Coffey like you've planned your whole life. I'm getting old. I don't need much, and you've got Carly to think about. We almost lost her." He began to cry again. "You've got more to worry about than me. It's okay here."

"No, it's not okay. It's not okay at all. You need to be drinking sweet tea on the back porch as the sun sets on the fields, not in a black hole like this place. You need to be killing snakes and Lord only knows what else with your garden hoe. You could use a hoe in here. I stepped on a roach walking down the hall just now."

"Yeah, the bugs and rodents are a little out of control."

"Rodents? What is this place, Black Plague Manor?"

Otis laughed softly and cleared his throat. "The truth is, I feel like that chicken Max used to talk about. The one that lost all its feathers in the tornado. I'm nothing but a naked yard bird."

"Yeah, but don't forget that chicken sure could run when the wind kicked up," Ivy said, and they laughed loudly.

The door flew open with a bang. Thelma's miniature frame stood in the doorway.

"Otis, visiting hours are over." She wrinkled her nose and her hairy lip twitched. She pointed her stubby finger at Ivy. "That woman has to leave."

Ivy looked at Otis. "Visiting hours? I didn't realize this was cellblock 8B."

Otis shrugged and scratched his whiskers. "They have a lot of rules here."

Thelma stomped into the room. "And no alcohol is one of them. I'll take that." She snatched up the bottle of scotch and pointed to the door. "Now, out."

Ivy jumped up. "Thelma, you have no right to take his things."

Otis waved at Ivy, signaling for her not to make a fuss. "It's all right Ivy. It's a rule. As long as Carly's all right, you can tell me what happened later. I'm pretty tired anyway."

The curtain of depression fell back over his face. When Ivy hugged him goodbye, she could feel his bones. Without her realizing, Otis had grown old.

"I was right. This isn't a home, it's a seniors' prison. I'll be back tomorrow with Carly."

Ivy stomped down the hall. She held back her tears until she was safely back in the truck. Resting her head on the steering wheel, she sobbed for Otis and for her grandmother. She wept for growing old and dying, and for those left behind.

Chapter 37

SENTIMENTAL JOURNEY HOME

The howling winter winds blew away summer's warmth and the barren trees in Grandma's backyard swayed and groaned from the force of the Midwestern gales.

Grandma slowly slipped away from Ivy, moving closer toward the unknown abyss of the world beyond, her so-called Great Hereafter. Her cancer created an emptiness around her, as if death were preparing to suck her away. Ivy sat on Grandma's bed and listened to her struggling breaths. Grandma squeezed Ivy's hand. "When I'm gone, I want you to travel and see all the places you've missed. Take Carly with you so she won't feel so trapped like you did. I should have given you the world."

Ivy nodded. "You did."

As the days passed, Ivy grew frightened as Grandma lost her hold on this world. The eighty-year-old seldom left her bed, sleeping on and off throughout the day. But whenever she was awake those days in late December, she looked out her window at the woods checking for signs of snow. She waited anxiously for the dance of the snowflakes to blanket the Iowa countryside, piling up big drifts and sending the remaining birds flocking to her backyard feeders. So far, the winter had brought cold brisk winds but no snow.

Dr. Kelsey and Matilda checked on Grandma every night after the clinic closed, telling Ivy that Grandma's time neared, perhaps a few more days or weeks, a few months at the most. Death was just a matter of time. And like most things, somehow Grandma knew.

One Saturday afternoon, Ivy washed Grandma's thin patches of silver hair that had finally grown back after the chemo. She propped Grandma up with pillows in the chair next to her bed. The winter weather put Grandma in a festive mood. She hummed her favorite Christmas song, "White Christmas."

Ivy held up a glass of cold water and Grandma sipped from the straw. "Ivy, see if Judy can make me look good before everybody and their brother comes trooping over here to say their sappy good-byes," said Grandma, touching her hair. She grabbed Ivy's arm. "And promise me you won't forget to pluck my chin hairs before I die."

"Grandma, I promise, I won't forget your chin hairs. And I'll call Judy and see if she can come over tonight."

Grandma nodded. "Good, good."

That night after Judy's Beauty Shop closed, Judy jingle-jangled into Grandma's bedroom, snapping her Doublemint gum and clicking her high heels. She hadn't changed much since Ivy first saw her step off the bus. Judy was still beautiful and lively.

Grandma smiled and shook her head. "Judy, you sure can brighten up a room."

Judy smiled and danced with the pink cape until she flipped it around Grandma's shoulders. "So, Violet, are you ready for a new do?"

Grandma gently touched what was left of her hair. "I don't have much hair left, but when I die, make it look good for my casket-viewing, if you can."

Judy stroked the thin strands of Grandma's silver-spun hair. "Now Violet, don't you worry on about that." She nodded in Ivy's direction. "Ivy will tell me when you pass, and I'll go down to Baker's and make you look beautiful on your way to heaven. You can believe that."

Ivy sat on the side of Grandma's big mahogany bed.

Judy's bracelets tumbled down her arm as she gently combed Grandma's hair. She looked over at Ivy. "I wanted to tell you something. Jesse and Raven are getting a divorce."

Ivy grew silent, remembering the betrayal of her friends. All her old feelings swirled around.

"A divorce? I knew that a long time ago." Grandma pinched her fingers open and closed. "Birds talk."

No one knew more than Violet Taylor.

The morning before Christmas, Ivy dipped the green sponge in a glass of cold water and dabbed it inside Grandma's dry mouth. Grandma swallowed hard and coughed, making strange gurgling sounds as she tried to breathe. She waved her trembling hand until the spell passed. "Ivy, don't forget, bring Justin home. Nothing will be right until we do right by him." She tried to clear her throat again.

Ivy pulled the quilts over her grandmother and kissed her cheek. "I will, Grandma. Don't worry, I will."

"He's Miss Shirley and Ben's boy for sure and we would never take him from them, but we need to stand up and claim him as family." Grandma closed her eyes and groaned. "And don't forget the birds," she whispered, her words harder to understand.

Ivy stroked Grandma's wispy strands of silver hair that Judy had somehow managed to tame. "I won't, Grandma. I'll feed them every day, just like always. Carly will make sure of that."

Grandma smiled. Her gums were black along the edges. There was so little of her left. Death was coming to claim its due. She sighed and sank back against her pillow. "The birds will be my sign." Grandma's eyes fluttered like the wings of the birds she loved, and she fell asleep.

Ivy was closing the red velvet curtains when she saw Jesse walking up the sidewalk to the house. When she opened the door, Jesse handed her a poinsettia plant.

"Merry Christmas, Ivy. I guess my mom told you. Raven and I didn't work out. You want to take a walk out to Beecher Pond?"

Ivy hesitated, then nodded.

They walked around Beecher Pond and went into Uncle Tommy's old duck blind. Jesse took Ivy's hand.

"I've been wanting to apologize for a long time. I just didn't know how to say it. I was so stupid, and I didn't treat you right. I didn't want to wait but I was wrong. I'm sorry."

Ivy gave in to his kiss, wanting the old dream, but then she stepped back. She stared at the place where the picture of her mother and father had been on the wall. "It's not enough, Jesse. I want someone who will wait through anything for me. I deserve that."

She had learned a long time ago that Grandma was right. Sometimes life's disappointments can turn out to be blessings. Jesse and Raven never made it past Stilton and ended up unhappy together. After all, plans change. Raven told her that when they were children.

She left Jesse in the duck blind and ran home, feeling the cold wind on her face. For the first time, she felt free from the darkness of her regrets.

On Christmas Eve, Ivy and Uncle Walter brought the already-decorated tree down from the attic and they re-arranged the bird ornaments on the branches. The holiday tree ritual would be Carly's job soon. The traditional unveiling of the perpetually decorated Christmas tree, like all things, would soon pass to a new generation.

Grandma settled on the couch in front of the fake white Christmas tree. She spent Christmas Eve, as she always did, with her family. Everyone gathered there except Angela, who hadn't been back home since high school. No one really talked about her, and Ivy and Russell's questions about her were avoided or left unanswered, until they rarely asked anymore. Ivy thought she saw her once in Stilton but decided it was just a trick of her mind trying to rearrange the pieces of her family to make sense.

Uncle Tommy, Aunt Hattie, and Russell went through the motions of the traditional Taylor Christmas celebration for Grandma's sake. But Ivy knew that Uncle Tommy and Aunt Hattie didn't really want to be there.

Uncle Walter never replaced his scorched Santa costume, but they still carried on the other Taylor traditions. They fed the birds, and when the eggnog and Christmas cookies were gone, they helped Grandma up the stairs to her bed. As Ivy pulled up the warm covers, Grandma reached for her hand. "I know my end is near. We got through Christmas Eve without a family fight this year."

"Well, it's not over yet."

"It is for me." Grandma closed her eyes. "Will you open the curtains, so I can see the snow before I go?"

"There isn't any snow."

"Yet," Grandma said knowingly, holding out her curled up palm. "Here," she said, opening her hand, revealing her wedding ring from Sam Taylor. "It's yours now. I don't need it. I'll be seeing Sam soon enough."

Ivy took the ring and slipped it on her finger. "Thank you, Grandma. I'll take good care of it."

Ivy pulled open the heavy red velvet curtains. Cancer slowly destroyed the hulking beauty of Violet Taylor. Her body whittled away until only the barest survival remained. Grandma lived through life's tornadoes, but the ravages of cancer had plucked the feathers of Grandma's life one by one and left only the soul intact. The reality of Grandma's impending death sucked all the life out of Ivy.

Grandma smiled and looked up. "Sam?" She closed her eyes and sank into the unconscious world. Ivy sobbed. Grandma's soul would leave a big hole when she left this world. Ivy kissed Grandma on the forehead. "Goodnight to the great surly one. May your mighty soul find its resting place in peace and bring joy to the Great Hereafter. We will miss you here on Earth."

Christmas Eve drew to a close, and Grandma remained unconscious, falling deeper into the unknown world. Then the snow fell heavy and wet outside Grandma's old Victorian house. The dance of the snowflakes finally arrived, but too late for Grandma to see.

Russell kissed his sleeping grandmother goodbye then joined his mother who had put in her obligatory holiday family appearance and was anxious to go. "Are you coming with us or are you going to keep worshiping the devil?" Aunt Hattie said to her husband.

"I think I'll visit with Jack Daniels for a little bit before I come home."

Aunt Hattie rolled her eyes. She pulled Russell out the door behind her. "I'll drop you off at your apartment." Russell still lived in the apartment above the Coffey Shop. He continued to enjoy working for the post office despite the unending ridicule of his father.

Carly was still up playing cards with Uncle Walter, so Ivy put her to bed. Then Ivy went back to Grandma's bedroom where her uncles avoided each other on separate sides of the room as their mother lay dying. Not even death could break the silence of the uncles' deep-rooted sandwich war. Ivy shook her head, still trying to understand all the years of long-standing muteness.

"Don't you think twenty-six years is long enough to hold a grudge?" Ivy asked.

Uncle Tommy pushed his glasses up the bridge of his nose. "Not for me."

Ivy sighed. "Like Grandma always said, time stands still in families."

Uncle Walter picked the lint off his sweater. "Tell Tommy if he wasn't so stupid, he might be worth talking to. And it wasn't his sandwich to begin with."

Ivy delivered the insulting banter. The uncles' bickering wasn't amusing anymore. "Uncle Tommy, he says it wasn't your sandwich, and you're stupid." Her blue eyes dimmed as the conversation triangle bounced back and forth.

An icicle broke loose from the front porch roof and shattered on the sidewalk below.

"Ivy, you tell Letter Boy he hasn't had a thought worth listening to in twenty-six years." Uncle Tommy tucked his wrinkled flannel shirt into his pants. He stormed out of the bedroom and thumped down the stairs muttering, "I need another drink." A moment later, Ivy heard him rattling around in the kitchen.

Uncle Walter ran his hands over his sagging face and through his salt and pepper hair. He closed his drooping eyes.

Ivy wandered over to the window. Snow clung to every branch and railing. A beautiful blanket of white fell, purifying the town as if preparing a final tribute for the exit of one of its oldest and most cherished citizens. The diffused light from the street reflected the white landscape onto Grandma's bed.

"Grandma, you should see the snow. It's beautiful. And listen, the birds are louder than usual tonight, especially for winter."

The quiet evening amplified the occasional bird songs. "Can you hear them?" Ivy asked.

Grandma's mind gradually closed, but Ivy hoped she heard the birds' farewell, their final salute. Although Grandma's frail body lay unresponsive, Ivy knew that if Grandma could hear, her heart would have rejoiced. Grandma spoke the language of the birds after all. Christmas Eve descended on the big Victorian house on Meadowlark Lane, and the silent sleep overtook Grandma's mind as the heavy snow turned the world white.

Downstairs, a bottle broke. "Don't do this to me, Mr. Jack Daniels," Tommy yelled.

Ivy thought perhaps even Uncle Tommy had surpassed his holiday cheer quota.

"I can barely stand to be in the same house with that man," Uncle Walter said to Ivy.

Uncle Tommy's voice boomed from the bottom of the stairs. "Ivy, I heard what the old mailman said." He huffed up to Grandma's room and grabbed his coat from the chair beside Grandma's four-poster bed. "Ivy, I've got to be getting on home."

Ivy knew Uncle Tommy wanted to escape the responsibilities and stress of his dying mother. But she sighed with relief, glad he was leaving before the never-ending uncle-battle raged.

Uncle Walter cleared his throat. "Too much work always makes Tommy nervous."

Uncle Tommy glared at his brother. "What would a mama's boy like him know?"

With no energy left to relay their insults, Ivy just waved her hand in the air. "It's okay, Uncle Tommy. Go on home. I'll see you tomorrow."

Uncle Tommy shook his head. "Can't come over tomorrow. Football's on." He pointed to Grandma. "Only did it all these years for her."

Uncle Walter rolled his eyes. He started brushing his mother's feathery gray hair and softly singing "Sentimental Journey."

"Look at him. He's nothing but a brown-noser. Always has been," Uncle Tommy said.

Ivy shook her head and walked Uncle Tommy downstairs. He looked around. "Hey, where's Carly? She hasn't been bothering me for a while."

Ivy tapped her watch. "Well, it's pretty late. She went to bed a while ago."

Uncle Tommy sniffed. "She didn't say goodnight to me."

Ivy could tell the ice of Uncle Tommy's heart was slowly thawing. Grandma used to say there was something about a heart that can't help but be touched by a child.

"I think you were still visiting with Jack Daniels when I tucked her in bed. But I'll tell her you said goodbye."

Uncle Tommy shrugged. "No big deal."

Ivy realized even the hardest hearts can soften. The narrowest path, given time, will find bends and curves and can eventually change course. Uncle Tommy scratched his chin and sniffed. "Yeah. You'd think you'd be more grateful to me, being that I shot that worthless father of hers."

Ivy stared at him. The shrill bird call she heard that night was Uncle Tommy! He shot Miles. "You? I thought you didn't want any part of it."

Uncle Tommy shrugged. "He was a varmint. Easy shot. Two points. Cats are harder to hit."

Stunned, Ivy stared at him. "Well, thank you. You saved my life."

He put on his coat. "Whatever. I just thought it was time I told you." He buttoned his coat and stepped out into the snow. "Merry Christmas."

Ivy shut the heavy front door behind him to keep out the winter wind. She pulled the curtain aside and watched her uncle trudge unsteadily down the sidewalk. Uncle Tommy's back porch post deserved a big notch.

She went back into Grandma's bedroom. "Uncle Walter, it's snowing so hard you can barely see the Christmas lights across the street." Uncle Walter's head lolled back against the back of the chair, his mouth open. "Uncle Walter?"

He startled awake. His dry tongue surveyed his mouth. "I must have fallen asleep for a second. I guess I'm just a little tired from the worry and all."

The heavy bags hung like dark crescent moons under his bloodshot eyes. Ivy rested her hand on his shoulder. "Saying goodbye can take a lot out of you. You better go on home, too. You must be exhausted."

Uncle Walter yawned again. "Well, I am a tad tired. I may keel over if I don't get some sleep. Anyway, my knee's been acting up again. I'm no spring chicken myself, you know. I'll come over tomorrow, bright and early, like always."

Ivy hugged Uncle Walter. "Sure. You go on home and go to bed, Uncle Walter. I'll feel better knowing you're getting a good night's sleep."

Ivy knew that caring for his mother and silently fighting with his brother took a heavy toll on him. Uncle Walter needed the solitude of his neat and tidy trailer to regain his strength.

"You deserve some rest," Ivy said.

Uncle Walter kissed Ivy goodnight. "She lived this long for you, you know."

Ivy nodded. "I know." Her eyes flooded with tears. "Merry Christmas, Uncle Walter."

"Merry Christmas, Ivy."

After Uncle Walter left, Ivy sat on the bed beside Grandma and gazed out at the shadowy woods and the moonlight glistening on the snow. She washed Grandma's face and spread lotion on her hands and arms. Then, keeping her promise, she took the tweezers and plucked Grandma's few chin hairs. Ivy knew that somewhere deep inside her silent sleep, Grandma smiled.

Chapter 38

WILL THE NIGHT EVER END?

As the night went on, Grandma's labored breathing became louder and more irregular. Her mouth hung open. Her eyes, darkly rimmed, remained closed. Her skillful, soothing hands, now gnarled with age and use, rested limply at her sides. Throughout the night, Ivy gently held Grandma's hand and stroked her sunken face, talking softly to her.

The night owls hooted mournfully, as if calling out their distress.

In the middle of the night, Grandma suddenly opened her eyes. Fear temporarily replaced the knowing. "Why won't this night ever end? I need to see the morning light."

Ivy patted Grandma's hand. "Just a few more hours now. I'll wait with you for the morning."

After that, Grandma slept fitfully. She shifted from side to side, fidgeting like an impatient child and moaning with each movement.

Before sunrise, a bad odor filled the air. Grandma's bladder and bowels stopped working. Death approached. Ivy cleaned Grandma's body with a warm washcloth. She changed her nightgown and sheets, the same way Grandma had changed Ivy's urine-soaked nightgown and bed when she was little.

"No need to worry, Grandma, it's easily fixed."

The end to Grandma's magnificent life approached. Faced

with her death, Ivy realized that the responsibility for her future belonged to her alone. She must be strong enough to accept the challenges of her life.

Grandma's strained breathing signaled to Ivy that Grandma's body was surrendering, and she had to give up the fight to keep Grandma on Earth. Time always wins.

Ivy stroked the loose-skinned arms of her beloved grandmother, once so vigorous and plump, and pulled the quilts around her. "Grandma, I'm glad my mother left without me. I would have been so alone in this world without you. And you were right about Coffey. It's home. I can explore the world from here. You can go now. I'll wait for your sign, when your soul's at peace."

Grandma stopped breathing. Many seconds passed. The empty silence screamed in Ivy's ears. Then Grandma sucked in a deep breath as if emerging from the ocean's depths, and she continued to breathe.

Ivy heard a sound, like the settling of a hawk's wings after a flight. When she looked up, Carly stood in the doorway, framed by the early morning light from the window. Ivy motioned for her to come over to the bed. As the five-year-old walked toward Grandma, she sang "Red River Valley," the song Grandma always sung to put her to sleep.

Carly took Grandma's hand. Violet Taylor opened her eyes and gazed at them both with a look of surprise, as if in disbelief that life's end had actually come and with regret at the leaving. But there was no strength left for words. Holding on to life's last moments took all her effort.

Ivy kissed Grandma's cheek. "The morning finally came. You can go now. Goodbye, Grandma. I love you more than the great blue sky."

Then the look in Grandma's eyes softened, as if recognizing

familiar faces. A tear, or perhaps the last of life's nectar, fell from Grandma's weary eyes.

Carly reached out and wiped it away. "Don't cry, Grandma. We'll never forget you. Go to sleep, Grandma. Mommy and I will be all right. We'll take care of each other."

Grandma's raspy breathing stopped and a shuddering bolt of loss surged through Ivy. The hollow silence filled her with dread. She raised her arms and gazed up at the ceiling as if she expected to see Grandma's defiant spirit hovering there.

"Grandma, where did you go?" Ivy said. Then she closed Grandma's all-knowing eyes and Grandma silently disappeared from the earth. On the quiet wisp of a snowy winter breeze, her spirit passed from this world. Violet Taylor was no more.

As night gently faded into Christmas morning, all of Grandma's bird friends startled awake and suddenly took flight. The sound of beating wings filled the air. Through the window, Ivy and Carly watched birds circling the house in an act of indescribable fury and unbearable misery, the birds expressed their grief. Ivy wrapped her arms around Carly, gazing out the window. "Oh, Grandma, I wish you were here to see this."

"She is," Carly pointed to the feathered frenzy. "Grandma's flying with the birds."

They sat by the body that once held the great spirit of Grandma and stared out the window at the flurry of suffering as the birds flew past the window. They listened to the loud fluttering until all the birds finally vanished.

Ivy knew what she needed to do. She called Uncle Walter. He arrived a few minutes later with his coat mis-buttoned, and his slippers wet and covered with snow. Ivy and Carly greeted him at the front door and hugged him. They cried from the pain seeping deep within the caverns of their souls. They did not cry for Grandma. Death freed Grandma from the devastation of her cancer. They cried for themselves and for having been left behind.

Together, they climbed the grand staircase to Grandma's bedroom. They sat beside her, unwilling to let go. But the great Violet was already gone.

As Uncle Walter said his final goodbyes to his mother, Ivy collected Grandma's burial clothing and the Hereafter quilt waiting on the closet shelf. Then Ivy called Dr. Kelsey. As she hung up the phone, unbearable fear swept through her with the knowing that soon, the last physical remnant of Grandma would be taken from her in a long black zippered bag, and she would have to face life without Grandma.

Ivy shook her head and sighed. "You know Uncle Walter, I've tried to get out of this old house and away from Coffey all my life. And now I'd do anything to live another lifetime here, with Grandma and you and Carly."

Uncle Walter nodded. "I know."

As they waited for Dr. Kelsey to arrive, they were startled by a loud crash. The largest limb of the old Maple tree in Grandma's front yard broke off from its strong base, splitting the trunk in two and barely missing the house. Nothing lasts forever. Plans change.

At twenty-seven years old, Ivy found herself an orphan again.

PART VI

THE RETURN OF THE BIRDS

(1985-1986)

Chapter 39

THE GERIATRIC SCUFFLE

A few days later, the heavens remained cloudy and dark during Grandma's funeral, as if the sky mourned her passing as well. The birds in the backyard had vanished after Violet's death, which was strange because they were usually so plentiful, even in the winter. But that winter, they flew away with their sorrow, their songs silenced.

The brisk wind tangled the skeletal branches of the weeping willows at the cemetery. Their slender tentacles bowed over the graves like grieving loved ones. The pallbearers: Uncle Tommy, Uncle Walter, Russell and Reuben, carried Violet Taylor to her final resting place, next to her beloved husband and youngest son Robert. Ivy, Carly, and Patty trudged through the snow, hand-in-hand behind Grandma's casket. The rest of the mourners, nearly the entire town, followed in a long sorrowful line except for Otis. Thelma had denied Otis' request to attend, saying the cold air would be bad for him.

When they reached the gravesite, just over the second hill, Carly dropped Ivy's hand and pointed to Reuben's field at the edge of the cemetery. "Look, there they are. There's Grandma's birds."

Ivy gasped at the long row of birds perched on a barbed-wire fence, reverently lined up in a final salute to their friend. When they lowered Grandma's casket into the ground beneath the weeping willows, the birds flew in unison into the dim, gray sky in a flutter of frenzied motion and lamentation. Ivy hoped Grandma could see the birds' touching memorial from her back porch in the Great Hereafter.

When Grandma's service ended, Ivy saw a woman who looked like Angela at the edge of the crowd. The woman with her hood pulled up, stepped back into the woods and hurried away. Ivy sighed. She knew she would have to face Angela about Justin eventually, but that would have to wait.

Many of the mourners returned to 4120 and Ivy was glad. She didn't want to grieve alone in a house that now seemed so empty. Ivy helped Matilda, Violet's mushroom companion, serve the food in the kitchen. She peeled back the aluminum foil to reveal each delicious dish.

Ivy looked outside and watched the snowflakes tumble in the wind. She remembered Reuben once told her that sometimes your home is worth the sacrifice. Ivy finally understood why he had stayed in the haunted house all these years.

This was her home. This was where she belonged. Coffey was her town. They knew her here. Everyone she loved was here. Well, almost. Nick wasn't there. But she understood. She had grown up. She'd learned to let go. Everyone has to find their own path and no one should have to give up their home. The ghosts be danged.

Ivy couldn't focus on any more sadness. She'd had her fill. She couldn't think of Nick anymore. If Nick could be happy without her, she had to accept it.

Matilda put her arm around Ivy and walked her into the large dining room set up for the potluck dinner. "Save your tears for later. Everyone's counting on you to be strong."

Ivy took a deep breath. If she could survive Grandma's death, she could do anything, including live without Nick.

Dishes of food covered the huge dining table. It resembled one of Grandma's family holiday feasts. Russell lined up the dishes in symmetrical order. "Ivy, you okay?"

Ivy nodded, afraid to speak. He shook his head and hugged her. "Me neither."

Miss Shirley bustled through the kitchen door, carrying an angel pie. Russell stopped fiddling with the dishes and held out his hands. "It wouldn't be an official funeral without your angel pie. Let me help you with that."

Miss Shirley smiled and handed him her traditional funeral contribution. The angel pie stood tall, piled high with pink creamy fluff and a whipped cream topping with a meringue crust and crushed Heath bars sprinkled on top.

He looked at the pie and then at Miss Shirley. "You only made one angel pie?"

She wagged her finger at Russell. "Now don't you go eating more than your share."

"Save me a piece," Ivy told Russell.

Russell counted the pieces over and over. Then he shoveled the largest piece onto his plate. He pushed the rest of the pie out of sight behind the roaster pan on the kitchen counter.

Bertha Tuttle, the perpetually hungry mourner, anxiously stood first in line for the food. Grandma's friends ate, shared their condolences, and soon went home to their own lives. The living had to go on.

Eventually, only Grandma's family remained at 4120, where Violet Taylor had held her family together for generations. But now, Grandma was no longer there to keep the tentative peace.

Everyone but Uncle Tommy gathered in the kitchen. Russell sighed and patted his hair. He pointed to the piece of angel pie on Uncle Walter's plate. "The only good part about today was the angel pie, huh, Uncle Walter?"

Uncle Walter leaned back against the kitchen counter, taking the weight off his bad knee. "That's true. There's nothing like a little angel pie to take the edge off of death." He took another a bite of the rich fluffy pie.

Uncle Tommy hustled into the kitchen. "Angel pie? Did you say angel pie?" He stared at Uncle Walter's plate. "How come Postal Boy got angel pie and I didn't?"

Uncle Tommy hurried back into the dining room and raced around the table, desperately searching for the angel pie. "Where is the dang pie, you selfish old mailman?"

They all watched from the kitchen as Uncle Tommy frantically looked around for the funeral pie. Uncle Walter shrugged and pointed to the empty pie tin on the counter. "I found it over on the counter, behind the roaster pan." He lifted his plate. "This was the last piece." He scooped another bite from his wedge.

The rest of the family stared at the two brothers. For the first time in Ivy's life, Uncle Tommy and Uncle Walter required no family interpreter. Pastrami on rye had started the uncles' sandwich war and a piece of Miss Shirley's angel pie was going to end it.

Uncle Tommy grabbed at Uncle Walter's plate. "Give me that dadgum piece of pie."

Uncle Walter pulled his pie away and took a step back. "This is my piece." He crammed another bite into his mouth. "Um. Um."

Uncle Tommy pointed his trembling finger at his brother. "This is just like that time you took my pastrami sandwich at Robert's funeral. Well, you're not going to get away with it this time, Letter Boy."

"It wasn't your sandwich. It was on my plate, just like this pie. And I'm fed up with your pranks and name-calling. You've been bullying everyone your whole life. I'm sick of it."

"Oh, right. What are you going to do?" Uncle Tommy trembled, pretending to be frightened. "Go postal on me with your bad knees and scaredy-cat fists?" He lunged for the pie plate again.

But Uncle Walter stepped out of the way just in time, dodging Uncle Tommy's attacks. He pushed his ruffian brother. Uncle Tommy stumbled and sprawled across the kitchen floor, his arms and legs splayed out like Bambi on ice. His glasses flew off his face.

Uncle Walter poked his finger at his brother. "You're the thug. The traitor. You're the one who takes things that don't belong to you . . . like . . . like Robert's wife."

Uncle Tommy picked up his glasses and struggled to get up from the kitchen floor. He raised his unsteady fists at Uncle Walter. "You've never had anything worthwhile to say your whole life. You better keep your dadgum mouth shut now."

Uncle Walter adjusted his belt and shifted his weight. "Why? Because then everyone might find out that if it wasn't for you, Robert wouldn't be dead?" He exhaled as if he'd been holding his breath for years. He set the pie plate on the counter.

Uncle Tommy balled-up his stiff fingers into fists. He stepped forward and swung at Uncle Walter. His attempted blow looked like the frustrated slow-motion of a dream.

Again, Uncle Walter dodged his brother's awkward strike, but the momentum of Uncle Tommy's lunge caused him to stumble headlong into Russell who held him upright. "Dad, get a grip. You're old. You're going to hurt yourself."

Uncle Tommy pushed Russell away. "Leave me alone, you hair-patting, thing-counting, food-separating weirdo."

Russell's eyes narrowed, but this time, when the insults came, he didn't fidget. Instead, he pushed his father back as hard as he could. The force made Uncle Tommy fly off-balance toward Uncle Walter, like a senior citizen projectile. Grunting and wheezing, the two men moved back and forth in a geriatric scuffle.

Russell stood his ground. "You shouldn't make fun of people." Then Russell stuck his foot out and tripped his father.

As Uncle Tommy fell, he grabbed Uncle Walter's belt. Uncle Walter's bad knee buckled, and he fell on top of Uncle Tommy. The two brothers wrestled clumsily on Grandma's linoleum kitchen floor. The rest of the family watched in disbelief and stunned horror as the uncles fought. Around them, the china birds rattled uncontrollably on the kitchen shelves. Aunt Hattie kicked her husband as he writhed on the kitchen floor. "Now you two old men calm down. Has Satan completely taken over your minds?"

Russell pulled Uncle Tommy off the floor and glared at the bully-father he had grudgingly endured all his life. Ivy helped Uncle Walter to stand up.

"What did you mean, if it wasn't for Uncle Tommy, my father wouldn't be dead?" Ivy asked, grabbing Uncle Walter's shoulders. Her face was pale and sweat beaded on her forehead. "Please, Uncle Walter, tell me what you meant." She squeezed his arms. "Tell me right now. I need to know."

Uncle Walter patted Ivy's hands and turned to Uncle Tommy. "Tell her. Tell her about you and Barbara. Tell her what really happened that night."

Aunt Hattie stepped between the two brothers as they tried to catch their breath from their melee and growled in her throat. "You two old worthless fools shouldn't be airing your dirty laundry now. That was the devil's work. It was over and done with a long time ago." She turned up her stubby nose as if she could smell something rancid. "Woe unto thee—"

Ivy put her hand up in front of Aunt Hattie's contemptuous face. "Be quiet, Aunt Hattie. For once, just be quiet. I deserve to know what they're talking about."

Aunt Hattie pursed her lips and pointed at Carly. "Shouldn't she leave the room?"

Carly went over and held Uncle Walter's hand, hiding her face in his sweater. Ivy shook her head.

"No, she's staying right here. No more secrets."

Uncle Walter wrapped his arm around Carly. "I think it's about time Ivy knew what really happened."

Ivy turned and faced the uncle whose heart always blew a cold breeze toward his family. "Uncle Tommy, did you have an affair with my mother?"

Uncle Tommy glanced at his holier-than-thou wife. Hattie's eyes glowed like a scared cat at the end of a dark alley with no way out. He looked at his son, but Russell stared back, his hands by his side, for once perfectly still.

Then everyone turned to Uncle Walter. After twenty-six years, Uncle Walter finally found his voice. With Grandma gone, no one could keep the lid on the buried family secrets. Uncle Walter faced his brother. "It's time. If you don't tell her, I will."

Uncle Tommy's face contorted. He paused, his eyes wide and darting around like a wild bird trapped in a cage.

"Okay. Okay." Uncle Tommy glanced at Ivy and then looked down at the floor. "Well, it started when her father tried to force her to go back to Stilton and it ended when she got pregnant and I refused to leave Hattie."

He turned to Hattie. "You never give me credit for that."

"Why should I, you whoremonger?"

Uncle Tommy shook his head. "To get back at me, Barbara talked Robert into marrying her. I tried to avoid her after that, but she came to me on the night of the accident and threatened to tell Hattie if I didn't run away with her."

"I found out anyway," Hattie said.

"Barbara said she was in trouble and had to leave. Guess Conrad had something to do with that. I shouldn't have gone." He sighed and looked away. "Robert saw us get on the bus. I think he was madder at me than her."

"He idolized you, don't know why," Uncle Walter said. "And you betrayed him."

"Shut up. I know what I did."

Uncle Walter looked at Ivy. "Robert chased after them in his car." He pointed to Uncle Tommy. "He was on the bus with your mother when Robert crashed into the semi."

His words echoed in Ivy's mind. Her hands shook and she covered her mouth for a moment. "So my father's not my father, is he?"

Uncle Walter slowly shook his head. "No. Robert knew you weren't his biological child, but he didn't care. He loved you. You were his world."

Uncle Tommy pushed his glasses up and tucked his yellowed dress shirt into his polyester pants. He took a deep breath. "I'm your father."

Ivy shuddered, and her heart quaked as lightning flashed, thunder roared, and torrential rains poured inside her mind. "No, that's not true. It can't be true."

Uncle Tommy stepped toward Ivy with his hands extended. "Ivy, listen to me."

She took a step back. "No. Stay away from me. I don't have to listen to you."

If Uncle Tommy hadn't been running away with her mother,

her father wouldn't have been driving so fast on the icy roads that night to stop her, and the tractor-trailer wouldn't have run into him. The shock of Uncle Tommy's horrifying revelation filled her with rage. She could never forgive him.

Uncle Tommy shook his head. "I didn't want Robert to die. I loved my brother."

"That's why you ran away with his wife?" Ivy looked at the man who had destroyed her family. "Why didn't you go on to Des Moines with her? Why did you come back?"

"He was my brother. This is my family. I got off the bus and stayed for Robert's funeral." His body went limp. "After that, it all seemed pointless. Barbara was gone. Hattie found out. Too much damage had been done."

Ivy's family, shrouded by secrets for so long, stood stunned by the revelations.

"If you knew you were my father, why didn't you want me?" Ivy asked in anguish.

Uncle Tommy's lip trembled. He glanced at Aunt Hattie and then back at Ivy. "After Robert's funeral, I tried to take you home with me, but Hattie wouldn't let me and mother thought it was best if you lived with her. I was just outnumbered. I had no fight left in me. And Mom was right." His tired eyes filled with tears. "But I've lived in hell because of it." Tears ran down Uncle Tommy face.

Aunt Hattie shook her finger at him. "A hell of your own making."

Uncle Tommy's hands quivered. "Never knew how to make it right. Just seemed like the best thing to do was to let you live with your grandmother."

Ivy looked at the man whose foolish love for her mother had altered her life forever. Sometimes, a single night can change a generation.

Throughout the years, Ivy had been disgusted by Uncle Tommy. She often disliked him, and sometimes felt indifferent to him, but now she didn't know what to feel. Uncle Tommy, the family traitor and agitator, was her father.

Grandma knew more about the sandwich war than she ever admitted. She should have told her, but Grandma came from a generation that believed some things were best left unsaid.

Uncle Tommy held out his shaking arms to Ivy. Ivy didn't move. She looked at Uncle Tommy and slowly shook her head. "Uncle Tommy, despite the truth, you'll always be my uncle. It's too late for you to be my father. You've already had a lifetime of chances. Besides, I thought I grew up without a father, but now I see I've always had one." Turning away from Uncle Tommy, Ivy walked into Uncle Walter's embrace, the man who had loved and protected her like a father all of her life.

That night, after everyone went home, Ivy and Carly paid a quick visit to Otis to tell him about the funeral and complain about Thelma keeping him captive. Then they hurried home so Carly could go to bed. Exhausted, she fell asleep as soon as her eyes closed.

Ivy cleaned up the kitchen and made a fire. The house settled too quiet without the constant sounds of Grandma. The night's silence stretched endlessly. Ivy could not endure the stillness that death brought. The stress of the day and the intensity of her emotions were exhausting. She stretched out on the couch in front of the fire, enjoying the warmth of the leaping flames.

After the death of Grandma, there was little strength left for life. Rosie, the old hermit lady, must have felt this way after her mother died. Only her wild dogs and cats kept her connected to this world.

But Ivy had Carly, Uncle Walter, and Otis to tie her to this life. Still, the emptiness swallowed her until she felt she would be lost in the hollow hole that Grandma's soul left behind.

Chapter 40

THE BENCHES

All through winter, Ivy and Carly put birdseed in the feeders for Grandma's winged friends. But only Grandma's old nemeses, the squirrels, feasted on the seeds. The birds in their bereavement, left the woods empty. Their nests abandoned. The echoing bird songs stilled. The only tune left in the woods was the breeze blowing through the bare branches—nature's song of anguish. The earth itself seemed to grieve the passing of the great Violet Taylor.

The loss of Grandma consumed Ivy as well, but she still needed to go to work, she had a little girl to raise, and her responsibilities to Uncle Walter and Otis prevented her from sinking too far under.

She picked up Carly from Patty's after work and often went to visit Otis. They tried to keep his spirits up, but living at Rose Hill pulled him even deeper into his despair. Ivy understood his sadness. Death and the feeling of overwhelming loss weighed heavily.

Spring came late and the snow lingered on the hard ground, unwilling to give up its reign to the resurrection of spring. But despite winter's reluctance to recede, the snow melted, and spring found its way. The little green buds on the trees sprouted. The daffodils and tulips raised their shy heads. The sun warmed the earth. The strong spring prairie winds blew in with the assurance that life goes on.

The warm spring wind brought the renewal of hope and the earth breathed with new beginnings. But the usually plentiful spring rains didn't come. The plants soon began to wither. The promise of the new growth shriveled and dried up, stunted from the drought. But like all things, that too changed.

Late one April afternoon, four months after Grandma died, the drenching rains finally came. The storm blew in from the south. The winds howled across the prairie, gathering an unstoppable force and speed. The dark clouds made the late afternoon look like the shadowy curtain of evening. Ivy sent everyone home early from the college alumni office. Uncle Walter was taking care of Carly that day, so Ivy got in the Monstrosity and drove home through the blinding rain. The windshield wipers ticked like the nervous beat of a metronome.

The heavens shook with thunder and lightning. The storm hovered, choking the atmosphere. It took all of Ivy's strength to keep the Monstrosity on the road. Sudden gusts sent it rocking to one side, close to the road's edge. She tightly gripped the steering wheel and drove on.

Ivy finally pulled into the long driveway of her house, relieved to have made it home safely. When she opened the truck door, the wind jerked it shut on its hinges. She pushed it back open and trudged slowly against the wind to the house.

As she opened the door, she heard the town's tornado siren faintly wailing against the roaring wind, meaning a tornado had been sighted near Coffey. She rushed in and struggled to pull the door shut behind her. "Carly! Uncle Walter! It's the tornado siren. We've got to get to the canning room," she shouted.

No one answered. The tormenting gusts rattled the windows. The chimney made a ghostly sound as the wind found its way down the old, brick shaft.

She ran into the kitchen. A note stuck under the bluebird magnet on the refrigerator read: "Carly and I are going to my place. Be back soon. Love, Uncle Walter." Ivy's heartbeat amplified in her ears. Uncle Walter's trailer. With a tornado coming, they'd have no chance. Trailers were always the first to go.

Ivy opened the front door. The wind threw the lid of a trash can against the porch wall. The menacing dark clouds changed shape, twisting and elongating as if some immeasurable force was pulling them down from the sky in a long funnel.

A trailer could be a death trap during a tornado. Uncle Walter didn't have a car and they would never get back home in time to escape the twister. She would have to drive to the trailer to get them. It was only a few blocks away.

Ivy fought against the rain and wind, and jumped back into the Monstrosity, pulling hard with both hands to get the door closed. The old truck sputtered but wouldn't turn over. "Come on! Start. Please."

She kissed her fingers and touched the dashboard like Nick used to do. She turned the key again. It churned and kicked over. She put it in reverse and backed out of the driveway. The drenching rain obscured her vision. The left wheel went off the driveway and spun in the ditch. She put it in forward and gunned the gas pedal. "Don't fail me now, you wily beast."

The tire slipped and then took hold. She rolled down the window and stuck her head out to see as she edged down the driveway. Rain pelted her face. She drove slowly through the streets, trying to avoid the streams of water pouring down the middle of the roads.

The windshield wipers pumped, pushing the torrential water away. For a few seconds, she could see clearly. The tornado funnel eased back up, disappearing into the mass of churning wind and clouds. Maybe she would have enough time to get to the trailer and back home.

The rain, a sheet of blurry liquid, prevented her from seeing the turn into the Prairie Hills Trailer Park. Ivy cut across the newly planted flowerbed and across the common lawn. She honked the horn. The trailers looked deserted and no lights were on. Maybe Carly and Uncle Walter sought safety elsewhere. Then Ivy looked at the street lights. They were off, too. The town's electricity must have gone out, so, Carly and Uncle Walter might still be in there.

She left the engine running, opened the door, and jumped out into the storm. Trash blew across the trailer park. She protected her face with her hands and glanced up at the sky. The funnel sprung down again from the clouds, this time bigger and more defined. The tornado headed her way at a tremendous speed. She ran up to Uncle Walter's trailer but the door remained locked, like always. She pounded on the door. "Uncle Walter! Carly! You've got to come with me. The tornado's here." No one answered.

She turned around to check the advancement of the twisting clouds. The curtain in Bertha's trailer opened. Bertha, with her nose pressed to the window, frantically motioned to her. Ivy ran across the small strip of lawn, dodging Uncle Walter's lawn ornaments. She opened Bertha's trailer door. Bertha, Uncle Walter, and Carly huddled under the kitchen table. The trailer began to sway. It creaked like an old wooden bridge about to give way. Ivy motioned to them. "Come on, you guys. We can't stay here. We've got to get home to the basement."

Uncle Walter and Carly got up and hurried toward Ivy. Bertha remained under the table.

"You, too, Bertha."

Bertha scrambled out from the table and they all ran for the Monstrosity. Ivy opened the camper's back door and they piled in. "Crawl under the benches along the walls. They're bolted to the floor. It's the safest place."

Then Ivy fought her way to the driver's door. As she got in the truck, a panel of Bertha's trailer tore off and hit the open truck door. Ivy gunned the gas pedal and the truck took off with the door open. She needed to get out of there, fast. The tornado, only a short distance away, swirled debris in the air. The strong wind slammed Ivy's door shut. Her foot fell off the gas for a second. Then she pushed the pedal to the floor. The Monstrosity jerked and drove smoking in front of the dark wall of the tornado with no other way out.

The camper windows weaved in and out as if they were made of liquid. The twisting mass of destruction chased them down the street with the tornado sounding like the trains roaring behind Mulberry Street, amplified.

Ivy looked back through the rearview mirror at the advancing black corkscrew of wind. Bertha's trailer roof tore off and its flimsy sides caved in. Then the tornado passed over Uncle Walter's trailer, picking up his home like a child's dollhouse, and sending its contents spiraling into the air.

Ivy was glad Uncle Walter and Bertha couldn't see the destruction of their homes as they cowered under the sturdy benches bolted to the floor in the back. The old haphazardly-constructed camper rattled and shook violently as the tornado's coiling edge got closer. The crooked nails holding the camper together groaned like a crowbar prying metal from a board.

Precariously held together at the best of times, the camper vibrated wildly.

Ivy turned around and glanced through the open cab window into the back. "Hold on tight to the bench legs. It's coming."

All she could hear in response over the wind was Carly's screams.

"Hold on Carly," Ivy yelled. "Hold on."

With a mighty jerk, the top of the camper pulled loose from its tentative grip on the old truck and was sucked away into the twisting cloud of the tornado hovering beside them. Ivy yelled as she made a sharp turn into 4120 and gunned it out of the path of the tornado.

What remained of the Monstrosity shuddered onto the driveway, as the black tornado shrank back up into the clouds as quickly as it came down. Ivy jumped out of the truck. She pushed her wet hair out of her face and ran to the back.

Bertha rolled out from under the left bench. She looked like a drenched cat, no longer proper, confident, lipsticked, and fluffy. Then Uncle Walter inched his way out from under the right bench. He slowly pulled himself up, grimacing in pain. His dark hair sprinkled with gray, still thick for an older man, stood on end, either from the power of the wind or pure fright. Ivy jumped into the ripped-open back. "Where's Carly?"

Carly's small hands still gripped the legs of the front bench, nearest to the cab. "I can't let go. My hands won't move. I think they're stuck."

Ivy crawled over, gently pried her little fingers from around the legs of the bench, and pulled her out. Uncle Walter and Bertha threw their arms around Ivy and Carly as the rain fell with a battering force. The storm was over and they had survived another of life's tornados.

However, the twisting winds of the tornado had destroyed all of Uncle Walter's years of meticulous collecting. The most careful life planning, disrupted again.

"Someone else will have to manage the trailer park now. I can't bear to live in a new trailer without any cookie jars," Uncle Walter told Ivy the next morning.

"You'll move in here. This has always been your home," Ivy said.

Bertha sat on the porch, wearing one of Grandma's old robes and drinking coffee. Carly sat beside her. The sky hung dark and wet with moisture. Ivy caught a quick movement out of the corner of her eye. Was it a bird? With summer approaching, the birds still had not returned. But no, it was just a leaf swirling to the ground. The woods stood silent, except for the constant rain.

After breakfast, they crammed into the front seat of the Monstrosity and Ivy drove Bertha to Edna Jean's house. When Edna Jean heard about the total destruction of the trailer, she invited Bertha to live with her. Now neither of them would be alone.

After making sure Otis was safe, hiding from the storm in the cellar at Rose Hill Nursing Home, they went to Uncle Walter's trailer park to look at the rubble and see if anything had survived the tornado. Uncle Walter's hands sank deep in his pockets as he examined the crushed remains. Only the trailer's base of cinder blocks remained. Uncle Walter kicked the debris beneath his shoes and stepped on a broken shard of a ceramic cookie jar.

Carly ran over to the mushroom-riding gnome. "Look, one

of your lawn creatures is alive!"

Uncle Walter examined his lawn art. "Well, sure enough, it looks a little wind-blown, but there it is, by golly."

They carefully transported it in the back of what remained of the Monstrosity and left the destroyed rubble of Uncle Walter's life behind. Then they ceremoniously placed it in the front yard of Grandma's grand Victorian house and the evil pixie continued to ride the mushroom.

Ivy put her arm through Uncle Walter's arm. "You lived in that trailer a long time. Did you ever want to get married?"

"It wasn't an option for me."

"That's what I thought."

"A small town isn't the best place for a man who likes men to find love."

"I love you."

"And that has been one of my only comforts."

Chapter 41

THE VANISHING OF THE GHOSTS

Spring, usually sunny and bright and blooming with new colors, remained drab and dreary. For a few days after the tornado, rain fell in full torrential force. The earthworms wiggled in the streets and on the sidewalks, forced from their comfort of the soil by the flood of water.

The saturated ground created puddles in every dip of Reuben's yard. The farmhouse gutters poured a steady waterfall of rain and the trees and plants drank until they choked. The ditches clogged with debris floating in the runoff. There was too much water, with nowhere to go. Reuben's fields filled with the endless spring rain. Great pools of water formed across his fertile land. The farm acreage could not absorb the non-stop rain.

One night in late May after spending the afternoon with Otis, Ivy and Carly went to Reuben and Patty's house to eat pizza and watch a movie. Uncle Walter wanted to stay home and sleep. After the frightening ordeal of the tornado, Uncle Walter missed his trailer, but he told Ivy he enjoyed the safety of living in a house with a foundation.

Ivy, Carly, and Patty looked out the living room window at the constant downpour. They watched Reuben's new puppy, Birddog, splashing in the huge puddles.

Carly tapped at the window dripping with rain. "When will the sky be empty?"

Patty sighed. "Soon, I hope."

Reuben walked over and stood beside them. His dripping boots left a trail of sloppy sludge behind him. "My crops will be ruined this year. Too much rain is as bad as too little. Nature always lets you know who's the boss."

Uncle Tommy stomped in to Reuben's house without knocking. He wore his black cowboy hat, the closest thing to an umbrella he had ever used. Uncle Tommy and Reuben were playing in the bowling league tournament at the Blue Moon that night.

When they were ready to go, Reuben called for his dog. It was too wet for Birddog to be out all night, but he didn't come racing around the house like he usually did when Reuben called him.

Reuben put on his John Deere cap. "Birddog's probably out back chasing those poor frightened chickens again. One of my chickens got so scared during that tornado, it lost all its feathers. Plum fell out. All of them. Dadburn strangest sight I've ever seen. Have you ever heard of such a thing?"

Ivy nodded with a smile. "Yeah, I have,"

Reuben and Uncle Tommy headed outside as Patty held the door.

"Ivy, will you go with those two old men to find the dog?" Patty asked. "You're the only one that's still young enough to see at night. One of them'll fall in a deep puddle, and we'll never see them again. But if it's Tommy, just leave him there."

Carly giggled into her hand.

Ivy nodded. "Sure."

She grabbed her jacket and followed Uncle Tommy and Reuben out into the rainy night. They headed around the house toward the barn, calling for the dog. The rain clouds cast a hazy film in the sky and dimmed the moon's light. The two old men and Ivy dodged the puddles and rivulets running through the yard as they hurried to Reuben's old barn.

Uncle Tommy adjusted his cowboy hat, tipping it to pour off the rain. "Sure is a hard rain."

They turned on the light in the barn. The bulb swayed from its dangling wires. Some of the old boards on the roof had blown off in the tornado, allowing the torrential rain to enter and make a muddy mess. The hay covering a corner of the dirt floor had a stale, earthy smell.

They found Birddog inside the barn, digging a deep hole. Birddog bounded eagerly toward them, carrying something in his mouth. The muddy dog proudly dropped his discovery in front of them. They stared, their eyes wide with shock and disbelief. What Birddog had deposited at their feet was a small human skull smeared with mud.

"What is that?" Uncle Tommy asked.

"Looks like a human skull," Ivy said.

Reuben stood upright in the old dilapidated barn, his face white as a ghost. He pointed to the hole in the barn floor that Birddog had dug. "My little brother was buried here, in the barn." He pointed to the muddy skull. "That's him."

Uncle Tommy stared at Reuben. "Have you completely lost your mind? What are you talking about?"

"That's right. How did I forget that? That's so weird. But I remember now. I was little when my brother died and the ground in the cemetery was too frozen to bury him. My father used a pickax to dig a shallow grave in the barn. I cried every time that axe hit the ground. My brother has been right here with me all along."

Reuben kneeled down in the mud and held his brother's

small skull in his hands. The old man wept a little boy's tears from his memories of his dead brother and from all the years of missing him. The rain continued to pelt down. Uncle Tommy held Birddog back and helplessly watched his buddy cry.

Ivy knelt down beside Reuben in the mud and wrapped her arms around him. They cried together. She understood the pain of losing loved ones and wondering where they went.

The next day the rain let up. Reuben dug up his brother's bones and buried them in a proper grave in Weeping Willow Cemetery next to his parents.

When Reuben returned to the farmhouse the ghosts had vanished.

Chapter 42

THE HALLOWEEN HEIST

The Iowa summer crept up unexpectedly. The windy warmth of spring turned into a roasting furnace without any warning. Nothing seemed right without Grandma. The humid stickiness of the air made Ivy sluggish. Her promise to Grandma about visiting Angela and bringing Justin home weighed heavily on her. But she didn't have the strength. It would have to wait a while longer.

One night at the end of August, the summer heat made it impossible to even sit on the back porch. Ivy had installed air conditioning that summer and sought relief from the heat inside the house. She flopped into a chair in front of the window air conditioner and stared numbly at the flickering picture of the television with the volume turned off.

Six-year-old Carly walked into the room and looked at Ivy. Then she pointed to the muted TV with a wavy picture. "Grandpa Otis stares at the quiet TV, too."

Ivy jerked away from the mesmerizing light, turned off the TV, and hugged Carly. "Grandpa Otis will come home as soon as his paperwork is approved."

Ivy knew that being a part of a family, however peculiar, created a sense of belonging and the comfort of home. She had finally convinced Otis that he did not belong in Rose Hill and helped him fill out the required departure request. Now, they were just waiting for it to be approved before Otis would be set free from his confinement of the nursing home.

When the cool air of fall blew into Coffey, Ivy breathed a sigh of relief. She had made it through the hazy summer. The fresh air of autumn made it easier to think. Everything seemed clearer, as if finally in focus. After several months without any response from Rose Hill regarding Otis's departure request, Ivy was tired of waiting. She had learned from Luther to go with her instinct, so she decided to spring Otis from Rose Hill without telling him.

Halloween night flew in on the dark shoulders of a witch's black cloak. Clouds covered the full moon's brightness. The wind blew so hard the dead leaves swirled across the yard like a small twister. Magic and power tumbled with the autumn leaves and the spirits swirled in the air.

The night grew dark and cold, and Carly was scared of the ghosts and witches roaming the streets. As Ivy drove Carly home from trick-or-treating, she saw two high school kids dressed up. The boy was dressed as an old man in a wheelchair. The girl had dressed up like a nurse and pushed him along, periodically stopping to hit him with a giant, inflatable hammer. The costumes were not so funny to Ivy.

"Guess what, Carly? Tonight, we're going to bust Grandpa out of Rose Hill and bring him to live with us."

Carly cheered. "Is that our Halloween prank?"

"Sort of."

At home, Ivy threw several empty duffel bags into the back of the truck where all that remained were the benches.

Ivy attributed the long life of the Monstrosity to the miraculous mechanical skills of Max and to the camper's defiant spirit as a misfit. It simply refused to give up.

They drove through town to the Rose Hill Nursing Home as little goblins, ghosts, and witches scurried along the sidewalks with bags full of candy. The light cast by the Halloween prank of burning bales of hay in the intersection of town illuminated the Halloween chaos as Charlie tried to put it out.

They pulled into the nursing home parking lot and Ivy grabbed the duffel bags from the back. The ground crunched beneath their shoes as they crossed the lawn toward 8B, which had a glowing electric pumpkin in the window that Carly had given Otis. Ivy tapped on the window.

"Mr. Norton, open the side door. It's us."

After a few moments, Otis opened the heavy locked exit door. Ivy and Carly tiptoed inside. Ivy didn't want Thelma to hear them. Otis put his arm around Ivy and reached down and touched Carly's cheek. "So, what's up with the sneaky stuff?"

Carly jumped up and down. Her shoulder-length curls bounced. "Trick or Treat. We're busting you out, Grandpa."

Ivy put her finger to her mouth. "Shh."

Otis smiled as he cupped the little girl's chin in his hand. "Is that right, sugar?"

Ivy went into his room and shut the door. "I'm tired of waiting for your paperwork to get approved. So, tonight is the night you're coming home to live with us. We've got to pack your stuff and then we're going out the back exit. Thelma can figure it out for herself. I don't want to deal with her right now."

Otis hugged Carly. "Well, what are we waiting for? Let's get going."

Ivy opened the drawers and the closet, gathering up Otis's meager belongings.

Otis slapped his legs. "Uh. Uh. Uh. Lordy. Lordy. I won't have to be alone in this room anymore."

It didn't take long to pack his things. His life whittled down to just a few belongings. With a final look around 8B, they left the light on to fool Thelma, and backed out, shutting the door quietly behind them. When they turned around, Thelma's menacing figure stood beside them.

"Witch!" Carly screamed.

Thelma scowled at Carly over the top of her half-glasses. Then she turned her accusing stare at Ivy. "I hope you're not taking Otis out of here on a night like this."

Thelma's breath reeked of alcohol, her own Halloween brew. Ivy faced the small woman who was blocking their exit. "Yes, Thelma, that's exactly what we're doing." Ivy nodded at Otis. "Mr. Norton will be living with us now."

Thelma, the peewee witch, shook her head. "His departure paperwork hasn't been approved yet. He isn't going anywhere." She emphasized each word with her stubby finger.

Ivy turned to face Thelma, now forty-four. "For months you've ignored our attempts to get the paperwork approved. We're tired of waiting. If we leave without Mr. Norton, I promise you I will be back with Mr. Norton's attorney, the county health inspector, and the *Coffey Gazette*. I'm sure you won't mind answering questions about how the residents are practically prisoners in this facility, not to mention the quality of health care, or how cockroaches and mice run unimpeded in these rooms. Perhaps you would also like to discuss with the authorities why you've been drinking on the job when you made it perfectly clear that alcohol is against the rules for the people who live here?"

Ivy heard a garden hoe swishing through the air in her mind. "Do I make myself clear, Thelma?"

Thelma folded her arms across her chest. "Oh, you're clear. I can see right through you."

Carly's fingers dug into Ivy's arms.

"Why are you like this? I saved your daughter from the corn all those years ago," Ivy said.

"So? I'm supposed to be grateful?" Thelma didn't give up. "What are you trying to do, go around saving as many black people as you can? I hate white do-gooders like you. You think us black people should be beholden to you because you pity us. Otis might be some poor community-service project to you, but you can't drop him off in the country like some old stray dog when you're tired of him."

Ivy paused, visibly shaken. "Mr. Norton is family and he's going home with us."

"Otis isn't leaving here!" Thelma yelled.

A soft growl escaped from Otis's lips. His sad eyes flashed alive. "Oh, yes I am, Thelma. Like the lady said, I'm going home."

Thelma pulled her shoulders back. Her mustache wrinkled into a tight half-circle. "Otis, your home isn't with that white girl."

Otis put his arm around Ivy. "It is now." He glanced around the shabby little room. "This was never my home. It's just a place to wait to die. But I want to live." Then he turned to Ivy. "Let's go home."

Ivy nodded. She picked up the duffle bags and quickly moved past Thelma, the evil pixie. The three of them walked down the dingy nursing home hallway for the last time and stepped into the dark Halloween night.

Early the next morning, Ivy found Otis in the metal glider on the back porch. He sipped a tall glass of sweet tea that Ivy made late the night before. Ivy wrapped a blanket around her shoulders, slipped on her boots by the back door, and joined him. They breathed the cool fresh air and listened to the trees rustling in the autumn wind.

"Something's wrong, Ivy. It's too quiet."

Ivy pulled the blanket around her shoulders. "I know. It's the birds. They left when Grandma died. Haven't been back since."

Otis sipped his tea and gazed into the empty woods. "Well, can't say that I blame them any. I left when Maggie and Pinky died. Thought it was all over when Miles took my Carly. But I came back. Maybe the birds will, too."

Chapter 43

FINDING YOUR SPIRIT

The cold Midwestern winter wind blew in across the prairie, but the rich black Iowa soil remained unusually bare without snow and ice that December. Nearly a year after Grandma died, Ivy finally felt strong enough to contact Angela. A lifetime of rejection made Ivy unsure of Angela's reception. Her anxiety increased with the knowledge that they shared the same father. By life's strange circumstances, they were sisters, another thing that Ivy would have to tell her.

The time had come for Ivy to mend the torn hole in the fabric of her family. She needed to open her arms a little wider and bring Justin home. Although a daunting task, Ivy intended to keep her promise to Grandma, who she imagined was anxiously watching her from the Great Hereafter.

She found Angela's number in Grandma's address book and called her. Angela refused to meet Ivy in Coffey. She had not been back home since she had Justin. But she agreed to meet Ivy at Ivy's college alumni office in Stilton.

At first, their meeting felt awkward. Ivy stared at Angela's hair. Her long beautiful hair that she'd had all her life, was gone. Angela self-consciously ran her hand through her short brown crop. "I chopped it off when I left Coffey. My act of defiance, I guess. I never let it grow back."

"Good for you." Ivy took a deep breath and decided to just plunge in. "Did you go to Grandma's burial?"

"Yeah, I just stayed near the woods. I didn't want to make it about me."

"I thought that was you. Grandma wanted me to talk to you. Before she died, she asked me to bring Justin back to our family."

"I was afraid that's what you wanted to talk about." She slumped back against the chair. Her blue-gray eyes turned soft. The frantic steel stare of her youth was gone. "I never wanted you to know. I was too ashamed. I knew you would hate what I did. You always seemed so confident. Russell and I were pretty much bullied by our parents." Tears ran down Angela's face.

"I never fit in, so I just acted like I didn't care," Ivy said.

"I haven't spoken to anybody since I left Coffey. I couldn't stay there and live with giving up my baby. So, when I gave up Justin, I gave up my family, too. Overall, losing my family was a small thing. I never had any other children."

"What happened back then?"

Angela sighed. "Well, Ben and I had been seeing each other for a while. Sneaking around, hanging out whenever we could. I really loved him, but I got pregnant my senior year. I didn't even tell my mom and dad until a few days after Christmas. Remember the year the Santa suit caught on fire? Anyway, Dad told me I couldn't raise him, that I had to give him up. He was worried about what everyone would think. I was so used to doing everything he told me, I just did it. I know you can't understand that because Grandma always let you think for yourself. You weren't scared of making mistakes."

"Where did you go?"

"Miss Shirley's house. Nobody knew, but Grandma and Dr. Kelsey."

"What?"

"Dad thought I went to live with someone Grandma knew in Des Moines. But I lived on Mulberry Street until the baby was born. Ben slept on the couch and I used his room. Ben and I became strangers and I spent most of the time just staring out the window. I used to watch you over at Maggie's house. You guys even visited Miss Shirley while I hid upstairs. I could hear you laughing as you watched that soap opera with Miss Shirley."

"That must have been horrible for you."

Angela grabbed a tissue from Ivy's desk. "I lost my spirit that year. I left my little baby three days after he was born. I couldn't go home to a father who considered me a disgrace and to a mother who believed I had given birth to Satan's child. I left my little boy sleeping in Miss Shirley's arms, and she raised my son as hers. I left Coffey, and I've never been back. I just couldn't stand to stay there, knowing that I'd given up my child because of the color of his skin. I should have fought harder. I should have stayed. I hate my parents for making me do that. I just hope Justin will forgive me."

Ivy leaned over and touched Angela's shoulder. "I know what it's like to feel empty about your family. There's always something missing. But it's not too late for you and Justin. If Uncle Tommy and Aunt Hattie can't accept Justin, we'll do it without them. We don't need their approval. They can't control you anymore."

Angela looked down at her hands. She pulled at the edges of the tissue. "Yeah, I guess you're right. You know, Grandma used to tell me I'd need you someday." She looked up. "She was right."

"She always was," said Ivy.

"Thanks," Angela said.

Ivy waved her hand through the air, imitating Grandma. "Ah, *pshaw.*"

Angela laughed. "I guess we have more in common than I thought."

Ivy smiled. Maybe some hope lingered for a friendship with her newly found sister, but one family secret at a time.

Ivy stopped by Miss Shirley's house the next day. They sat on the same brown tweed couch where she sat as a little girl. Miss Shirley turned on the TV to watch her story. Ivy leaned forward and pointed to the TV.

"Hey, what happened to *As the World Turns*?"

Miss Shirley waved her hand back and forth in the air. "Oh, child, I had to move out of that town. Everybody kept getting amnesia. I'm over at Pine Valley now with *All My Children*."

"Sometimes life is like a soap opera, don't you think, Miss Shirley?"

Miss Shirley nodded. "Yeah, except I never knew one soul who got amnesia for real. Some people wish they could forget." Her deep laugh boomed. "Speaking of soap operas, I sure got a good laugh when I heard how you stood up to old Thelma. Thinks she's Miss It, she does. That was a nice thing you did for Otis."

Ivy smiled and shrugged. "He's family."

Miss Shirley slapped her knee and waved her hands in the air. Then she sang Leon Wilson's words. "Dig down deep" She pointed to Ivy. "Sing it with me, Snowflake."

Ivy threw her head back and they sang together. "Until you find the fight in your soul."

They laughed in the warmth of their shared history. Then Ivy cleared her throat.

"Miss Shirley, I came here today to do something Grandma asked me to do."

Miss Shirley clasped her hands together in prayer and shook them back and forth. "God rest her soul. Your grandmother was a fine woman. A fine woman."

"I came to talk to you about letting Justin know he's also a part of our family."

Miss Shirley threw up her hands. "Ah. Lordy. Ivy girl, I don't know what it will mean to a black child to find out he has white family." She rocked back and forth on the couch. "Mm. Mm. Mm."

Ivy put her hand on Miss Shirley's shoulder. "Grandma said her soul wouldn't rest until our family did right by Justin."

"You listen to me. Your grandmother was very generous to Justin. She had nothing to feel bad about."

"Our family turned our backs on Justin. It's time we make it right. Angela, Uncle Walter, and I want him to be a part of our family."

Miss Shirley's eyebrows raised. "What about Tommy and Hattie?"

"We're going to do this with or without them. Their reign over our family has passed. It's a new generation of Taylors now."

Miss Shirley stood up. "I'm not sure how Justin will feel. That boy thinks I'm his mother. He never even asked who his father was, just assumed it was Max, and Max embraced the role. Max made sure Justin didn't miss out on anything, but Justin doesn't know his real father is his brother." Miss Shirley paced around her living room. "Have you considered that some people in this town aren't very forgiving sometimes?"

"Grandma's secrets weighed her down. I don't want to live like that."

"Yes, I suppose so." Miss Shirley let out a heavy sigh. "I'll talk to Justin."

Ivy put her hand on Miss Shirley's arm. "Thanks, Miss Shirley. Thank you for loving Justin and taking care of him all these years."

"Girl, having Justin in my life has been a pure gift of joy from heaven."

Then the two women, who had faced fate together many times, embraced each other with the knowledge that nothing would be the same again. A tear from Miss Shirley's face fell on Ivy's cheek. "Ivy child, there must be some black in you somewhere, because you're too good to be a white girl."

Chapter 44

NOTHING WORSE THAN BEING CAUCASIAN

A few days later, Ivy hurried to the Coffey Shop before it opened to meet Justin as Miss Shirley had arranged. Ivy pulled up her collar as the wind whipped her hair in front of her face. The cold weather kept people indoors and downtown Coffey stood deserted.

Ivy stepped inside. The old steam heater always made the restaurant cozy in the winter. Seventeen-year-old Justin sat in the back-corner booth drumming his fingers on the table. Ivy hurried over to him and touched his shoulder. "Justin."

Justin, a junior in high school, slid out of the booth and stood up. "Well, if it isn't my long-lost relative."

Ivy wrapped her arms around him. "Where've you been all my life?"

"Stuck in the corn."

They laughed and sat down at the table. Kitty came over. Her light-blue uniform had not changed over the years, but now she wore thick support support hose and Nike tennis shoes. She took their order for Green Rivers. Then she disappeared into the kitchen. Miss Shirley anxiously watched Ivy and Justin from the grill.

Ivy searched Justin's gray eyes. "Grandma told me about you right before she died."

"How come she never told you before that?"

"She was sort of big on family secrets. She felt that Angela had a right to her decision. When you were born, Angela thought if I knew, I would go and get you. Drag you home in my bike basket, I guess." Ivy shrugged. "She was probably right."

"Yeah, I can just see us, like Elliot and ET, with my little blanket around my head like a hood, flying through the air on your bike."

They both laughed as Kitty approached with their drinks.

"You guys telling secrets over there?" Kitty asked.

"Yeah, sort of," said Ivy.

When Kitty went into the kitchen again, Ivy leaned across the table. "Anyway, when Grandma got really sick, she told me. She said her soul couldn't rest until I brought you back into our family. She made me promise. I guess she should've considered that you might not want to be a part of our family."

Justin gritted his teeth. "Well, I always liked your Grandma and Uncle Walter, but there's a few others I'm not too thrilled about."

Ivy laughed and nodded. "Yeah, well, me, too." She paused. "Angela—your mother— hasn't been back to Coffey since you were born. She hates her parents for making her give you up. She never got married or had any other children."

Justin's gray eyes watched Ivy. He always seemed older than his years. "Ivy, my brother is my father. My mother is my grandmother, and I'm part white. Do you realize how weird all this is for me?"

Ivy imitated Virgil Jackson's voice. "Nothing worse than being a Caucasian."

Justin laughed. "You got that right, Doll Baby."

They both laughed loudly. Miss Shirley looked over at them from the grill and smiled.

"Anyway, you owe me big time for pulling you out of the corn when you were little," Ivy teased.

"Yeah, I was a goner."

"So, I heard. You know, you and I were both raised by our grandmothers." Ivy held her glass in the air in a toast. "Here's to grandmas."

Justin bumped his glass with hers. "God bless grandmas."

They sipped their drinks in silence for a moment.

"I know it might take a little time to get used to all of this, but do you think you would like to meet Angela?"

Justin looked down. "I don't know. What if she's disappointed? I mean she didn't want me because I'm black. I haven't changed."

"Oh, she wanted you! She won't be disappointed, I promise you. Why don't you come over for supper and see?"

"Okay. I guess I can do that. When?"

"How about next Sunday?"

Justin took a sip of his drink and set the glass down. "All right, I guess. If you're sure."

"Good, it's settled then." Ivy pointed her finger at Justin. "You can't back out now, I'm going to tell Uncle Tommy and Aunt Hattie."

"You know where I live anyway," Justin said.

"That's true. Don't mess with me. Did you hear we busted Otis out of the Rose Hill maximum security facility?"

Justin laughed. "Yeah, my mom told me. She said you had a knockdown, drag-out fight with Thelma and you won."

Ivy wiggled her fingers at him. "What can I say, the spirits were restless on Halloween. The evil pixie went down. I heard the county's investigating. Thelma might actually have to be nice to people."

"Don't know if that'll happen." He laughed. "I guess I'd better not back out of supper."

"I'm glad you understand my power."

Chapter 45

THE PIES

The cold winter left the rich, black soil frozen and bare. The snow that usually transformed the Iowa landscape into a magical white illusion still refused to fall that dry December night of Justin's reunion supper. Otis had gone over to Virgil's to play poker with Max and to give the family a chance to get to know each other.

Angela waited inside the house with Uncle Walter and Carly. Ivy stayed on the porch, pacing nervously. She had to make this reunion successful. She had promised Grandma.

At five o'clock, Uncle Tommy, Aunt Hattie, and Russell walked around the back of the house and up to the porch. Uncle Tommy chewed on a mouthful of sunflower seeds. The tilt of his black cowboy hat almost covered his eyes. "Well, we're here. Are you happy?"

He turned his head and spat sunflower shells into the backyard. He tipped his cowboy hat up a little.

Aunt Hattie flipped her hand at Ivy. "That boy is an abomination in the sight of the Lord. God made his skin black to pay for the sins of his ancestors."

"Oh, shut up Hattie. Please, not today. I'm tired of your Bible-thumping," Uncle Tommy said.

"Aunt Hattie, you know what the Lord doesn't like?" said Ivy. "All your hate."

The back door opened, and Uncle Tommy looked up. Angela came out on the porch. Nobody said anything. Aunt Hattie stared at Angela. Uncle Tommy cleared his throat and adjusted his glasses, looking at the daughter he had not seen in sixteen years. "What'd you do to your hair?"

"I cut it," Angela said.

Tommy nodded. "It looks short."

Russell rolled his eyes at his Dad and hugged his sister. "It looks good."

"Thanks, Russell. Listen, Dad, I want my son back and I'm willing to do whatever it takes," Angela said. "If you and Mom don't want to be a part of it, I want you to leave."

Uncle Tommy shuffled his cowboy boots. He cleared his throat and ran his hand over his balding head. "I guess I might not have been completely right when I made you give that boy up."

Angela leaned against the porch railing. "His name is Justin."

Uncle Tommy put his hands in the back pocket of his jeans. "Yeah, I know. Ivy told us."

"Are you trying to say you're sorry?" Angela asked.

"If that's what it sounds like," Uncle Tommy said as he tapped the old green glider with the toe of his black cowboy boot. "Then I guess that's what it is."

Angela held out her arms to the father who had turned his back on her. Uncle Tommy walked into her embrace. Aunt Hattie stared at her husband and daughter as if she didn't recognize them.

"You were so weak back then, wanting me to let her keep that boy and you're weak now. It's an abomination unto the Lord," said Aunt Hattie.

"You wanted to let me keep him?" Angela asked.

"Didn't exactly like the idea but giving him up seemed worse. But Hattie was determined and I owed her one. But she's right about one thing. I was weak. Shouldn't have made you give him up."

Justin strolled up the path to the porch. He seemed confident and eager, but Ivy knew he was worried about the reception he would receive. The rest of the family automatically moved aside and let Angela step forward to meet her son. She held her arms out to him.

"Welcome home. I'm sorry I've been gone so long," Angela said, touching his face. "Having you was the best thing I ever did. You're beautiful."

"So are you," Justin said as he wrapped his arms around her in an embrace that was seventeen years in the making.

Ben appeared on the path, wearing his EMT uniform. Angela smiled at him over Justin's shoulder. Ben smiled back.

When Angela and Justin stepped apart, Russell held his hand out to Justin. "Hi, Justin."

Justin shook his hand. "Hey, Russell, how's it going?"

Uncle Tommy took off his cowboy hat and fondled the brim in his hands. He cleared his throat and looked around at his family. "Justin, I'm not promising anything, mind you." His voice cracked. "But, well, don't expect too much."

Justin smiled. "Okay."

Ben walked up to Angela. "You look good."

"So do you."

"So, does that mean you're all staying for supper?" Ivy said.

Uncle Tommy shifted his weight and tapped his cowboy hat against this thigh. "I reckon. We're having Miss Shirley's pies, aren't we?"

Ivy put her hand over her mouth. "Oh my gosh, with all the fuss, I forgot to pick up the pies. I hope Kitty left the back door open."

"The door is broken again. It sticks. I'll go with you and show you how to get it open," Justin said.

"Okay. Justin and I will go get the pies. We'll be back in a second," said Ivy. "Sorry, everyone."

Uncle Tommy put his cowboy hat back on his head and pulled his keys out of his pocket. "I'll drive you."

Ivy looked at Justin and raised her eyebrows. He shrugged. "Sure, why not?" He turned to Angela and Ben. "I'll be back in a minute, Mom, Dad. This is really weird, but don't go anywhere."

Angela's eyes teared up. "I'll be here waiting for you."

Ben nodded at Justin.

Ivy and Justin climbed into Uncle Tommy's truck. Uncle Tommy started the engine but left it idling. He nodded as if deciding what to say before turning to Justin.

"Hey, I guess I should've driven you to the doctor's clinic when you fell in the corn."

Justin nodded back. "That's okay, Reuben did."

Uncle Tommy nodded. "Yeah, he did. He's a good man."

Then Uncle Tommy backed his truck out of the driveway and drove to town. As he parked in the lot behind the Coffey Shop, the deputy sheriff pulled in behind them. The three of them walked toward the back door of the restaurant as Charlie leaned out of his car window.

"Hey, Tommy, looks like criminal activity afoot. You breaking and entering the Coffey Shop?"

"Hey, Charlie, just picking up our pies. Ivy forgot them." Uncle Tommy adjusted his cowboy hat.

Charlie stared at Justin and pointed his chin at him. "What's he doing with you? He letting you in?"

Uncle Tommy shook his head. "No." He took a deep breath. He scratched the back of his neck and nodded at Justin. "He's my grandson."

Charlie's mouth fell open. "Good God, Tommy, have you lost your mind? Do you realize what you're saying?"

"Yep, I reckon I do." He put his hand on Justin's back. "He's Angela's boy."

Uncle Tommy held the Coffey Shop door open and turned to Justin. "Hurry up, son. I've got a hankering for some pie."

Ivy followed them in, smiling. Maybe it was worth it, even if it took a lifetime to find your family.

Chapter 46

THE WINGS OF HOPE

After everyone went to bed that night, Ivy felt anxious, as if she had forgotten something. She went down the hall to Grandma's old bedroom, untouched since Grandma last slept there. Ivy had completed her promise to Grandma. Justin had come home. Grandma's soul could rest peacefully now.

Ivy pulled aside the red velvet curtains and looked out Grandma's bedroom window at the vacant trees and the spot where the big, old maple tree used to stand, empty now in its absence.

"Are you sitting on your back porch in the Great Hereafter, Grandma? Because I've done what you asked. Did you see Justin come home? The secrets are all gone. It's going to be okay."

She closed the curtains, still unable to shake her unease. At midnight, snow began to fall. The feeling that something remained undone still gnawed at her. She lay awake, watching the world transform outside. The woods lay sleepy and quiet, wrapped in a blanket of white.

Ivy got up early, unable to sleep and anxious for the morning. She put on baggy sweats and fixed hot tea in the kitchen. A commotion, like muffled chattering, stirred in the backwoods. Probably those nasty squirrels. Ivy slipped on her boots by the back door and went to investigate what new mischief the squirrels had created.

Pushing the heavy snow back with the bottom of the storm door, Ivy stepped out onto the porch. The sky hung low, cloudy, and gray. The limbs of the trees sagged with the weight of the new snow, like the snow that fell the night Grandma died. A heavy dampness settled around Ivy's heart.

She walked into the backyard, listening for the strange noise, straining for something familiar. She had grown used to the quiet of the woods since the birds vanished. But something sounded in the trees. A low fluttering like eyelashes brushing against a pillow whispered in the cold hush of the morning.

Ivy stood still and cocked her head. Her ears strained to recognize the sound. Then a small bird flew out of a nearby juniper bush, the first bird in the backyard since Grandma had died. It fluttered in the air, as if uncertain where to turn. The chickadee paused on top of the full but unused bird feeder. The bird tilted its head back and forth as if receiving some awaited message, and then it flew straight at Ivy.

Ivy took a step back and closed her eyes, preparing for the impact of the bird. But nothing happened. She felt the light fluttering of wings and opened her eyes. The gray and white chickadee with a black cap and a black stripe over its eyes sat on her shoulder. She froze in wonder. Then with gradual recognition, she relaxed her tense muscles. Ivy spoke in the sing-song tone Grandma had used with her bird friends.

"Well, hello, Sweetie Pie. Where have you been?"

The nearby trees rustled. A thrush sang a sweet solo in the unearthly stillness. When it finished its hymn, it flew up into the air and was joined by another thrush. Then together they landed on Ivy's other shoulder. Ivy gazed in amazement.

"Why, Miss Susie, you finally found Sir Lancelot."

Then the murmuring began again. The bare branches of the trees whispered, and the woods rumbled. Snow shook loose from the branches and floated to the ground. Then the hushed sound of small wings moving against the air, like pages quickly turning, grew louder.

More birds landed on Ivy's shoulders. She stood with her arms outstretched as the birds came to her from all over the woods. They lit on her shoulders, arms, and head until the winged creatures covered her. A wave of warm electricity rushed through Ivy's body and the smell of lilacs filled her nose. The hair on the back of her neck stood up and her body tingled. She shuddered from the impact of knowing.

The birds were Grandma's sign that another world existed after this one and everything was all right. Wherever it was, Grandma waited there in peace. It was proof of the power of love and the indestructibility of the spirit.

The bushes rustled, and footsteps sounded up the back path. It was Nick.

He stopped and stood in awe when he saw the birds resting on Ivy. She looked over at him. "Nick! It's Grandma's sign. They're back. The birds have come back to the woods."

He smiled. "The birds know that if you're here, this is home."

"You're back?"

"This is my home."

"Are you staying?"

Nick slowly reached out and held Ivy's hand. The birds didn't move. "Wherever you are, that's where I want to be. You can visit other places, but Iowa is where you can live."

"Grandma brought you home, too."

The swirling snow danced around them and covered them with the soft white blanket of winter. But Ivy and Nick didn't notice. They had finally come home, together.

"I'm sorry about Grandma V. I should have come to the funeral."

"It's okay. She was already gone."

"I should have come for you."

A goldfinch landed on Ivy.

"Look, Nick."

Then the birds took to the sky and circled the house in the triumph of returning home and the joy of new beginnings. They flew together in the celebration of the continuity of life and death, and the assurance of a home in the Great Hereafter. And the squirrels watched from the trees.

The End

RECIPE FOR ANGEL PIE

Ingredients:
　　6 egg whites
　　¼ teaspoon salt
　　2 cups sugar
　　1 teaspoon vanilla
　　1 tablespoon vinegar

For the topping:
　　½ pint of stiffly whipped cream
　　½ teaspoon vanilla
　　2-3 tablespoons sugar
　　3-4 drops food coloring
　　2 refrigerated Heath candy bars

1. Mix together six egg whites and ¼ teaspoon of salt with an electric mixer until fluffy.

2. Measure one cup of sugar and add one tablespoon at a time, beating with an electric mixer until well mixed.

3. Add one teaspoon of vanilla and mix.

4. Beating continually, add one cup of sugar and one tablespoon of vinegar.

5. Grease and flour one large pie tin. Heap mixture in center of pan and bake for 30 minutes at 275 degrees. Then bake for 30 minutes at 300 degrees. Cool completely to room temperature. The pie will fall a little bit on top.

6. To prepare pie topping, mix together ½ pint of stiffly whipped cream with ½ teaspoon vanilla, 2-3 tablespoons sugar and 3-4 drops food coloring to get desired color. Spread topping over pie.

7. Crush two refrigerated Heath candy bars and sprinkle on top. (Tip: Put Heath bars inside two baggies and crush.) You can also replace the Heath candy bars with strawberries or raspberries.

8. Refrigerate for at least 4 hours. Better if left longer. Serves 8.

ABOUT THE AUTHOR

Jana Zinser writes stories about people fighting against all odds. Versed in TV, features, and books, her background is in politics, public policy, and the media. She is a graduate of the University of New Hampshire School of Law, received her Masters in Journalism from the University of Iowa, and her undergraduate degree in political science and history from Graceland University.

Jana is the author of the award-winning book, *The Children's Train: Escape on the Kindertransport.*

OTHER BOOKS BY JANA ZINSER

The Children's Train explodes with a tale of the ultimate fight against the vilest hatred known to mankind as Hitler seeks the total annihilation of the Jewish People. It is a story of sacrifice, violence, determination, betrayal, revenge, love, and hope. The goals of the children in this story are to stay alive, to live each day with the hope that they will see their families again, and to fight hatred with every ounce of their dwindling strength.

Violin-playing Peter escapes Nazi Germany on a train to England filled with just children, but after his Coventry farm is bombed, Peter returns to Germany to try to save his family and childhood friend Eva and with the help of underground rebels, sabotage the Nazis.